SEARCHLIGHT

A. DAVID BARRETT

Paperback: 978-1-957332-05-5
Hardcover: 978-1-957332-06-2
Audiobook: 978-1-957332-07-9
Ebook: 978-1-957332-08-6

First Edition March 2023

Edited by Cole Girodat
Proofread by J. Flowers-Olnowich
Proofread by Maddy D.
Cover Art by Stefan Koidl
Illustrations by Andrea Figuera
Latin Consult by Nate Kolpin
Formatted by Kari Holloway
Future Fossil Fiction Publishing
https://www.fiddlerandshoots.com

Dedicated to:
My Father, Dave.
You have always been the best father you could be,
thank you for all you have sacrificed for us.
And thank you for being my hero.

Preface

The second time around was not easier. Well, maybe a little. But, I want to thank you, my steadfast reader, for enjoying this adventure like I did. The story has progressed in a path I thought it would, for the most part at least. As always, I just watch what my characters do. Whether it is to laugh at them or cringe at what they say.

I also want to apologize if the topic of WW2 is a sensitive one for some, and, I want to express my sincere apologies for the victims and their families.

And, ultimately, I hope you enjoy this story, Grandpa.

*'Every time you take on a new responsibility,
you are more them and less you."*

— Mr. Fiene

Chapter 1
Jinx

24th December, 1942
Hackney Borough, London, England
4:30 P.M.

The sun began to set on the crumbling city that lay before us. Glaring rays of a weary day fell upon the landscape in abstract shades of black and gray, giving life to the otherwise inanimate objects. An eerie silence snaked through the rubble from the collapsed buildings, only to recoil off a random clack of a stone or piece of debris falling from an overhead ledge.

My team and I walked single file, mindful of where our next steps rested in case any traps awaited us. I eyed the ground, watching for a tripwire or pressure plate hidden underneath a pile of stone or wood.

Those Germans are bastards, using electricity as weapons. I can't believe we have to worry about shock grenades.

I hadn't even realized I drifted off into thought when I was yanked back to reality. My little brother, Woodrow, asked me something I didn't quite make out.

"What, Drow?" I asked, glancing back at him behind me. "What did you say?"

"How are we going to find the source?" Drow asked.

Behind us, Phillips let out a booming laugh. It echoed off the skeletal remains of the city's framework that towered above and could be heard for a few moments after he finished, repeating for anyone and everyone within earshot.

"Can't you tell Deck is busy ignoring you?" Phillips asked, nudging Drow forward.

I rolled my eyes at the question, knowing that Drow could not see or tell that I did so. I took in a few steady breaths to calm my fraying nerves and looked back at them. "We'll use the detector Frank procured for us. Remember?"

Drow tilted his head in thought, cocking an eyebrow for good measure. "I remember now. The warbler. Sorry, I was lost for a moment. Have had a lot on my mind lately."

"I know. Me too. I just hope we can find the source soon. It's getting colder by the minute, and it's Christmas Eve. I'd rather be spending it back at the church, being merry. Let's hurry it along to get back there as quickly as possible," I said, shivering.

We all stopped as I reached into a pocket on the side of my fatigues, pulling out the warbler. The cool metal device was heavy in my hand and almost cold enough to freeze right through my glove. It was about the size of a pack of cigarettes, which made it relatively easy to hold. But to prevent from dropping it, I slipped my covered fingers through the tight leather strap on the backside.

On the right side was a button that, when pressed, supplied power to the unit. While on the front was a gauge with a needle that moved like a compass, leading you to the source of a particular radio wave you were tracking. On the left side of the device was a knob the size of a dinner mint, used to cycle through the various frequencies, with a small numeral wire indicator on the bottom of the face. A small speaker on the bottom of the device played the station it was dialed in on.

My thumb pressed the button to implement power to the device, and the speaker crackled softly, surprised at its sudden, rude awakening. Static filled the air around us, humming and buzzing without a care. I turned the dial on the side to scan through the stations, attempting to find the one we were searching for.

"*Deux-trois attendez, un-cinq attendez, trois-un attendez, trois-cinq, terminer,*" the voice said, feminine and distant. The audio was laced with more static, making it difficult to make out clearly.

"Help?" Drow asked.

"With what?" I asked.

"No, she's saying, *Help.*"

"How'd you know what she was saying?"

Drow let out a stunted chuckle. "Grandad taught me about word ciphers. It's just a bunch of numbers. That's a simple one: a Polybius cipher."

"Yeah, simple," I snorted as I began our march again.

"You mean we went looking for the source of a signal you don't know anything about?"

I sighed. "Well, we reasoned that since it's in French, it is probably someone that needs our help. Maybe a small pocket of resistance fighters."

Drow rolled his eyes and sighed. "It's convenient she's asking for help. Here we come, I guess."

"That's not the only reason we are out here, remember? The source of the station may be someone that knows a thing or two about Jakobus. We are also out here to try to meet with the group transferring the American to our headquarters," Phillips said.

"What if we miss them?" Drow asked.

"Don't you remember anything?" Phillips asked.

"No. Why do that when I have you two?" Drow chuckled.

I paused our forward momentum and sighed as I glanced back to Drow for a moment before moving again.

"So?" Drow asked.

"They have the coordinates for our Headquarters. If we miss them, we will still see them there. You happy?" Phillips asked.

"Yes, thank you," Drow exaggerated.

My foot caught onto something, causing me to turn forward again. My eyes scanned the layout of the world around me before I looked at the ground to see what tripped me up.

Laying across the path was a wooden pole with a flag attached to the end. I looked to the left and saw it was a red fabric with the symbol for the Third Reich plastered over the surface. It rippled in the light breeze, causing the frayed end to snap angrily at nothing.

"Watch out; there's a pole across the path. Be careful," I said over my shoulder.

Drow was the one right behind me, tall and stocky. His uniform was the cleanest of the group because he was our sniper, and I usually had him wait in the back or stay in cover while we had skirmishes. He still had that ridiculous mustache like Errol Flynn.

Drow certainly has grown, even in the last four years.

Right behind him was Phillips, who didn't care for his first name, so he went by his surname. I didn't think Rodney was such a bad name, but I suppose, to each his own.

Out of the corner of my periphery, I saw Phillips had his helmet off like he usually did, even though I had repeatedly scolded him for it. I noticed this because the sunlight reflected off his slicked-back hair. The steel skull cage lay across the front of his chest, doing its best to protect what it could.

At least, the other two men in my unit have maintained good personal hygiene. I have fallen short with that for some reason. Not sure why. When we get back to base, I need to get a haircut and maybe shave. My beard is getting scratchy and if I let it get any longer, the gray hairs I had developed over the last few years would change my light brown hair into a hodgepodge of colors.

"Phillips, could you please put your helmet on? Your head can be seen for miles. Don't you want to keep it on your shoulders?" I asked, still glancing back.

"Well, then why don't you put that sword of yours away? That thing is like a damn lighthouse," he retorted.

Instead of arguing further, I shook my head and looked back down at my feet. I kept up the pace by being careful and paving the way for my unit, forcing down a few laughs myself.

Even though we were in freezing temperatures, sweat began forming on my face from the stress of having my body shocked to the core by 70,000 volts of pure German blitz.

"Shut up, Phillips, unless you want to be the one in front, taking the chance to be turned into crispy schnitzel," I said with a tone fit for a parent to their child.

"But Deck, I'm just having fun. You know that," Phillips said.

"Well, then quit it. We need to pay attention. Never know what is around the next corner," Drow said.

"Come on, Drow. You know I don't like it when you do that," I said.

"What?" Drow said.

"Oh, come on, you know I believe in jinxes. I hate it when people say things like that."

"Sorry, Deck, I forgot. I'm sure I didn't jinx us, though."

The three of us neared the end of the street we were currently on. On either side, shops and pubs lined the sidewalk at a ratio I really didn't want to talk about. It would reveal something about myself and the people of the city I wouldn't like to admit.

Since the sun sank lower in the sky, the light that illuminated the ground began to recede with it. A sense of uncertainty followed on its heels, not knowing if the next step would be our last.

"Boys, time to get out the spotters. Don't want any surprises. Drow, you stay in the middle and keep an eye on the right corner just up there," I said, pointing up the ways toward the opposite side of the street in front of us. "And Phillips, keep a lookout behind us. Wouldn't want anyone catching us with our trousers down."

"Copy that, sir," Phillips said.

"Alright, Deck," Drow followed up.

We stopped near the entrance of what I presumed was a pub and crouched. I slung my modified haversack off my back, hitting the ground with a soft thud. It cast off motes of gray dust that flew in all directions. The other two men followed suit, adding more noise to our surroundings.

I undid the clasp on the front of the bag and flipped the cover flap to the back. In the growing darkness, I reached inside, pawing at the contents to find what I was looking for. My peripheral vision picked up the movement of two new light sources, and I looked back to see that both Drow and Phillips already had their own spotters out.

"Boy, you guys are quick. Have your ladies ever complained about that?" I asked, smirking at my quick wit.

"Oh, shut it. We all know Drow's girl left him for me," Phillips heckled.

Drow elbowed Phillips as a rebuttal, catching him off guard. Phillips smirked as he rubbed at his side.

I zoned them out as they bickered among themselves for a few seconds. Their back-and-forth banter was a welcome change to the dull, constant, and persistent droning that sounded in my ears the rest of the time from the Wavergy. To our surprise, the Tesla Coil Substations were the one thing the Germans kept going since they took London, while everything else was left to be decimated by the Luftwaffe and their blitz.

I reached into my haversack to pull out my own spotter. My fingers felt for the switch on the side to be sure it was flipped off for now. The cool metal body of the light in the palm of my hand felt somewhat warm compared to the chilled air around us.

When I pulled it out the rest of the way, I turned it over in my palm a few times. It was about four inches tall and was a round metal tube with the top bent at a right angle at the lens. The slender steel frame reflected the light of the other two beams into broken fragments, peppering the walls and ground in a kaleidoscope of yellow-white shards.

I pointed it at the ground and flicked on the switch, completing the circuit of electricity. The beam of light lit up the ground just next to my feet, where a tent sign lay on its side. It was about a foot from the doorway on the corner of the street, advertisement fading away with the rest of London.

I tilted my head to the side and read it aloud, "The Lion's Den."

Isn't that odd? Small world.

I let out a light, almost inaudible, chuckle before I continued, "I used to come here. I have a lot of fond memories of this place."

The faint rustling of canvas from either Drow's or Phillips' web gear sounded behind me as it rubbed against one of their rifles. I glanced over my shoulder and saw Drow as he got closer to me.

"Oh hey, this is The Lion's Den, isn't it?" he asked. "We used to meet up here with Grandad all the time, right?"

"Yeah, I remember. We'd drink till the cows came home," I said.

Fond memories of our past washed over me in a wave of warmth. The late nights and early mornings filled many weekends when we turned of age—or at least old enough for Grandad to convince the barman we were of age.

All that time, and he never told us about any of this. All those moments, we could have asked him for help or just some good advice.

The darkness of the doorway crept back into the foreground, pushing at the light and love that made up the past. It bled into the edges of the explicit pictures in my mind, like a fresh watercolor painting as it settled. The crisp lines of the world around me muddled into grays and blacks, eventually giving way to what was in front of me.

"Hey, you okay, Deck?" asked Drow.

"Yeah. Sorry, I was just thinking of Grandad," I whispered.

"I miss him too, you know," Drow said.

I held onto the memory for a few more seconds, not wanting to let go. My gaze fell to the ground again, thinking of times which passed too quickly for our own good. I shook my head and looked at the tent sign once more, still thinking of many fuzzy nights. But this time, I noticed a newspaper folded up neatly, lying underneath one of the legs. I reached to grab it from my crouching position, straining to stay on the balls of my feet and not fall flat on my face from overextending myself.

"What's that?" Drow asked.

"Not sure. An old newspaper?" I guessed.

"I wonder how old it is. What's the date on it?"

After scooping it up, I scanned the front page for the date while my eyes skated over the headlines and article names. *The Battle of Britain* stood out in bold characters compared to the muted grays of the paper.

It reminded me that at one point in time, things used to be much more cut and dry, like good and evil. At that point, it was a little easier to tell who the bad guys were. We had been watching the rise of the regime for quite a long time, and it hadn't been easy figuring out all the details, like who was actually pulling the strings behind the scenes. Since the start of the war and of the Keepers Division of the military, we had a hunch about who Jakobus resurfaced as at this point. The problem was that it could have been a few different people. Anyone, really. To be honest, he was a very mysterious character that could cause panic in the smallest of ways.

"What is the date?" Drow asked.

I shook my head and said, "Oh, yeah, sorry. It says here that this paper is from—wait. Could it be?"

"What?"

"This paper is from the day the streets went dark. From the day they invaded. Tenth of July, 1940."

"No. Really? How? That was over three years ago. It should be mashed bits by now if it's been out in the elements this whole time."

"I know, it's crazy. I never did see the paper from that day. I never would have guessed they got anything printed out before the shadows took over." I said as I scanned the page again.

"Is there anything about how they did it since it was printed on the day of? I wonder if we knew anything then as they stormed the city," Drow said.

"Let me look," I said as I searched for the headline.

Drow shifted his weight behind me, causing the canvas of his haversack to ripple some more.

"This one here." I pointed at the paper as I found the right heading. "*Darkness Prevails Over King George VI.*"

"What else does it say then?" Drow asked, fidgeting to know more.

"The article says:

> *The kingdom falls as the streets run black. All power has been deactivated around the city, and the defenses we have in place will no longer keep us safe. We urge all citizens to practice the utmost caution, stay calm, and collect their necessities as they undergo the evacuation methods specified in your borough of residency.*
>
> *We have received reports that the Abwehr, the German equivalent to the CIA or MI6, infiltrated the city and set devices to sabotage our electrical infrastructure, thus our defenses and lifelines. After they crippled our ability to respond to further attacks, the Luftwaffe took to the skies above and rained death down over the city in waves of metal and fire. The RAF attempted to rally and fight the good fight, only to be stalled before their wings could even leave the ground.*

> *Since our source of electricity, TEA, was damaged by the Abwehr, our military could not power up the planes to defend us. Our ground forces could not assemble quickly enough to meet them head-on, but they do plan to hold the city as long as possible. God save the King'."*

We were silent for a moment or two, the air rushing around us and lifting puny clumps of ashen snow into the air. I felt the frigid cold nip at me some more, reminding me that we were still deep into German-occupied territory.

"They must have reactivated the TEA coils after they took London after the fact," I said. "Strange."

"Yeah, it is. But it seems like they knew enough. I am surprised we got sixty percent of the population out when we did. It's a long trek across the pond to Nova Scotia," Drow said.

But not the one most important to me: Hope.

"Yeah, we almost didn't have a—" I began.

I was interrupted by a noise off in the distance.

"Guys, did you hear that?" Phillips asked.

I stayed crouched as I turned to look at him. "Hear what? Do you see anything?"

Phillips glanced down to the end of the road. His hands were trembling with the decision of whether he wanted to shine the light or not. Eventually, he made up his mind and slowly lifted his spotter to see what lay in that direction.

I grabbed his wrist before he could lift it further. "What are you doing?"

He snapped his head toward me and stammered, "I-I want to see what's making the noise."

"That—that's a bad decision. We need to be smart about this, Phillips," I whispered.

"Yeah, we are in the middle of German-occupied territory. We don't need to be shining a searchlight in their faces," Drow added quietly.

"*Scheiße!*" yelled a voice.

At the sound of someone else's voice, Phillips, Drow, and I went prone. We simultaneously turned off our spotters, not wanting to draw attention to our location.

"*Sheiße, sheiße, scheiße,*" sounded the voice again.

I focused as I listened, trying to determine whether they were speaking English or not.

"What are they saying?" Drow asked.

"Either someone didn't pick up after their dog on a walk after they pooped, or they just aren't happy about something," I whispered. "Phillips, do you see where they are?"

Phillips reached for his haversack about three feet in front of him. It scraped against the concrete with a noise that thundered in the quiet surroundings as he pulled it toward himself.

I glared at Phillips and hissed, "Shh, quiet!"

As I feared, it was too late. I felt like chiding him over being so stupid, making so much noise.

"*Was war das?*" boomed a different voice. "*Wer ist da?*"

"Phillips, what are they saying?" I asked.

Phillips pulled out a pair of binoculars from his bag. "I think they are asking who is there. They don't seem to know where we are."

Luckily, we were surrounded by a decent amount of cover where we lay on the sidewalk. To the left and front of us were a few mounds of rubble, consisting of stone, glass, and wood. Behind me, I heard the wind creak against an old decrepit Bentley. I glanced at him, watching what he planned to do next.

"I'm just gonna have a quick peek, see if I can make out where they are," Phillips murmured.

"*Ich glaube nicht, dass jemand da ist, Klaus,*" said another voice.

"What else did they say?" asked Drow.

"Something about not seeing anyone, I think," Phillips said. "One of them is named Klaus, though."

Phillips switched to a crouched position, trying to stay as quiet as possible. He then moved closer to the furthest rock pile, putting the binoculars to his eyes.

"Damn, I can't see anything from here. I have to move up some to get a better look," he said.

"Don't go any—" I started.

Before I could finish talking, he was already walking closer to the voices, and just as he got to the edge of the corner pile, the air filled with deafening thunder. More claps followed in a cacophony of echoes, causing me to flinch. Surprised more than scared, I lowered my head to the ground after the first strike.

CHAPTER 2
Scaredy Cat

Silence followed the reverberation of the gunshots, heavy with a menacing weight.

"Phillips? You okay?" I mumbled through my arms.

Without lifting my head, I already knew the answer. The taste of salt and iron filled my next breath, coating my nostrils with the stench of hopes and dreams now vacant and missing.

Dammit, Phillips. I told you to wear that bloody helmet. Why didn't you listen to me? Why?

I slowly raised my head as my eyes fell upon his body, now just a motionless heap lying in the rubble. A mess of carmine and gore spilled out on the concrete, like the beginnings of a Duncan Grant painting. I needed to keep calm if Drow and I wanted to make it out of here alive. I couldn't let this get the best of me. I told myself that I could mourn him when we were away from there.

"*Ich Habe etwas!*" yelled a voice.

They have something? Yeah, it was Phillips.

"*Hans, du weißt doch nicht, wer das war,*" said the other voice, presumably Klaus.

Why is this Klaus so concerned about who they shot?

"*Es interessiert mich sowieso nicht,*" Hans said.

Well, Hans, you will be the first one I kill.

I heard the cool scrape of a metal slide rub against the body of a heavy machine gun. I assumed they were checking a jam in the buzzsaw they just used to cut Phillips down. The two Germans began to argue, giving me time to make a quick decision. I flipped off the warbler, wanting to keep our presence unknown, and slipped it back into a pocket on my fatigues.

"We lost our translator, and I don't know if they will come looking for him," I said, looking back at what was left of Phillips. "We both know a little German, but I am not confident in my own translations."

"Oh God, oh God. I jinxed us. Why did I say something?" Drow said.

He was on his knees, hands holding his head as he rocked back and forth.

"Dammit, Drow, don't do this to me now. You didn't know," I said. "*Hey*, look at me."

I looked him in the eye and took his hands from his head, trying to help calm his nerves. He started to shake, arms trembling like an earthquake. The adrenaline probably dumped into his bloodstream at this point, causing him to hop more than a rabbit in a garden.

"Y-yes?" he trembled, looking at me.

"Do you have your bio-electric rifle?" I asked.

"Yeah, I do. It's in my pack," he said, pointing at his haversack.

"Good. I need you to see if you can take them out. I can't hit anything from this far away," I said.

"Okay— I can try," he whispered, his body still shaking.

Drow dropped to a prone position as he grabbed for his pack. He reached in and pulled out a slender metal device. In the last bit of twilight, I could make out the Mason Model 1937 Sharpshooter in Drow's hands.

Definitely not as clunky as the 1870 model.

I glanced over it to compare it to the one my Grandad would have seen in his day. It had a new version of the focusing disk built into the side of the gun itself, upgraded from the plain wire one that sat on the side. It gave it a much quicker response to your connection, as well as cutting the amount of recharge time in half.

The receiver was like most guns, complete with breach, magazine, bolt, and trigger. Its barrel was about two feet long, blued to help combat rust. Mahogany was the wood of choice for the stock, with a quick detach button to help with storage.

This military issue wasn't as luxurious as some civilian models you could buy: no-mother of-pearl inlay or gold trim. It was just a bare-bones rock 'em sock 'em kraut killer.

"Ready?" I asked.

"Yes," Drow said. "Do you see anything?"

I closed my eyes to focus on the noises around us. At first, it was silent, but the closer I listened, the more I could hear. The Germans weren't arguing anymore, which made me unsure if it was good or bad.

The next thing I heard was the slow, guttural growl of diesel truck engines inching closer to the intersection ahead of us. I opened my eyes to look at Drow again as he removed the telescopic sight that he kept in his breast pocket.

It was the size of a little canister of balm, an inch wide by half an inch thick. On either side, a hinge connected the protective covers, allowing it to be more compact to shut. With a quick flick of his wrist, he pulled on the ends, causing the sight to expand to its full length of five inches.

"Give it to me before you attach it. I want to look at what is coming up the road," I said, holding my hand out to him.

He handed it to me without fuss, and I stuck my head up to see over the piles of rubble that acted as our cover for the time being. I brought the scope to my right eye and peered through it, gazing through the protective camouflage of a broken car window.

A few hundred feet near the corner of the intersection, I saw the front of a German VW type 82 pull into view. I held my breath while it continued forward, anticipating who could be in the passenger seat. I felt my jaw hit the floor when Himmler appeared in the telescopic sight, causing me to lose my breath momentarily.

"It's Himmler," I whispered.

Drow choked. "W-what?"

I watched as the VW came and went in my view, followed by another Type-82 and half-track pulling a 20mm anti-aircraft gun. Just like that, they were gone, continuing down the road and away from us, taking any slight chance we could have had to take him down.

There's no way we could have; we weren't ready for it. We didn't plan on seeing him here, and we've lost—we've lost Phillips.

"Are you sure?" Drow asked.

I nodded and took the sight from my eye. "That's him, all right. But they are already long gone, and there would've been no way we could have taken him on right now. Not just us two."

I looked at Drow as he pursed his lips and nodded in agreement, focusing on what he was doing. Drow had calmed down quite a bit, measured breathing replacing the ragged and random ones that took hold of him moments ago. He ensured the stock was attached securely while flipping up the sight connectors on the top of the Mason 1937.

"Okay. I can do this. Which way are you going to go?" he asked, attaching the sight to the bio-electric rifle.

Looking to my right, I scanned The Lion's Den, glancing at the second floor. I pointed to the bar, gesturing for us to go in. "Maybe we should get higher up, to a better vantage point."

Drow nodded as he duck-walked to the pub's front door, careful not to stand up and give the Germans a clear shot. I pulled up the rear, falling into step right behind him.

The entrance opened into a moderately sized room. Everything was cast in shadows as the sun's rays no longer reached into the pub. I flipped the switch on my spotter, wanting to look around. Its light illuminated everything in a yellowed glow, leaving only a few spots in the darkness.

Shattered pint glasses and bottles littered the floor between the peppering of random refuse and crumpled newspaper. I turned my head, and immediately to the left was a cramped corner with a couple of seats tucked neatly underneath a window, broken out long ago. The bar top started as a curved corner, going about ten feet toward the back of the space. Only three stools stood tight to the bar top.

Boy, what I would give for it to be six years ago, sitting here enjoying a pint with the ones I love.

Behind that was a wall of mirrors with shelves holding a poor selection of drinks. To the right were a few booths underneath mostly intact panes of cylinder glass, reminding me of the wonder of the mysterious open sea. Just beyond that was a brick fireplace, cold and long dead. The room was spacious, with tables and chairs scattered close to the far-right wall. I brought the spotter up to look straight back, ash and bits of dust floating through the beam. In the furthest corner was a flight of stairs leading up to the second floor.

"There, let's go check," I whispered. "Just be careful. I'll go first just in case."

I turned to Drow to make sure he understood before we quietly walked to the back. My hand started reaching for Excalibur slung across my back but stopped.

It would be better to use my sidearm in this situation.

Before ascending the staircase, I pulled out the standard issue Kestler Mk IV and pressed down on the charging button. I felt as it connected the circuit with the built-in power source, using my hand to complete the loop. In the same motion, I pulled the slide back to load a round into the chamber, revealing the charging pin for a split second. The white light from it gave off a minuscule amount of heat from the warming effect of the electricity.

"You keep an eye on our backs. Stay behind three steps. Okay?" I said.

He nodded and followed me up the steps. They were steep and uneven looking, creaking from the weight of our feet. The walls were decorated on either side with framed photos that seemed to go on forever. Upon closer inspection, it looked like they were post-mortem pictures from the mid-1800's.

They look like the ones I used to see with Grandad. Damn creepy, they are. Why do they have to have an entire staircase of them?

We walked to the right, down a narrow hallway past about eight closed doors. At the top was a small table with a decorative lace doily and a vase resting atop it. The doily was surprisingly crisp and white, while the vase was broken about halfway down with muddy, brown water inside. I did make sure to check each one carefully and quickly before moving on to the next.

Not finding the one we were looking for, we turned around and went in the other direction. We wrapped around to the street side of the building and came to the last room we hadn't looked in yet.

This will provide cover for us and make it easier to sight in on the Germans.

"I think this one will do," Drow said while pushing open the door.

"Okay, I'll come check it before I try and make my way around to flank them," I said, scooting past Drow into the room.

The tattered curtains billowed from the light breeze that began to pick up outside the pub. It filled the inside with a cold air that started to work its way into my bones. A light glow could still be seen on the horizon, giving us some much-needed light to finish up this recon.

I surveyed the room and saw that the bed was pushed off to the side, lying crooked on the wooden frame. My attention shifted as I heard a crackling noise from a bathroom off to the right. When I looked over at it, I saw that the door was not entirely shut.

My eyes adjusted to the room's dimness as I clicked off the spotter and slid it into a small pocket on my chest harness. I pulled my pistol up, readying it in front, just in case there was someone, or something, in the loo. I took a deep breath to calm my nerves and placed my free hand on the door.

Okay, Deck. On the count of three. One. Two. Three.

I forced the door open, gun raised to defend myself if need be. Light flooded my eyes from a narrow window in the shower, causing me to bring up my left hand to cover them. I panicked from the lack of sight, hairs on my neck standing on end from the fear welling up in my guts. Between my fingers, I feverishly looked around for the source of the noise, struggling to focus. Movement out of the corner of my eyes caused me to look over to the shower curtain just in time to see it flutter.

"Come out now. I have my gun on you. I don't want to shoot, but I will if I have to," I said.

The response I received was scratching followed by rustling. I cocked an eyebrow in confusion, still staring down the sights of my pistol. Without warning, something burst through the shower curtain with a flash of black. My gun went off, burning holes in the plastic of the curtain and the scuffed, battered linoleum behind.

The roar of the charged projectile thundered in the confined space, causing my hearing to be consumed by ringing. Some bullets went left, striking the porcelain throne and shattering the bowl all over the floor. The others went to the right, sinking into the walls with a thud, tendrils of smoke leaking from the holes.

"Deck, you okay?" Drow asked.

"Wh— what was that?" I choked out.

I turned to look at Drow, lowering my pistol in the process. Knowing I didn't need to be firing off any more shots, I rested my pointer finger on the side of the trigger guard. My arms shook as I reached to my forehead with my sleeve, wiping the sweat from it.

"You almost shot a bloody cat. Why are you shooting at a cat?" Drow asked.

I opened my mouth to talk, but I just shut it, breathing heavily from the surprise. Drow's shoulders relaxed slightly, slumping as he lowered his rifle. He chuckled when he realized there wasn't currently a threat. I raked my hand through my hair and rubbed at the back of my neck in the process.

"Dammit, Deck. You're such a scaredy-cat," he said, chuckling.

I looked at Drow and rolled my eyes. "At least I didn't—"

The thundering sound of machine gun fire tore through the air, interrupting my sentence. We hit the ground in seconds, trying to stay low, out of the firing line. Plaster flew everywhere in the room, exploding from the impact points of the hot German lead.

"I think they heard you!" Drow yelled.

The bullets stopped raining upon us after a few seconds, replaced with an eerie silence. Drow and I scrambled to the wall underneath the windowsill. I looked around and saw the Germans were shooting at center mass level, giving me a slight sense of security with our choice to stay low.

I looked around, mind and body clenching in anticipation for the guns to start back up again. A chair next to us lay on its side, probably because of the missing back leg. The plush leather seat was an off-color brown, almost tan. Or maybe it was tea-coloured with some milk added to it. Facing the threat of death, I couldn't help but turn my thoughts to my loved ones.

That's just like how Mum used to like it. When was the last time I saw her, anyway?

Chapter 3
Awake

18th July, 1937
Spitalfields Borough, London, England
1:45 p.m.

Rain struck the windowpanes gently, filling the only void it was able to. Thunder began rumbling in a low, gravelly tone, following up from the flashes of light that sprang to life every few minutes. The somber chatter of people filled the rooms and hallways of the house. Rich laughter mingled with an array of sorrowful tears, echoing throughout, most of which were for the memories remembered and cherished by all that knew Davey O'Shea.

"Mum, how are you holding up?" asked Deck.

He sat gently next to her on the loveseat, placing his arm around her. Eleanor sank into Deck's embrace, sobbing softly as Deck tried to be of some comfort. Her body shook with a constant sadness as she tried to shed more tears. By now, Deck had noticed that a few days of crying left her face red and puffy around the eyes, giving her a pained expression.

"I will be eventually," she whimpered.

She tried to say more but was rewarded with a cough, leading into a fit that made her previous shaking look like a ripple in a pond. Deck tried to hold her tight, making sure she knew he was there.

It pained him to see his mother this way, sad and defeated, but after a few moments, a hand rested on Deck's shoulder. He looked up to see his father standing over them both, casting a comforting shadow over the two of them.

Deckard took in his father's appearance, noting he was still a strong man even at sixty-two. He was wide in the shoulders and gut, standing about five feet, eight inches tall. His hair was a mess of black curls, accented by a beard and mustache to match, which always seemed to look professional.

"Son, there is someone here that wants to talk to you. I can stay here with your mother," he said.

Deckard looked down at his mum, then back up at his father. "Where is this man?"

"He is outside on the steps. I believe he is just out there smoking," he said.

Deckard nodded to the information, trying to shift his mother in his arm without disturbing her. His father came around and carefully switched spots on the couch, permitting him to leave and meet the man. As Deck stood, he patted his father on the shoulder before turning away.

Deck looked around the room in a slow arc, taking in all the people who came by for the wake. He honestly had no idea of how many lives his grandad had touched throughout his long life. But Deck shrugged off the sense of grief that sat in his gut, deep and heavy. It was churning away at his psyche, threatening to derail any sense of hope or happiness that came his way. Suddenly, someone walking past bumped into him, causing him to stumble forward slightly.

"Oh, oh, oh. Sorry, my boy. I was trying to sneak past you," said the older gentlemen.

Deck raised his hands in an understanding gesture and said, "It's quite alright. It was me. I wasn't paying attention."

"No, no, no. It was my fault," said the man. He extended his hand. "I am sorry about your grandad. I knew him long ago."

Deck rubbed his neck, glancing at his shoes. The mention of his grandad threw him off a little bit, scattering his train of thought.

"You did? Oh, sorry. Where are my manners? I am Deckard," Deck said, extending his hand to the man.

The man reached out and shook it, firm yet gentle. Upon contact, the ring on Deck's middle finger began to glow with a faint yellow hue. The soft ambiance of the light helped warm the dull grays and muted happiness in the room.

Deck looked down at his hand. "You're a—"

"Yes," the man said, smiling. He shook Deck's hand three times. "My name is Nikola Tesla. Nice to meet you."

"I know y—" Deck started, then faltered. "In memories from me grandad."

"Yes, and I see you have found it, haven't you," Nikola said, pointing to the ring on Deck's finger.

Deck looked down at his hand once more, watching the light as it started to fade. "How do you—Wait, you know about this?"

"Why yes, yes, yes. I know quite a bit about it, actually. But you will know more in time. I must be going," Nikola said as he excused himself.

Deck stood there silently in awe, sifting through his thoughts to unearth the right one. The man who stood before him was the famous Nikola Tesla, behind the visionary company called Tesla Electric Association.

Since his grandad passed away just a few short, but long, days prior, he had been trying to come to terms with everything. Not only did he have to sort through all of his stuff, but many things were compacted on top of that. One was that he was experiencing hundreds of years of memories for the first time, pushing against the tide that threatened to engulf him. Another thing to come to terms with was that his grandad was a descendant of

King Arthur. This revelation only made him part of one of the most important bloodlines ever to walk the earth. No pressure.

"Someone is looking for you still. I believe he is just outside," Nikola said as he stopped.

Deck watched as Nikola turned and walked off, blending into the sea of mourners spread thickly throughout the foyer. He thought that the man was odd. Very peculiar. Maybe that's what you get when you run a company like TEA. He knew that his grandad had met him before. It was one of the first memories he saw the morning he found out about his grandad's heart attack.

Deck rolled his neck slowly from side to side, causing it to crack and pop, releasing a tension built up from the day. He then started off to the front of the house, passing the hall filled with the same old black and white photos. They made him think about what he had seen in the sword. Each one represented a brief second in time, captured for eternity in a chemical reaction on a piece of paper. He wondered how different it was from a memory in someone's mind. *They're both just chemical reactions, right?* He reached the front door, and noticing it was open just a crack, he opened it and went outside.

"Hello?" Deck said, looking around the weather-beaten stone steps.

A man stood leaning against the railing at the bottom left of the stairs, looking off at the street. He had a pipe in one hand that was bringing it up to his lips, while the other rested in the pocket of his plain black dress pants. Deck looked him up and down, cataloging what he saw and cross-referencing it with everything floating around in his head.

Deck watched as the man turned, giving him a better look at his features. He wore a rich black suit jacket that covered a vest of the same color. Underneath all of that was a white dress shirt with pearl buttons, crisp and clean. The tie around his neck was also black, with an outline of a sword and wings stitched into it with a dark maroon thread. Deck didn't think the man looked familiar.

"I believe you are looking for me?" Deck asked.

"Yes, I presume you are Deckard O'Shea?" the man asked.

"Yes, sir. But most people call me Deck. Who might you be?" Deck asked, looking at the man's face more closely.

His face was scarred from pubescent pimples, potting his face around the cheekbones and the nose. His hair was filled with pomade with slick, dark waves that snaked back and forth from the top of his scalp to his neck. Below his bottom lip was a scrubby patch of hair, neatly trimmed into a triangle. His steel-blue eyes hid behind a pair of horn-rimmed glasses, calm and calculating. It made Deck think that this was what a Frenchman probably looked like.

The man brought his pipe to his lips and inhaled a large amount of tobacco smoke. On the exhale, he said, "My name is Frank. Frank Matthews. I am here on behalf of TEA."

The smoke plumed outward from Frank's nose and filled the air around him. Deck inhaled some, and it tickled the back of his throat, burning his nostrils and causing him to cough violently.

"Why are you here? Didn't me grandad only work for TEA for a few years?" Deck rasped.

"Yes, that is true. I am here on a different matter," Frank said as he took another slow pull from the pipe. "I am here because I am also a part of another organization. One that you may or may not know about."

"The Order of *Est Aequum*," Deck blurted.

Frank cocked an eyebrow. "You have found it, haven't you?"

"The sword? Yes, among other things. Wait, why on behalf of TEA as well then?"

"You know what happened prior to 1889, then?"

"Uh, yeah, I suppose. It all seems fuzzy, though. Everything is kind of mashed together, not much difference between anything."

Frank rubbed his chin for a moment before speaking again. "Hmph, there's time for that later. Right now, all you need to know is that after the events involving your Grandfather Davy, the order eventually joined forces with TEA, allocating everything under one roof, so to speak."

"What does that have to do with me?" Deck asked.

"Well, son, it looks like we got the luck of the draw."

"What do you mean by that?"

"The reason you have all those memories floating around in your head can only mean one thing. It isn't a good one either."

Deck thought for a second, looking for the right picture in time, thinking of back when Davy first received the sword from the strange man named Merlinus. The clack of Frank's pipe hitting the railing helped Deck find the correct memory, almost as if he was pointing it out.

"Jakobus is back, isn't he?" Deck said.

The gravity of the situation sank in, and Deck realized what it meant. Not only for him but for his family. His friends. Everyone.

"Bingo. I don't think Jakobus is just after prostitutes this time either," said Frank.

Chapter 4
Distractions

24th December, 1942
Hackney Borough, London, England
5:15 p.m.

 droning in my ear brought me careening back to reality, like a wayward artillery shell hitting off its mark. After a moment, I realized it was Drow trying to get my attention.

"Deck, Deck!" yelled Drow.

I shook my head, ridding myself of the memory. "What? What is it?"

Drow shouted over the rapid gunfire, "You just zoned out. What happened?"

"Nothing, but we need to move something in front of you, so if they start up again, you can be covered," I whispered.

My eyes danced as I cataloged our surroundings. There was the mattress and frame from earlier in the corner. To the left was a vanity, dark brown with smooth carved edges, complete with a broken mirror at the top.

Won't be telling anyone who is the prettiest of all any time soon.

"Do you see anything?" Drow asked.

Shaking my head, I swept right to see what was there. Nothing popped out as being any more bulletproof than the mattress, and even that wasn't a good option. I checked to the left once more, hoping to God I would see something else I could've missed. To my relief, I spotted a small ottoman neatly between the wall and the vanity.

"That," I said, pointing it out to Drow.

"It might work. Let's grab it and drag it over here," Drow said.

"Let me go get it; you stay here and ready your Mason," I said, turning to him.

I started to crawl toward the ottoman, keeping low to avoid being seen. The rapid noise kicked in again, causing me to jump as I reached it. I holstered my pistol, needing both hands to grab the makeshift cover.

The obnoxious noise of gunfire made it hard to think, hard to focus on what to do next. The cushion was soft and supple, a crimson velvet fashioned to the frame with five buttons. Surprisingly, the faint smell of a flowery perfume wafted out of the fabric when I took hold of it. I grunted as I pulled it over to Drow, astounded at the thing's weight.

What is this made of? Stone?

Drow reached for the piece of furniture and helped me push it over onto its side, sliding it up to the wall. I leaned back on my left leg and backside, lifting my right into the air to ready myself. With a quick kick of my foot, I broke off the first leg pointing outward in the air.

"You do it on the other side, so you don't lean into it and hurt yourself. Okay?" I asked.

"Right," Drow said, leaning back as I did.

Just as he broke the leg off, the booming noise from outside stopped abruptly. It caused the cracking sound to cry out in the still surroundings, timed as perfectly as a joke in poor taste.

My face snapped up to Drow. "At least they already heard me."

Drow made a face at me, childish in nature. He was lucky I was his brother. That certainly wouldn't fly with just any soldier.

"Wait here. I will try and make it around. I want to try and take one alive."

"Why would you want to do that? They killed Phillips," Drow said, anger flashing across his face in red. "We need to get back at them for doing that."

"Just listen to me. It could help the order," I said.

Drow made a show of frustration, his face contorting in an angry look once more. He stared at me for a few moments, trying to convey that he wasn't happy about that. I watched as my brother picked up his rifle off the splinter-ridden hardwood floor.

"Okay?" I asked.

"Yessir," Drow said in a monotone, flat, and emotionless voice.

He's not happy about this, but neither am I. It doesn't mean we can't make some good come from the situation, though.

I quickly walked while staying crouched to the door of the room. Before I left to flank them, I looked back at Drow to check if he was in position yet. He was propped up and leaning against the left corner of the furniture. The gun was resting gently on the frame of the window, nestled in the crook of his shoulder. His measured breathing made his back rise and fall in an even rhythm. He lifted the bolt back to load a round into the chamber, cueing me to do my part.

"Just watch out for the next burst of lead. If they shoot, make sure you aren't leaning out for them to hit you," I said as I crossed the doorway's threshold.

I gotta get outside and make it around to the Germans across the way. It would be good to bring one in for Frank to have a crack at. He might know something valuable to get one step ahead of Jakobus.

"And comm silence unless I initiate, alright?" I asked.

I looked back in his direction, knowing full well he wouldn't answer. I'll have to trust him on this one. For now, the element of surprise was out the window. So far back, it was down the block and into last week. I jogged out of the room to the steps, glancing at the flowerpot we had seen earlier.

What a sad-looking vase. I wonder how long it has been broken.

My hands fidgeted with the cuffs of my shirt as I flew down the steps of the staircase, keeping my eyesight forward. The photographs of the dead were creepy as hell, and the last thing I wanted to do was get sucked into looking at them and their odd, morbid gravitational pull.

My feet hit the ground with a light but solid thud at the bottom of the stairs. It caused dirt to rush outward in small comets, spreading and floating into the air like a flock of birds, thick and moving as one. I bolted past the bottles of alcohol, a wall of simulated and artificial happiness, thinking about the last time I was there with my grandad.

Those were good times. Only thing we needed to worry about was getting home before the sun came up. When life was full of simple problems and even simpler solutions.

I pulled out my handgun and brought it up to my face, pulling back the slide to see if it was loaded yet. The already loaded round flew from the breach in a small arc into the air in front of me. I let go of the slide to chamber a new bullet into place while I reached out to catch the previous one before it could hit the ground.

My feet carried me further, and once I got to the doorway, I was stopped by the automatic thunder of lead hitting the sidewalk in front of me. My heart leaped from my chest as I fell back a step, trying to avoid being hit. I could feel a new adrenaline injection gush into my veins, causing my blood pressure to spike higher than a deathly tsunami wave about to hit an unsuspecting harbor.

Come on, Deck, keep low and run like hell. Your life only depends on it.

My brain forced my lungs to take in a few huge breaths, doing its best to calm my scattered thinking. All my gauges were flickering in the red, systems overloaded. The extra boost would help with the running, but it would be counterproductive to planning things out. I readied my arms and squared my stance to make a go for it.

The options and variables in front of me were a lot to consider. An overwhelming consensus was met: *get the hell moving and do your damn job.*

I bent my knees with my Kestler Mk IV out in front of me, deciding to get it over with. The muscles and tendons in my legs and feet screamed with anger and resentment as I took off from The Lion's Den.

The loud pops of light machine gun picked back up the millisecond I left the pub, trailing inches behind my feet. I focused on the path I was going to take, running to the left. I planned to go to the side of the building to find an access alleyway behind this block of buildings. Hopefully, without my luck, there would be one.

I was notorious for having horrible luck, which I blamed on my dad. We have a little Irish in us, so growing up, he always said we had the luck of the Irish. Now, after many years of countless examples, I have realized that it is, in fact, bad luck. No good, rotten, bad luck.

Just as I rounded the corner of the building, a small burst of dust sprang out next to my head. A bullet slammed into the bricks just as the corner shielded me. Luck, for once, was actually on my side. The twang of the ricochet made my heart skip a few beats. Definitely not a comfortable feeling.

The road on this side was a little less crowded, with some mopeds and cars scattered randomly along the refuse-ridden sidewalks. The streetlamps pulsed with an odd humanoid rhythm, keeping up with one another. On the left, past the end of The Lion's Den, was a small break in the fence, presumably the entrance to an alley.

Here's hoping my good fortune will continue.

I reached the gap and was happy to see that it was just a rickety gate blocking my way. Only about half of the wood remained on the cross boards of the frame, sun-bleached and peeling. I pushed my way through, listening for anything that was out of the ordinary. At least anything that was out of the current situation's sense of ordinary.

The gate opened into a small passageway extending about a hundred feet. It stopped at the end, where it looked to open into a small courtyard. Shadows engulfed the area, leaving my imagination to run amuck.

Should I pull out my spotter? No, I would just have to put it away again sooner or later.

I started to jog slowly down the narrow path, glancing at my feet to check for anything nefarious and hazardous to my health. My boots clattered against glass bottles, bouncing off the tips and colliding into the walls, causing more noise.

You need to be quieter. You're trying to sneak up on them.

The ambient glow of a few lights flooded the small courtyard, giving me a better look at my surroundings. I slowed as I reached the alley's end, eventually stopping at the corner. My hand pawed at my pocket as I pulled out the compact mirror I kept in my right breast pocket. It was a gift Hope gave to me before everything became horrible and the city was evacuated. You wouldn't believe the teasing I received from the other men in the group, constantly heckling me about my makeup and stupid things like that. Maybe they would be more sympathetic if they had known why I carried it.

I miss you so much, Hope.

I popped it open and used it to look up and around the clearing. There were two different mirrors in it with a sturdy brown plastic case. The top one was for closer inspection with a convex curve, and the other was a regular piece of reflective material. The curved piece was cracked slightly, but that didn't hinder the other one, which I'd use right now. I wanted to see where the lights were, just in case I needed to shoot them out for added cover. I also wanted to check the windows of the buildings for anything that could kill me.

About thirty seconds passed while I moved the mirror around, not finding anything hazardous. I looked around and counted thirteen lights, a combination of some on poles, in the rooms of some windows, and a few next to about five different doors.

Alright, time to get going. I think I need to go through a door on the left side. That should lead me right to the Germans.

I flipped the compact mirror shut, the clasp coming together firmly. It slid into the padded front pocket with ease, keeping it from cracking any further. Next, I reached into a slot on the opposite side, pulling out a pocket watch. My thumb clicked the button on the top, springs squeaking from the stress of old age. I closed the lid and glanced at it, worn and scratched from many years of use, Atlas staring back at me in agony.

How appropriate it was. You felt like you held the world on your shoulders. Now everything feels like it is on mine. I won't let you down, Grandad. But you're wasting too much time; get going again.

I slipped the watch back into its hiding place and entered the courtyard. Most of it matched what I saw in the reflection moments prior, except the hulking beast of a man standing right in the middle of it. He wore a German infantry uniform, squashing my hopes of him being someone friendly. He was facing the corner in front of us with his back to me.

Damn, I didn't see him. Maybe I just need to trick him with a riddle or something.

Before I could turn back around and go back into the alley, the mass of a man turned to look at me. He towered over me at about seven feet even. His arms and legs were about the size of a small child—each one, not combined. His hair was buzzed to the scalp, revealing a series of scars that crossed and stretched like the stitching on a baseball. The wool tunic he wore was tight against his skin like it was made for him before he had started hitting the gym twenty-four-seven, three-hundred-sixty-five days a year. I gulped harshly as I slowly raised my pistol toward his chest. He gave me one look and growled in a low guttural tone, animal in nature.

"Hey there, Spike, can't imagine we can't talk this out?" I asked, hopes fading as quickly as my confidence.

Spike let out another grunt and growl as his body started to shake violently. His joints cracked and popped loudly, adding to the already tension-filled atmosphere. He looked down in front of his feet, staring at the ground. He heaved a deep and heavy breath, eyes staring me down again as steam curled from his nostrils in an upward arc from his ragged exhalation.

How did I not see this guy? He's as big as a damn house.

"Are you sure we can't talk? I really don't have time for this," I said.

I barely finished talking before he started to sprint at me. Dirt kicked up from each step he took, flying back every which way. I fired a few shots as quickly as possible, firing at center mass. They collided with his chest, doing as much damage as rocks skipping across a pond surface.

"What the hell are you?" I yelled in panic.

I tumbled to the side in a heap, trying to steer clear of the runaway train. He flew past me, shaking the ground beneath my feet. I rolled onto my shin and planted my foot, ready to spring up and away again if need be. A crash came from behind, and I turned to see that he had collided with a few garbage bins and some wooden crates. He yelled, struggling to free himself of the mess that entangled him.

Well, the pistol isn't cutting it. Maybe it's time for me to try Excalibur for real.

"Deck, are you in position yet?" Drow asked, voice breaking up.

"Not yet. But I'm a little busy with something," I said as I stood up. "I'll let you know when I am."

I slid my pistol into the holster against my hip, looking up in time to see the man start at me again. I leapt out of the way, causing him to strike a door behind me. My eyes turned to look at him as he burst through the wood, splintering it into shards and chunks. The adrenaline rushed through me again, turning the screams of my muscles from exhaustion to ones of primal reactions of flight and fight.

In a quick motion, I pulled Excalibur from its sheath on my back, bringing it in front of me. I planted my feet instinctively, left one in front, pointing toward the abyss of a doorway. My right was sideways, firm and steady, waiting for its next order. It freaked me out to realize my back was almost up against the tree he had been standing near. I exhaled, trying to catch my breath. It spewed forth in a thick fog, heavy and fleeting. It took shape from the light from the lamps, disappearing just seconds after they took life. Some noise sounded from the doorway in the form of creaks, groans, and sneers that bounced off the walls out to me.

"Come on, Spike, can't we just calm down?" I asked, staring patiently into the dark, "Maybe go back around to the pub and grab a pint?"

A guttural growl was the response I got from him, low and deep. It sent shivers down my spine, splintering off in every direction. I shifted my weight on my feet, waiting for anything to happen.

"No? Okay, maybe this'll do the trick. Toro, toro," I said.

Scraping from the hall filled my ears, followed by more animal noises. I focused to keep calm as I took some deep breaths and counted to thirteen. At the end of the first round of counting, I saw a spark of vibrant orange, a stark contrast to the dark background. I looked at it, squinting as it swayed back and forth. Before I realized what was happening, it flew in my direction. A split second went by, and I raised Excalibur to block whatever was flying at me. Impulsively I swung the sword at the glowing orange mass, slicing through it with ease. I quickly looked to the ground, checking what Spike had thrown. The object was now in two pieces at my feet, smoldering and crackling.

What the hell is it? And why is it on fire?

The ground shook softly, vibrating from added weight under my feet. I snapped my eyes back up to see Spike five feet from me, his own seemingly glowing with hatred and anger. He opened his mouth as if he was going to say something, but sparks and pulsing particles drifted from it as he let out a harsh breath. I shifted Excalibur in my hands, leveling it with his abdomen to be ready for him to collide with me. A strange heat pushed on my skin. It was almost too hot as it brushed against my face, and I could feel it starting to burn.

What is going on with this man? I don't understand what's happening right now.

The second he was within striking range, I dropped to the left and sliced through his body, feeling the blade catch on what I assumed was his spine. It cleared his body a second after it came in contact with it.

Two loud thuds sounded as I rolled out of the way after my strike. I immediately turned to see if I was going to be gored by him or not but on the ground next to the tree was Spike's body. Well, more or less. One half was on one side of the street, and the other half was on the opposite. I glanced around to check for more strangely large men looking to kill me. Luckily, there were none, so I was safe for a little while. Well, momentarily, anyway.

Get going. God knows how much longer Drow will keep in cover. Who knows when they will get sick of shooting at a wall, and I wouldn't want them to start after him.

The distant popping of gunfire sounded off through the building in front of me. The repercussions echoed through the hallway and out into the courtyard. I leaned over and wiped Excalibur on the dead man's shirt, cleaning off the slick black sludge from its blade. I looked closer at it, wondering why it wasn't a typical red stain like blood usually was.

Better save some of that. Quite peculiar. I'll have to bring it back for Dr. Thatcher to look at.

I slid Excalibur back into the sheath slung across my back, nestled between my haversack and my uniform. As I knelt next to Spike, I reached to a small pocket on the side of my bag, pulling out a tiny, cigar-sized vial. I took my knuckle-duster out of my right boot and used it to scoop some of the muck off his back.

Carefully, I pried the stopper out of the vial and scraped the blade over the mouth of the metal tube, depositing the strange substance into it. After I finished, I wiped off my knife like I did with Excalibur and replaced it into its sheath. Then, I put the rubber stopper back in the vial and deposited it in the small pocket. My mind nagged again, reminding me to get going, so I stood up, jogged over to the doorway, and went inside.

The blade was not only sharp but it was also enchanted. It was created to be able to cut through anything. Literally anything. Trust me, I know. I caused a few accidents when I was training with it. Let's just say that when I cut clean through one of the supporting beams in the basement of The Keepers Division Recruitment center, it didn't end too well.

Chapter 5
Good News, Maybe

I tried to tread lightly as I entered the hallway, keeping my ears focused on the noises around me. It was very dark and unnaturally damp for this time of year, giving my body a different kind of shiver.

I reached into a pocket on my left leg and pulled out my spotter. Since it was dark, I fumbled with it at first, not wanting too much light that would alert the Germans that I was coming up behind them. My hands found the right end of the spotter, and I twisted the lens on the end to limit the amount of light that could come through. I flipped the switch, and the articulated lens let through a small amount of the luminescence, adding a light glow to the objects around me. The hallway was long and narrow, with nothing in the way of doors on either of the walls. But I did see a few reflections at the far end where it turned into a narrow staircase.

I heard some inaudible yelling come from the same direction, cueing me to quit dawdling. As I ran toward the noise, I could feel the temperature fluctuate from cool dampness to a warm and dry atmosphere. The uncomfortable feeling lingered until I reached the steps as it quickly changed back to the dry cold I felt outside.

What the hell is going on around here?

The walls of the staircase were lined with more photos in frames. There were hundreds of memories of dead loved ones trapped in glass forever. Forever in company, but alone in silence.

"Why does it always have to be post-mortem pictures? It must be Scare Deckard Day," I mumbled to myself.

I kept my eyes trained on the top of the stairs, ignoring the faces of the lost peering into my soul. Nervousness bared down on me, making my steps come faster. I reached the top and released a heavy but silent sigh of relief.

Down the hallway, a door was cracked open slightly, about halfway down. Piercing white light shone through, beckoning me to come. More shouts in anger came from up ahead *not that the German language didn't sound angry enough.*

Probably a good bet they are in there.

Still wanting the element of surprise, I flipped the switch on the spotter as I placed it back into a pocket on my pants. As if on cue, gunfire picked up again, giving my footfalls a good cover noise to make it to the door. The noise stopped when I pulled out my pistol, deciding it would be a quicker dispatch of one of them if Drow hadn't had a chance to take the one out that was manning the MG42. I took a few deep breaths and peeked through the crack of the door, hoping to get a good look at what I was dealing with.

I could make out one of the men to the right of the room. He was leaning against the wall with a pair of binoculars to his face, probably keeping an eye out for Drow. I moved my gaze to the left, scanning over the rest of the room. Crouching in front of a window was the other man, gun propped up on the windowsill as he leaned against the buzzsaw.

Like always, I went through the rigamarole of counting to three and preparing myself for another heart-clenching situation. I flipped the pistol's safety off and readied it in my hands. A few more deep breaths, and I'd be on my way through that door and taking the gunman down.

I reached for the doorknob and started to open it slowly, my Kestler Mk IV leveled to fire center mass at their chests. When the door was open enough, I slipped through, my eyes trained on the person to the left. I lined up my shot when a tinny voice chimed through the Warbler's speaker without warning.

"*Deux-trois attendez, un-cinq atten—*" said the feminine voice.

My blood went cold, chilled with fear and a surge of anxiety-infused adrenaline. I fumbled with my pistol in my right hand as I tried to reach for the device with my left, struggling to turn it off before it gave away my position.

"*Was war das?*" asked the man to the right.

Yeah, what was that? Come on, you damn infernal device.

They whirled around to look in my direction. I tried to take a few shots at them, but the growing panic sent my bullets wide, missing by miles. I looked back and forth as they dove to the ground, hands reaching for guns themselves. The thwack of a bullet from a large caliber bolt action rifle slammed into the wall next to my head, crackling from the leftover charge slowly dissipating into the air.

"Dammit Drow, *not at me!*" I yelled into the comms, retreating to the hall behind.

Static broke through the communication system. "He was standing just before I shot. Not my fault you're a klutz."

I pressed my body up against the wall outside the room I was just in. The sound of slides and bolts clacking from guns filled the air right before the thumping of bullets followed. A few bullets whizzed through the plaster next to my face and torso, pushing me back further down the hallway. I let off a few shots myself, putting the barrel of my gun to the wall and pulling the trigger wildly.

"What if I just wanted to talk? Is that such a bad thing?" I said, my voice stifled by the ruckus.

"Are you alright, Deck?" Drow asked.

"Yeah, I'm fine. Are they still in the room? Have I hit one of them yet?"

"No, I don't think so. I see one of them. I think he was the one manning the gun."

Another loud thwack of the heavy caliber rifle echoed through the air, followed by Drow's voice coming through the comms again. "I think I got him. The other one looks like he is wounded on the floor. Go have a look."

"Okay, keep an eye on my back, though."

I holstered my pistol again, my nerves frayed and my heart pumping a million miles an hour. The last rays of the disappearing sunset peeked through the bullet holes in the walls, cutting lines of light through the darkness of the space in front of me.

If he thought one of them was down and the other was injured, then I shouldn't need to use force. I should be fine.

I nervously rolled my neck from one side to the other, popping from the habitual act. The plaster crunched underneath my boots as I walked into the room. Bullet casings and more debris littered the floor with the furniture strewn about. Cautiously, I looked around, just in case.

The maid won't be happy about the mess she has to clean up.

To the left, like Drow said, was one of the Germans on the floor. Blood pooled around his body, arms and legs contorted at unnatural angles. The bullet that Drow fired hit him in the back of the head — fitting, considering what he did to Phillips. I heard raspy and heavy breathing from behind me. Turning, I saw the other one propped up against the wall. He had a bullet wound on his right shoulder with blood soaking the entire front of his uniform.

I walked over to him, staring to ensure he didn't do anything idiotic. His eyes flickered from me to the ground just in front of his hands. I looked down to see a Luger just inches out of reach. He made a struggling effort, fingers aggressively clawing at the ground, trying to reach it before I did. The sweat poured from his face as a look of fear, anger, and understanding danced across it.

"Deck, there's another behind you; look out!" Drow yelled.

Without thinking, my hand reflexively drew Excalibur, blade singing as it slid from its sheath. I spun around and dropped to one knee, swinging the sword in a horizontal arc. The German in front of me had an MP40 raised and pointing at my head. Excalibur sliced through his midsection just as a gun went off. My right shoulder flew forward, causing me to lose my balance. The sword flew off to the left, clattering against the wall. I went with the momentum and rolled onto the injured arm as the man's body hit the ground next to me. I looked behind me to see the wounded man had successfully reached his Luger, the barrel steaming from the energy of the hot lead forced through it.

He looked at me, face still contorted with conflicting emotions. "Es tut mir Leid."

Sorry? That's all you have to say for yourself?

I didn't have time to do anything. I couldn't get out of the way or stop him from doing this, so I closed my eyes and waited for the light, yearning for the sense of ease that came with death, the promise of no more worry or pain.

Next, I heard the metallic click of a firing pin hitting home with nothing to send off, and I did not see the white light I had expected. I opened my eyes to see that I wasn't dead and that the misery was to continue. The Luger skidded toward me across the floor, scrapping and clattering off shards of glass, porcelain and metal.

"Ich gebe auf." Whimpered the man.

Give up?

"Deck! Come in, Deck! Are you okay?" Drow asked.

I grunted at the pain, "Yeah, I am. Come over here. I got the one that had the MP40. Be careful, though."

I sat up and struggled to my feet. With each new heartbeat, my shoulder pounded in pain, causing my vision to blur momentarily. The blood oozed from the shoulder wound I sustained, trickling down my uniform and dripping to the ground. I meandered over to Excalibur, leaning over gently to pick it up. Pain coursed through my body when I straightened my back, causing me to let out a strained yelp. Just then, Drow came through the doorway, skittering to a stop.

"Deck, are you okay?" he asked, looking at my arm and shoulder.

I glanced down at it for the first time. The skin, muscle, and fabric exploded outward from a small, jagged hole. A wave of nausea washed over me, my body's way of telling me not to look at it.

"Yeah, it looks just great. Went clean through, for the most part," I grimaced.

A soft grunt came from the corner, followed by a few heavy coughs. It made Drow's head snap in that direction. He lifted his rifle, ready to fire on him, but I reached over and put my hand on the barrel before he could do anything.

"No, we need him alive. I know you don't want that, but we need him to answer our questions," I said as I pushed his gun down to the ground.

"But Deck, they killed Phillips. We don't need them," Drow said, his voice filled with venom.

I turned to Drow, giving him a stern look. "That's an order, soldier."

His face was filled with anger, eyes boring into me. I hated to resort to ranks, especially to my brother, but sometimes he just didn't listen to me. I shook my head and walked over to the man in the corner. He looked at me through pained eyes, watching my movements with each ragged breath.

"Can you understand English?" I asked, crouching next to him.

He nodded slowly, still watching me. I shifted on my feet and dropped to one knee. The pressure from crouching was relieved, taking it off my shoulder. I winced from the pain, coming and fading slightly.

"What about speaking? Can you speak it?" I asked.

The man just stared at me, not saying anything in response. I looked over my shoulder at Drow to see if he was paying attention. Of course, he wasn't. He was busy searching the bodies of this man's fallen partners.

I looked back at the man. "What about a name? You got a name?"

He swallowed hard. "Klaus."

I studied him before responding. The man known as Klaus had a clean-shaven face. His thick black hair was shaved on the sides and a few inches tall on the top. It was parted at the side, combed up and back to the other side of his head. He had sharp features that resulted in a pointy nose and stark cheekbones that jutted outward. The next thing I noticed was his uniform. It lacked any specific insignias or ways to tell he was a German soldier. For some reason, the uniform was very similar to what we were wearing: just gray. That in itself concerned me more than a little bit.

"Alright, Klaus, I am going to have to take you with us. You understand?" I asked.

"*Ja.*"

"Okay. We have some questions that we need answers to," I said.

He just stared blankly at me again.

"We will get you fixed up. Make sure you get some food in you while we talk to you. But you've gotta behave yourself. Most of my men don't take too kindly to Germans. Especially ones involved with killing their friends," I said.

He nodded in understanding, putting his hands above his head. Klaus winced from the pain of the shot to his shoulder, but he kept his hands up. I looked back over at Drow again, seeing if he was done.

"Hey Drow, you got one of those new bindings handy?" I asked.

"Uh, yeah. Gimme a sec," he said.

Drow walked over to me, slinging his Mason Model 1937 Sharpshooter onto his shoulder. In the same motion, he pulled a wrist binding from a side pocket on his haversack. I turned to Drow and took it from him as Drow looked at Klaus with disgust, turning away immediately.

"Klaus, hold out your hands," I said, reaching out to him.

Klaus put his wrists in front of his body, waiting for me to slide the loops around them. I got the right hand in with no issue, tightening it to prevent him from sliding it off. As I went to slide it to the left, my hand brushed against his skin.

Without warning, the ring on my right hand lit up in a magnificent golden glow, showering the small space in the bright light. I looked at my ring in amazement, confusion starting to form in my mind. I looked from the pulsing ring to Klaus' face, bewilderment and shock painted across his expression.

Drow's voice sounded over my shoulder, "Well, damn."

Chapter 6
Questions First

24th December, 1942
Hackney Borough, London, England
10:06 p.m.

We entered the church a little after ten with the German in tow. I wasn't sure what to make of it. The fact that he was a descendant rattled me. It seems that's just my luck; having to convert an axis soldier over to the good side seemed like something I would get stuck with.

We made our way to the back of the crowded nave, skirting past the grimy pews. They lay in somewhat disarray, covered by piles of bibles and other books. Other miscellaneous items I couldn't make out were hidden underneath white linen sheets now gray from the recent bombings throughout the city.

"I don't think I can tell him," Drow mumbled.

"I can. We did everything we could, Drow. Phillips knew the risks of the mission," I said.

In the early moonlight, I could faintly make out his face. The look of anger and frustration stretched across it put my mood on edge.

"That doesn't mean it needed to happen," he said.

I began to reply but stopped myself. Anything I said now wouldn't change much, and definitely wouldn't bring Phillips back. I decided to bite my tongue, continuing to follow as Drow led the way to the hidden passageway in the altar. I adjusted my grip on Klaus' arm, keeping him out in front. Before we had even left the room where we found him, I had removed my ring, not wanting it to glow every time I nudged him along.

Drow stopped in front of the massive expanse of candles standing in attention, row after steady row. I pulled on Klaus' arm to signal him to stop as well. Drow reached into a pocket and silently pulled out something small and metallic. With the flick of his wrist, it sparked to life, burning strong in the dark expanse of the church. He leaned forward with the flame, lighting a few, what seemed to be random, candles.

After he finished, he moved to the side. "Did I do it right?"

I looked over Klaus' shoulder and said, "Lemme see."

My eyes moved over the expanse of candles as I counted to thirteen about five times as I scanned them over. On the second to last count, I noticed he missed it by two, throwing off the next one as well.

Without sounding judgemental, I said, "You have to fix the last two. You're off."

Drow looked at it again, lifting his hand to help with the count. As he was doing that, the German let out a pained groan, causing Drow to growl in frustration. He turned to glare at Klaus, then returned to his count. Drow sighed as he finally finished extinguishing the wrong candles and lighting the new ones. The floor beneath our feet began to shake and vibrate violently after bringing the last candle to life. The stones separated at the seams and lowered into the ground, creating a spiral staircase in about five seconds.

I looked at Drow and said, "You go down first. I'll follow behind and blow out the candles."

Drow shrugged and started down the staircase, head disappearing in seconds. I nudged Klaus to follow, having him go first. When my head was eye level with the flames, I drew a deep breath and blew the candles out. The room grew dark once more as we descended into the abyss.

The staircase led into the underground about fifteen feet, not too far, but far enough to stay out of earshot of anyone we didn't want to hear. The bottom opened up to a small chamber with a large set of doors set into a wall that stood ten feet high. On either side of the stained oak was a cast iron torch holder complete with a primitive wooden torch. Drow crossed silently over to the doors and pushed gently. They opened with ease, perfectly balanced on their axes.

Our eyes adjusted to take in a heavy, thick cloud of candle and cigarette smoke lay in the air across the space. It spread along like fog, causing spots to be less than visible. The room beyond the doors was large, extending thirty feet in either direction. Large, three-foot wide support columns were spread evenly at five feet intervals holding up the ceiling. Along each wall were banks upon banks of massive radio relay consoles, including a few electromechanical computers. Each station was manned by a soldier, a mix of both male and female. Guards were standing at half of them, watching their surroundings like hawks eyeing their next meal.

Frank was standing in the middle of the room, leaning over an expansive table, the top filled with maps, diagrams, and small figures representing the land's current lay. We garnered Frank's attention as we took our first few steps in.

"You made it!" said Frank as he stood and turned with his hands outstretched in welcome.

Drow, Klaus, and I filed into the room one by one. Drow was in the front, and I followed up the rear, making sure Klaus kept the direction we wanted him to.

I looked over to Frank and said solemnly, "Yeah, we did. We have a prisoner that needs some medical attention, though."

Frank looked us over, meeting Drow at the entrance. "And where is Phillips?"

Drow looked away, trying not to meet Frank's eyes. He skipped over the German momentarily as his gaze stopped on me. The smile faded slowly, realization taking its place.

"He didn't make it, did he?" Frank whispered.

I shook my head, not needing to say more. Frank's shoulders slumped only for a moment before returning to their usual rigged and confident position.

He clapped his hands together gently. "He knew the risks. I trust you took care of it properly?"

I nodded and motioned to Klaus in front of me. "Yes, we did, immediately after we apprehended this man."

With a frown, Frank said, "He will be remembered and honored as if he was a true member of the round. Arthur will have a place by his side for him, from fire to ashes."

"I still don't know why we have to do that to any of us that die. I feel like it is an insult to our memory," Drow said.

Frank nodded but replied, "Since our division is considered highly secretive and classified, anyone that perishes in the line of duty is dealt with promptly. You know that."

Drow shook his head in anger and disgust.

"It sounds inhumane, but the scientists employed by the opposing forces have technology that can do unthinkable things. The last thing we need is our classified information used against us," Frank said.

As we spoke, a soldier walked near us. Frank stopped the man and pulled him close. He saluted Frank and stood attention without saying anything else.

"Young man, what does every one of us bring into battle to prevent our secrets from being used against us?" Frank asked.

"'Every Keepers soldier is sent into combat with a device called SPARC, which stands for Spontaneous Personal Accelerated Remote Combustion. When activated, it causes the person's body and anything on them to combust spontaneously'," the soldier recited from memory.

Ah yes, during basic training, the other men in my unit affectionately called it, 'the flight of the phoenix.'

"Thank you, soldier. You can go back to what you were doing."

He nodded and saluted once more before continuing his tasks.

"I collected half of Phillips' dog tag and the postcard he was carrying on him, in his helmet of all places. We said a few prayers before our goodbyes, sending him off in a blaze of glory," I said as I handed them to Frank.

Drow finally spoke up, "It was this man's fault."

He violently jabbed a finger into Klaus' abdomen, pushing harder than was needed. Klaus let out a strained cough, taking a few steps back. He regained his footing while simultaneously barking out something in German. Drow then got into his face and started yelling as well.

"What did you say to me? It's your fault! It was the day you started the war!" Drow yelled.

"Wait a minute here. Let's stay calm, okay?" I said, getting in between them.

I put a hand on Drow's chest, keeping him from knocking the other man down. Meanwhile, Klaus was pushing against my shoulder. I grunted in pain, looking at the bullet hole, still very tender and sore. Before I realized what was going on, Klaus had grabbed my pistol. He took a few steps back and pointed it at me, face pale and drenched in sweat. I turned and looked at him, putting my hands out in front to signal cooperation.

The guards, Drow, and a handful of other soldiers pulled out their guns. I raised my arm, motioning them to stop and lower their weapons.

"Klaus, please. Don't do this," I said.

His arms swayed weakly. "Was ist going on here."

I turned to Drow and then to Klaus. "You can speak English?"

"*Ja*, some."

I wet my lips and said, "Okay, that makes things easier. Please, lower the gun."

Time felt as if it slowed to a crawl. The overlapping noises sounded in the distant background. A light buzz from the radio relay consoles gave way to the slow ticking of a clock on an unseen wall.

"Was ist going on here? Why did das ring glow when you touched me?" Klaus asked.

The gun switched from me to Frank, hovering at him for a moment before finding its way to Drow, jerking and overcorrecting at his chest. It eventually trained back on me, causing me to flinch involuntarily.

I chuckled nervously. "Just give me the gun, and I'll tell you. Trust me. We don't want to hurt you."

Klaus snapped the gun back toward Drow.

"Look at me, not at him, at me," I said.

His eyes darted back at me, pupils wide and deep. They were extremely dilated, and he was struggling to focus on me. He opened his mouth to say more, but before anything escaped, his eyelids fluttered. Without warning, he crumpled to the ground in a heap, the gun still firmly grasped in his hand.

I rushed to his side and dropped to my knees. I reached for the pistol first, wanting to get it away before it went off accidentally. Frank was right behind, yelling out some orders, "Eileen! Is the sick bay ready?"

"It is, sir!" she yelled, voice carrying off from the left of the room.

Dr. Thatcher came rushing up to our sides, two men following behind carrying a stretcher. She motioned for us to move so she could take a look at Klaus. We took a step back and allowed her men to lay him out gently on his back. I abruptly holstered my pistol and carefully snapped the safety latch to ensure that didn't happen again.

"He has lost a lot of blood. Let's get him over to the sick bay," she said.

One of the men that followed Dr. Thatcher took a spot at Klaus' head while the other crouched near his feet. They gently took hold of him and lifted him onto the stretcher they had laid next to him. They then grabbed the handles and lifted him, carrying him off to the infirmary. Dr. Thatcher followed next to them, a stethoscope fixed on Klaus' chest, looking for any sign of life.

"That was close," I said.

Frank sighed heavily. "What was that all about?"

I rolled my neck from side to side, letting out a sigh myself. After a few seconds of silence, I reached into one of my many pockets. I dug for something in particular, my hand sorting through the contents: A few extra bullets, some loose change, a small spool of dental floss, and empty candy wrappers. My hand finally found what it was looking for, making me happy that at least I still had some. I grabbed it and took it out, placing the ends in my fingertips. I pulled on the fanned edges of the wrapper and undid it, exposing the sugary nugget of goodness.

"Still needing to use the pear drops?" Frank asked, looking at my hands.

I popped it into my mouth and said, "Yes, and it's my last one, so don't ask."

He rolled his eyes as he pulled his pipe from his jacket pocket. He checked the bowl, seeing if there was tobacco still packed inside. Nodding with satisfaction, he put the pipe in his mouth and lit it with his lighter.

He took a huge breath of the vile burning smoke and said, "Never mind, I suppose. You didn't answer my question, though. What was that about?"

"It's complicated."

"I have time," he said through the rolling cloud of pipe smoke.

My shoulder flared in pain from the movement of digging in my pocket. I flinched and said, "Okay, but you gotta help me with this bullet wound first."

Frank agreed, putting my left arm over his shoulders. We walked slowly to the infirmary, dismissing the soldiers who offered to help. I glanced over and saw a field nurse standing near the desk next to the archway looking over the shoulder of Dr. Thatcher.

Once inside, I plopped down onto one of the beds located in the small alcove. There were three short rows of beds consisting of three in each. Privacy curtains that usually separated them sat unused, tucked away in the corner. Klaus was lying on his back in the first row on the bed nearest the front entrance, while I was in the last row.

"Lisa, can you help Frank and Deckard out? I need to keep an eye on this one," Dr. Thatcher said, busy attending to Klaus.

"Yes, ma'am," she replied.

Lisa hurried over to us in a blur, shoes clicking and clacking on the hard stone ground. She reached into her nurse's apron and pulled out a small medi-spotter.

They were a version of the military issue spotters. Designed with size in mind, small enough to be easily carried, but strong enough to work well.

She clicked the button on the end and waved it over her hands for a moment, checking to see if it was working correctly.

Happy with the results, she shined it into my eyes without much warning. I blinked, head shaking in surprise from the bright light.

"Well?" Frank asked.

"You know how I said it was complicated?" I asked.

"Yeah, why is it, though?"

Lisa finally moved the medi-spotter from my eyes, freeing me from the searing blindness. I blinked hard, chasing the spot in my sight around the room.

"For lack of another way to say it, he's a descendant."

"Sir, I'm sorry to bother you, but I am going to have to ask you not to move so much. Please keep still," Lisa said, light trained on my shoulder.

I heard Frank choke on some of his tobacco smoke. Some heaving followed, so I tried to look at Frank to see his expression.

Before I could finish the movement, Lisa took my jaw in her hand and moved my face forward again. "Sir, please. Keep looking straight."

"Okay, sorry," I said.

I heard her clear her throat expectantly, so I turned and focused on her once again. She was frowning at me with a cocked eyebrow, causing me to smirk slightly.

"What are you eating?" Lisa demanded, prying my mouth open and shining her light inside it.

I mumbled, "It's candy."

"Spit it out. I can't have you choking on it," she said.

"No, it's my last one. I'm in charge, and I say let me be," I said.

She shook her head and started back at my shoulder again.

"What did you say?" asked Frank, exhaling another acrid cloud of smoke.

"I said he is a descendant of a knight of the round."

"You're right. That is complicated."

I heard Frank make a few humming noises; a tick he does that when he is thinking. It is usually only when the situation is difficult, so I guess we are in for some real fun.

I could hear the burning of the tobacco as he inhaled, crackling quietly against the competing noises all around. My gaze shifted from Klaus' bed to Lisa, the nurse in front of me.

"Ma'am, is it bad?" I asked.

She clicked her tongue and said, "No, not very. It went clean through. Let me grab the mender."

I felt the blood flush from my face. "The mender? Do you really need to?"

She gave me a gentle pat on the cheek. "Oh, hush. You'll be alright. You've been through worse."

Lisa turned and walked briskly across the alcove. I could see she had to rummage through a few crates of things to find what she was looking for.

Frank unexpectedly stopped humming and turned to me. "What do you think? Can we trust him?"

I laughed obnoxiously. "How would I know?"

"I trust your judgment, Deck. That's why you're in charge of the men."

I looked around the room, my gaze hopping from person to person. "I think we need to administer the test first to see if it takes."

My gaze eventually fell on Frank as he let out another plume of the vile smog. I tossed the pear drop in my mouth, thinking about the last person we administered the test to. If we had known that some people do not react well to the sudden implant of a few hundred years' worth of memories, we would have tied them up or something. Let's just say it didn't go as planned and ended badly.

Lisa quickly came back with the mender in her hands. It gleamed maniacally in the light from the Tesla Bulb chandeliers. I didn't know the device's real name, but it was a big soldering iron for your skin. It was made of metal and was about the same size as a beer bottle. It used a high focus of electricity to stimulate the natural healing properties of the human body. And it hurt a lot.

Lisa approached and sat down in the small rolling chair she was pulling behind her. "Okay, are you ready?"

"Uh no. I am not. But that doesn't matter, does it?" I asked.

She smiled deviously as she flipped the power switch on the mender. My body shuddered from the memory of the last time I had to use one. I looked away just before she started on my shoulder.

"Okay, we will have to see if he can pass," I said.

"Sounds like a good start. I will go check on Drow, see if he is okay," Frank said. "How long do you think this might take?"

"It should only take about ten minutes, sir," Lisa said.

"Send him our way when you are through with him. It's Christmas Eve. We should try and use this to boost morale," he said with a smile.

"Frank," I said, "is Himmler still a prime suspect for Jakobus?"

He paused. "Yes, why?"

"We saw Himmler while we were out there."

He raised an eyebrow. "You did? Were you able to do anything? See where he was headed?"

I shook my head. "It was right after we lost Phillips. We were under fire from the POW and his cohort."

Frank pursed his lips. "You did the best you could in the worst situation."

Chapter 7
Briefing

2nd August, 1937
Kew Gardens, Richmond Borough, London, England
8:20 a.m.

The mechanical grumble of the motor car shook the frame beneath Deck's feet. The man across from him leaned forward from the backrest of his seat, causing the brown leather cushion to squeak underneath him. The vehicle's weight shifted gently to the right as they turned the corner onto Kew Road as the morning sun kissed the rooftops of the buildings and outlined the smoke lazily rising from the chimneys.

"How are you this morning?" asked Frank.

Deck turned from his view through the window and looked at him. "I'm doing alright. Thanks for asking."

"Not a problem at all, just wanted to check and see if you had any second thoughts about all of this."

Deck's gaze turned back to the window once more. He watched as the street raced past in a blur, people forming large, continuous blobs. "I'm sure Grandad would want me to help."

"Good. Good. We will need it."

The automobile slowed almost to a stop and picked up again as it turned to the left. They drove down a winding driveway lined with plants consisting of thorny bushes, thick tall trees, and vibrant summer flowers. Eventually, the dirt path opened up to a large steel structure of thousands of gleaming windows reflecting the morning sun.

"Why are we at the Temperate House?" Deck asked, gazing up at the expanse of glass and metal.

"You've been here before?" asked Frank.

"Yeah, quite a bit, actually. Grandad took us here when we were younger. He always said it was an important place to him."

"That would make sense. It seems that he did expose you to some of these things."

"He did." Deck paused. "He never spoke of Nikola, Arthur, or The Keepers, though."

"Fair enough, but either way, you know all about it now."

The motor cautiously creaked to a stop in front of the front steps of the greenhouse. The driver killed the engine, causing it to heave and groan, relieved to be free of the strain of combustion. The driver turned and placed his arm on the back of his seat, looking at both of us.

"How long will you be, sir?" he asked.

"Shouldn't be long. Oh, I'd say maybe an hour or so. Do you mind staying around that long, Harry?" Frank asked.

"Not at all, sir. I will keep her right here waiting for youse."

Frank nodded and opened the left side door with a quick motion, gesturing for Deck to go first. He obliged and exited the car, taking in the view again. It was just as beautiful as the first time he'd seen it all those years ago.

"Come along, Deck. We still have a few things to take care of. You can look around again when we are finished. This way," Frank said as he started up the step.

His stride was rather large, taking two or three steps at a time. Deck rushed after him to keep up the pace, jumping from one to another. He struggled to stay with him, almost tripping on his own feet.

"He makes it look so easy," Deck thought.

Once at the top, they quickly walked over to the double doors directly in front of them. They swung open with ease, leading into the expanse of tropical plants. The thick, muggy air hit Deck like a crumbling brick wall, a mixture of cool and hot air in lieu of small sections falling from its surface. Sweat started forming on his forehead, beading and beginning to fall. He wiped it with his forearm, trying to keep it from his eyes.

"Why are we here? Is this really a suitable meeting place?" Deck asked.

"Yes. Trust me, this way."

He led Deck down the main path made of cut stone through the middle of the greenhouse. After about fifty feet, they came to a crossroads in the center of everything before taking a sharp right, walking another fifty feet. They passed more plants from many different regions of the world, all brought together, living in thriving harmony. Finally, they reached the end of the second path near another set of doors leading into a smaller greenhouse filled with even more flora. Just before them was a spiral staircase that led to an upper level of catwalks that provided an aerial view of the garden.

"What now?" Deck asked, looking around for something obvious. "There are only plants. Are we early?"

Frank smirked and chuckled. "No, we are actually right on time."

He walked to the staircase and made it seem he was going to ascend it, but instead, he stuck his foot underneath the first step and tapped around for a moment. Frank felt around for something, the clacking noise bouncing off the walls as he did so. He eventually found what he was looking for as the clacking was replaced by a hollow, thunking sound. The floor underneath the staircase shook as the bricks started to shift and drop below the ground. Deck watched in awe as they formed another set of stairs going the opposite direction.

"I stand corrected. This is definitely the place to meet people in secret," Deck said.

"There's always more than what's in front of your eyes." Frank chuckled as he circled the railing of the spiral staircase. He then reached into his jacket pocket, pulling out a small reflective object.

"What's that?" Deck asked, pointing at his hand.

"Oh, this?" He lifted his hand to show me what it contained. "It's an Embyr, a handheld, copper-encased light that you carry in your hand. This one happens to be your grandad's."

Deck's eyes glazed over as memories fluttered through his mind. He remembered the fateful night of the first time Davey met Steven, finding the woman who Jakobus and his followers killed. He remembered the seemingly random events leading to the moment their lives became intertwined. He recalled the struggle between good and evil, dark and light in conflict, demanding they were right, and the other should grovel at their feet.

"I really gotta stop zoning out like that," Deck thought.

They started to descend into the dark abyss, the Embyr keeping the shadows at bay. It took a minute or so of winding in a downward spiral to eventually reach the bottom, opening up into a large meeting room. It went for a few hundred feet, brightly lit with hanging Tesla Bulb chandeliers cascading light upon the furnishings.

To the right was a wall made up of bookcase after bookcase, extending to the back. Blues and reds mixed with muted browns and tans with green and black mixed in at random intervals making up the spines of books.

To the left was painting after painting of landscapes, people, and animals with a beautiful array of colors which rivaled, if not overtook, the beauty of the books. Deck walked over to the painting closest to him and studied the content. On the left wall hung a bewitching oil painting depicting a woman with the skin of porcelain and hair of scarlet that rivaled the fierceness of any fire. She lay upon what seemed to be a simple fishing boat guided along by a man in mourning.

"Frank, this one is familiar. How come?" Deck asked.

"That was a gift from the Commissioner of the Scotland Yard after the year of the reaper. Your Grandad received it as thanks for stopping the menace known at the time as The Leather Apron. You probably know him better by the name Jack the Ripper."

"He turned out to be Jakobus, didn't he?"

"Yes. And that was just one name he went by. But you know that."

Deck rubbed his neck. "I do. It's quite a lot to have ricocheting around in my head. Sometimes it's a little hard to differentiate the memories. I know that there were three people under Jakobus' control. Weren't they Dr. Henry, Herman Mudgett, and Constable Jules?"

"Yes, they were. But only two were confirmed to be killed, and there could have been more. Here, try this." Frank held out his hand, fingers uncurling from his fist to reveal a pear drop.

"What's that for?" Deck asked, reaching for it.

"Think of it as a tether. It will keep you linked to the memories that are yours. Keep you anchored to the present."

Deck unfurled it and popped it into his mouth. As he began to suck on it, it brought back memories of his childhood.

He raised his eyebrows in surprise. "It worked!"

"Good. Now to get down to business."

They turned to the center of the room. It had an arrangement of leather couches in a circle around a small coffee table. A crystal vase filled with birds of paradise sat elegantly in the middle of fine white china with intricate yellow floral design placemats. Next to the flowers was a silver serving tray with sugar cubes and milk for tea. Sitting on the couches were three men and a woman holding cups to their lips, buried with idle chatter.

"This is the group you'll be working with from this point on, sans Mr. Tesla. He won't be on the frontlines with you. I hope you can understand."

Deck waved to the group sheepishly, trying to keep his cheeks from turning red and burning up. Everyone turned to him and nodded, returning to their conversation and tea.

"On the left, we have Mr. Tesla, the one who is helping tremendously with The Keepers lately."

"I met him at Grandad's funeral, didn't I?"

"Yes, you did. Next to him is Thomas, who is our weaponry engineer. He is the leading developer currently employed by TEA."

Deck nodded, eyes bouncing along as Frank continued.

"In the middle is Eileen, a pioneer in her field. She has been pertinent to developing medical devices in the Asclepius Division."

Deck's gaze hovered on her longer than he'd like to admit, taking in her flowing brown hair.

"Wow, she's very beautiful," Deck whispered.

"Breathtaking, really," Frank murmured. He looked at Deck and cleared his throat. "She is a beautiful young woman."

Eileen looked toward Frank, peering over the ridge of the cup. Her eyes twinkled with a mischievous mixture of attraction and embarrassment.

Deck's eyes shifted to the last person on the group's far right. "Who is that? Have I met him before?"

"That is Steven, but I don't think you have. He is just in from the States." Frank spoke up for everyone to hear, "Gentlemen, and of course, Lady, may I introduce you to Deckard O'Shea. He is Davey's grandson."

The man introduced to Deck as Mr. Tesla put his cup and saucer on the table and stood up in one quick motion. He turned to Deck with the same sense of urgency and took a slight bow.

"It's good to see you again, my boy. My name is Nikola. But, but, but we have already met. Again, sorry for your loss."

Nikola was wearing a light brown tweed suit, hair gray and parted down the middle, combed in waves to the sides. His face bore a respectable but rather small mustache, clean-shaven besides. His ears and cheekbones were a prominent and noticeable feature, along with his very slender stature.

"Thank you. I do remember you. I have actually heard a lot about you from—" Deck paused for a moment before clearing his throat. "Sorry, had heard a lot from my grandad."

Deck grew silent from the surge of pain and loss still very fresh in his mind. He shook it off, not wanting him to get the wrong impression.

"Hmm, yes, yes, yes. He was a fine man. One of the best that I have ever known. He was the reason after all that I was brought into the fascinating world of Sir Arthur Pendragon." Nikola turned to Thomas and said, "This will be the man to talk to if you need anything. Think of him as your own personal butler."

Deck looked at Thomas once more, taking in his well-kempt appearance. The suit he wore was black with pinstripes, a pure black vest, a white dress shirt, and a burgundy tie. His black hair was slicked back with the front pushed off to the left, accented by bushy sideburns.

"If you need anything, just let me know. You want that blade of yours to be electrified, I'm your guy. Maybe you just want a gun that shoots grapes as fast as a bullet? I can do that. You dream it, and I can make it." Thomas winked and took another sip of his tea.

"He's very good at what he does," Frank chimed in.

"And the lovely young woman next to him can fix anything you put in front of her, as long as it is flesh and bone, that is," Nikola said.

Deck's heart fluttered erratically as he took in her beauty once more. She was wearing a simple but elegant baby blue dress and bonnet. The dress had white trim along the lapel's edges, accentuating her bosom, ending at the collar.

"Hello, love, try and stay healthy, so you don't need me to poke and prod," she said with a devilish smirk.

Deck turned to the last person: Steven. He looked at the man, and they caught each other's stare. The thoughts tugged at the back of his mind as hazy and foggy pictures fluttered to the front, so he chewed on the drop more, trying to push everything back.

"Hello, Deckard. My name is Steven, but you can call me Steven for short."

Within seconds, Deck's grandad's cherished memories became clearer. They sifted through the other millions to form a cohesive series of events for him to understand.

Deck smiled and said, "Hello, sir. I believe I have you at a disadvantage, though."

He cocked an eyebrow and asked, "Why's that, my boy?"

Deck turned to have Excalibur shift on his back for Steven to see. "I feel like I already know you. It's a strange feeling."

Chapter 8
Rough Mornings

25th December, 1942
Hackney Borough, London, England
7:00 a.m.

I awoke to a consistent chatter laced with an unbearable amount of static. With each heartbeat, my brain knocked against my skull, causing it to hurt from pressure and noise.

I opened my eyes slowly, rubbing my neck gently as I tried to roll it from side to side to crack it. Sadly, my efforts were to no avail. I looked around to try and deduce how the night played out, catching blurry glimpses of the past twelve hours in my mind's eye. The smoke of candles and cigarettes from the night prior was thinner, making breathing more manageable, which was always good.

"Ugh, my head," moaned someone to the right of me.

I glanced at the source of the voice and noticed I was lying in the infirmary. Sprawled out in a cot next to me was Drow, still dressed in the clothes from our latest mission.

"What happened last night?" I asked, closing my eyes again.

I reached up to rub my temples with my right arm, only to be rewarded with pain. It shot down my arm and exploded through my shoulder. I let out a grunt and looked down at it, wondering why it hurt so much.

My shirt was cut away, revealing my pale, bloodstained skin. A fresh scar about the size of a penny almost centered perfectly on my shoulder. I heard Drow's bed creak from movement and turned my attention from the pain to him.

"Too much eggnog," moaned Drow.

He sat upright, for the most part, and swung his legs around the side to face me. Drow hung his head low, staring down at his feet. His fatigues were grimy and full of dust and dirt. I scoffed as I noticed he didn't even take the time to kick off his boots.

"Who had the brandy?" I asked, still trying to crack my neck.

"Me. I snagged some from The Lion's Den when I came after you," he said.

"You took the time to grab alcohol even when you thought my life was in danger?"

Drow chuckled. "Uh yeah. I knew you'd be fine. You have a sword. I mean, come on. Who's gonna mess with someone carrying a sword?"

I shook my head. "I suppose you're right. Where is the rest of it? The brandy?"

Drow pointed to the ground at the foot of his cot, where a half-filled bottle of dark brown liquid sat. I reached down and scooped it up, causing the alcohol to slosh around idly in the glass. I leaned over and slipped it into my bag that was hooked over the bedpost of my own.

I glanced at a lump, presumably Klaus, lying on his side in the furthest row of cots. Each new breath he took caused the blanket to rise and fall in a smooth rhythm. The sound of scraping from boots pulled my attention to the left, away from the man that may have been responsible for Phillips' death.

"Oh good, you two are up!" said Frank, slapping both of us on the shoulder.

Thankfully he hit my good shoulder, only giving me minor discomfort. On the other hand, Drow let out a shriek of pain, swearing in the process.

"Frank, why? I'm hurt and tired and don't want to be awake. Can't we do this later?" Drow asked, putting his head in his hands.

"That's what happens when you smuggle alcohol into a prohibited area," Frank said. He looked over to the nurses' station. "Lisa? Do you have anything to help Drow with his hangover?"

"Yes, sir, I'll be right there," she said.

"While she helps you, I'll steal your brother away. We need to prepare for the test," Frank said, turning to me once more. "By the way, Merry Christmas, gentlemen."

After four or five minutes of trying, I finally popped my neck. I sighed with satisfaction. "Okay, let's see what we're dealing with."

I got up from the bed, patted Drow on the arm, and lazily followed Frank to the think tank, a small conference room at the back of the larger operations room.

We passed soldiers at their posts as we made our way to the back. Some seemed like they took the night easy, beaming good mornings to us in cheerful voices. Others were zoned out, quietly murmuring mornings to us in pained and strained tones from a night of bad decision-making. Frank held the door open for me, ushering me inside.

The room was lit with a few Tesla Bulbs, swinging gently in a breeze from no discernable location. It was a decent-sized space, stretching back about twenty feet in either direction. Fittingly, there was a large round table placed in the center of the room with thirteen chairs spaced evenly and a few benches lining the three walls. Above them hung paintings illustrating grand Arthurian legends and quests from the time of the famous knights of the original round table.

When The Keepers contacted me in 1937, I quickly worked my way through the ranks. After all, I was the first of my generation to find their artifact. Soon, we realized we would need a place of residence to work from—a base of sorts. We finally found the perfect location to use as the permanent headquarters in the city. When we approached the church about our needs and specifications, they were more than helpful. Originally this was just a basement, but we had Thomas Kestler retrofit the entrance with the one we have now. I made it impossible to enter without knowing where the two entries were. The one we did not use the night prior opened up into the sewer that led into the city near the ports.

"Have we figured out how old the table is yet?" I asked, looking it over, drumming a finger on the wood surface.

Close to us, covering up some of my favorite carvings, was a large crate. The top was worn and well-used, and the original stain rubbed away from time passed. The table's edges, bottom and legs were the only places still dark brown from the original coating. Carvings decorated the expanse with depictions of old war plans and stories of better times.

"No luck, I'm afraid. You know there's a theory this is actually the original," Frank said.

I blew raspberries. "I would say there is no way, but we have seen crazier things. I mean, there's a trunk full of things linked to knights of the round table. That's crazy."

Frank chuckled. "Yes, we have. So, what do you think? Should we try to explain everything to the man first? Or just have him start grabbing things and see what happens?"

I thought about it for a second, weighing the pros and cons of the strange situation. As I mentioned earlier, we have had one bad situation with the test. So far, I am the only successfully activated Keeper.

"I suppose we should just go for it. The last person we tried knew all about what's going on, and it really messed him up," I said.

"Hmm, maybe. It could work. You didn't know about any of this before you got the sword, so it stands to reason that might help with the initial shock," Frank said.

I nodded intently while reaching for the trunk. I flipped the latch on it and pushed it open. The lid fell back and thudded against the table, causing me to jump a little. I saw Frank get out his pipe and matches in my periphery, reach into the same pocket, and pull out his snuff. He opened the small container and pinched some of the dried loose-leaf tobacco between his pointer finger and thumb before packing it into the heavy bronze bowl. I glanced at it, noticing the bowl resembled a three-clawed dragon foot clutching an intricately molded heart. The stem came out of the wrist of the foot, slender and sleek. I looked away again, focusing my eyes on the contents inside the trunk. In the background, I heard the dry strike of the wooden match on the uneven red phosphorus strip, igniting in the first go.

"Marvels of modern technology," I said, attention still mainly on the box's contents.

I turned to him as he spoke, watching the flame intently. It flared to life for a few moments before dying out completely, tiny tendrils of smoke from the chemicals mingling with the smoke from the pipe.

"What do you mean?" Frank asked, letting out a steady stream of pipe smoke.

"The matches. Not but forty-five years ago, those things were made with a very poisonous compound, white phosphorus."

He turned the since-burned piece of wood in his fingertips. "Ah yes, phossy jaw. I remember hearing about that from my grandfather, Hubert."

I turned back to the artifacts that lay dormant in the trunk, watching the pulsing light of the swinging bulbs dancing across the surface of reflective objects. Some of them consisted of steel or iron, meant for use and wear in the heat of battle, while others were of glass and lacquer for less practical and more superficial uses.

Frank cleared his throat before saying, "We have that transfer due today. After you returned yesterday, we reached out to them, and they informed us they were running behind anyways."

I turned to him once more. "Where's he from again?"

"The States. New York, to be exact."

More smoke seeped into the air, adding a strange sense of secrecy to the situation. I wondered how lucky we were to find someone, even if it was that far away. Even better is he's already on the good side.

"How'd we find him?" I asked.

Frank snorted. "He found us. He claims to be a descendant."

I looked at him and cocked an eyebrow. "What basis does he have for this?"

"He says he found out by going through his grandfather's things, who didn't want him to know."

"Does he already have an artifact?"

"No, he said his grandfather left it here when he left England, fifty-two years ago."

"As far as we know, we have the other twelve, right?" I asked, rubbing my neck.

"Correct. The twelve we have collected over the last fifty years are split between the trunk, and in Nikola's possession, besides the sword you carry on your back," he said, pointing to the trunk on the table.

It really must've been something back in the day to go around collecting the remaining eleven artifacts around the world. I wish me grandad had told me some of those stories when I was young. I think I would have enjoyed them thoroughly. It's strange; I can't remember when he collected them.

"Frank, how come I am having a hard time remembering when me Grandad and Steven collected them?"

He rubbed at his chin. "That is strange. I honestly wouldn't know why. We will look into that at a later point."

I nodded, and the irritating pain in my neck swelled again, making it hard to focus on anything besides. I remembered the bullet wound in my shoulder from last night and started to feel a dull ache. I reached the spot and rubbed carefully at the warm mound of scar tissue, freshly grown through the magic of electricity.

I closed my eyes as I began to talk again. "We're forgetting it's just eleven. We may have twelve, but we have Lancelot's descendant locked up in a padded room for the foreseeable future."

Frank let out a frustrated grunt. "Ah yes. I forgot about him. What was his name again?"

"Chadwick Streaker. I never liked him, to be honest. But I suppose I would never wish permanent insanity on anyone," I said, chuckling and rubbing the sore spot on my neck. "I know me grandfather left me an extensive number of notes, but he didn't document why only certain relatives could access the artifacts more than others. Why is that?"

"They are all mostly Dimmers. They are related in some shape or form to an original knight," Frank said.

I processed that momentarily. "Does this happen to them?"

"The memories? No, it doesn't work like that. Only Brighters have the power to access the artifacts," Frank said. "Since Chadwick tried accessing his artifact, even if there are any other descendants of Lancelot alive right now, they will not be able to activate it. It is now effectively locked to him until he dies."

I nodded my head, waving some of the smoke away. "Okay, I think I underst—"

The door behind us opened with a prolonged creak, cutting me off mid-sentence. Frank and I turned from the table to see who decided to interrupt in such a slow way. A clean-cut man of about twenty-five peeked around the door. His hair was a deep brown combed, neatly to the side and back.

"Uh, sir," said the man, clearing his voice. "Sorry to interrupt. But I have the POW here with me as you asked."

"Ah yes, bring him in. We should probably get started then," Frank said.

Frank ushered them into the room, closing the door swiftly behind them. The private pushed Klaus in front of him, directing him to a chair in front of the trunk at the edge of the table. Frank pulled the chair out for him as the private sat him down.

"That'll do, Private. We will handle it from here. Could you let me know when the American transfer gets here?" Frank asked, looking at Klaus.

"Yessir, will do!" said the private.

The private did an about-face and left the room, opening the door with the same grueling, sloth-like movements as before. After the slow ticks of time had passed, the door shut with a gentle click.

Frank rolled his eyes as he and I looked back at Klaus, sitting quietly in the chair. He had his hands clasped together in the front with handcuffs, pink and red circles on his wrists where the metal dug into them. A pair was also around his ankles, restricting him from running off. He was now wearing plain gray wool pants and a white cotton shirt. The boots looked the same as he had before: mid-calf-high black marching boots.

Frank paced back and forth while I took a chair on his left side. I sat with one chair between us, giving him a little bit of room. I also didn't know what he was thinking right now. I certainly didn't want another episode like last night.

"So, your name is Klaus?" Frank said, stopping to the right of him.

Klaus stayed quiet, staring forward at the wall ahead of him.

"Come on now, don't you know your own name?" Frank asked.

The man did not move; his head was still trained at the same spot in front of him.

I did tell him I would explain what was going on, so I might as well do that now. It might get him talking to us.

I reached into my pocket and pulled out my grandad's ring. The cool metal of the faded gold felt comforting in my palm, easing the aches and ailments of the night prior. I slid it onto my ring finger and extended my hand across the table toward Klaus.

"Klaus, shake my hand."

His eyes fluttered over to my hand. I watched as his gaze hovered there for a second before promptly returning to the spot he was boring into the wall.

I kept my hand outstretched while I continued, "For me to explain what is happening, I need to show you something."

A handful of moments passed as I shifted uncomfortably in my chair. The extended period I was keeping my arm out made my shoulder start to throb again.

"You mean the glowing ring?" he asked, eyes still looking forward.

"Yes, the glowing ring. Now please, shake my hand so I can show Frank."

Klaus turned to me, chains shaking and clanking together as he shifted his weight. He was now facing me with a blank and patient expression. His vacant, tired eyes stared me down and watched my every move down to the last muscle. Klaus lifted his right hand and took mine with a firm grip, causing the ring to light up immediately with the familiar golden yellow glow, warming and pulsing with hope.

Frank sighed and said, "You're right. That does make things difficult, doesn't it?"

Chapter 9
The Test

9:00 a.m.

The room stayed quiet for a moment, only giving way to the chatter seeping through the crack of the door.

"That's what Drow said. I don't know what to think. It's a risk," I said.

Klaus let go of my hand and rested his upon his lap, handcuffs clanging. I looked over to Frank, who was now chain smoking on his pipe. The smoke wafted up in an undulating cloud, spreading above our heads in an even layer. Klaus moved in the chair, causing it to squeak and groan.

"So, what does it mean? You said you would tell me what it means," Klaus said. "Why did your ring glow?"

Now's a good time as any, I suppose.

"The easiest way to do this is to have you take the test," I said.

"But you said you'd tell me. How will a test help *mich* understand?" Klaus asked.

"As I said, it's a little complicated and hard to believe. That's why the test will help. It will show you what we mean."

Klaus stayed quiet again. He turned his body in the chair to face the wall once more. I scoffed and turned to Frank.

"Let's get this started then. It seems to me like he's done talking without getting any solid answers from us. Like you said, let's just show him," Frank said.

I nodded in agreement, knowing it might be the easiest way. I stood up and began to reach across to the trunk. Before I got too far, I removed my pistol from my holster and set it aside, out of reach. I undid the button holding the security strap in place and pulled it out to see if the safety was set. The bio-connection indicator was dull and lifeless, devoid of its usual royal blue glow.

He could've shot me yesterday. When did I disengage it?

I rubbed my neck, thinking about how bad my day could've been, as I slid the gun out and placed it on the table to the left. With that out of the way, I resumed manually removing the artifacts from the trunk.

The first item I pulled out was a simple dagger, about four inches in length from pommel to tip. The handle was solid bronze in the style of fish scales with a cross guard about two inches wide. The sheath was a simple brown leather accented with gold wire. Two grape-sized maroon stones lay encrusted in the cross guard on each side with the design of Roman chapiters or capitals in the small space between the two.

"Hold out your hands again, please," I asked.

Klaus reluctantly lifted his hands off his lap and placed them on the table, palms up. Glad to have him cooperate, I placed the dagger in his hands. I looked at him and waited calmly for a response. Anything would do. Perhaps a sign, like a sudden realization of a world larger than he first thought, or he could begin to laugh hysterically. Or fear and confusion could cause his face to lose all of its blood. The last option wouldn't be the most desired scenario since we would be out another descendant. But time passed unhurriedly as nothing interesting happened.

"Anything?" I asked.

"*Nein,* aside from just getting an absurd itch on *mein* nose. How ist this showing me?" Klaus asked impatiently.

"This one's funny. Aren't we lucky: sarcastic and infuriating," Frank said as he puffed feverishly on the pipe.

I hastily plucked the dagger out of his hands, remembering that it was also a deadly weapon in the hands of an Axis soldier. I put it near the original seat I had taken earlier, far away from him.

"On to the next one. This obviously isn't the one," I said.

I peered over the edge of the trunk as I reached for the following item. My hands glided across a few smooth surfaces, and eventually, my fingers rested upon something fashioned from rough wood. I pulled out the object and looked at it while I spun it in my grasp. It was an old mahogany cross about two inches in height with a worn leather necklace attached to the top with a simple iron loop. Nothing seemed unique or exciting to it, but I suppose not all the pieces had to be extravagant. The dry, untreated grain was bleached from years of sitting in the sunlight.

"What about this?" I asked.

I silently coiled up the necklace and put it in Klaus' hands lightly. I took mine away and waited patiently, curiosity keeping my attention on him. But the same thing happened as before. Nothing was my reward for watching intently.

"Anything for that one?" I asked, looking from the cross to his face.

"*Nein*, nothing. What am I supposed to feel?" Klaus asked.

"It's not just a feeling; it will be more than that. Trust us, you'll know," Frank said.

I picked it up from his hands and placed it next to the dagger, so they were lined up. At this point, I was losing my patience, so I blindly reached in and pulled out the next piece to try. In my fingers was a pristine metal belt buckle reflecting the light of the Tesla Bulbs off its surface. The design was of a creature with the edges carved out around it.

"What do you think it's supposed to be?" I asked.

Frank paced around Klaus and reached out to me, gesturing for me to hand it to him. He took it and brought it closer to his face, embers still burning wildly from his inhalation as they illuminated his face in an orange hue.

"Looks like a mule or a donkey to me. But I am sure it isn't. I mean, why would a knight of the round table choose one of those for a design on an important, existence-saving artifact?" Frank asked, handing it back to me.

I took it and immediately placed it into Klaus' palms. As before, but with much less anticipation, I waited for something to happen. The crackle of Frank's tobacco in his pipe got my attention, dry and dead but somehow alive once more. Something else broke through my focus: my chair's creak and groan. As I sat entranced by the anticipation, I had not realized I had begun to lean forward slightly. Klaus spoke, startling me as I did not expect a response from him.

"It's a Griffon," Klaus said.

At this point, I teetered off my seat and stood up. The excitement was bubbling up inside my guts like a warm babbling brook after a winter's thaw. Frank had stopped pacing and looked at Klaus, waiting to hear more.

Before he could say another word, Klaus' body began to shake violently. Suddenly, he fell from his chair and hit the ground with a sickening thud. His eyes snapped shut as he tucked his chin into his chest tightly.

"Klaus, are you okay?" I asked, rushing to his side.

He was on his side now, convulsing in brutal spasms, legs kicking madly. I tried to steady him as he shook, to no avail. He vomited, spewing bile over his arms, and dribbling onto the cold stone floor. It was a sickly green color and smelled of bile, devoid of any real substance.

"Go get help! Get Dr. Thatcher!" I yelled to Frank.

He turned and ran out of the room to get her. His heavy boots thudded on the stone floor with each receding step.

I turned back to Klaus to try and steady him again. The distraught shaking subsided to a series of small intermittent tremors, quickly fading as fast as they began. I reached into one of my back pockets, pulling out a muckender to try and wipe the expelled mess away from his mouth. The slimy discharge was easy enough to clear away, giving me enough room to kneel to hear if he was still breathing. I put my ear close and listened for anything. It was raspy and light, faint almost, but even, nonetheless.

"What happened? Is he still breathing?" asked Dr. Thatcher.

"Yes, but it's faint," I said.

"What were you doing?"

"We were administering the test. We gave him an item, and he just locked up," I said.

I backed away to let her take my place. My gaze shifted over to my pistol as I grabbed it, sliding it back into my holster reflexively. At this point, all motion had stopped as Klaus was deathly still.

Dr. Thatcher reached into her apron and pulled out her medi-spotter. She flicked the switch and began shining it over his face, body, and legs to check for abnormal signs. She looked back at his face, prying open his eyelids with her left hand while looking at them with the medi-spotter with her right.

"His pupils are dilated," she said, moving her hand to his neck. "And his pulse is weak. I need to move him to the infirmary again."

She looked over her shoulder through the doorway expectantly, waiting for what I assumed was help. She glanced back at Klaus, took the rag from my hands, and started to wipe away more of the vomit from his face. Frank returned to the room just a few moments later, a look of frustration plastered across his face.

"Did you get the other two as I told you to?" Dr. Thatcher asked.

"No, they are still indisposed from last night. What can I do?" Frank asked.

"Help me get him to the infirmary. I'll deal with the other two later," she said, scowling.

Dr. Thatcher walked over and held the door open for us as Frank and I grabbed Klaus by the shoulders and legs. The two of us hoisted him up and slowly walked to the doorway, mindful of his head and appendages, not wanting to hit anything on the wood. We navigated that easily and followed the doctor to the beds in the infirmary, carrying him carefully and swiftly.

"Place him in the same bed. No sense in dirtying another on account of him," she said as she turned to the nurses' station. "Lisa, I need your help, please."

Lisa rushed over. "Alright, Doctor, what do you think is wrong?"

"I think he is having or had a seizure. He seems to be done for now. We will just need to monitor him for a few hours or until he wakes up," Dr. Thatcher said.

We watched as they started their regular duties. Lisa reached over to a small white enameled medical bowl on a bedside table as she pulled out a rag. She squeezed the liquid out of it, giving it a few more twists to ensure she got it out. Then she dabbed at Klaus' forehead and face, getting the last small remnants of the bile off his chin, neck, and cheek.

Frank walked over to Eileen and placed a hand delicately on hers. She stopped tending to Klaus temporarily and looked up at him. Her stern expression softened for the briefest of moments before returning to her usual self.

"Let us know when he wakes. I hate to put him through this, but we need answers. We need to know what caused this to happen," Frank said.

"Okay, I will see that you will be the first to know. Now, if you'll please excuse me, I need to tend to the patient," she said with a hint of nervousness and annoyance.

Oh yeah, the vial of black goop I took from Spike the other night. I'll have to grab that and give it to Dr. Thatcher to have a look at.

Frank and I decided to let them be so they could do their job and started back towards the main area of the HQ. As we walked past the very last bed in the infirmary, I noticed Drow lying in the fetal position.

He was still in his uniform, complete with gear, except for his shoes. At least he had the decency to take those off. We wouldn't want to track dirt under the covers. Besides, if he were still in rough shape from the night prior, he probably wouldn't be very pleasant to the new arrival, especially if he was American. I decided to leave him alone for now. I could handle the recruit.

"So, what was that back there?" I asked, looking at Frank.

"Hmph? What do you mean?" he replied.

"That. The soft caress of Eileen's hand. You two a thing now?"

He let out a nervous chuckle as he tugged at his collar. "What are you talking about? Of course not. I was simply consoling her. Helping her with the rough situation."

"Sure, of course, that's what it was. Her knight in shining armor," I said, teasing him by jabbing my elbow into his. "I am going to check in with Thomas for now. Let me know when the recruit shows up, alright?"

"I will do that. We received word that he would arrive today, so it shouldn't be much longer," Frank said.

I fell out of step with Frank, trying not to tangle my feet, and back peddled to the cots Drow, and I stayed in the night prior. I decided I should probably bring him with me when I spoke to Thomas to ensure he wasn't having any issues with his rifle. I stopped at my bed first to grab Excalibur.

It's a habit from being in times of war to, even if you think you're safe in the confines of the headquarters, make sure you have your weapons always within arms reach. I crouched next to the head of the cot and grabbed aimlessly for it. My knees popped loudly from the relaxation of a solid ten hours of not standing for every second. It was satisfying and painful all at once. Finally, my efforts were rewarded with the cool, comfortable leather wrap cushioning my calloused fingers and palm. As always, I felt a wave of calm wash over me like silky water in a slowly receding tide. I let out a grunt and a groan as I stood up from the floor, glancing down to my haversack tucked near the support leg.

Oh yeah, I need to bring the vial to Eileen.

"Would you stop making so much noise?" Drow protested.

I glanced over at his still form on his cot, chuckling at his pain. "Why don't you just get up now?"

He didn't even respond with words; all I got out of him was a growl.

"Come on. We need to check with Thomas. He needs to look over our firearms to see if they are still in proper order," I said, reaching down to the pocket that held the liquid.

"Can't you just take my rifle? My head is pounding furiously right now."

"No, I can't. You know that. The bio-electric connection is not calibrated to me, so I can't operate it to test it."

Silence followed my statement. In a burst of fury and anger, Drow sat up hastily, kicking his legs out over the side of the cot. "I don't see why not. Thomas can activate it."

"That's because he built the damned thing," I replied.

Drow stood up quick and impatient, just like his decisions in life. His stance wavered, but leftover alcohol still sluggishly inhibited his movements for a moment. I reached out to help keep him upright, only to have my hand swatted away in a feverish slap.

"I have this. I don't need you babying me all the time. I'm an adult too, you know," sneered Drow.

I scoffed, "Fine, but you don't need to be an arse about it."

Drow gave me an apologetic look and gestured to me to lead the way. He never did like apologizing for anything, so to get a look was enough.

I shook off the annoyance I felt creeping in and decided to make my way to Thomas. As we passed the nurses station, I looked down to see what lay on the counter near the podium. At first glance, my eyes gravitated to the mender, and my body let out an involuntary shudder. I started to remember the countless occasions I have had to have it used to fix my wounds, some minor and others major.

I couldn't believe the technology we had. It was a significant advancement in modern medicine we used on the frontlines. It was one of the many inventions Nikola Tesla's TEA company had produced in the last twenty years. Since the Great War, TEA wanted to specialize in healing the injured and prolonging life for humanity rather than being the source of destruction, pain, and agony.

This device could heal minor wounds such as cuts and scrapes caused by enemy bayonets and barbed wire and more extensive injuries, including broken femur and bullet wounds. The process was quite painful, but luckily, it was also quick. A broken or shattered bone took about five minutes to heal completely, and a gash on the forearm from a bayonet slice only took about thirty seconds.

Next to that were some scattered loose papers, with some only having the edges or half of the sheets sticking out of Manila folders labeled in black as *TOP SECRET*. I could make out a few diagrams of the human body, presumably to indicate where it hurt the worst.

"Stay here for a second, Drow. I have to talk to Dr. Thatcher," I said.

He grunted and leaned against a support as he shut his eyes.

I looked over to Eileen and called to her, "Dr. Thatcher, I have something I need you to look at if you have a moment."

She glanced over her shoulder as she hovered above Klaus, scrunching her nose like she usually did when annoyed. Eileen said something to Lisa that I couldn't hear before walking to me.

"What is it?" she asked, curiosity worming its way into her voice.

I reached over to hand her the small glass vial. "I had a bizarre encounter yesterday. This was what came from his injuries."

She took it and looked at it incredulously. Holding it up to the light cast off from the ever-swinging Tesla Bulbs, she scrunched her nose further.

"Well, it's definitely not blood. At least not anymore," she said, taking out her medi-spotter.

She clicked the button and held the light to the viscous liquid. It was thick and black like tar or motor oil, slowly inching its way from top to bottom as she turned it up and down like an hourglass. The high-focused beam from the handheld light didn't even make it through, only shining on either side of the glass.

"You said it came from someone's wounds?"

I nodded. "Mhmm."

"Was there anything else that stuck out about this person?"

"Most definitely. But I'm not sure what was real and what could've been a hallucination."

"What do you mean by that?" she asked, still twirling the vial in the light.

I reached into my right front pocket and dug around while I talked. "For starters, he had stitches crisscrossing his entire head. They were very close to stitching on an American baseball."

"Really? Very interesting. Anything else?"

"This one was the one I wasn't sure about." I paused momentarily as I found the thing I was searching for. I took out a pear drop from my cavernous pocket and pulled on the ends of the wrapper to open it. The wrapper crinkled as I flicked it into my mouth and started to suck on it. "He spit a ball of fire at me."

Eileen stopped twirling the vial and looked at me, mouth dropping open before she began to talk. "He spit *fire* at you? Are you sure? Maybe you ran into a pocket of leftover pseudo-gas."

The candy clacked against my teeth as I moved it around with my tongue, making my mouth itch. I gave in to the urge to start chewing, reveling in the hardened sugar's crunchy fruitiness. I hadn't realized I closed my eyes because when I opened them; I looked at Eileen and noticed she was staring at me now.

I cleared my throat and said, "Sorry, no. It wasn't that. The air was pretty clear and fresh from what I can remember. And it was a *ball* of fire, not just fire. It had substance because Excalibur was able to cut through it like it was a ball."

Eileen shook her head and said, "That is a new one. I haven't the faintest idea of what it could be. The Reapers have devised some devious weapons, so this isn't entirely surprising."

I shrugged in agreement. "When you have a chance, please look at that and let me know what it might be."

She slid it into her apron and nodded. "I can. It's right up there with letting Frank know about Klaus. Speaking of Klaus, I should check back with Lisa and see how he is."

"Okay, thanks again," I said as I turned away to walk back to Drow.

Chapter 10
New Fish

12:30 p.m.

I turned on my heels and started towards Thomas once more. For the most part, Drow was standing right where I had left him. His face was in his arms which were lying down across the podium. I gave him a hearty pat on the back and said, "Up and at 'em. On your feet, soldier."

"I am. Doesn't it count?"

I looked at him standing there and said, "Yes, but no. Come on, let's get going."

A long and drawn-out moan of false pain and agony escaped his lips. I looked around to see if anyone was paying him any attention. But just as I thought, everyone was so used to his outrageous behavior that they went about their regular morning duties.

I led the way through the headquarters past the clamoring relay consoles and the men standing at attention. The air was thick with smoke from morning cigarettes and coffee, keeping the hazy secretive feel to the place. We slowly skirted past the large operations table in the center of the room, not wanting to agitate the stacked papers and laid out diagrams of the frontlines.

Frank took heavy influence from his ancestors by planning and depicting the current situations with painted and whittled figurines. I stopped and scooped one up gingerly, peering at the level of detail that went into the things. The one I happened to pick up was the one that probably represented me. He was tall, strong-shouldered and gave off a sense of valor. The figure had everything to match, even the sword strapped to my back. I chuckled and placed it back in where I picked it up from, not wanting to confuse Frank.

Thomas and his armory, of sorts, was located on the side opposite the infirmary. There he took care of a manner of things, including but not limited to gun repair and maintenance. He was my outfitter, supplying me with anything I needed as well as the other useful inventions that he created on a usual basis for the Keepers.

Not everything he invented was practical for everyday use on the battlefield, but for the most part, they were. His grandfather, Emmet, was a key element when Nikola first formed TEA. He joined the ranks among one of the first engineers to help with Nikola's vision after the Year of the Reaper. Naturally, he taught his son everything he knew when he was old enough, continuing with Thomas.

As I approached the armory, I stopped and slapped my hand on the counter. "Thomas, how are you?"

Thomas turned to me, his trademark slick black hair and bushy sideburns being the first thing I noticed. He had on a brown workman's apron covered in dark, coal-colored smudges from the early morning's projects. A smile crept across his face as he brought a sandwich up to his face between his grimy fingers.

"Doing just fine, Deck. Working on another great project that I think you'll love. But what brings you here this morning?"

"Maintenance," Drow grumbled.

Thomas turned to Drow with a smirk. "Ah, and still not a morning person I see, are you Woody?"

Drow cleared his throat. "I'm not a morning person because I always have to see your ugly mug. And don't call me Woody."

I chuckled. "Alright, you two. We need to work together, not apart. Thomas, mind checking on our weapons to see if anything is out of order?"

He looked back at me and smiled. "Of course."

I pulled my sidearm out of its holster and pressed my thumb to the hand grip on the side to disengage the bio-electric connection, just in case. Satisfied, I put it on the counter and slid it across to him. The metal frame of the pistol scraped quietly against the hardwood top of the counter, scratching lines through the caked-on grease and grime. Thomas then picked it up and turned it over, squinting and inspecting it thoroughly.

"How'd it do in the field?" Thomas asked.

I finished chewing the candy and swallowed. "Well, except for the fact that I forgot to reconnect to it. I had a POW pull it on me just as we returned yesterday."

"That definitely wouldn't be a good thing. Did he actually try shooting?"

"Luckily no, we talked him down before he did anything. I only realized the next morning he could've blown me away. For once, I had decent luck."

Thomas shrugged, flipped the pistol into the air and caught the barrel with his hand. He extended it back to me and said, "Why did you break the connection anyway?"

I shrugged. "Not sure, to be honest. I guess I am not into the habit of seeing if it's connected."

"It could be faulty at the moment too. It is not supposed to disconnect," Thomas said as he rubbed his chin. He then turned back to Drow. "How's the new rifle doing, Drow?"

Woodrow gave Thomas a short but serious smile. "Thanks for the professional courtesy. It performed very well. The recoil was half it used to be since you tinkered with it. Much easier to line up consecutive shots."

"Not helpful enough, I'd say. You almost hit me," I said, looking at Drow as I took my pistol back from Thomas.

"Or too well?" He winked. "Also, the charging time is much quicker than before, which helps a lot too."

Thomas nodded with appreciation and smug satisfaction. His face switched to surprise as he put up a finger. "I got something else for you too."

He bent down and started rummaging through something underneath the counter. Clanking and scraping were followed by him muttering about how he needed to clean the months-old, half-eaten sandwiches out of his workspace. With something in his hand, and excitement plastered across his grubby, oil-smeared face, Thomas sprung up.

"This!" he said.

"What is it?" I asked.

I held out my hand as he dropped something into it. The small metal device hit my palm with force, causing it to give slightly. I looked at it and noticed it looked like a ball of tied metal chain. Curious, I gave it a few investigative hefts to feel the actual weight of the object.

"Again, what is it?" I asked.

"It's an electrified net."

I looked at him. "What's with you and electricity?"

"I'm not sure. I just enjoy it. It's shocking, I know."

Drow groaned and rolled his eyes as I chuckled softly. I stifled it quickly and resumed my regular, business-like demeanor.

"How do I operate it?" I asked.

"Simple." He grabbed it from my hand to show me. "Just press the pressure switch in the middle and throw it at the anemones."

"Oh, come on, that's it. I'm going to shoot you."

Before Drow could even pretend to aim his gun at Thomas, I turned and put my hand on his shoulder, stopping him from acting on his anger.

"Boys? Everything alright?" Frank asked.

We turned to see him walk up to us with the private from earlier in the morning next to him. Frank had an eyebrow raised over the top of his horn-rimmed glasses, confusion on his face.

"Yes, he's still a little drunk from last night," I said, patting Drow on the shoulder.

"Ah, well, maybe he should check in with Eileen then. I know she has a lot on her plate, but I think she can handle another numbskull."

Drow sighed heavily and grunted as he shook my hand off his shoulder. He did a snappy about-face and walked off in a rush, brooding the whole way. Drow pushed past the two out of frustration, hitting the private and making him trip to the side. Frank just shook his head as the private chased after him.

"Again, sorry, sir," I said.

"It's alright, I understand. I may be in charge of many people, but I am young too." He clapped his hands together and said, "But alas, we have the recruit in from the States. I have him waiting for us in the conference room."

I started off from Frank, only to be stopped by Thomas. He signaled me to come back for a moment, so I jogged back to him to see what I had forgotten. He held the newest invention in his hand for me to take it.

"Don't forget this. You may need it," he said, dropping it into my outstretched palm once more.

I thanked him and placed it into one of the side pockets of my pants. As I returned to Frank, I waved goodbye to Thomas as we started to walk towards the conference room again. We stayed silent most of the way until we reached the door to the room. He stopped me, and I turned to look at him.

"I have to warn you about something." He paused, looking for the right thing to say. "He's quite clueless. I have tried preparing him for his artifact and telling him some about Jakobus, but he just has an innocence about him."

"I think I can handle it. We will ease him in and help him realize what's happening and what's at stake. I deal with Drow too often, and he is usually a lot of trouble."

Frank nodded and smiled. "He certainly is, isn't he?"

"Is Klaus up and moving around?"

"He is. I have him waiting in there as well.

"You have them together in one room?" I asked, my jaw dropping in disbelief.

"Don't worry. I have Klaus in handcuffs sitting far enough away from the American. I already explained the situation to him as well."

"Has Klaus said anything else since his seizure?"

"No, he hasn't, and Eileen doesn't know what caused it either."

I shook my head, and Frank pushed open the door to the conference room. Sitting in the same spot Klaus was earlier was a young man with blonde hair fashioned into a crew cut. He had an average-sized nose, medium lips, and sideburns that reached beyond the bottoms of his ears. His eyes were hazel with streaks of green that shimmered in the light.

I walked around him and took the same seat I was in before, as did Frank. On the opposite side of the room was Klaus, staring at his lap, still silent and brooding.

"Hello, my name is Deckard. But you can call me Deck for short," I said as I offered him my hand.

"Howdy-do there, Deck. My name's Gary Diedrich," he said, reaching out to shake my hand.

Gary was in the standard American Army Field uniform, complete with the helmet resting on the table just in front of him to the right.

"Nice to meet you, Gary. I'm assuming you've met Frank then?"

He glanced back at Frank. "I did. He met me at the door, actually. Mighty fine place you have here. Kind of on the beam it's hidden so well."

"It's been an integral part of keeping the Germans at bay over the last four years. We've been able to hold them off from completely overrunning the city because of our placement," Frank said. "But anyways, let's get down to business. It's nice to have you here finally. How was your trip?"

Gary rubbed his chin and said, "It was interesting. Some parts took longer than others. The hardest part was sneaking into the city without alerting anyone. No wonder they had me come by myself."

Frank nodded and asked, "Do you have your SPARC they gave you when you landed in the country?"

"Yeah, I do. They explained it to me somewhat. But I wasn't really sure how to engage it."

"Don't worry, for now. You made it here before anything happened, so we will show you later. Hold on to that and just keep it someplace safe." Frank looked at me and then back to Gary. "Sometimes they are faulty if they get hit too hard."

"What do you mean?" Gary asked.

"You'll have a very bad day," I said.

Gary shifted in his seat uncomfortably as he patted his breast pocket. "Okay, I'll keep that in mind."

"All right, down to the real reason you are here," Frank said. "The first thing we need to do is administer the test. I assume you are up to speed on the basics of this particular division?"

"Yessir. Before leaving America, I was briefed on the details. Not to the extent I would like, though," Gary said.

"In due time. That's what the test is for. I would ask if you knew who you are related to, but ultimately it doesn't matter since we haven't found a way to sort out what goes to who besides the ones we have already tested," Frank said.

"We can give him a brief rundown of the situation. It won't take long," I said.

Frank twitched his lips. "I suppose. Just keep it brief."

"May I ask questions?" Gary asked.

"Three. But that counts toward one of them," I chuckled.

Gary furrowed his brow. "Really?"

"That's number two."

"Are you being serious?"

"Not really. It was more of a joke. Drow would have laughed. Never mind, I'll start with what we are currently working toward."

Gary raised his hand, gesturing that he already had a question.

"Not yet. I haven't even started."

Gary lowered it and got comfortable, deciding to listen instead of talk.

"We are currently in the process of holding the Germans at bay here in London, ensuring they don't completely take over all of England. So far, we have been successful in that regard, but they have been continually hitting us harder and harder in the last couple of months. They have had a surge of reinforcements from Germany, making their numbers swell dramatically."

"Where do I come in then? Why did I transfer here from the States? Even if I am a descendant like I think, how will I be able to help?"

"Glad you asked. This unit is special. We are tasked with finding and training descendants of the knights of the round table, like yourself. There are quite a few people in every generation that are Dimmers, but only the true-bloods, Brighters, can access the artifacts and activate the memories."

"How do you know if they are Brighters then?"

"Here." I reached out to shake his hand.

He took it, and my ring lit up with the magnificent yellow glow that by now seemed so familiar to me. This was only the third time I had seen it glow this brightly with my own eyes, but I had seen it glow dimly several times when brushing up with Drow. I let go of Gary's hand and returned to my explanation.

"The brighter the glow, the better chance the person is a true blood," Frank said.

"Is there more than one descendant per generation that can access the artifacts?" Gary asked.

"No, one per. It would be very confusing to have more than that running around," I said.

"It's confusing enough to just have one," Frank chimed in.

"Right." I looked at Frank and nodded. "The other thing we are currently tasked with is finding the source of a numbers station that has clogged up the airwaves in the last few weeks. We do not know where it is coming from nor why, until now actually."

"What do you mean?" Frank asked as he raised an eyebrow.

"When we were out on patrol, and before getting ambushed, we activated the Warbler and picked up the transmission. Little did I know that Drow could decipher it. I never even thought to check with him before," I said.

"What did it say?"

"It was just a simple, 'Help.' I think we would need to go out and try to locate it again to see if whoever was behind it really needed help or not."

"Could it be a trap?"

"Very well could be. But we won't know until we make contact. Anyways, Gary, do you have any more questions?" I asked.

"No. Not that I can think of. I assume the test will explain everything else?" he asked.

"It will. Let's get testing then," Frank said.

For the next fifteen minutes, we went through the rigamarole of grabbing items from the chest and having Gary hold them. So far, we had tried the two that we had Klaus hold before the one he ultimately ended up with, but sadly, the cross and dagger were not the correct artifacts, so we then moved onto the rest.

The one that belonged to Lancelot, which was out of commission, was a beautifully crafted, long-flowing cloak. It was a deep maroon color with a gold trim accentuating the edges and corners. We had it tucked away for the next generation of descendants, just in case all went to hell with this attempt.

We only have four others in the headquarters, making for a quick but incomplete attempt to decide which is the right one. The items we tried were an ornately designed shield, a chainmail shirt known as a haubergeon, and a simple leather flask. The last was a boot. It wasn't an all-purpose leather boot that'd be usable in any situation, but a full-on suit of armor boot.

Boy, would I hate to be the person with that one.

"Well, that's kind of disappointing. I would have thought the right one was here," Frank said.

I rolled my neck to see if I could get it to pop, "Maybe Nikola has it."

"He may—"

Frank was abruptly cut off when the door to the conference room crashed open. We turned to see what could be so urgent to warrant the commotion.

"Sir, we're under attack!" yelled a private.

The lights slowly dimmed from the vibrant yellow to a dark, thick honey. All of us were bathed in a smothering blanket of darkness as the power was swiftly cut off.

Why can't anything good ever happen?

Chapter 11
Big Trouble in Little London

1:15 p.m.

The stone floor pulsed and heaved with a force I'd never felt in person. I was startled as the chest thumped and thudded against the tabletop as the artifacts shook against the wood. Explosions and thunder sounded distantly through many layers of sediment and rock, echoing in the hollow space. The room lit up with a carmine red brought on by damage to the primary power source.

Gary, follow Deckard! Frank mouthed, voice lost in the commotion. Faintly, I heard, "Deck, you know the drill! Meet at the rendezvous point."

"What about everyone else?" I asked.

"I'll take care of everyone else. Grab the POW and make sure you get them there!"

The walls shook again from the impact somewhere nearby while dust and debris dispersed into the air. I watched out of the corner of my eye as the Tesla Bulbs pulsed from the connection being strained to the Wavergy.

"What about Drow?"

"He'll come with me. Just get going!"

I ran to the other side of the table and yanked Klaus up by the collar, pulling him along to the front. Then I grabbed Gary by the arm and pulled him from the seat. "Come with me. We need to grab my things from my bunk."

All four of us ran from the conference room and into the main area, Frank departing from us off to the left as Gary, Klaus and I went right. The air was filled with heavy gray and black smoke, unlike the kind a typical buzzing afternoon usually had. It was full of soot and ash floating lazily above our heads, raining down upon the right person it deemed worthy. I felt some plaster against my sweating face, smearing as I wiped at it with my sleeve.

Men and women were running around shouting in the hazy atmosphere, trying to grab what gear they could while hastily setting the self-destruct sequences to the machines they worked with. We hurriedly jogged toward our bunks, dodging everyone around us like a lone flopping fish in a hostile crocodile pit. I glanced back to see if Gary was keeping up with me while pushing on Klaus' back to keep him moving forward.

I can't even fathom what they may be thinking. This stuff in general is a lot to take in, especially if you haven't connected to your line.

We came up to the bunks to see they were turned in different directions from the shaking of the assault. Some were now sideways, creating a makeshift walkway resembling planked paths, while others had the mattresses and blankets and pillows shaken to the grown. I scanned the minefield of comfort for my bag and Excalibur.

"Wait here. I have to grab my bag!" I shouted to them over the noise.

I handed Klaus off to Gary and leaped over the first bunk, landing on a cotton and wool pillow, allowing me to keep going with relative ease. My eyes glanced around as I slipped between two more, trying to keep pace.

Finally, I reached my bunk and hit the floor, scanning underneath for my stuff. All my stuff was at the foot of the bed near the far side, just out of reach. Instead of struggling to get it from there, I flopped onto the bed and stood up.

I looked at the bedposts and saw my jacket, gear webbing and haversack dangling back and forth with each new rumble. My hands shook as I snatched them up and threw everything on sloppily, just well enough so nothing would fall off. After that, I slung my haversack on my back, Excalibur sliding into place, complete with matching scabbard. I turned and navigated my way back to the two, trying not to waste any more time.

"Follow me!" I yelled.

Gary nodded and pushed Klaus along behind me. At this point, the air was thick and dense, causing us to breathe heavily and cough from the strain. Most personnel had made it to the escape tunnels that started in the armory, hopefully making better progress than us.

"Gary, where is the rest of your gear? Your gun?" I asked.

"Frank had me leave it near the entrance."

I shook my head in frustration before saying, "Okay, we will grab it before we leave."

After navigating the disaster that was now the headquarters, we were about five feet from the front entrance before the doors flew off the hinges. They exploded inwards toward us, narrowly missing me by what felt like centimeters. Time felt as if it slowed down as we all flew backwards from the force, throwing me to the right and the other two to the left. I hit the ground hard, Excalibur's hilt clanging against the floor, my bag cushioning my head from following suit.

My ears began to ring, loud and disorienting, from the force of the concussive blast. I rolled onto my stomach and struggled to get up, my eyes glued shut from the dust mixing with the moisture from the tears. My trembling fingers made it difficult, but I pried them open and gawked aimlessly in the direction I assumed the other two flew. The lights above fluttered sluggishly from the added stress of the latest explosion, fading and glowing in a strange sequence.

"Gary! Are you okay?" I yelled.

The ringing in my ears ensued, blocking my voice and hopes of hearing a response. I finally saw a heap in front of me, lying motionless, covered in rubble. Instead of waiting for them to move, I crawled to my feet and bolted to them.

I glanced at what was left of the doorway and saw the Waffen entering the headquarters. Through the growing thickness of the air, I could make out the metallic stitching of their emblem patch emblazoned on their arms as the warning lights danced on the shiny thread. The simple design of a scythe set in a diamond made it clear that these were not normal Waffen. They were the elite squadrons of Jakobus' Harvesters sent out into the world to hunt down descendants. Watching them show up here sent shivers down my spine, regardless of how many times I had been able to hold my own against them.

I hit Gary and Klaus head-on, pushing them over and shaking them. "Get up! We need to leave. Now!"

Gary shook his head, dust flying from his hair in every direction. He coughed and wheezed, rubbing his eyes to try and see. I shook Klaus, pulled him up, and had Gary help me drag him along. The ringing ceased enough to allow the thunder of machine gun fire to shake through my daze, raining down around us. The deathly lead bit the floor around our feet, creating small craters in our path. We made it to the counter of the armory and dove over it, trying to hide from certain demise. The thunk sounded from more bullets hitting the thick reinforced walls.

"What in the hell is going on here?" Thomas yelled.

I looked at him in surprise. "What are you still doing here?"

"I had to make sure I took a few of the bastards down before I left and had to set the charges on my equipment. We wouldn't want any krauts to take our tech, would we?"

The noise from the guns stopped, and worry filled me quickly. I reached into my pocket and pulled out the gadget Thomas had given me earlier, rolling it around in my hand. Looking for the button, I turned to him. "Let's see if it works, shall we?"

I pressed the big red button in the middle of the device, causing it to emit a loud beep and a bright red light from the center into my eyes. With the offensive being the only thing on my mind, I rushed to my feet. I turned towards the enemy soldiers as I tossed the device in their direction. The light started flashing quicker, turning to a solid red right before the woven strands expanded to a large net, wrapping itself around two people. The second it closed around them, the strands lit up with an electrifying azure light, followed by screams of anguish and pain.

I dropped back to the ground with a smile and said, "That packs quite a punch, doesn't it?"

"I'm glad it actually worked," Thomas said.

"You mean you didn't know if it would?"

I turned to him to see his hands in the air as he shrugged his shoulders and smiled. "Nope. But thanks for being my guinea pig."

The shrieks ceased as the gunfire resumed, causing me to jump. "Thomas, do you have any extra gear? Gary needs weapons!"

"Of course I do. There are some bags and guns in the back near the tunnel. Good luck!"

I patted Thomas on the shoulder. "Thank you!"

"Don't mention it!"

"You two ready?" I asked, turning and looking at them.

Gary gave me a thumbs up as he huddled against the wall, and Klaus nodded in understanding. I started to duck walk to the back, keeping low to avoid any bullets to the head. The two followed behind, Klaus in between us.

I looked back to Thomas to see him heft a large machine gun from a shelf under the counter to the top of it. He racked back the bolt and fired, sending blue, glowing masses of electrified lead back at the Germans.

We ran past three rows of iron racks half filled with rifles and machine guns, grenades, and handguns. In the back, a door led into the tunnel that extended into the British underground. The utility light at the intersection of the wall and ceiling was blinking an amber hue, bathing the area in a limited amount of clarity.

The rock wall was crumbling as bits and pieces fell to the floor, fragments of dirt hovering like slick muck in cloudy water. Two bags rested on top of the filthy metal counter with a rifle and a shotgun hanging on the wall on hooks within arm's reach.

I grabbed Klaus and said, "Gary, grab the bags and the guns. We'll need them."

He reached for the bags, handing one to me in the process. I hooked it onto the scabbard of Excalibur and let it slide behind me, resting up against my haversack. Gary reached up and took the rifle, sliding it onto his shoulders via the sling. He fidgeted, shaking his back to ensure it was secure. Then he reached back up to the rifle, brought it down, and pulled the bolt to load a round into the chamber. I turned to the mayhem behind us.

"Thomas! Are you coming?" I yelled.

"I'll be right behind you! Get your arses moving!"

Dammit, Thomas. You can't hold them off for long. Please make it out alive.

I turned and pushed Klaus toward the door. "Gary, keep an eye on our backs. Let's move."

Holding onto the chain of Klaus' handcuffs, I ran through the exit door into the fathomless black tunnel. The minute we stepped through the threshold, I heard a metallic clunk as a blast door dropped, blocking us from the rest of the headquarters.

The deep red light that bathed us just moments prior disappeared, submerging us in blinding darkness. I fumbled with one of my front pockets and pulled out my spotter, hooking it into my jacket with the clip as I flipped the switch. A small beam of light lit the space in front of me, stretching forward about twenty-five feet.

Dammit, Thomas, you better make it out of there; otherwise, I won't ever forgive myself.

"Gary, are you okay? Did you get hit?" I asked.

"No, I am in one piece." He paused as he patted himself down. "You?"

"I'm fine. Klaus, you?"

A few seconds of silence passed before he answered, "*Nein.*"

I turned to face Klaus. "I'm going to let go of the chain. Will you follow me?"

The glow from my spotter filled his face with a dull light causing him to squint and cover his face with his hands. I turned it to the right to keep it from shining directly into them.

"*Ja.*"

"Alright, the minute I feel like you're going to try something, I won't be so nice anymore."

He nodded in understanding, keeping his hands where I could see them. I thought for a second and decided it'd be safer with his hands behind his back. I reached into one of the many pockets and pulled out a pair of handcuff keys. In the relative darkness, I reached up and slipped the key into the lock, turning it until I heard the audible click. The right cuff slipped off his wrist, falling and dangling as it was still connected to his left.

"Gary, lock the cuffs behind his back," I said.

Klaus complied and put his hands behind his back, allowing Gary to click it into place. I went to draw my pistol for protection when Gary slipped the shotgun off his shoulder and handed it to me. I took and clicked the safety off, racking the slide in one quick motion. The contact of my skin on the gathering plate caused the electricity lines to glow a bright blue, gathering power for the first shot when it was needed.

"Thanks," I said.

I turned and led the three of us down the path of roughly cut stone, spotter dancing off every reflective surface it saw. The further away we got, the quieter the tunnel grew, thunder and explosions giving way to water rushing and dripping in the darkness. We continued for a few hundred feet, boot heels scraping rhythmically as we walked. The walls were bare, except for a few torch holders randomly strewn about the path.

By that time, the ringing in my ears had all but ceased, easing my adrenaline-battered nerves. Earlier, when we first came through the threshold to the pathway, I was still dealing with residual discomfort from the unexpected explosion that greeted us at the main entrance. Luckily though, that seemed to be the worst of the current predicament. We had weapons, plans and hopefully other helpful supplies for the journey there. Eventually, we reached a junction of three other tunnels, one leading straight in front while the other two went off to the left and right.

"Which way?" Gary asked.

I glanced over my shoulder at him. "When we originally planned the escape route, we made it to where it'd be confusing and disorienting to anyone that followed us."

"So that means you know where you're going?"

I chuckled nervously. "Uh, yeah. I do."

You'll always know which is best, a choice of three to pass the test.

I recited the phrase in my head a few times, trying to remember the correct path to take.

Which is best, a choice of three to pass the test. Test, test, best of three? Why did we have to make this so confusing? Ah, screw it.

I led us to the left, hoping it was the right way. We walked down this tunnel for about another hundred feet before seeing a small light ahead. I squinted to try and see what was giving off the little flame. To help see, I reached up and turned my spotter off to make it out better. I stopped and crouched down, signaling the other to do the same.

"We need to be quiet and vigilant. I'm not sure what's ahead," I whispered.

I stayed low to the ground and continued to the opening. My ears strained to listen for any voices or noises that would be out of place, but all I heard was water dripping and rushing nearby.

The tunnel opened to a dimly lit room about the size of a sitting room with a few rows of bookshelves on the left. They connected to the brick wall on one end, jutting out to the center of the room. To the right was a small altar with three sections cut into the wall on either side. The ceiling was low, only about seven feet high at its tallest point.

A knee-high bench connected to the floor and walls stretched along the whole room, odds and ends scattered about the tops. Included in the random objects were old glass jars filled with dark goop, while others held chunks suspended in a semi-clear liquid.

"What is this place?" asked Gary.

"*Mein Gott*," said Klaus.

My God is right.

"I'm not sure, but I think I took a wrong turn," I said.

What the hell is this place?

I crept into the room, still cautious, in case anyone else was there. As far as I could tell, this place was abandoned because dust covered most of the surfaces. I turned my spotter back on and started with the bookshelves, curious to see what could be contained in them.

I quickly skimmed the spines on the first shelf before me, spotter illuminating names and titles. Various colors and materials bound the pages in the rows of books, from brown and black to rough and sleek leather. Out of the corner of my eye, I saw something move. I turned my head toward the source, not seeing anyone. Movement in my periphery caused me to flinch once more. It made me twitch and I snapped the gun toward the new source and pulled the trigger without thinking. The explosion of electricity and lead shot flew at a bookcase, striking at least fifteen books and turning them to near dust. Behind the hole created in the bookshelves was a man's head, perfectly centered in the jagged and crooked edges of paper and wood.

Who is that? What the hell?!

I took in the features of what seemed to be a ghost standing in front of me. His skin was as white as bleached bone, with black hair cut short and combed back. He had mutton chops and a handlebar mustache, oiled with what seemed to be motor oil. His lips were stretched in a grin, pencil thin and inhuman as he stared me down with beady eyes.

The man looked so familiar, but I couldn't quite place it. I sifted through the many memories storming around my head, trying to find the right one. After a moment, I found something. Maybe it was a memory from my grandad, but I wasn't sure. It was the first night he got the sword when a man talked to him. The man seemed out of place, strange even. He asked what was fun to do at odd hours of the night. It was the man he saw in America when he, Steven, and Nikola went there.

How could it be him? That was almost fifty years ago. He would be an old man by now. They thought he was…they thought he was connected to Jakobus.

I brought my mind back to the here and now, eyes shifting from not focused to looking back in front of me. The man was gone. He was no longer there, his ghost white face and scary smile missing from the homemade frame of stories.

"What the hell was that?!" Gary asked.

"I- I don't know. I thought I saw someone. Something," I said.

"Whatever it was, I didn't see anyone. You just shot the books. I mean, I don't like to read, but I'm not gonna go shooting at them," he said.

"Yeah, sorry. I flinched and got scared," I said as I trailed off.

I don't know what's going on here. What's with the collection of books? Especially in a place down here, definitely not light reading.

Trying to ignore the fact I was seeing things, I moved my gaze to the altar nestled between six coffins opposite the bookshelves. Upon closer inspection, the altar did not facilitate the usual items you'd find on one in a church or place of worship. There were six candles the color of fresh gray clay eerily flickering, moving in unison to an unheard deathly tune. Curiosity peaked, so I walked over to the shrine of torment to see what else lay atop the altar.

"Deck, I think we should turn around and move on. I'm not sure we should be here," Gary said.

"Hold on, let me see what this is," I said.

A book was opened halfway with a large red ribbon down the middle, separating the two pages. The right page was blank while the left was filled, but oddly, half of it was crossed out. Next to the top right corner was an ornate metal inkwell with a quill made of a stark white owl feather sitting inside.

"What is it?" Gary asked.

"It's a notebook of sorts. Part of it's filled out, but some is scribbled out," I said before reading it aloud. "*You will soon hear of me without funny little games. I saved some of the proper red stuff from the last job to write with, but it went thick like glue, and I can't use it.*"

"I don't like this place," Gary gulped.

That phrase was written out three times. The top two were crossed out. From what I could tell, it was smeared, and he tried to fix it twice. I reached for the quill to see if it was stuck in the inkwell or not, trying to pull it out. The thing wouldn't budge by itself; it was just lifting the metal along with it. I dropped it in horror, realizing what it was. It fell to the altar and bounced, careening towards the edge. It slipped over the end and twirled in the air as it fell to the floor.

"*Gevatter Tod,*" muttered Klaus.

I turned to look at him. "What are you saying?"

He shook his head. "We should not be here."

"Why?" I asked.

"*Gevatter Tod.*" He paused. He shook his head and muttered, "The Grim Reaper."

Wait a minute. Reaper, creepy ancient books, jars with organs?

"This was Jakobus' lair, of sorts. One of them, at least. When he was parading around as Jack the Ripper," I said, eyes wide in surprise.

I spun while looking around the room, taking it all in. Everything surrounding me made sense now. My grandad told me all about the stories when I was young. How Jack the Ripper terrorized the streets of London the year before my mum was born, how he took the lives of innocent people.

"We need to leave. This place is evil," Klaus said, voice quivering.

"Okay, we will leave. But later, you need to tell me everything you know about this person you call the grim reaper, alright?" I asked.

Klaus nodded as he started to back away from the altar, inching towards the entrance. I surveyed the room again, looking for anything that might be useful later. My eyes stopped on a small jewelry box resting menacingly on the clean-cut stone next to the notebook. Dead rose petals were placed around it in a half circle, crisp and black. I began feeling dread as I stared at it, my body feeling like its energy was being drained. An odd droning slowly filled my ears, drowning out the raggedy and raspy breathing of the three of us. As if it was a black abyss calling for me, my soul, to join it in an everlasting night of nothingness.

"Deck?" Gary asked.

I looked at him, then away, noticing my hand was outstretched to the box. His hand was curled around my bicep, shaking it to get my attention. I blinked a few times, ridding myself of the trance I didn't know I was in.

"What is it?" Gary asked.

I shook my head. "I'm not sure. But it feels important, like I need to bring it with me."

"Well, if you think it's important, I wouldn't touch it with your bare skin. I don't know much about this magic business, but that seems like it'd be a big no-no."

I nodded, eyes still locked on the box. I rifled through one of my jacket pockets and pulled out a pair of worn leather gloves. I pulled them on, inching little by little to get them to fit.

That's what you get for not letting your gloves dry out after getting them soaking wet. Serves you right.

I reached out and took the jewelry box in my gloved hand, being careful not to let it touch my skin. Reaching back with my left, I pulled the spare haversack off Excalibur and gently placed it in front of me. I undid the clasp and nestled the box into the main cavity of the bag with a small cloth from the med kit wrapped around it. After letting go, the droning disappeared completely, along with the great cocktail of emotions that came along with it.

I took one last look at the altar and everything that lay upon it. My mind checked to make sure there was nothing else that may be useful at a later point in time. To my surprise, I noticed a set of keys just beneath the spot that held the box.

I really need to start being more observant. I could see a hot cup of tea right now and miss the bloody thing.

"What about this?" I asked, shouting at them.

They both stopped and turned to me, looking at the keys I was holding up.

"They might be of use later. Should I bring them?" I asked again.

"You can. I won't touch the damn things," Gary said.

I did an about-face, slipped it into one of my pockets to save for later and followed them from the room of nighttime horrors.

CHAPTER 12
Decks Labyrinth

4:15 p.m.

We made it back to the crossroads in the underground cat-acombs and decided that the other way was, in fact, the right way to go. For the next few hours, we wandered through the maze of switchbacks and dead ends, hoping the next turn would bring us an opening to the outside world.

"Deck, mind if we stop for a few minutes? Rest our feet and maybe eat something?" Gary asked, still following behind the two of us.

"Uh, sure, let's find an exit to the surface or another room so we have a better watch on our surroundings," I replied.

I kept up a steady pace while we continued looking for some sort of sanctuary. Klaus and Gary followed without a complaint or suggestion, matching my speed well. The small tunnel turned from rough rock and compacted dirt with wooden supports to masonry brick walls and ceilings. The smell shifted from wet earth and insects to old, damp, and musty. Further ahead, I noticed a small fragment of light that splintered down from the ceiling, illuminating what seemed to be a larger area. I crouched and motioned for Gary and Klaus to do the same, glancing back to see if they listened.

"I think there's a room to take a break in up ahead. Let's be quiet just in case someone lurks in the shadows," I whispered.

"Or something," whispered Gary.

I turned to him again, eyes wide with a pained expression of disappointment. My head shook with frustration as he shrugged and mouthed sorry.

I turned forward, and we began to duck walk to the room, carefully lifting each foot with precision, so they didn't drag or scrape against the floor. When we were within three feet of the opening, I signaled for them to stop so I could continue without them. I paused and reached into one of the front pockets of my jacket, pulling out a pear drop. Ritualistically, I pulled on the tabs and unfolded the fruity perfection. I plopped it into my mouth and began to toss it around while I turned the safety switch to the off selection on my shotgun. This enabled the charging disk to accumulate enough electricity just in case I needed to discharge a shot hastily. A faint crackle filled the immediate vicinity, accompanied by the beautiful azure hue of the power lines for which the charge travels on the gun's surface.

My grandad always told me I had the luck of the Irish, but what he didn't mention is that it was bad luck. I took a few deep breaths, readying myself for sudden death because my luck could only hold up for so long. Reluctantly I pulled it up to my shoulder to brace it for a shot and stood up to walk into the room.

At this point, I won't be able to stay quiet. I don't know what lay beyond, but whatever it is, please be like a crocodile or something. It would be strange, but I can deal with that.

I quickly jumped out into the open, sweeping the shotgun sights around the room. My aim started to the left, circling to the right, taking in anything that could be alive and moving. My heart was racing by the millisecond, eyes moving ever faster. I took a few more cautionary glances around at my surroundings.

To my surprise and relief, nobody was there. The room was rather mundane; nothing seemed out of place, and I saw no sign of movement. I looked up to see the light's source, only to have my gaze fall upon a small crack in the ceiling. I squinted one of my eyes and closed the other to try and see up through the crack, hoping I could make out a land marker or street sign. Sadly, I couldn't make anything out, so I turned and called over to the men. "It should be fine. Come on in."

I took in the room with fresh eyes, this time without all of the adrenaline and fear convoluting my ability to observe thoroughly. The opposite side to the one we came from held an old wooden door with metal trim riveted to the outside edges. Light from my spotter glinted off the various steel parts, remarkably untouched by the elements and time.

The ceiling, which seemed to be made of interlocking cut stone, extended further up than the rest of the tunnels and rooms we'd previously been through. It overshadowed them by at least ten feet, arched and gothic in style. The coffins embedded in the walls were the only resemblance between this room and the unnerving one full of jarred organ trophies. This time, it was seven on either side, with two stacks of three with one above. Each spot was filled with coffins except one, adding a strange and macabre feel to the place. I motioned to the other two that it was safe for them to enter.

"What's with these underground rooms and coffins? It's kinda creepy. Why can't it just be chests or something? I mean, you can put a body in a chest, and it wouldn't be as freaky," Gary said.

"*Do sollst mehr Respekt vor den Toten haben,*" Klaus said. "You should respect the dead more than that."

"I do. I'm just saying it'd be a helluva lot less creepy. I don't think that's too much to ask for," Gary said as he shrugged.

I walked further into the room and stopped in the center, or at least what I assumed was the center. With a nod, I decided this was a decent spot and dropped to the ground as I slung the two packs from my back, plopping them in front of me. I grunted and said, "Well, it seems like this is as good a time as any, so let's have a rest while we can."

Gary gave Klaus a little nudge, pushing him to the center of the room. Klaus stopped within three feet of me and said, "Ist here *gut?*"

"Yes. Gary, would you mind switching his hands to his front again?" I asked.

He nodded and undid Klaus' bindings, allowing them to move it to the front. I then began unclipping the top of my bag and reached inside. My journal was the first thing I pulled out and set to the side. The second was my mess tin, followed by spare socks and laces.

I then grabbed the rest of the contents to take stock of everything I had, sans the bottle of brandy; I left that in there for a later date. In a pile at my feet were some spare tinned rations, extra iron rations, my water bottle, and some spare handgun ammunition bundles. With the other two looking away, I slid the small box I took from the altar into a small pocket of my haversack. I felt a minuscule electrical charge as my hand curled around it, causing the hairs on my arms to stand up on end.

I don't see why I need to worry about touching it with my bare skin. It seems perfectly fine to me.

Gary took a seat on the cold stone floor, completing the triangle we sat in. He did the same, dropping his bag in front of him and placing the rifle within arms reach just in case. He then began to rummage through the haversack himself, seeing what wondrously dangerous toys Thomas left for us.

I opened the second flap on my modified haversack. I pulled out the extra food tins I stuffed away for these situations. The first can that caught my eye was bully beef. This made me sigh in disgust as I looked at the rest of the foodstuffs. There were a few packages of loose-leaf black tea, a tin of tooth dullers, aka biscuits, and two tins of M&V.

"Klaus, how are you feeling?" I asked, eyes still trained on my supplies.

I saw him fidget for a moment in my periphery.

He settled and spoke, "I am alright. I do not feel like I will have another seizure if that ist what you are wondering."

"More or less." I turned my attention to him as I handed him a can of bully beef. "So, how *do* you feel?"

He was silent for another few seconds. "I feel *seltsam*, strange. I am not quite sure what to make of it."

I chuckled. "Yeah, it can be like that, to begin with. Trust me. I went through the same thing."

"I have all of these *erinnerugen*, these memories that are not mine. It is confusing."

"Yup, that is also something you'll have to deal with. My suggestion? Find something to think about, something that's yours. Something that means very much to you and think of that anytime you feel confused or lost. It'll help."

He nodded thoughtfully and remained silent, looking at the ground with the can resting between his fingers. I glanced in Gary's direction, seeing what he was doing now. He emptied all the contents of his bag onto the ground between his legs like a kid on Christmas.

"So, what do you all have there?" I asked.

"Some stuff I've never seen, along with a mess tin, first aid pouch, and a canteen."

I got to my feet and crouched near him, "What do you mean things you've never seen?"

In a pile between his legs were three of the electrified nets Thomas had shown me just a handful of hours prior. The other two objects were a set of smooth, shining metal cylinders about six inches long.

"Huh," I said as I picked up one of the nets. "This is a trap of sorts. It's a net you throw at your enemies."

"What makes it so special then?" Gary asked.

He picked one up himself, starting to reach for the big red button in the middle.

I yanked it from his hand before he could. "Be careful. It's electrified. You press the button and throw it, and it wraps around the enemy and shocks them."

"What is it called?"

I shrugged. "Not sure. He never gave it one."

"You guys need to start putting directions on things. Almost everything you have seems severely dangerous if not used correctly," Gary said as he sighed.

Klaus snickered somewhat, breaking his stoic attitude. He stopped abruptly to try and maintain the little amount of mystery he had left.

Gary shook his head and said, "What are those then? I don't want to pick it up."

I put the net trap down and carefully picked up one of the cylinders. "This, I'm not sure. I have never seen anything like this before." I gently placed it back on the ground. "But knowing Thomas, we should be careful with it. Anyways, are you hungry, Gary?"

"Uh, sure. I should probably eat something," he replied. "Good thing I just dumped everything out."

I walked back over to my pile of supplies and bent down to pick up one of the M&V tins. Gary carefully put everything back into his sack, keeping the metal cylinders level so as not to excite anything they may contain.

I whistled to get his attention, and he turned to me just as he finished sliding them back into the bottom of his bag, sweat visibly forming on his brow. He dabbed at his forehead as I tossed it to him, catching it with remarkable agility and ease.

"What is this stuff?" he asked, turning it over in his hands.

"It's M&V," I replied.

"Okay." He paused, turning it over again. "That doesn't really explain what it is."

I chuckled. "It's a meat and vegetable stew, thus M&V."

"That doesn't sound that horrendous. I'm sure it's pretty decent."

"Yeah, let's go with that," I said, grabbing my own can of mystery meat.

I reached into my pocket and struggled as I pulled out my keyring. A lucky rabbit's foot dangled loosely back and forth next to a few keys and a small hunk of metal. The p38 can opener gleamed in the light shown down from above as if the angels were answering my stomach's prayers. I hastily dug into the rim of the tin with the opener, hunger growing rapidly in the pit of my stomach. In anticipation of the meal, I finished chewing the piece of candy and swallowed it. By now, Klaus had already pulled the top off his bully beef and was eating it with a knife.

"Oi, how'd you get a knife?" I asked, almost dropping my tin of food.

He shrugged and continued to eat, carefully slicing pieces from the gelatinous meat blob. Without much luck, I tried to ignore the fact that he had a knife this whole time, returning most of my attention to my own bully beef. I carefully glanced back at him periodically as we enjoyed, no, tolerated the food we had.

"I am not a huge fan of the food," Gary said.

I looked at his face to see a sour expression plastered across it. "Yeah, sorry. It's better warm. Sadly, we are kind of lacking basic necessities."

We all ate in silence for a little while, only to be bothered by water droplets echoing off a surface somewhere out of visible range. The room temperature was surprisingly warm, gnawing at my aching body and tired mind. It mingled with the comforting feeling of a full stomach, coercing me to forget the world's pains and ignore my problems. It told me it was alright to lay here, fall asleep, gather my strength, and let the night tend to my wounds. I shook my head to rid myself of those threatening thoughts of comfort.

Now's not the time, Deck. We need to keep moving toward the rendezvous to meet everyone. Or at least everyone that's left.

I felt more than exhausted, and my eyes became extremely heavy like they were made of lead. The droning I heard earlier in the altar room returned, but this time more than just a sound. I could feel my hands and feet start to vibrate faintly. My arms, legs, and torso followed them, delicately pulsing to a non-existent rhythm. My vision began to blur and tunneled to nothing but an everlasting, engulfing black.

Scrape, scrape

Train whistles sounded all around me, blowing in short and long bursts. I opened my eyes to see people hurrying to and fro walking to catch their train or meet someone for lunch. I looked around to see where I was and how I was there. I turned to my left and saw my Grandad sitting right next to me, journal clutched in his hands.

"Grandad, why are we here?" I asked.

Why is my voice so squeaky and high-pitched?

I looked down at my hands and moved them in front of my eyes, only to see they were tiny. My heart started to beat rapidly, threatening to burst from my chest.

"We're here to watch for someone, Deckard," he said as he wrapped an arm around my shoulders.

The worry of my sudden de-pubertization immediately became less urgent, eventually floating to the back of my mind. A sense of ease and comfort washed over me as I scooted closer to him.

"Who are we waiting for?" I asked.

"Oh, just an old friend. He said he would be visiting any day now."

"What's his name, Grandad?"

Before he could answer me, the memory started to ripple and become fuzzy in my mind. Without warning, I was pulled from the safe place, crashing back to the here and now.

Scrape, scrape

Chapter Thirteen
Nothing Worse
Than Brandy

5:11 p.m.

I struggled to reconcile what just happened.

"Deck, hello? Deck, are you with us?" Gary asked, shaking my shoulder.

"Uh yeah, sorry. What happened? Did I fall asleep?"

Gary scoffed. "No, you just went extremely quiet, and your eyes rolled into the back of your head."

"Sorry." I rubbed my neck and chewed the rest of the meat paste in my mouth. "Sometimes memories flash through my head, and sometimes they aren't even mine. It can be hard to deal with."

Gary nodded as he processed this.

I cleared my throat. "Time to get moving. We need to get topside to get an idea of where we are and how far away we are from the rendezvous."

"Where is the rendezvous, anyway?" Gary asked.

I turned to him as I scraped the last of the bully beef from my can. "I can't tell you yet. I'll just have to ask you to trust me. In the meantime, I'll have to look over this journal."

I picked up my journal from the pile at my feet and reached out to Gary. He leaned over to take it from my hand, settling back to his sitting position after he took it. As he flipped through the pages, I put everything else back into my own haversack. I started with the food tins, followed by the extra socks and laces, my water bottle and iron rations. I placed the spare ammunition bundles at the top because they would likely be the first thing that I'd need next. The rustling of turning paper filled the air as Gary flipped through the journal, eyes dancing as he read random sections of entries on non-specific pages.

"Did you write all this?" Gary asked, nose still glued to the pages.

"No, it's actually Frank's. I have it in case I have issues sorting through memories. It helps me remember the specific details I need to know about The Keepers," I said.

"This is quite extensive. It'll take a while to even go through a fourth of it."

"Well, of course, it is. It explains almost everything we know of The Keepers for the last fourteen hundred years. Most of that is basically cliff notes, but the more recent stuff has more substance to it."

I finished gathering my things and started to stand up, swinging my bag onto my back, only to be interrupted by Gary.

"Wait, I have some questions before we leave. You want me to trust you? I need some answers first."

I stopped myself from standing and sat back down. "Fair enough. Ask away. I'll answer a few."

"Was about me? Do I have to trust you?" Klaus asked.

My blood pressure rose, skyrocketing through the roof as my breathing sped up. I started to stand again but stopped and sat back down. The frustration and anger swelled deep in my guts, boiling, bubbling, and swirling like molten hot lava. I closed my eyes and took a few deep breaths, trying to calm myself enough to talk to him. "You don't really have a choice. You don't need to trust me. I certainly don't trust you yet. You still are the reason one of my men is dead."

For all I know, you were the one that spotted Phillips and told your friend to pull the trigger.

"I am sorry about your freund. I never wanted to be in this war." Klaus shuddered.

I looked at him, taking in his expression and body language. He was shaking, breathing raggedly with a pained look on his face. The tin he had in his hands was now crumpled and crushed lying at his feet. His knife was tossed to the ground as well, lying between the two of us.

Maybe he's right. There are men on our side who never wanted to be drafted. They just wanted to stay home and live their lives. They wanted a simple existence of finishing high school and starting college or their first job. Find a lovely lass ask to marry and create a family. Why couldn't it be the same on their side?

"Everything in *mein* head is conflicting, fighting to be the driving force in my decisions. I keep seeing things that aren't my life, things I've never lived. I feel myself talking in a way I wouldn't normally," Klaus said.

After he said that, I noticed he wasn't talking with as many German words mixed with English as he had been.

"I never wanted to be in this war. I don't agree with any of it," he continued.

I'll have to watch him. He may be a descendant, but he is also the enemy. I can't even imagine how different this is for him.

"Okay, if you want me to be able to trust you, then you need to tell me how they found the headquarters."

Klaus' body slowly stopped shaking as he turned his face towards mine. "Ich have a tracking device on me."

"Where is it? In a pocket or something?" I asked.

"*Nein*, sorry. In me. I have one inside me."

"Where in you?"

He lifted his hands to his face, pulled open his mouth, and turned to the side. He mumbled through his fingers, "One of *mein* teeth. They started implanting them a few months ago on most soldiers. At least the ones interviewed by Himmler and his team of doctors."

"Who was involved in the team of doctors? Do you remember?" I asked.

"*Ja,* one man I knew. You may know him by another name: *Todesengel.* The Angel of Death."

I closed my eyes and rubbed my temples. The new information came as a shock to me and may complicate things further. I felt my mind slipping again as I drifted off into thought. Still, I quickly snapped my eyes open and began talking again to focus on the conversation. "Josef Mengele. He's bad news. To think he is working with Jakobus. I can't even fathom what they might be doing together."

Maybe that would explain Spike. He could be the product of an experiment or something.

"Can you remove the tooth without discomfort? How is it held in place?" I asked.

He grabbed his second premolar with his index finger and thumb and wiggled it. The tooth didn't budge regardless of how hard he tried. "It will not move."

"Sorry, Klaus. You know what we need to do."

Klaus looked at me as his face went as pale as marble, visibly gulping. He nodded slowly, knowing what needed to happen.

I slipped my haversack off my back once more and dug into one of the side pockets. I pulled out a small green bundle of canvas and placed it on the ground. Pulling the neat knot that tied the strings to keep it shut, I unrolled it out to reveal the stainless-steel tools I carried around. A variety was fastened in fabric loops to hold them in place and spread evenly on the rolled-out canvas. I had a few knives, screwdrivers, wrenches, and a pair of pliers. Without looking, I reached down, withdrew the pliers from their spot, and held them in my hand, flipping them up in the air and catching them to have the handle pointing out.

"Do you want me to do it? Or would you prefer to?" I asked.

"You can't be serious," Gary interrupted.

I snapped at him, "I am. He needs to take it out if we want to make it to the rendezvous and see everyone again. He's one of us now, a Keeper, which means making the right decisions. They aren't usually the easiest or the most comfortable, but they are the right ones. That's what it means to fight back against evil incarnate."

"Do you have schnaps? Alcohol?" Klaus asked.

"I have brandy. Would that do?"

He scowled. "No, I hate brandy. But I don't have a choice."

"So, you'll do it?"

"*Ja*, hand me the brandy first."

I grabbed the bottle by the neck out of my haversack and handed it over to him. He took it and uncorked it quickly, sniffing the opening first. Gagging, he shook his head from the stench and swore before lifting it to his lips in both hands. He took one large swig of the liquor and coughed as he pulled it from his lips and put it between his knees.

He then reached out to me and said, "Pliers."

I handed them over and watched with a macabre interest as he readied himself for the pain. He took four large breaths and lifted the pliers to his mouth. I didn't expect him to go through with it. Maybe for him to try once and not get anywhere, to give up immediately. Or perhaps it was all a ruse, and he had another knife to stab us with when we weren't expecting it. I even expected him to scream at the top of his lungs if he, in fact, did try. Teeth are quite strong, but I know from past trips to the dentist that they can also crack and crumble, making it difficult to remove all of it.

But he did do it. He got it on the first try. I also expected lots of blood to start pouring out. But to my surprise, he was as quiet as a church mouse, not a single grunt or groan. Not only that, but it didn't bleed whatsoever. Not even on the tooth itself. He held it out to me and dropped it and the pliers into my hands, immediately grabbing the brandy and taking another big gulp from it.

"Will you be alright?" I asked.

Klaus took another drink of the brandy and put the cork back on the top of the bottle. Handing it to me, he said, "*Ja.*"

"Alright, let me know if it hurts too much at any point. I can probably find pain relievers in my first aid kit," I said.

He nodded and returned to staring down at his feet. I slipped the pliers back into the canvas tool roll and folded it shut, tying the bow again. Next, I lifted the tooth to the light from the crack in the ceiling, looking at it more closely. It had cooled down after being torn from his mouth and was cold as stone.

For the most part, it was a typical-looking molar until I noticed it warmed back up since he had placed it in my hand. I turned it around and looked at the tooth's roots, seeing tiny filaments of wire starting to pulse with a bright red color.

"Well, that's pretty ace. I think it's powered by body temperature. Activated by warmth," I said.

"How can that be?" Gary asked.

"Not sure, honestly, but we have guns powered by collecting electricity in the air. It's not too far-fetched to see other kinds of technology."

"What will we do with it?" Gary asked.

"Leave it. Let them find it down here as we try to get away. That is if it stays activated without being in his mouth."

I took it and threw it back down the tunnel we came from, being content with ridding ourselves of that problem. It clattered and bounced off the walls and floor, coming to a stop further away. Satisfied, I picked up my tool roll and slid it back into my pack, clipping it shut.

"How do you know Mengele is working with Jakobus?" Gary asked but then corrected himself. "I suppose rather, how do you know who Jakobus is?"

"We don't particularly know who he is, but we think it may be one of four people, including Hitler," I said. I started counting fingers on my right hand. "It could be Mengele, Himmler, Goebbels and, well, Mr. Fuhrer himself."

"Hmph, it would have seemed to me you guys would have a better idea who he would be," Gary said.

I scoffed, "I'm sorry. We will get right on that, sir. We've only tried to figure it out for the last six years and narrowed it down to four people. But excuse me if that's not good enough. I'll get back at it."

I stood up and shook my head in frustration. I slung my pack on my back and started trudging toward the metal studded wooden door.

Stupid yank. Not like we aren't trying, dammit. Do you know how many people have died for this? How many homes destroyed, and families torn apart just because someone was egged on by an evil warlock?

Gary got up to follow me, scrambling over his packs. He reached out and grabbed my arm to stop me. "Deck, I didn't mean anything by it. I'm sorry. I only meant that there should be an easy way figuring out who exactly he is."

I stopped for a second, turning to him. My face grew red with warmth as I bared my teeth and gritted them tightly. "Do you have an idea I'm not thinking of? Any insight you might have that I'm missing?"

"No, I don't. I'm sorry, Deck," Gary said.

Gary backed up a few steps, tripping over the bags he just scrambled around. He lost his balance and fell to the ground in a heap, thudding hard on the rock floor.

"What about *das* ring?" Klaus asked.

I turned to him, trying to let my anger subside and slip away. "What about it?"

"*Das* ring tells if someone ist a descendant. Couldn't it tell if someone is Jakobus?" Klaus asked.

Could it? Grandad never told me if he tried it with Jakobus before, not that he told me anything anyways. I can't recall anything from the memories I have from anyone who has been in contact with him. Then again, what is the box I found at the altar? Could that be used to find him somehow? Could that be like the ring? It may have been a way for Jakobus to find the right "vessels" to be able to control or abuse.

The buzzing returned to my ears, faint and distant like the sound of thunder many miles away. It made everything go fuzzy in my head, causing me to lose focus again.

"Maybe. I'm not sure. I don't recall there being a mention in the journal either. We could always try it. But that poses another issue. We need to get in close contact with one of them to try," I said.

Wait a minute.

Gary and I turned to each other, broad smiles creeping onto our faces. We were definitely thinking the same thing as we turned to Klaus. His face went even whiter than it had from pulling the tooth from his face. He shook his head and let out a small groan.

"*Scheiße*," he muttered.

"That'll be something to worry about later on. First, we will camp here for a few hours, get some sleep and go from there," I said with a smile.

We all sat down once more, getting as comfortable as we could. I nestled the shotgun next to me and flicked off my spotter, bathing the room in shadows.

CHAPTER 14
Questions

2nd August, 1937
Richmond Borough, London, England
9:00 a.m.

Deck caught himself staring into the distance, gazing upon the wall of paintings. He heard the conversation among the others fluctuate from serious talk to random bouts of rich joking and hearty laughter.

"Deckard, are you okay?" Steven asked.

Deck shook his head and looked back at him. "Yeah, sorry about that. This is all just a lot to process at once. I was looking at the painting of the woman in white laying on a boat with a man in mourning guiding it."

"Mhm, yes. I remember the first time I saw that painting. It was during the year of the reaper. When your grandad and I were deep into the investigation trying to find Jakobus."

"Yeah, that's the thing that is quite odd. I have that memory. I feel like I was there meself. But I wasn't, clearly. That's me grandad's memory."

"It was the same for me when Davey first found me. When I touched my artifact, it was a lot to deal with, but I think my family's line wasn't as involved as yours was. Less for me to deal with in terms of information."

Deck smirked. "What was he like when he was younger? Seems like he had an answer for everything to me."

"Who? Your grandad? He was a good man. Strong-willed and a damned good fighter. He always wanted to do what was right and help anyone that needed it. The answer part, well, I think that probably came with age." He chuckled.

"It seems like it was hard back then, trying to find Jakobus?"

Steven pursed his lips. "It was in some ways, and in others, it seemed like it was right in front of our faces the whole time."

Deck looked over at the paintings again, scanning over the years of creativity. Some were landscapes of lush greens and browns, yellows, and reds. There were pictures of wheat fields stretching for miles, while other images displayed green pastures dotted with animals like cows, sheep, and horses. Looking around some more, Deck saw trees on the cusp of a crisp fall morning, orange leaves shaking and drifting with the cool gentle breeze.

They all told a story. They told us something the artist felt was important enough to share with future generations. Something clicked in Deck's head: That's what all memories are. Meaningful experiences he needed to use. They were for his advantage, to keep him going further than any other descendant had gone before him.

"Me grandad never told me about you. Why was that?" Deck asked, eyes still glued to the wall of color.

"I am not sure about that. Maybe because I never came back. Maybe it was easier for him to move on if he didn't talk about it," Steven said.

"About what? Jakobus and The Keepers? Or how you left and never came back?"

"Most likely all of that. He had a life he needed to live here. Easier to forget something that wasn't happening anymore."

"Why did you leave, anyway? I don't seem to have any memory of it from me grandad," Deck asked, turning back to him.

Steven sighed heavily. "I originally left because I felt I had unfinished business in America that needed care. When we went to the USA with Nikola, we ran into a man who seemed to me involved with this whole mess."

"Did you ever find him?"

"Not right away. About seven years after I moved to America, I heard the news of a man in Chicago who was killing people for their insurance policies. Turns out it was the very same man I went there to find."

"What happened to him, then?"

"He was found guilty of his crimes and was hung to death. That was that."

"Did you come back to London, then?" I asked.

"Before that, yes. Your grandad and I actually helped Nikola collect the artifacts, too. Over a few years, we went around the world collecting them. I thought you knew that?"

Deck rubbed at his neck. "I didn't, actually. I thought Nikola just hired people to collect them."

"No, we helped. After that, it had been seven years, and I had already fallen in love and had a child of my own. A daughter. So that's why I never stayed," he said.

Deck fidgeted in the momentary silence.

Steven then pulled out a pocket watch and clicked the button to release the cover. Inside was a picture of a beautiful woman wearing a flawless flowing dress. Steven peered at it intently. "She was a wonderful woman. So caring and loving."

"Did your daughter have any children of her own?" Deck asked, hopeful.

Steven quickly replied and stuttered, "No, s—sorry."

Why did he respond that way? Is he lying to me? Could he be trying to protect someone?

Frank sat next to Deck on the couch and said, "You two catching up?"

Deck turned his attention to him, wondering why Steven was acting strange toward his question. "Yes, sort of. He was just telling me what happened after me grandad and gran had me mother."

"Ah yes, near the end of 1888. My grandfather Hubert told me all about it," Frank said.

"I was just wondering why I remember some things about them and not others. Do you know why this happens?" Deck asked.

"I'm not sure why, no. Maybe you only remember the things that relate to Jakobus?" Frank asked.

Deck thought about it, quickly sorting things in his head. Everything he could remember related almost directly to Jakobus. What Frank was saying seemed like it made the most sense.

"Wait, your grandfather is Hubert? How is that possible? He was a man of the cloth. Isn't that frowned upon?" Deck asked.

Frank chuckled, "Yes, it is. But my mother was from another life of his, before he devoted himself to The Keepers. But that's a story for another time."

Chapter 15
The Door

25th December, 1942
9:35 p.m.

I awoke from the small amount of sleep I afforded myself, feeling all the aches and pains from the last day finally seep into all of my existence.

These dreams are almost more vivid than the memories themselves. Just gotta keep reminding myself of what's important.

I stood up and looked at Gary and Klaus, who had fallen asleep back-to-back, one toward the wooden door and the other pointing down the hall from which we came. My fingers curled around the shotgun as I kicked both their boots and woke them up, wanting to get going.

"Come on, you two, time to get a move on," I said.

They both let out groans of disapproval, rousing slowly and rolling to their feet. Gary dusted off his pants while Klaus stretched, cracking his back. We all walked to the wooden door and looked at it, deciding the best thing to do.

I turned on my spotter to help see everything better, but the door was locked when we tried opening it. We wanted to stay quiet since we were not privy to what lay beyond the indestructible door of iron, causing the whole situation to last much longer than was necessary.

So far, we had tried the handle, hoping it would work, but my luck must have been rubbing off on everyone else. That, or they too were from a long line of unlucky Irishmen.

"Can't we just shoot out the handle with the shotgun?" Gary asked.

"We can, but that would surely mean our demise. Knowing how things usually go for me, a three-headed dog is on the other side, ready to take me to the underworld," I said through gritted teeth.

I pulled and yanked on the doorknob with all my strength, straining beyond belief.

This must be tougher than pulling the sword from the stone. I lucked out with that one. Conveniently I got it from a box in a dusty basement. The only tricky thing about that was the sneezing I got afterward.

"What about using the sword as a pry? Just wedge it in there and shimmy it loose," Gary said.

I turned to him, face drenched in sweat. I took a few deep breaths to calm my scorching nerves. "No, we can't use Excalibur as a glorified tin opener."

"What about *das* keys?" Klaus asked.

I stopped pulling on the door and realized he had a point. My fingers fumbled as I reached into the right pocket to pull out the rusty, pitted metal keys.

Damn all these pockets. I can't keep track of how many I have.

I held them out into the light cast off from my spotter, looking at each one. Four were hooked on the ring, the first being a simple skeleton key. The following two were barrel keys, exactly the same as each other, while the last was a pipe key that would be used for a safe. I took the skeleton key in my hand and guessed that this was the right one.

This is definitely not a lock that requires a key to a safe, and I don't think it'd be one of the matching keys. Who would keep both of them on the same ring? Wouldn't it just be confusing?

"Here, I'll try this one first," I said.

I gingerly pushed the key into the keyhole and took a deep breath. On the exhale, I gripped the bow and turned it gently, letting the bit catch on the lock's inner mechanism. With a creak and groan, the bolt rolled in and unlocked the door, giving us access to open it with the knob.

"We don't know what's on the other side, so like I keep saying—"

I was cut off by Gary. "Yeah, we're soldiers too. It's not like we're complete idiots, right, Klaus?"

Klaus looked from me to Gary, then back to me once more. "Do not bring me into this."

I rolled my eyes at them and returned my attention to the door in front of me. Once I righted the key, I pulled it out. My eyes squinted in anticipation as I turned the knob slowly. More noises from it argued with me as I kept turning, proving some valid points on how I wasn't ready to open the door.

I stopped and contemplated what could be beyond; maybe it was a mime pretending to be stuck in a box? Or perhaps it was a door to a cliff I would be leading us off, or could it be the depths of hell? Maybe this was just another way to get down there. On the bright side, perhaps we could meet Dante? I shrugged and pulled to see what lay beyond the door of secrets.

The other side was dark and cool with a breeze that picked up and blasted us with a frigid wave. The second thing I noticed was the semi-decomposed German body that fell onto my feet when I opened it.

Surprise and horror brewing in my mind, I shuffled my feet to get them out from underneath the corpse. On the other hand, Gary freaked out royally and screamed like a little schoolgirl. After the small outburst of fear, he straightened his clothes, attempting to bring the attention away from the fact that he was caught off guard. We nodded, and all agreed silently that it'd be best to just push on and act like that didn't happen.

I slung the shotgun from my shoulder and pointed my spotter down at the body. The glacier-white skull protruded in stark contrast from the uniform. Most of the skin and meat had rotted away. The brightness of bone was outlined with small trace amounts of black and brown decay that clung on like lively green moss to the north side of boulders and stones. The empty shadowed eye sockets stared up at me with an emptiness I felt I knew more about than I should have.

"Klaus, do you know anything about this man?" I asked, looking at the uniform.

"*Nein*," Klaus said.

He bent down and went for his neck to look for identification, pulling the man's collar apart in the process. With no luck finding dog tags, he started looking for another form of identification or other pieces of paper that may hold any information. After rummaging through the countless places things could be, Klaus pulled out a small leather-bound journal. It was the size of a standard hardcover novel, made of a caramel brown color with a thin cord wrapped around and tied in the front on a brass button.

"What is it?" I asked, reaching for it.

"I do not know," Klaus said.

"Regardless of what it is, we should take it with us. It might hold some information we could use to our advantage," I said while I took it from Klaus. I then slipped it into my haversack and asked, "It doesn't seem normal to me that he doesn't have any dog tags. Why wouldn't he?"

"I'm not sure, but I think das uniform would be useful," Klaus said.

"Yeah, it probably would, actually. Good thinking, Klaus. Considering we don't have your old one, this will do if we need you to infiltrate your own army," I said.

He began to take the clothing from the corpse, undressing him gently with a sense of respect. He started with the tunic, undoing the last few buttons, still holding on for life.

I noticed he had a gas mask that lay just out of arm's reach a few feet away. The hairs on the back of my neck stood on end as my eyes grew wide. I looked at the dead soldier's hands, shining my spotter on them. The palms were facing upward, and strangely most of the skin was still attached. I reached down and turned them over to look at their top side. The fingernails were all broken away, leaving bloody finger beds with chunks of black and scarlet streaks running down the backs of the hands.

I dropped them in horror, realizing why the skin on his face was gone. I quickly reached back and pulled my gas mask to my face. I barked out, "Masks on."

Did I breathe some in? Oh God, I hope not.

"Why? What's going on?" Gary asked.

"*Traumgas*," Klaus replied. "Dream gas."

Klaus reached for the mask on the ground before crouching again and sliding it down over his face. He then began to strip the corpse of his clothing once more, ensuring he collected all the garments.

"Was there a mask in either of the extra bags?" I asked, pulling my mask down over my face.

I turned to look at Gary, fear and confusion flooding over his face. He scrambled as he grabbed for the haversacks on the ground, digging furiously through the pockets he must not have checked before. The panic on his face grew as he switched to the second, empty-handed from his search with the first. He did all but rip the flaps from each pocket as he rushed to look in another. I started to look around the room and hall, checking for anything else he could use, not seeing anything.

"What is dream gas? What happened to that man?" Gary asked.

I didn't respond, still trying to find something for Gary. He was now on to the last pocket of the haversack, still no luck with finding another mask. He pulled out various objects, throwing them in different directions. The last thing he pulled out was a mask.

"I have one!" he shouted in triumph.

"Good, now put it on. We don't have time for you to celebrate your good fortune," I said.

Gary pulled the mask on hastily, adjusting it snuggly, so he didn't have to worry about leaks or an ill-fitting seal. His breathing sounded labored through the muted protective layer, coming out as short rasps in the silence.

"Are we all okay then?" I asked as I looked at both of them.

Klaus looked at me through dusty round circles of glass just as he finished taking the clothes off the dead man. The garments were now tucked neatly under his arm as he stood to face us. I crouched down, stuffed most of the supplies into one of the haversacks, and handed that one to Gary, giving him something to do other than hyperventilating.

"What is dream gas?" Gary asked again.

"It's something the other side cooked up in their labs. You don't want to have to deal with it," I said, grabbing the last sack. "It causes a plethora of different effects, mainly bad ones. It is a hallucinogenic, causing visions so vivid they feel real, nasty stuff it is."

"Have you dealt with it before?" Gary asked.

"I have. The problem with pseudo-gas, or as Klaus referred to it as *traumgas,* is that it was really dangerous. It has different effects on different people, being severely unpredictable. There have been some instances that I have seen it react well to some, creating a euphoric type of situation. But most often, it isn't forgiving, making the inflicted see things only their greatest nightmares could dream up. It was a nasty invention the Germans cooked up when they invaded England, using it to help confuse and scramble our forces and cause mass panic."

Gary didn't respond. His eyes were wide with what I assumed was horror. I stood up and glanced inside the second haversack. The contents left over were rations and a canteen. Nothing dangerous or that could be used as a weapon was left inside. I held the top open and motioned to Klaus. "Put the clothes in here. I'll let you carry this bag."

He took the clothes from under his arm and put them in the bag. Klaus then slung the bag over his shoulders, adjusting its position by jumping and rearranging it. I realized he no longer had his bindings on and asked, "How did you get the bindings off?"

Klaus shrugged and pulled on the straps to tighten the pack to his back some more. He then crouched and looked at the body once more. "*Das* body is not very old. A day or two, maybe."

I crouched down next to him and showed my spotter on the death at our feet. The same darkness stared back up at me as I took in the rest of his body. His torso, arms, legs, and other extremities were devoid of markings, blood, or damage. The only indication of expiration was that his face and flesh were gone.

Did I imagine the rot and decay? Did I breathe any of the gas in?

"Why is dream gas a thing?" I asked.

"It is an idea by Himmler. He is death incarnate with no respect for human life," Klaus said.

"Do you think he really could be Jakobus? I mean, out of anyone, that is who I would assume it would be," I said.

"Maybe," Klaus replied.

"I'm sorry. I know this is all confusing to you. Especially since we are supposed to be at war with each other. I just need to know I can trust you."

Klaus stayed silent for a few moments. I decided I wasn't going to get a confirmation out of him, so I pulled another set of bindings from my bag. "Hold out your hands, Klaus."

He complied, placing them in front so I could slide them on. They went on easy as I tightened them, making sure I went a little snugger this time since he somehow found a way to take the last pair off. I gave them another tug and decided they would be suitable for now.

"Let's get moving. We still need to make it topside and find a way to get to the rendezvous," I said. "Gary, you stay behind Klaus like we did before. Klaus, please behave."

I pointed the shotgun in front of us and took off down the corridor, light from my spotter focusing on random spots as I moved. After about a hundred feet, we were far enough away from the body that I decided we should be out of any remnants of dream gas. With my free hand, I reached up and took my mask off, breathing in a breath of the relatively fresh air. The other two followed suit and tucked theirs away for later use. The smell of the tunnel shifted from the earthy stench in the previous room to one of wood smoke and cooking food, wafting around our nostrils and tantalizing them with a promise of a warm meal.

"Is that food I smell?" Gary asked.

"It is, but we need to practice caution. We don't have any outposts in the city. Probably Germans knowing my luck," I said.

We kept going for another forty feet, eventually reaching a set of stone stairs leading up toward the surface. At the very top, I could make out a small amount of light peeking through cracks in what seemed to be a rickety wooden door.

We crept up the steps, trying to stay quiet, making sure we took each step softly. Reaching the door, we crouched and listened intently to see if anyone was directly on the other side.

Definitely got lucky when we opened the last one.

"Who wants to open this one?" I asked, glancing back at them.

They both shook their heads no, looking in different directions, acting too busy to bother themselves with the task.

I sighed and shook my head. "Fine, I can do this one too."

CHAPTER 16
Topside

25th December, 1942
St Katharine's & Wapping Borough, London, England
10:00 p.m.

I pulled the shotgun into the crook of my arm, ready to grab it with the left after I opened the door. My nerves were fraying like a strained rope as I reached for the knob and slowly turned, pushing it open. The light poured through at first, blinding me momentarily as my eyes adjusted to the change in brightness. My vision returned as I peered through the door's crack, looking around at the surroundings. The door opened into a small arch-covered alley of some kind with the light coming from the right, and from what I could tell, there was nobody within earshot.

I gulped and pushed the door open the rest of the way as I duck-walked out. My eyes followed the shotgun's sights as I brought it up to my face and peered left around the open door. The alley stopped at a dead end that looked to be boarded up manually about twenty feet down. There was nothing too exciting besides some piles of trash and wooden crates that were pushed up against a wall. I swiftly turned to the right, shotgun following my lead as I aimed down that direction. The alley went on for about fifteen feet. Eventually, it stopped, opening up and intersecting the road with overhead lights illuminating the area. Smoke visibly floated lazily from that direction, dissipating into the nighttime air.

"It's clear for now but be careful. I think there are enemy soldiers down there," I said. I looked at Klaus and smiled sheepishly. "They're your enemies now too."

They followed me as I crept down the alley toward the delicious smells trying to play tricks on me. Trying to get into my head and persuade me to let my guard down with a promise of a full stomach. I could hear an accordion begin to play close to us, starting off slow and quickly changing into something with a fast pace. Some singing shortly followed, joining the music in a jolly melody.

"I'm going to peek around the corner. You two just stay back a little," I said.

Reaching up, I turned off my spotter to keep my position a secret and ensure nothing took me or us away. I crouched at the corner and gradually inched my head around to see what was down to the left.

Halfway down the road was a checkpoint that sat menacingly in front of The Tower of London on the side that faced the river Thames, searchlights and a few fires adding to the artificial daylight. There were about six or seven men I could make out, walking in random bursts, looking out for trouble that might join in the festivities. The shadows created from their bodies danced on the walls, conjuring a dangerous show of string puppets being used for a weightier cause unknown to them.

Near the checkpoint entrance was a large bonfire where three other men sat, backs straight as if they expected the Fuhrer himself to join them. One of the men sat with an accordion as the other two were busy tending a boar roasting on a spigot. I could hear the crackling of the wood as the drippings fell unceremoniously upon them, sizzling and smoking as the smell wafted to me.

God, that boar smells so delicious. What I wouldn't give for a taste of the juicy meat slowly cooking for hours.

I shook my head to remind myself of what was at stake, ridding myself of the silly notions of a hot dinner. The sling snagged on Excalibur for a moment as I slung my shotgun over my shoulder and head. After adjusting it, I slipped my hand into one of my breast pockets and pulled out my dime glass, wanting to make sure that they were the only men there.

I'm glad I had Thomas make a version of the telescopic lens we used on the Mason Sharpshooter Model 1937's to be used without the rifle. It's smaller and more manageable for use out in the field.

I popped off the ends and twisted the sides to extend outward, allowing for ease of use. Pulling it up to my face, I peered through and scanned ahead more carefully. From what I could tell, it was the same as what I saw before taking out my dime glass.

I looked to the left, scanned the makeshift docks created near the water, and saw a couple of dinghies tied to the wood. Without looking, I took the dime glass from my eye and collapsed it down to size. I placed the caps back over the lenses and slipped the scope into my pocket as I crept backwards and returned to Klaus and Gary.

"Klaus, do you know anything about the checkpoint up ahead?" I asked.

"A little. Not much. I was not stationed over here." Klaus said.

"Where did we end up anyway?" Gary asked.

I sighed. "On the opposite side of The Tower of London, next to the river."

"Is that bad?" Gary asked.

"Yes and no. Yes, because there are quite a few German soldiers off to the right," I said.

"What's the good thing about it then?" Gary asked.

"The good news is if we happen to make it past them without alerting anyone, we can commandeer a boat and take the river to the rendezvous," I said.

"Oh yeah, simple. Just sneak past and not make a peep. I can do that in my sleep," Gary said.

I rolled my eyes at him and sighed. "We need to do this the right way—"

Without warning, heavy machine gun fire ripped through the air around us, echoing off the walls and thundering deep into the bone. We all hit the ground, getting as low as possible to help keep us from being shot.

Aerial artillery roared, adding its own percussion to the medley of the brass of war. I looked into the opening and saw flashes of light fill the night sky, lighting it momentarily and fading almost immediately.

"What's going on?" Gary asked, muted by the gunshots.

I looked at him and shook my head, unsure of what caused this. The music had stopped shortly after, replaced by the cacophony of off-tune gibberish. We all got to our feet, still crouching, and duck-walked to the edge of the wall, hoping to catch a glimpse of what caused this commotion.

The German that manned the accordion was now jogging to the nearest doorway while the other two were no longer tending the boar. In fact, the boar was no longer on the spit. It was gone. Completely and utterly gone from the fire, leaving it to its own devices, arguing with itself.

The other seven men were watching the skies, firing aimlessly into the darkness of the night. The streaks of phosphorus arced in lines as they followed an unseen target. In front of us was a small stone fence that stretched for a few hundred feet, separating the river from the tower.

"Up there. Let's hide behind the fence!" I yelled.

They both agreed and said, "Okay."

We took off and sprinted to the fence while the attention was on the stars. After a moment of what felt like millennia, we all dove to the ground behind the stone lifeline. As we hit the ground, it shook with an unearthly force as the artillery shot to the heavens again, exploding soon after it left the smoking hot barrel.

"What do we do now?" Gary asked.

I peeked over the stone fence to see if any of the Germans were looking our way. Two lay motionless in front of the fire, which now roared out of control, while a third shot into the air, swearing in German.

Before realizing what happened, I saw a black mass hit the earth where the man stood and then vanish into the sky, leaving nothing but snow and clattering rocks in its wake. A shrill streak cut through the gunfire as I ducked back down and said, "I don't know what just happened, but a man was there, and now he's gone."

Were we too late with the masks? Is this a side effect of the pseudo-gas? Why do I see these things?

I looked to the sky to see if I could tell what they were shooting at, to find what could pick a man off the ground like he weighed nothing. The large black mass zipped from right to left, blurring beyond recognition. Another artillery shell was launched into the abyss after the mass, missing by miles. With my attention on the Germans, I was caught off-guard when the ground shook with a thud, and the boar fell from the sky, landing right next to us. Gary let out another scream that was swiftly silenced by Klaus covering his mouth with his hand.

"Shh," Klaus said as he brought a finger to his mouth.

Gary shook his head, eyes still wide in understanding as Klaus took his hand from his face. I looked at the boar in front of us, taking in the damage that was done to it. The seared flesh had jagged slices that scored up and down the length of the body, while chunks were missing from near the neck and thighs. I could still hear the meat sizzle as the bottom cooled rapidly against the cobblestone pathway. Lifeless eyes bore into my soul.

"What the hell caused that?" Gary asked, eyes still wide.

I glanced around. "I'm not sure. I couldn't make it out."

"Were we too late with the masks? Are we experiencing the dream gas?" Gary asked.

Gary began to breathe heavily as he patted himself up and down. He ran his fingers through his hair and began rubbing his eyes, trying to rid himself of the awful things he thought he was witnessing. I grabbed his hands and pulled them down, bringing my head to his and pressing my forehead to him.

"Gary, I need you to calm down. We are okay. We will make it through this," I said.

"No, we won't," he said, batting at his hair again. "I feel them in my head. I can't handle it."

I shook him. "You're okay. We're okay. We got the masks on in time. There is nothing in your head."

He shook his head some more, rocking back and forth on his knees as the skies thundered. Heavy clouds of gun smoke sat in the air like early morning fog with a stench of acrid sulfur. The explosions lit up his face, revealing a canvas of pain, confusion, and horror.

"Gary, I need you to get a hold of yourself, soldier! We need you to be ready to help us make it to safety. Are you ready?" I asked.

He shook his head and whimpered, "Yessir."

"Okay, Klaus, are you ready?" I asked.

"I am," he said.

"Alright, I need you two to follow me and keep low. We are heading for the makeshift docks to take a boat down the river. Ready?"

They both nodded.

"Now!" I yelled, my voice being masked by another artillery shot.

We all took off at a sprint heading to the edge of the ledge. Bullets bit the ground in front and behind us, making small bursts of dust spit into the air. The ricochets twanged every which way as I leaped over the small rock wall, hoping the dock was closer than I was expecting.

Within seconds my feet hit the wobbly wood, queuing me to tuck and roll to a standing position. I felt two more sets of feet hit the deck, causing it to shake and strain against the weight. The gunfire continued overhead as I heard whistling and a thud close to the ledge. The next thing I knew, a body was falling toward us, hitting the deck with a sickening thud like a fifty-pound sack of flour on a baker's tiled floor. The strain of the added force of the body that just fell to earth caused the deck to make one last ornery sway as it gave way, collapsing underneath us.

My body convulsed from the immediate change in temperature of being submerged in frigid water. It caused a few moments of confusion as I tried to figure out what happened, going through the series of events that led to the cruel game of dunk the soldiers.

I felt the cold seep through the many layers of clothes I wore, chilling me to my core. I started to panic as the current pushed me down, and my lungs began to burn from the lack of oxygen. My arms flailed wildly to counteract the waters hold on me as I tried to paddle my way to the air above. After what felt like a hundred years, I breached the surface and took in lungfuls of the ice-cold air. I looked around as I continued breathing in as much as possible, trying to find Gary and Klaus.

"Klaus! Gary! Where are you?" I yelled.

I kept looking feverishly for them, moving my arms rapidly to move me in circles. The fire from the roasting pit now engulfed more of the wooden structure the Germans had attached to The Tower. The building had drifted further away from me than I expected, giving me more reason to panic.

"Deck? I'm over here," Gary yelled.

I turned toward the direction of his voice, squinting to make things out in the darkening skies. About thirty feet away from me was a mass floating along with the current, gaining speed from being closer to the middle of the River Thames.

"Gary! I'm coming. Hold on!" I shouted.

I tried to swim to him only to realize I could not properly complete a full breaststroke because my gear was waterlogged from being submerged. Panic was on the verge of taking over as I struggled to slide out of my haversack and webbing. I couldn't shake it from my arms because of the swirling water around me. My eyes locked on Gary's direction again to see if he drifted further away or if I had actually closed any of the distance. He was bobbing in the current about thirteen feet away from me now, renewing my effort to try and make it to him.

"Deck! Help!" Gary yelled.

The sound of a small outboard motor putted behind me, causing my heart to go into overdrive. Adrenaline rushed into my veins, doubling down in my efforts to make it to Gary in time. I could feel my hands and fingers begin to tremble, and I wondered if it was from the freezing water or the adrenaline booster shot.

The noise of the motor got closer, and I knew the electricity-based weapons wouldn't work in the water. Quickly, I pulled my right foot up to my hand and pulled out a plain jane powder and primer revolver from my boot. In anticipation, I turned around in the water and kicked my legs to keep my propulsion to Gary. The small boat was about twenty feet away as I slammed into Gary.

"Are you okay?" I asked, glancing at him, and noticing he was floating on a body.

"Yeah, luckily, the Germans still float when they're dead. I can't swim and wouldn't have made it otherwise," he said.

I smirked. "What about Klaus?"

Before he could say anything, I turned back to the boat as I heard a gunshot go off nearby. I couldn't determine how many people were on it, so I took a few shots at it. The revolver kicked in my hands as a burst of fire spewed from the barrel, funneling outward in a hot blast of lead and leftover trace amounts of burning gunpowder. The bullets ricocheted off the boat's hull and skipped off into the water or air. I got off a few more shots before the hammer clicked down on nothing but the gun's firing pin. The boat stopped about ten feet away, and the outboard motor was cut, bathing us in the soft roar of the fire in the distance and the splashing of the water around us.

"Are you done shooting at me?"

I squinted again, looking at the man on the boat. A match struck against a surface and rushed to life. The flame floated in the air and moved to the left, lighting a small lamp at the front of the boat. The light from the wick lit up a face next to it, revealing a smiling Klaus.

"Dammit, Klaus. Why didn't you tell me it was you?" I asked.

Out of his bindings again? How?! That slippery bastard.

"I was trying to stay quiet. But you do not seem to try really hard," he said. He threw a rope at us so we wouldn't drift further away from each other.

"I was trying to get to Gary, but apparently, he was okay," I said, gazing back at him.

"What? I needed help. Until Frank drifted by and saved my life," he said.

"Frank?" I asked.

"You know, Frank? As in Frankfurt? Because he's German."

I rolled my eyes. "You're lucky I don't have any bullets left."

Klaus laughed and said, "I actually liked that joke."

"Yeah, let's all laugh about it out in the open, just floating like bobbers in the water, ready for the picking," I said.

I grabbed onto the rope and tossed the other end out to Gary. He caught it without grace as he flailed his arms in anticipation. He eventually got his hands on it and began pulling himself to the boat. I followed suit and reached the side. Klaus extended an arm and pulled me up onto the swaying deck. Gary reached us, and we both helped him aboard. He scrambled at the side and still managed to make a beached whale seem nimbler than he. We all plopped down and sent the hull teetering back and forth again, lamp swaying with us. The glow was dim and cast a small amount of light on the surroundings, being engulfed by the blackness of the dark depths of the river.

"Did I actually hit you?" I asked, looking at Klaus.

"*Nein,*" he said as he wound the rope up and placed it on a hook next to the lamp pole. "You are *scheiße* at shooting. Maybe stick to that sword of yours."

We all laughed at that, filling the semi-silence with the joyful noise of momentary happiness. The artillery exploded in the distance, interrupting our celebration of living for a bit longer.

"We should get going. We still need to make it to our destination. Klaus, can you start up that motor again?" I asked.

Klaus nodded and shifted his body to the back of the boat. He flicked a few switches and pressed the starter button near the top. The engine shook to life as the electricity stored in the battery coaxed it on.

We are lucky the electricity was still being collected from the surrounding Tesla Coil Substations throughout the day and stored for later use. It is an efficient design to keep up with the demands of daily use.

"Just follow the river west. We have a ways to go, and I want to try and make it before sunrise," I said.

"Aye," Klaus said.

He revved up the engine and started us off toward The Kew Gardens, our destination. The boat picked up speed as it glided across the top of the water, lapping at it as we bobbed up and down from the minor disruptions in the current.

"I'm surprised that thing still starts. It looks like it's about ten years old," I said.

"Some small checkpoints like this have been repairing and maintaining equipment for us to find and weed out the resistance. It has a lot of replacement parts from Germany," Klaus said.

I nodded in understanding. "Wouldn't surprise me. Hey, Klaus, I just remembered something."

"What was that?"

"I am assuming you knew what the belt buckle was because of the memories, but I wanted to know, who was your ancestor then?"

"You want to know now?" he asked.

"Why not? We have a little bit of time to kill."

CHAPTER 17
Infiltration

Klaus kept the boat straight, following the river's curves as they came. He didn't answer my question right away; I'm not sure why. Maybe it was because he was still processing it all, or perhaps it was because he wanted to keep me in suspense.

Over the last day and a half, I had found myself taking a liking to the guy. I wasn't too happy about it. Deep down, I still thought of Phillips and how it could've been Klaus' fault he is no longer with us.

I put my hand over the boat's edge and let the rushing water flow in and around my fingers as we moved along. The coolness of it helped me stay awake and clear my mind of the ever-encroaching memories of my relatives. I was about to tell Klaus never mind, but before I could speak again, he told me.

"Bors The Younger," he said.

"Really? That bastard?" I asked.

He looked at me with a sour expression.

"Sorry, that was a joke," I said.

"Wasn't he sworn into celibacy?" Gary asked.

"*Ja*," Klaus said.

"Then how can he have descendants? That doesn't make sense," Gary said.

I cut in, "He was, but he was tricked into bedding with King Brandegoris' daughter, Claire. It is the only known time he broke that vow."

"Once was enough, I suppose. Especially when you eventually need to have your lineage continue in an eternal struggle with an evil warlock."

"Wait, so that makes us warlock hunters? That's so cool!"

I rolled my eyes and sighed. "Yes, we are warlock hunters."

"It does sound more interesting," Klaus added.

I noticed Gary shivering from the cold temperatures and the wet clothing, so I reached into my haversack and pulled out a small tube. The light from the lamp illuminated the white powder that filled it about three-quarters full.

I took off the cap, and it slid around as I poured some into my palm. "Gary, hold out your hand."

He looked at me and said, "Why?"

"Because I said so. Just do it."

He held his hand out for me, and I poured some of the white powder into his palm. It tumbled out and fell in a neat pile as the water droplets that covered his palm were absorbed.

He raised his eyebrows and asked, "What is this stuff?"

"It's quicksand. Well, not real quicksand—it was made by Thomas. It is used to absorb water from gear," I said.

"How do I use it?"

"Just rub it in your palms and then run your hands over the wet portions of your clothing."

Gary nodded and did as instructed, rubbing his hands together as the powder formed into a paste consistency. It stuck to his palms as he rubbed his hands up and down his body.

"My hands feel really warm. Is that normal?" he asked as he continued to rub.

"Yes, just keep doing it," I said.

I leaned over and offered some to Klaus.

"No, thank you. I did not land in the water," he said as he patted his clothes.

"Okay, fair enough," I said.

I put the cap back on the tube and tossed it back into the pocket I took it from. After that, I did the same, rubbing my hands together to make the putty and then I proceeded to rub it up and down my body. The water began to seep from the fabric and was absorbed into the paste. It grew larger as more of the water switched from me to it, expanding to the size of a baseball.

"This stuff is amazing," Gary said.

I turned to him as I finished myself. "Just toss it into the river. It will deteriorate in the water."

We both threw the balls of watery paste into the river. Gary eventually turned away from us, and I figured he was most likely thinking about some of the entries from the journal and the events of the last few days. A lot of information was contained on those pages. By the time he was done with it, he could know more than me.

I turned to Klaus and asked, "Are you doing better in keeping everything straight?"

"*Ja*. Mostly."

"Anything I can do to help? Any questions you might have?"

"*Nein*. I will have to sort it out *meinself*."

"Okay, let me know if I can help at any point, then."

I turned to Gary and asked, "How about you? Are you feeling better?"

Gary nodded, his face illuminated by the lamplight at the front of the boat. He looked down at his hands as they gripped the mask he took from the German soldier at the tunnel entrance.

"I'm sorry," he said.

"It's okay. Don't worry about it. You haven't been exposed to this kind of thing yet," I said.

"Yeah, but—" he began but paused. "I need to be ready for anything. I'm here to help, and I can't do that if I think things are crawling inside my head."

I thought about it for a second. "If it makes you feel better, you are the only person I know to have been exposed in any fashion to have made it out unscathed. No matter the amount, even if it was just minuscule."

"It does a little. But I need to be stronger than that for my grandfather."

A heavy sadness hit me in the heart. Wave after dull aching wave flooded through my being at the mention of his grandfather reminded me of mine. It echoed around in my consciousness, causing me to drift off. The memories of swap meets and afternoons in the markets swam their way to the front of my mind.

In fact, it was one of those days I met my fiancé, Hope. My grandad was the one that told me I was a dunce for not noticing her flirting with me. I owe a lot to that old man.

"I know what that's like, to want to be strong for someone. Especially if that someone is your grandfather," I said, eyes still looking back on the old times.

We sat in silence for about twenty minutes and continued to our destination. The sounds of the fighting had ceased as we got further away. Klaus had revved the engine down to two or three knots at some point, slowly chugging us along.

I felt a nudge on my shoulder as my mind wandered the plains of blissful randomness, queuing me to turn my attention to it. I turned toward Klaus and saw him holding something in his hand. I looked at it more closely in the light and realized it was a chunk of meat in his palm.

"Is that boar?" I asked.

He nodded. "Yes."

"Where? How—" I began.

"I took a few chunks of the boar when it landed close to me."

I looked at him and said, "Isn't it waterlogged from the nice swim?"

"*Nein.*"

"Oh, yeah, because you probably hopped in the boat immediately."

"*Ja*, want some?"

I smiled and took a piece of the roasted boar meat from his hand. Klaus got Gary's attention and tossed the rest to him. I began to nibble at the hunk I took, my mouth exploding in wonderful flavors of salty meat and savory wood smoke. The skin had a satisfying crunch when I took another bite, adding another dimension to the chorus my taste buds were enjoying. I reveled that we were all experiencing our small heavens in the middle of war-torn London. Who knew the next time we could enjoy a simple pleasure like that.

I broke myself from enjoying my late-night snack and took in the surroundings. Klaus still had the boat inching along so we did not raise suspicions or unwanted attention from anyone on land. We were coming up on parliament around the next bend. From what I had heard from other scouting parties, the Germans held a Headquarters there. There were many places in London they infiltrated and began converting into hubs for troops to pass through. I didn't even want to know the damage or vandalism that had been done to some of our landmarks, especially good ol' Big Ben.

"Klaus, from the reports I have seen on our end, you guys have Parliament heavily fortified, right?" I asked, still focused ahead of us.

"*Ja*, that was the last place I heard Himmler would be. They were constructing a state-of-the-art labor— How do you say?" He stopped as he looked for the right word. "Laboratory?"

"Like a place for science and experiments?" I asked.

"*Ja.* That is where quite a few of the captured soldiers are brought to," he said.

Klaus shuddered as he finished that last sentence, his body tensing as he shook his head in disgust. The way he said it haunted me and made me think of the horrendous things they could be doing to my fellow Londoners, let alone anyone else.

I could ask Klaus about Spike, the hulking Wienerschnitzel that tried melting my face off like a damn dragon.

"Klaus, who was that man guarding the building you and the other soldier you were with?" I asked.

He cocked an eyebrow. "Who?"

"The large man with the stitching all across his head," I said as I traced lines along my scalp.

"I am not sure of who you are speaking about. I was sent there with the other soldier, that was all," he said.

What does that mean, then? Was it just pseudo-gas, like I thought? Pseudo-gas wouldn't melt holes in walls and bleed a thick, black substance. It definitely wouldn't account for the mass I cut in half as it fell to the ground.

I turned and looked at him, taking in his features and trying to decipher if he was lying to me or not. His stare ahead of us didn't waver, expression still blank and unreadable.

Can I really trust him? Would I be able to count on him in a life-or-death situation? Honestly, I'm hoping I never have to find out.

"Never mind then, I must've seen something that wasn't there," I said.

Klaus cut the engine, and we drifted to a stop. The boat nodded up and down in agreement, deciding this spot was best over all others. The night was now completely dark, black nothingness spreading far and wide over us in the night.

A large bridge spanned the river's width, giving us more cover from direct sight. There was a dock consisting of steep steps and a small platform hugging the rock wall a few hundred feet from Parliament. Big Ben stood guard, towering in the air, and reaching for the heavens as it held time for all to see.

"Here," Klaus said.

I looked at the clock tower and over to Parliament. "What about it?"

"Himmler should be here," he replied.

"Do you know that for certain?" I asked.

"*Ja,* now would be the best time to test the ring to identify him."

I rubbed forcefully at my temples. "Do you really think now is the best time for that?"

"*Ja.*"

I pulled out my pocket watch and clicked it open. "At 10:49 p.m.?"

"*Ja.*"

I shook my head and started to say something, but I was interrupted before I could get anything out.

"Um, I don't mean to interrupt, but I would like to point out that they would know he is missing by now, right? I mean, they trashed the headquarters looking for him," Gary said.

I looked from Gary to Klaus and cracked my neck. "He has a point. Do you think you can get us in without raising any alarms? Let alone get close to him?"

Klaus didn't reply, but instead, he slipped his haversack from his back and placed it between his feet, letting it thump softly against the bottom of the boat. He undid the clasps, opened the cover flap, and reached into it. Next, Klaus pulled out the uniform from the unlucky soul from earlier as the lamp's light bathed it in a warm yellow glow. The light highlighted the folds of the wool. It reflected the metal buttons and ribbons that decorated the collar and shoulder loops, adding detail to the bleakness of the surroundings.

"I can wear this. It will get us far," he said.

I sighed and rubbed the back of my neck. "Can we trust you? We would be walking right into a den of wolves."

"I kinda like being alive. I'm not sure if I like this plan very much," Gary said.

Klaus looked me in the eyes and said, "This would be the best time to do this. They will still have men looking for me elsewhere. This would be the last thing they would expect me to do."

I reached into my pocket and pulled out another tootsie. I tossed it into my mouth with practiced effort and chewed on it immediately. I thought about it and mulled everything over in my head. On the one hand, he was right. This was the last thing I would expect him to do, let alone bring a British and American soldier. We may never get another chance to get this close to Himmler.

But on the other hand, Klaus may have been lying. This could have been a ruse to get me to trust him completely. He put on a compelling show by pulling his tooth out in front of us.

All my instincts told me I could trust him, but my common sense said I could not. I didn't want to be caught with my britches down in the middle of German infested parliament with no foreseeable way out. I suppose this would be something that would either help the cause tremendously, or this would be the end of this line of King Arthur. The next generation would need to be found if the Keepers lived to keep up the good fight.

"Gary, you will stay with the boat while Klaus and I infiltrate the compound. I will leave my sword and gear with you in the boat and go in under the disguise of being a prisoner, while Klaus will pretend that he is the soldier lost to the dream gas," I said.

"I don't like this. I do not like this at all," Gary replied.

"Doesn't matter if you like it. This could be the best opportunity we have to test out the theory and finally know who Jakobus is," I said as I shifted my gaze to Klaus. "Will that work for you then?"

Klaus nodded. "We will need to get ready here on the boat. Deck, as you said, you need to strip yourself of all your gear. You will also need to remove identifying markings such as your dog tags."

"Okay, fair enough. But why?" I asked.

"I do not plan on it, but it is just in case we do not make it out alive."

"Ah, that makes sense. Anything else?"

He thought for a second. "Nein. Let me do the talking, though."

I nodded, staying silent.

Klaus turned the engine over and started it up, moving the boat close to the small dock. I looked around for something to attach us to it when a lasso flew through the air toward a post protruding from the water.

I turned to Gary with my eyebrows raised, "Of course you know how to do that. You're American."

He smirked and said, "My father was from Texas. He wanted to make sure I could prove him proud."

As we got close to the dock, Klaus killed the engine for the last time as Gary pulled the rope tight. He tied the loose end to a loop on the railing in the middle of the boat. Klaus got up with finesse and used caution as he stepped onto the wooden dock. "I will change now. Can I have some privacy?"

"Oh yes, sorry," I said.

"Definitely," Gary added.

We both turned and let Klaus go about his business of switching out clothing for the correct attire. Gary moved to the back of the boat and took up residence next to the motor just in case we needed a speedy getaway. I leaned over and turned the dial on the lamp to dim the incandescent glow to a semblance of dying embers, casting a less exuberant light.

I took my haversack off and put it on the front of the boat to offset the weight distribution. Next was Excalibur, followed by the shotgun I had slung next to it. I pulled my dog tags out from my shirt and looked at them before removing them completely, leaning over and slipping them into the pocket of my bag closest to me. My fingers brushed against the small box I took from the shrine room in the tunnels below London, sending a chill up my arm.

"Deck, you okay?" Gary asked.

I looked over my shoulder. "Yeah, just putting things away."

I turned back to the bag and made a split-second decision by grabbing the box and putting it into my pocket. A strange sense of understanding washed over me, starting at my fingertips as it glided across my skin and flowed to the rest of my body. It was different from the sensation I got when grabbing Excalibur or having it with me. It wasn't the warm and vibrant feelings of duty and honor. It was one of calm, cool, and calculating. It filled me with a sense of knowing if someone disobeyed, they would feel my wrath. Knowing that things were absolute and would be bent to my will, bowing down to my decisions.

"I am done. We should be leaving now," Klaus said.

I pulled myself from my bag and stood up, still shaken from the thoughts that just filled my head. To focus, I bit down hard on the candy and felt my teeth dig into the side of my cheek, altering the flavor from sweet to savory. The tried-and-true process brought my focus back to the present and helped me remember the task at hand. "Okay then. Let's go test this out or die trying."

Chapter 18
Parliament

25th December, 1942
Westminster Borough, London, England
11:00 p.m.

To be more believable to the Germans, Klaus put the bindings on my wrists and walked behind me with a pistol held to my back. The metal dug deep into my wrists, causing flares of pain to shoot up my forearms every time I took a step. I realized the pain helped keep me focused on my surroundings and the situation I was walking voluntarily into. I also now realized what I was doing and decided I was certifiably off my rocker.

We climbed the steep steps that clung to the wall worn away by water like barnacles on a buccaneer's sea vessel. We paused to look at the street that ran along the river to Parliament. We glanced in the opposite direction, ensuring no returning units searched the area for disturbances.

"Looks good to me," I whispered.

"Be quiet. Might have someone listening," Klaus said.

I gave an apologetic look and zipped my lips, not wanting to blow my cover. We made up our minds and started off toward the towering timepiece looming over us in the near hour of twilight. My feet felt quite heavy the closer we got to the entrance, especially when some German soldiers came into view. They seemed very nonchalant, leaning against walls and arches as they puffed on the youth drainers between their fingers. It struck me as odd that they weren't paying much attention to the things happening around them. Especially since the two of us were approaching them without resistance.

Klaus stopped me by pulling on my shoulder and walking around in front of the others. He stopped about five feet away and waited for them to see him. They finally noticed Klaus standing there almost fifteen seconds later, only because he cleared his throat twice.

The soldiers immediately stood at attention, flicking the butts of their cigarettes off in different directions. They flew in large arcs of yellow and orange, burning with the fire of momentary life and fleeting confidence just before hitting the ground in the eventual deaths they were destined for. Smoke curled in a lazy cloud that floated just above their heads, comparable to early morning fog rolling in from the cold front, disagreeing with the heat of the night.

"*Du sollst doch mal besser aufpassen!*" Klaus yelled.

I leaned forward near his ear and asked, "What did you say?"

Klaus gave me a cursory glance and whispered, "I told them they need to pay better attention. Stay quiet."

"Why would you tell them to stay quiet?" I asked.

Klaus cleared his throat and looked forward again, helping me realize he meant for me to stay quiet and not them.

I wish I didn't have to keep asking what people were saying. I know a little German but not enough to understand everything. It puts a damper on things and throws suspicion our way. Wait a second, if Klaus is from a line that has German mixed in, then maybe I am too. It wouldn't be too odd, I don't think. I mean, there are plenty of other things that I have realized or weird situations I have been through that seem much more far-fetched.

The soldier closest to Klaus began to speak, "Sorry, sir, please forgive me."

"What the hell did you just say?" I blurted out loud.

The soldiers, including Klaus, turned to me as their jaws dropped open. The man in front switched between Klaus and me, mouth still agape. He then regained his composure and moved his hand close to the pistol strapped to his hip, "What did you say, Tommy?"

Did I just understand what he said? Could the understanding be from my past lives?

"I can understand you! How can I do—" I began to say.

I felt a surge of pain in my right cheek as my head snapped to the left. Sparks of bright white filled my vision as stars flew from side to side. I threw my shackled hands to my face and cupped them around the stinging skin. The flesh started to swell a small amount as the metallic and salty taste of blood seeped over my tongue.

I looked at Klaus, surprise and anger fanning to life in my guts, sparking quickly and filling me with a rage that seemed more than what the situation required. An urge to strike him back and to hit him harder than he did me washed over. I wanted to take him to the ground, choke the life from him, and watch it slowly drain from his bleak eyes.

What am I thinking? This isn't me. He did that to preserve our cover. Get ahold of yourself, Deck. This isn't who you are or how you handle things.

I met Klaus' gaze, red hot embers still burning in mine. For a split second, I knew he could see what I wanted to do, what I intended to happen to him if I gave in to the sudden urge. It passed almost as quickly as it came crashing in, replaced by my normal temperament. I took a few deep breaths and straightened my back, standing upright while still maintaining eye contact.

"Leave him. He is wanted by Himmler," Klaus said.

The lead soldier glanced between us again, eyes resting back on me. He sneered at me as he pulled his hand away from his pistol and stood at attention again. His face returned to a more controlled expression. "Sir?"

I could tell the frustration and worry were getting to Klaus because his voice became stern and confrontational.

"Did I not speak clearly? He is wanted by Himmler," Klaus said.

The soldier shook his head no and said, "Sorry, sir. Please forgive my insolence."

"Just let us pass. We must go, as we are on a schedule," Klaus said.

The soldier in the front nodded and took a step to the left. As he did that, the others followed suit, putting their arms up in a salute.

Klaus turned to me and gave me a harsh stare. "Come along, Tommy."

He walked behind me and pushed me along, being gentle enough to keep from knocking me over but hard enough to make it believable. I acted a little and stumbled to add some flair to the part of the prisoner.

By God, if I wasn't going to be the best at it.

Instead of the doors opening into Parliament, they opened to a small room that was boarded on every wall. From what I could tell, it was only about ten feet by ten feet.

I realized that the Germans utilized our equipment in terms of being electrified. However, from what I could tell, they still used quite a bit of the old style of thinking, using a lot of oil-powered tools like lamps and mechanized armored tanks. They never shifted to the new age like the rest of the world; instead, they reinvented gasoline-powered engines and machines to use on a grand scale of smog-producing destruction.

"What's going on here?" I asked.

Klaus leaned forward and whispered, "They are building underneath."

I was shocked at that response, not wanting to believe they would do anything like that. My eyes shifted to the ground and noticed a rectangular manhole cover at the back of the room.

Klaus pushed me to it. "Open it up, prisoner."

Not wanting to make a scene, I complied and reached for the manhole cover hook to pull it open. I bent down, wedged it in the small slot, and stood on the opposite side to pull it toward myself. I took a few deep breaths, pried, and tightened as I leaned back.

The cover was quite heavy, and I began to sweat as I struggled to open it all the way. After fighting with it for about thirteen seconds, I won and grabbed onto the edge and dragged it from the hole. Leaning it up against the wall, I noticed the other soldiers left the room and let the doors shut behind them.

"Why underground?" I groaned aloud from the straining of lifting.

"I am unsure. We started this sometime after we took the city three years ago. I was not brought into the city yet, but from what I read in the reports, it took them a year or two to decide what they really wanted to do," Klaus said.

When he started talking, I leaned against the wall to regain my strength. I wasn't sure why it took so much of me to do that. I just couldn't catch my breath. My hands and feet felt like they had lead weights tied to them, pulling me closer to the floor. I reached up and ran my wrist over my forehead to wipe the sweat away but was shocked when all I felt was cold, dry skin.

"Any particular reason?" I asked, voice quiet and distant.

The lights in the room pulsed with an unnatural quickness that seemed to further my weakness.

"Deck, I already said I did not know why. Are you okay?" he asked.

I felt my head swim and swirl into a vortex of icy cold water, flowing into the depths of nothing. My legs gave way, and I slumped to the floor with a heavy thud, unaware if I had hit my head or not. I felt Klaus fall to my side and tug on my arm, his voice fading further away as I slipped into the deep.

Scrape, scrape.

The air was cool and crisp, nipping and biting at my cheeks. The overcast sun was hidden away by the clouds and did little to warm my skin or help deter the colder weather. I looked around at my surroundings and saw the puzzling scenes before me. It was the train station again, and I sitting in the same spot as the vision I had before this one. The silence was the first thing I really noticed. No bustling patrons were waiting to board the next train or the others rushing off to their jobs or destinations.

"Grandad? Are you there?" I asked.

I was met with no reply besides the howl of the wind, picking up in speed through the vacant structure. There was snow covering everything in a fine, thin layer of half an inch or so. Lifting my hands closer to my face, I saw no scars or wrinkles of overuse from years of training and hard work with the Keepers. I looked down at my body to see if I had puberty to look forward to again, only to see that I was now a teenager.

"Hello? What am I here for?" I asked again.

As I assumed, the wind was the only thing that would talk to me. The sky grew darker as the clouds changed from almost translucent to a rumbling and angry black. Thunder sounded as lightning arced and spiderwebbed across the sky while the snow started to fall over the area. It floated down in lazy swaying motions, and I held out my hand to catch a snowflake.

It landed at my fingertips, and I peered closer, wanting to see the pattern. The flake wasn't snow. It didn't have a beautiful design that seemed like something out of a fairy-tale. It was ash. Lighter than a feather but spoke louder than anything man could create.

The incarnation of eradication and desolation reminded me that we were nothing but what we destroyed. It wasn't a miracle or God's gift to humanity. I smeared it between my thumb and fingers in anger and frustration that swelled in size, growing larger until I felt as if I would explode.

"What does all of this mean?" I screamed.

I tried to get up but was held in place, something invisible shackling me to the bench. My body thrashed, and I screamed and yelled, trying to break free of the unseen hold. Instead, the world around me swirled and faded as the sky flowed down and became one with the land, engulfing me entirely.

Scrape, scrape

It felt as if my head would be shaken from my shoulders as I came to. I took stock in how I felt and noticed my body seemed to be its usual, pudgy self. My hands and feet didn't have the phantom weight plaguing them anymore.

I guess that's a positive.

The one thing I did wish was gone was the annoyance of my situation. Maybe if I didn't open my eyes, I would magically transport back to the headquarters or something like that.

I get the random visions. Is it too much to ask for to get spontaneous body displacement? I guess so. A shame, really.

"Deck, are you okay? What just happened?" Klaus asked, shaking my shoulder still.

I grabbed his other hand as he pulled me to my feet. A groan escaped my lips from the sudden change of gravity, and I could feel my body sway again. But instead of falling head over heels for no discernible reason, I managed to keep my balance.

"I had a vision," I groaned.

"A vision? Of what?" he asked.

"Of meself—" I paused. "Wait, your first question isn't even about how or why? It's about what?"

He thought for the slightest of seconds. "Yes. I have had a few myself."

"When?"

"The first time I touched the belt buckle."

He motioned to buckle as he lifted the folds of his shirt, revealing the metal and leather. It reflected the light of the few lamps in the small space we were confined in, shining with a different sheen than before. It felt like it portrayed purpose and reason. Or maybe I just felt that way because I was getting to know him better than I did previously.

"What was it about? How come I am only hearing of this now?"

"I have been unsure about all of this. All of the things in my head and all of the things happening to us now. I am ready to accept it, I think."

I mulled it over and reasoned that it was fair. It was a lot to believe. Especially if you were part of an opposing force, hellbent on destroying everything wholesome and good. Not only that, but it was all orchestrated by the force you now were obligated to oppose. "What was it about then?"

"I am not sure. It was all muddled and distant. I couldn't move or speak. All I could do was watch as a man vowed to uphold a lady's honor. She was accused of poisoning someone, and the man then volunteered to fight for her to prove her innocence."

The door creaked open as one of the German soldiers peered into the cramped space. Klaus backed away, and it caused me to stumble and falter back to the ground. Luckily I was paying attention, and I hit the ground with grace and skill, catching most of the blow with my hand against the wall.

"Sir?" the soldier asked.

"Yes?" Klaus asked.

"Any problems? Do you need me to teach this prisoner some manners?"

"No, I can handle this. Now leave me and return to your post."

At first, the soldier just stared at Klaus, eyes trained on him as if he recognized him or the uniform he was wearing. The tension in the room grew, causing the air to run thick and heavy like woodsmoke wafting through a sleepy camp. He then nodded his head in acknowledgment, closing the door as he backed away. It clicked shut with a soft, almost inaudible noise of the wood and latch sliding back into place. Klaus turned back to me and helped me regain my composure.

"Are you okay?" he asked.

"Yeah, I believe so. I think we should get moving. They may be getting suspicious of us," I said.

"Most definitely. Let us go. I will let you take the lead since you are technically my prisoner. Here," he said as he held the bindings out for me. "Slip these on when you reach the bottom. It will be easier for you to navigate the ladder without it on."

I took it and put it over one of my wrists so I wouldn't lose it as I walked over to the manhole that led into the ground. Wanting to know before I threw caution into the wind, I leaned over the edge to peer down and see how deep it went. Every ten feet or so, I could see a small light or lamp fastened to the wall opposite the ladder. With that to judge the distance, four of them meant that the ladder ended about forty feet down.

"Here goes nothing, I suppose. Should be fun. Climb a ladder to your death far beneath the surface where it's safe and secure." I turned to Klaus once more. "How will we get back out?"

He waited to respond, making my patience fray and anxiety ignite like short-fused fireworks.

"I honestly do not know. But you will just have to trust me on this."

"Well. We've come this far. Might as well bet it all on red."

CHAPTER 19
Tunnels and Ladders

11:45 p.m.

I began to descend the cold iron ladder into the belly of the beast. After halfway down, the air and temperature shifted from frigid and light to temperate and thick. The heat radiated around me as it seeped through my jacket, warming my chilled bones. The shallow breaths I took in felt like they lacked the correct amount of oxygen, making me feel somewhat light-headed.

I hate dirt. I hate climbing. I hate ladders. I hate being so far underground and getting the sense of tons of dirt pressing down on you. At any moment, a support could give, and you would be buried alive.

I reached the bottom of the ladder and felt my foot hit the solid floor with a heavy thud, sending a wave of reassurance coursing through me. Klaus was just a second or two behind me, his feet hitting the floor with more grace than mine, sending a much smaller echo bouncing off the walls.

I looked around and saw a hallway, which went on for forty or fifty feet. The hall was lit with good ol' fashioned fire torches on either side, spanning the whole way. The black smoke from the burning oil and rags filled the air, probably causing the thickness I was experiencing on the way down. The ceiling was held up with wooden supports that seemed strong, so I tried not to worry.

Easier said than done.

"After you, Deck, I need to keep up the ruse," Klaus said.

I agreed, nodding, and slipped the bindings over my other wrist and pulled on them to tighten them ever so much to create the illusion of being secure. Klaus motioned for me to go, so I obliged by starting down the hallway.

Looking up as I passed under the first support, I realized they were ornately carved with scenes of fire and brimstone. Some were of creatures prowling and monsters in flight chasing humans to their death. While other parts had men at stakes burning or women tied in barbed wire, faces contorted in agony and contempt.

"Klaus, what's with all the gory décor?" I asked, still looking at it.

He peered up at them and whispered, "Josef Mengele. He is a very sick man."

I shuddered from the thoughts the carvings provoked in my head. The awful nightmares that this man brought to life every day to unsuspecting victims were horrid. My heart began to race as I started to feel light again, and things flashed before my eyes. I could see myself tied up, the rope holding my hands above my head as they dug in painfully, causing me to bleed. Fire was all around me as I felt my body start warming up, beginning to cook from the heat. Men in white surgical gowns prodded and poked me with needles as they spoke in a language I couldn't understand. The world began to spin as I felt every little prick on my skin, going deeper and deeper than the last.

I felt a hand on my shoulder, and my mind cleared once more. The hallucinations dissolved in my mind's eye as quickly as they came to it.

"Deck? Are you okay?" Klaus asked.

"Yeah," I said as I shook my head. "I keep seeing things, and I don't know why."

"I'm sorry you are, but we need to keep moving. Someone might see and get suspicious."

I cracked my neck and stood straight, "Okay."

We continued down the hallway as I kept my eyes straight. I didn't want to fall into the rabbit hole again and see things that couldn't possibly be real. This place was evil in the purest sense, the atmosphere reeking with the stench of it. It permeated the air around us, death and pain lingering, tainting everything it touched.

The end of the hall ended at a three-way intersection with lights coming from either. I glanced down both. To the left was another narrow hall lit by the same oil rag torches that ended at the door. The right was a larger path, almost double the width of the last two, but this time, it was lit overhead with incandescent, knock-off Tesla Bulb strips.

"To the right, please," Klaus whispered.

Without stopping again, I turned to my right and headed in that direction. I looked around as we continued that way and noticed some piles of wooden boxes and crates stacked in pyramids off to the right, while others had linen sheets tossed over them.

At the far end on the same side was a guard sitting in a chair, head drooped with his arms crossed over his chest. I looked at the other side and realized some cages were built into the walls. There were five in total, and the first three had the doors slid open, lit up from within and casting the shadows of the bars across the floor at our feet. I peered inside the first, curiosity always present in my mind, not seeing anything of interest. The following two were the same as the first: a small paper-thin mattress on the cold floor with a pail in the corner for God only knows what.

"Of course, he is sleeping," Klaus said.

"Maybe it's for the best?" I asked.

Klaus scoffed, "I suppose. If I behaved the way the men that we have run into have, I would have been reprimanded into regretting being born."

I tried to stifle the laugh that wanted to pry itself from my lips. It was challenging to do, but I succeeded and kept myself quiet. I kept walking and passed the fourth cell, getting a sudden strange and bewildering surge of cold. It caused me to stop in my tracks, shivers shaking my body involuntarily as I looked inside the steel and stone cage. More feelings engulfed me, wrapping around my arms and legs as they slithered over every inch of my body. Dread and a sense of loss weighed heavily on my mind. Other feelings that accompanied them confused me, being ones of familiarity and trust. This one had no light on the inside, making it very difficult to see anything that lay within. The overhead light strip was on but not strong enough to shine anything into the dark cells.

"Klaus, what are the cells for?" I asked.

He looked into the one we stopped in front of. "As far as I know, they are for prisoners of war."

I looked deep into the darkness again, eyes scanning for any signs of movement or life. Squinting, I saw something in the back near the corner, eyes glowing in the shadows. They moved back and forth as if it was an animal stalking its prey, burning and pulsing with a strange brightness I didn't know could be natural. Before I could reply to Klaus, I heard the loud clang of the creature flinging itself against the metal bars before I actually saw it do so. Klaus and I jumped almost three feet, staggering back so as whatever it was could not reach us.

"What the hell?!" I yelped.

An arm jutted out between the metal, swiping and swinging as it tried clawing at my flesh. I saw the light reflect off three-inch razor-sharp talons, five in all on the one hand. It scrabbled as it attempted to gain another inch of reach, still slicing the air in front of our noses. I heard an audible swoosh as the sharp talons cut through the air repeatedly. Its arms were matted with patchy brown and black hair that started at the claws and went up the arm, presumably even further than I could see myself.

Time felt as if it slowed to a crawl as I looked at its face, taking in the features of the strange beast. It had an elongated nose, almost snout-like in nature, that ended in a nose shaped like that of a large cat. The same fur or hair was present on its face, only it was very short and flattened to define facial features. The eyes were set deep into its skull, sunken and feral as they seared brightly into mine. They throbbed with a primal lust for blood mixed with anger and anguish.

What is this creature? Am I seeing things? Could this be dream gas from before? Or did we go throw any on the way down here?

I looked at Klaus, hoping to confirm or deny my suspicions of what was happening. To my surprise, his skin had gone as white as alabaster, eyes wide with disbelief. I wasn't sure if that was a good thing he saw it too or if it just meant we both were being influenced by the dream gas.

The creature threw itself against the metal bars harder than before, causing it to creak and groan from the strain. Its mouth was gnashing at us, snarling as drool flowed from its gums and pooled on the floor.

"Back!" someone yelled from the left.

My head jerked toward the yell, and I saw the German soldier scramble to his feet. He reached out to grab something that leaned against the doorway as he stood and bolted toward us. I saw him flick a switch near the pole's handle and heard a zapping noise as the tip began to spark with electricity, arcing a gap between the two tips.

The soldier stuck it into the cell at the beast, crackling as it made contact with its skin. I started to smell burning hair and flesh as it howled in pain from the electricity. The creature pulled its arm from between the bars and skittered to the back of the cell, eyes still focused on me as they quivered dimly.

"What was that?" Klaus choked out.

The German stood up, chest heaving from the effort of sprinting to our aid, regardless if it was more for Klaus or not. He flicked the switch on the device's handle again, and the electricity died without a fuss.

He looked at Klaus and said, "Sorry, sir."

"What was that?"

"It was just an animal, a wolf, I think."

"A wolf? In the middle of London?" Klaus asked.

"Yes, I believe so," he said as he straightened.

"Why is it here?" Klaus demanded.

"I am unsure of that, sir. Sir? Why are *you* down here? I was given strict orders not to let anyone through this way."

"Oh, why yes. Of course. I was sent down here by Himmler. He wanted me to stay out of sight of any British soldiers in the area."

The soldier looked at us incredulously, peering around Klaus to have a better look at me. He eyed me as he spoke again, "And what makes this man worth being so careful?"

"Never mind that. You would question Himmler's orders? What is your name? I will be sure to mention it to him when we talk next. Tell him how you would not let us pass."

The soldier went rigid on the threat of being reported for insubordination. He stammered, "N—no sir. I will let you pass right away, sir."

"Good, thank you. Wise choice," Klaus said.

What in the seven gates of Hell was that?! It looked like it was human. It had a man's reach, but a beast's features: hairy and nightmarish.

He returned to his seat near the door and rested the pole against the wall where it met the doorframe. I glanced at his hand as he took it away, interested in the tool he used to keep the beast at bay. As I did so, something else caught my eye.

A rifle made of wood and steel was propped alongside it, with the light reflecting off the accented spots made of metal. It struck me as odd in the aspect that I had seen rifles like that before.

It was a military issue Mason Model 1937 Sharpshooter that we gave out at the beginning of the war, making it increasingly curious as to how they have one here. As far as I remember, about sixty-five percent of them were recalled within the same year due to random and unpredictable charging of the firing system even when not in use.

"Klaus, how do they have those?" I whispered.

The more I thought about it, the more familiar the rifle looked. It had burn marks near the bolt resembling lines to count kills and a charging coil built into the stock. I tugged on his sleeve to get his attention and pointed toward it.

"It looks like my brother's rifle." I paused. "It can't be though. He should be with Frank and the others."

He glanced at it before looking back at the other soldier, pulling me through the door without giving me a reason or letting me continue. The German had put his arm up in salute, keeping it up as we disappeared through the door. The door shut with a loud slam, closing the door to any other answers I could get from it.

We walked for ten or fifteen seconds before coming to an open room at the end of the hallway where we were standing. The ceiling was fifteen feet above us, held up by the same style of wood beams, arches and supports. It looked to me like it was a small meeting room with an even smaller round table offset to the right.

Well, smaller compared to our round table standards.

The rest of the room was occupied with longer, but thinner rectangular tables, papers, and candles scattered across the tops lining either side. They had a few chairs pushed up tightly against them with other chairs pulled further away, ready for someone to take their seat.

Klaus stopped us in the middle of the room. "I am not sure, Deck. Like I have said on many occasions when you have asked, I was not a part of this area. I am not privy to the reasons or things they are doing here."

Still doesn't make me feel good about any of it.

"Fair enough. I am sorry for asking so many questions. It's just that I have seen that gun before. It's really nagging at me."

"It is alright. But we really need to keep moving. Every second we waste talking or looking at beasts in cages is another second that they could be onto us."

He's right. Usually, I am the one that calls the shots and makes sure people are doing the things they should. Why am I so out of it right now?

"You're right, sorry. One last question, though, if that's okay?"

"Yes, what is it?"

"Where do you think Himmler is? I mean, do you know where he could be right now?"

He glanced around. "Not sure on that either. He could be anywhere, and I am just going on basic layout right now."

"You mean you don't actually know where we are going right now?"

He grinned sheepishly. "No. I am just— how do the Americans say it? Winging it?"

I groaned. "Klaus now is not the time to be adventurous. You really don't have a clue?"

"No. But judging from the other soldier's words, I think we are going in the right direction."

I was about to respond with my usual spiel about following him and making sure I kept up when we heard a door open from up ahead of us. The noise of pounding feet sounded against the floor, echoing off the walls and resonating throughout the room. My eyes snapped to the source as panic filled me to the brim.

"Let me handle this, be quiet and stay vigilant, okay?" Klaus whispered into my ear.

I nodded, being mindful of the plan while I felt my heart fill the back of my throat, trying to beat its way out into the open.

A group of four dressed in dark colors came from the other side of the room. Two of them wore the typical German battle dress, complete with their stahlhelms. They stood on either side of a smaller petite figure with their arms hooked under the prisoners, dragging him along as his boots slid limp on the wood planks. The prisoner's head was draped forward, pointing his face to the ground.

I looked closer at him, trying to make out any identifiable markings or features, when I noticed the blood dripping from his face. It fell to the floor in a thick, steady stream like freshly harvested maple syrup, sickly sweet stuff. The two soldiers were not of much interest. Basic goons you would find manning the next buzzsaw like every other soldier in their army. They continued toward us slowly and methodically, allowing me ample time to see the last man behind the three.

Who is that person they are just dragging along? We just passed some cells in the last hallway. Maybe they are bringing him there? Wait— is that? It can't be...

The man behind the group was of average height, almost blending in with the rest if it wasn't for the difference in uniform. His facial hair was slightly larger than a Chaplin mustache with no more besides that, sitting with prominence over his top lip. He had a receding hairline that would rival the quick surrender of the French, the enemy forehead gaining ground by the second. He wore rimless glasses with circle lenses that fit his shrewd and close nit features.

That's him. It must be. From all the briefing photos and the sketches we've received, I'm sure it's him.

"Klaus," I whispered.

"I know, be quiet," he whispered back.

Can I still trust him? Will he turn me in the minute he talks to Himmler? I've grown fond of him and the teamwork we all have done to stay alive. He must be trustworthy. He pulled a tooth from his mouth. There's no way that was a trick. Could it have been?

Klaus pulled me aside to the right to clear the way for the group. He then saluted his hand to the officer behind everyone, waiting quietly for them to pass. The two men in the front kept moving as if we were not even there, not stopping to wait or talk to us. When Himmler came within a few inches from us, he first made eye contact with Klaus, holding his gaze for a moment in heavy silence. It then shifted to mine, dissecting every muscle movement or nervous twitch I had. While we held that look, locked in a decisive battle of pure will, the other soldiers and the man continued out of the corner of my eye. I finally broke the cold tension and looked away, feeling my skin crawl with goose-bumps, trying to move as far away as possible from this man.

"Sir, your—" Klaus began to say. He was cut off mid-sentence by a strong booming voice, firm and sinister.

"What are you doing?" Himmler asked.

"Excuse me, sir?"

"What. Are. You. Doing?"

He stared at us still, face empty of emotions. I could feel the strain on time, threatening to have the situation go sideways in the blink of an eye.

Klaus stammered as he said, "I-I was bringing in this prisoner."

"If that's the case, the cages are this way," Himmler said as he lifted his hand and pointed the direction we came from, arm as still as a rock.

"You mean cells? Sir?"

"Whichever you prefer to use. They still act the same: containing filth where it belongs."

His lips drew back in a smile with haste, too quick to be natural. It wasn't one of warmth or comfort, no hint of happiness or compassion. It was evil, reiterating that he was a cold and calculating monster.

I don't even need to use the ring to know he's evil. I can sense it in my bones, in my gut. But in a way, it's familiar, something that I might be missing in life. Stop it! Stop thinking that way! This is not you. You do not have these kinds of thoughts!

I shook my head, trying to get out of it. I wanted to get away and be far from there.

I want to be back at home with Hope, held up tight in a cottage tucked away in the countryside. The only thing I should be worried about is the fish biting my hook and pulling the drowsiness from my holiday relaxed soul. Why did it have to be me? Or my family tree being that of King Arthur? Why couldn't I have been born as a cobbler's son or something less dangerous as a knight of the round table and a Keeper?

I noticed someone was watching me. I could feel their heavy stare bore into my head, threatening to see what I was thinking. The vertebrae in my neck creaked as I looked up at Himmler, meeting his eyes again. A feeling of confronting my demons before they consumed me washed over me.

My blood ran cold, frigid as the Thames, slowing its pace to what seemed a stop. My heartbeat thumped against my rib cage as hard as the boots of a thousand soldiers marching to war. I felt lost, but I also felt like I was found, like a piece of me had been missing for a long time.

My pocket started to feel warm, nagging at me for my attention like a dog wanting a bone. It continued to grow in warmth, reverberating throughout my body. It came to a crescendo as searing heat like lava burning my flesh. Without warning, and to my relief, Klaus pushed me toward the direction of the cells. It cut through whatever I was feeling and made it all melt away in a flash.

"This way, Tommy, let's go," Klaus said.

I felt myself get angry again as I thought about it all. He pushed me again with more force, causing me to trip over my feet. I gave it my all to keep from crashing to the floor, equilibrium still thrown off from earlier in the night.

Get it together, just get moving and get on with it. Make a good show of it, ol' boy.

Once again, I started walking like the good monkey I was acting to be. We made quick work of the short distance to the cells and met up with the other two soldiers and their prisoner. The guard was positioned near the door while the other three were standing at the cell. Himmler passed us and stood next to them, staring at the prisoner with an intenseness I couldn't begin to explain.

"So?" he asked, eyes still focused somewhere other than us.

"Yes, right this way," Klaus said.

He pulled on my arm as we walked next to them. We stopped just short of a few feet from them, light shining from the room into our eyes, making it hard to see anyone clearly. Klaus put his hand out to Himmler to shake his, testing out our theory if the ring would glow for him.

It would be great if this worked and even better if we could make it out of here in one piece.

I stared intently, just waiting to see if it would work and if the ring would light up. The tension and anxiety of waiting started to grind at my fraying nerves, threatening to reduce them to nothing and causing my sanity to snap away from reality.

I can't believe that was his plan all along. Just walk up and shake his goddamn hand. We're dead, plain and simple. We are just dead. Why doesn't that surprise me, though? I should've guessed he didn't have a plan besides being that direct and blunt about it.

Finally, after what felt like a fortnight, Himmler turned and took Klaus' hand in his own. I could see sweat bead on Klaus' temple and run down the side of his head in an erratic, slow line, pausing then continuing at random. The vein in his neck was thick and visible, beating along with the stressful seconds.

Himmler again had a blank look on his face, unamused by the situation mixed with a bit of menace. I watched as their hands shook up and down, eyes locked on the ring with extreme intent, trying not to blink and miss anything.

Since we were trying to see if it would glow with Jakobus, we didn't know what would happen. It could maybe only glow for mere seconds, or it may even turn a different color in general.

"It's a shame," said Himmler.

Scrape, scrape

"It's been quite an adventure for you, hasn't it?" said a voice.

The voice was familiar but not something I had heard for quite some time. It may not even be someone I have talked to in my own lifetime. I think I recognized him as the old man that gave Grandad the sword. It looked like Merlin.

"It has been something, you could say. Stressful and full of difficulties mostly," I said.

My surroundings hadn't changed since the last time. They were still snowy and cold. I looked around and noticed how perfect the thick layer of fluffy white snow was over everything. There was a strange calmness to it all, serene and patient. Almost as if no one has been through here in a very long time.

"You're on the right track, though. You just have to keep going."

I turned to the source of the voice and realized it was right next to me. There was a man older in age with gray hair that extended past his shoulders. He had a beard of the same color, falling gracefully to his lap. His clothes were vibrant and beautiful, contrasting heavily with the surroundings. It was composed of blues and purples, swirling in designs of far-off galaxies with small swashes of bright red and burnt orange. His face was soft but weathered with lines of happiness and even deeper ones of sorrow and regret. Perched atop his pointy nose was a set of wire-rimmed half-moon glasses.

"How close am I? How can I keep going?"

"You just have to be one step ahead of him. Think of the things he wouldn't see coming."

"How am I going to get out of this alive? He's right in front of me, and I just don't know how to escape."

I waited for a response in the cool overcast of the winter afternoon.

"Just as before you and Davey, I cannot tell you how to conquer the obstacles in your way. I am simply here to tell you to keep going and that all hope is never truly lost. I am here to tell you that you are close to the end of this chapter of the story, but you have a long way to go. Sometimes to stop something unstoppable, you need to go back to the beginning."

"What does that even mean? How am I to go back to the beginning?"

The man began to dissolve, outlines of his body and face fading into nothing. Soon he was gone, and nothing but the beautiful stark white snow was there in his place. Fresh, new, and blank.

Scrape, scrape.

CHAPTER 20
Escape

26th December, 1942
Westminster Borough, London, England
12:30 a.m.

I almost didn't realize he had said anything until I looked him in the face. I was so intent on not missing a thing like the ring glowing or pulsing that his voice barely registered in my head.

"What is, sir?" Klaus asked.

"I was interested too. You silly Keepers have had that dainty trinket for a thousand years, and I always was curious how it worked. So it's a shame that it didn't work for me," Himmler said.

I was in shock. Did he really just admit to us that he was Jakobus? Did he just blow his cover? I mean, we've had a hunch for the whole war, but we didn't have the proof we have now.

"I am not sure what you are talking about, sir," Klaus said.

I could tell this was all an attempt to keep our cover. I was just as dumbfounded as he was, almost unsure what to do.

"It's also a shame that they found you first. I would have killed you as soon as I found you, but I am sure we can make a deal. You leave the silly little band of merry men and join me.

Together we can continue my work and take what's rightfully mine: the world," Jakobus said.

Time slowed again, making me really wish I had a watch. I looked at Klaus, pleading silently with him to not believe him. I would never leave there alive if he agreed and chose Jakobus over the Keepers.

Jakobus glanced at me again. "And you, you have something that belongs to me. It's been quite a long time since I've been whole, and I will enjoy having myself all in one place for a change. It was a stroke of luck for you to stumble into my chamber in the tunnels."

I sneered at him as my rage became almost uncontrollable at this point. I was about to say something before he cut me off.

"Don't you worry, I have ways of getting the things I want. Maybe a trade is in order? You might find I have something you would desperately want back."

"You are the devil. We would never make a deal with you," Klaus said. "I can't sit idly by while you try to destroy things meant to thrive."

"Very well. I suppose this is fortunate for me, then. Two fewer piggies for this big bad wolf to go searching for."

With a flash of light, Klaus pulled a knife from somewhere in his jacket and swiped at Jakobus. It cut through the air with a metallic ring, slicing the front of his uniform. I pulled my hands from the bindings and dove for the rifle I had seen earlier in the corner near the doorframe.

The ruckus of Jakobus and Klaus struggling in the background filled my ears as I took it in my hands, rolling onto my back, facing them. I maneuvered the rifle into the air and leveled it at Jakobus as I pulled the bolt back to chamber a round into the gun. The wires illuminated with a soft yellow glow as the contact with my skin was complete, sending a quiet droning noise into the air as the charging process started.

"Klaus, move!" I yelled.

Klaus glanced over his shoulder and saw me, jumping back hastily to allow me a clear shot. I aimed the iron sights at Jakobus' head and pulled the trigger. To my surprise and abject horror, the gun didn't fire. It just fizzled and powered down in my hands.

"Really?" I yelled.

Jakobus laughed and smiled as I flailed and struggled with the rifle in my hands. As I awkwardly fumbled with it, he enjoyed his luck for a moment. He was silenced abruptly by me throwing the gun at his head, giving me a reason to smirk in amusement for the slightest of seconds. It surprised him as it struck him across the face, scraping his cheek, eye, and temple. The rifle flew to the left and fell to the ground, bouncing as it hit the stone floor inside the cell.

Instead of speaking, Jakobus sneered at me with hatred brewing in his eyes. His facial features warped and writhed as he let out a guttural growl, becoming sharper in shape. His nose curved to a point, fierce enough to pierce steel, while his eyes sunk deep into his eye sockets. The color of his skin shifted to an almost translucent sheen to it.

The soldier at attention near the door dove at me as I lay on the floor, eyes wide and crazed. I rolled out of the way again to a crouching position. My arm swung wide at the man's stomach before he could barrel into me. I heard the air rush from his lungs as he choked, coughing and sputtering as I pushed him to the floor. His body hit with a loud thud as I looked behind Jakobus at the prisoner still locked in the other two soldiers' arms. I saw him struggle before he wriggled free from their grip and elbowed them. Crimson rivers poured from their noses when he removed his arms just before he flung his fists into their groins. I twitched involuntarily from the impact, immediately feeling their pain and agony as they slumped to the ground.

"Klaus, I think it's time to go!" I yelled.

Jakobus swung around with his right arm raised to strike the prisoner in the chest in one fell swoop. He saw it coming and ducked before it could connect with his chest, quick as lightning struck a tree. He reached down, pulled a small push dagger from his boot, and stabbed it into Jakobus' side as he bolted under his arms toward me.

"Get up," yelled the prisoner.

He rushed at me, eyes being the only thing I could make out in his dark hooded face. Klaus dashed behind the prisoner and grabbed my arm as I struggled to get up, pulling me to my feet with the raw strength of not wanting to die.

"Follow me," the prisoner said as he passed me.

Klaus and I ran to catch up to him, not stopping to look back at Jakobus. We ran away from the direction we came in and went what seemed like deeper into the compound.

Behind us, we heard a loud, animalistic bellow from the cells in the distance. It made me wonder if it was from the creature, I thought I saw in one of them or if it came from Jakobus himself.

We ran into the meeting room with all the tables and rushed to the other side, wanting to get as much distance between Jakobus and us. The lights around us went black without warning, bathing us in an inky rich blanket of comfortable uncertainty. Within seconds, blood red flood lights lit up our surroundings as the alarms started to blare, echoing off the walls and filling our ears with screams.

"Where do we go?" I yelled over the noise.

My eyes darted left to the rectangular tables and chairs, checking for any kind of door or hatch. I did the same with the right, only seeing a mirror image. I could not find any other way of getting out of here but to keep going deeper into the mouth of the Kraken. I looked to Klaus for an answer, but I saw he was turned to the prisoner for answers.

Go figure.

"Follow me," the prisoner said.

Another roar from behind came crashing through the alarms, overpowering them in the menacing and creepy department. That helped us make up our minds, and we left through the set of doors in front of us. Just beyond were a few chairs next to the doorframe. I made a split-second decision and grabbed one, wedging it underneath the handle.

Definitely won't hold 'em for long but should delay them for a few minutes.

The same red floodlights washed over the next hallway from the room, extending thirty feet with more cells on either side. We started jogging down it to get to the other end, keeping our guards up as we passed each steel and stone cage.

Most of them were uninhabited and unlit as we passed them, while some had the same crimson light. In one, a man lay on his bed wrapped in a straight jacket-style full-body stocking, while another had a man reaching out through the bars with his feet, standing on his hands.

His feet? Why?

The next one was filled with what seemed to be at least thirteen people, wall-to-wall tightly packed like sardines. One of the last cells was filled with a mass of fur the size of a cow, packed tightly into a ball. I looked at it and saw it twitch, causing me to almost void the contents of my bladder all over the floor in front of it. Thankfully that did not happen; almost, though. Another prisoner put his hands on the handle of his own door, straining and struggling against it.

"It's locked. It won't budge," he said.

Klaus reached for the handle to try himself, only to grunt and groan against it too. "He is right. It will not move."

The screeching of bending metal brought our attention to the wedged door on the other side of the hall. We all turned to see the doors fly off the hinges, smashing against a few empty cells and bending the bars at odd angles.

I squinted to see the beast capable of that amount of damage, breaking it apart like a twig. The gray and black form of a beast sauntered from the doorway in our direction. Its body seemed as if it shifted like smoke or fog, changing shape as I stared at it. I rubbed my eyes, hoping all I saw was a trick of the mind.

"Klaus, what's happening?" I asked, fear filling my voice.

"I— I do not know. I simply do not know," he whispered.

"Reynard le Renard. Reynard the Fox!" shouted the prisoner.

"What are you talking abo—"

A snarl leapt from Reynard's throat, biting at us from thirty feet away. I jumped from the threatening menace it carried, sending shivers down my spine. He eyed us for a few more moments before taking off at a sprint in our direction.

"Any ideas?" I yelled.

I looked at the wall, running my hands up and down, hoping to find something. My hands stopped on a set of buttons at waist level to the right of the door. Without much thought, I slapped both in a panic, hoping it would do anything helpful. One by one, the cell doors slid open on their tracks, metal scrapping against metal as they slammed home. At the same time, the one behind us clicked as it opened inward, almost too silent to hear over everything else going on.

"It's open. Let's go!" the prisoner yelled.

Someone tugged on my shoulder, trying to pull me back. I glanced at Klaus, eyes open wide with dread and shock. "Deck, come on. It's heading this way!"

I started to speak but stopped when I noticed the color drain from Klaus' face. Somehow it was as white as a ghost while still drenched in the bloody red light. I turned to follow his gaze, dead on the monster behind us. It was bounding in our direction, claws digging into the hard-packed earth, throwing chunks and bits behind him. Its mouth was wide in a snarl, teeth gleaming as drool poured from it. Each long stride came closer to shortening the distance between us, bringing our dreams of a long life to a swift end.

"I think we really need to leave!" I yelled.

I scrambled to push Klaus through the doorway. We ran into the prisoner, sending us all sprawling to the ground. I frantically tried to get up from the pile of arms and legs. Eventually, I succeeded in getting to my feet. I kept to the wall, immediately feeling for a way to close this door. I reached for a button on the wall, and as I slammed my hand on it, I saw the eyes of the beast. My hand fell from the button as the same familiar eyes I thought I had seen earlier locked on mine. It caught me in a trance, pulled in by its curiosities and oddness. Klaus pushed it the rest of the way, cutting off my eye contact with it. When it clicked shut, the prisoner slid a chair underneath the handle to keep it from opening again.

"What the hell was that?" I shuddered.

"Like I said: Reynard," huffed the prisoner.

I turned to him and said, "What does that even mean?"

"It is an old French story. He is a wolf-like man," Klaus interrupted.

I turned to him. "And how does that help? This means nothing to me. You know what, never mind."

"He is a little more than that, but that is the basics of it, yes. That's a story for when we are not staring death in the eyes, though," the prisoner said.

I turned back to him, ready to start asking more questions. To demand to know how he knew so much about the area and why he was here. I then realized something I didn't catch before.

You know, minor details often slip from people's minds that could be considered very important in most situations. Things like the fact that the prisoner is a woman.

"But you're—" I started.

"French, yes. Let's keep going, so we do not become anyone's next meal," she said.

Something hit the closed door with brute force, shaking the chair we wedged up to it. I flinched back from it, reeling in fear that with the following charge, the wood would splinter, and we would be the dog's next meal.

"I'll trust you to get us out of here. But after we do, you need to answer questions, okay?" I said.

She smiled as she nodded. "Deal. By the way, my name is Madeleine. But you can call me Del for short."

"Okay, Del, let's get moving."

Without any more argument or discussion, we followed her down the next hall. The further we went, the more I felt like we were in a maze that was winding and twisting in directions that seemed to not make any sense whatsoever.

More cells and meeting halls flew by as we weaved in and out of guards trying to stop us by tackling us. Bullets ricocheted off walls with wild pangs and bounced from the floor with pings, adding more things to worry about in our attempt to make it out alive.

Our escape came to a crashing halt when we rounded the next corner. In front of us was a dead end of brick and mortar ten feet away. We heard shouts and gunfire peak above the still-blaring alarms.

"Great. What do we do now?" I asked.

I saw Del survey our quickly dwindling prospects of ways out of this mess. To sum it up, we had five choices that were all pretty solid. We are not going anywhere.

She started patting the walls, looking for a spot that could be a pressure plate or any way to open up a hidden door or hatch. Anything would be a godsend. A way out of here to prevent us from becoming fish in a barrel would be preferable. Del stopped with her hands firmly placed halfway up the wall in front of her.

"What is it? Did you find anything?" I asked.

She continued to feel the mortar around one particular brick with her fingertips. "Maybe."

"Anything would be nice," Klaus said.

"A hole in the wall, some way into the ceiling. Hell, I'd be okay with a trap door in the middle of the floor that drops into a mote of sewage, as long as I make it out alive," I said.

"Be careful what you wish for," Madeleine chuckled.

I was jerked from my good mood by the German shouts and the beast's snarls. My head snapped back to look at the corner we came from, waiting and anticipating something to come hurtling around it. I noticed my heartbeat shift from a low gear of paranoia to a high gear of panic. An almost imperceptible click sounded behind me.

I nervously asked, "Klaus, did it work? Do we have a door to go through?"

I heard a loud splash, queuing me to turn my head and look. Del was the only one standing there. Klaus had seemingly disappeared. I couldn't see a door or anything. "Where'd Klaus go?"

"I told you to be careful what you wish for," she said, smiling.

I kneeled to look at the spot he was standing, hoping to see how deep it was. As I peeked over the edge, I saw nothing, just black and shadows. In a panic, I yelled, "Klaus?!"

I waited for a response in anticipation, straining to make out anything besides the noises that seemed normal at this point.

I yelled once more, "Klaus?!"

Another second went by when I heard a reply, "I am okay. Come down here!"

I was going to reply. I was going to prepare for it and leap into the dark unknown. But before I could gather the courage, my mind was made up for me with a little push from Del. It was accompanied by flailing, screaming, and panicking like a schoolgirl.

Chapter 21
Rough Waters

12:55 a.m.

As I hit the water with a stinging thud, the air around me turned from a muggy thickness of fear to cool, calm, and smelly. The cold enveloped me as I sank to the bottom in a fetal position.

My lungs started to scream in agony for the sweet taste of life. I unfurled my legs from my chest and pushed off the floor, rocketing to the water's surface. Upon cresting, I could hear Klaus and Del laughing, adding a minuscule distraction to the situation.

"Not funny. I was going to do it meself. I didn't need the help," I grumbled, still choking on some water.

Del giggled and said, "I just gave you a nudge. Takes forever for you Brits to make a decision. I just use a small amount of diplomacy to help the situation along."

I made a sour face which made the two laugh some more. It was infectious, which caused my lousy mood to lessen. Their chuckles died down after a moment, letting the echoes fade into the distance.

"I am assuming by the smell we are in some sort of waste disposal tunnel?" I asked.

"Yes, it is an old one from long ago," Del replied.

"How did you know about it? And how does a waste tunnel just get forgotten about?"

"Not sure how it gets forgotten, but I knew about it because of the blueprints I was given. Enough chit-chat, though. We need to leave."

"Where does this empty out into?"

"The River Thames. Once we get out of here alive, we can continue with pleasantries. Until then, we should focus on staying alive," Del said.

"If you get us to the river, we have a boat and another man waiting for us. We can use that to get somewhere safe," I said.

"That works for me," Del said.

As we talked, the trap door above us slid shut, robbing us of the valuable light. I patted myself up and down, instinctively looking for the spotter I always kept on my person. I then concluded that I didn't have it, only for the simple reason of not having any of my gear.

"Klaus? Have anything? I left all my gear with Gary."

I heard him do the same, looking for something to see with.

"I have an idea," he said.

I felt a hand touch my arm, interrupting me and my attempt to tread water. He let go in time for me to resume and not let my head go below the surface. A soft yellow glow radiated from the water in front of me, rising to the surface slow and steady.

"What's that?" Del asked.

"Ah. That's what you were doing. Great idea, Klaus," I said as I looked at Del. "We'll explain later. You have to trust us."

He lifted his hand above the water, which illuminated the room, cascading a small aura of light into the cavern. I took in my surroundings and saw we were in a small void designed to be used as an entry point. To the left was a platform that stretched the length of the cavern with steps leading into the water. A door sat in the middle of the wall, sealed, locked, and barred from this side. I wadded over to the steps, pulled myself out of the murky liquid, and walked over to the door.

"Klaus, toss me the ring," I said.

"Are you sure?" he asked.

"Yeah, I can catch it. Played on the rugby team when I was young."

I saw him shrug as he pulled the ring from his finger. He then tossed it to me, arcing it through the air like a flaming attack from a catapult. I caught it with ease and slipped it on my own finger. It lit the door and wall in front of me, shedding light on the task. From what I could see, the door and frame were metal and not only welded shut but also had locks and bars.

"Not getting out through here. Bollocks. I guess we have to take the tunnel," I said.

"Alright, this way, gents," Del said.

With great regret, I walked back into the human sludge and swam over to them. Del had already started down one of the tunnels, leaving small waves in her wake. The water rippled and bounced off the confined space, agitating chunks to the surface. There was something calming about the sound of swimming and splashing. I would have been in Heaven if it weren't for the foul smell and the chunks of waste brushing against my fingertips as I swam.

I will need to take a bath in radioactively-heated water after this.

"Klaus, I blame you for this," I said.

He didn't respond, but I somehow knew he was laughing. I eventually tried to ignore what was happening in the water around me, but at some point, I could have sworn something was moving around my legs. It was easier to assume it was an octopus or eel, maybe a snake in the water. At least that would be preferable to the reality I was currently dealing with.

"Do you hear that?" I asked.

"Yes, rushing water, right?" Klaus asked.

My stomach dropped to the bottom of my feet as the tunnel ended abruptly, sending me into a free fall.

Before I knew it, we hit more water with considerable force. But this time, it was frigid and toe-curling, just what you need to wake you up. Because I was already on edge, I was more ready for this one, allowing me to get my bearings and reach the surface with haste.

I rubbed my eyes and saw the tunnel emptied into the pale moonlight that peeked between midnight clouds. Klaus and Del were floating to my left, bobbing up and down in the water like lily pads. The alarms still sounded in the background, almost drowned out by the noises of the river.

"That was easier than I expected," Del said.

"Yeah, I kinda thought we wouldn't make it out and that we would die in that crappy tunnel," I said.

Klaus splashed *clean* water at me. "Stop it."

"Why? Someone needs to ease the tension," I said.

"Boys, come on. Where is that boat of yours?" Del snickered.

Behind Del, I could see a golden ball of light swaying back and forth. Right on cue, we heard the low rumble of a boat motor growing louder as the luminous orb grew closer. I looked at Klaus and saw that worry was plastered over his face. It threw my mind into doubt. I panicked and searched for something to conceal us. Anything to hide behind would do. A large boulder jutted out from the rock wall just below the tunnel. It was submerged in the water, creating something we all could fit behind.

"The wall! We need to hide!" I said as I pointed to the boulder.

Del and Klaus saw where I was pointing, and both started to swim to it with haste. The mechanical growl of the engine kept growing louder as the lamp lit up the water only twenty feet away from me. I followed them, pushing my worn and weary bones to their limits.

I hope that isn't a German patrol. If it is, we will certainly not make it out of here. We've come so far and done so much. We know who Jakobus is now. Finally, at long last, we have solid and concrete evidence! We need to make it back to Gary and then to the rendezvous.

I pushed myself against Klaus and Del, huddled in the corner where the boulder met the wall. It made me feel like we were a bunch of penguins in the heart of winter, trying to survive till the next thaw. The yellow beam from the boat was now in front of us, bringing the dark water dancing to life before our eyes. I held my breath, waiting for the boat to pass so it wouldn't hear my ragged gasps for air.

The bow eased to a stop mere feet from us, nodding up and down with the reverberations of the waves it just caused when it was still moving. Whoever was in the boat killed the engine, causing the chugging of the overworked engine to a stop.

"Hello? Deck? Klaus?" asked a voice.

Is that Gary? He's supposed to be waiting for us over near the docking area. What is he doing over here? What made him decide to come over this way?

"Gary?" I asked, pushing myself off the rock wall.

The lamp was extremely bright, making it hard for me to see anything past it. I squinted as I put my hand up to cover the blinding light. I swam out a foot or two, trying to be careful just in case it was all a trick.

"Deck! You made it!" Gary yelled.

"Shh! Are you trying to get everyone's attention?" I asked.

"Right, sorry. Deck! You made it!" he whispered.

I rolled my eyes as I turned back to Klaus and Del. "You can come out here. It's only Gary."

They both came swimming over to us as Gary reached out and helped me into the boat. I pulled myself over the side and rolled into it as Gary returned to the stern. I sat up and settled on the bench, reaching over the side to help Del in. She gave me her hand, and I pulled her in with ease, surprised by how light she was. She got into it with more grace than I could ever muster and took a seat on the other side of me.

The lamp lit up her features as it swung back and forth, playing tricks on my eyes as the shades and shadows danced with her. Her beauty was stunning, taking my breath away even when I couldn't make it all out. She had brunette hair that flowed to her shoulders, curling upward in ringlets at the ends. Her features were soft but prominent, strong jawline and noticeable cheekbones with caring but knowing eyes.

As I was busy drooling over Del, Klaus was able to pull himself over the ledge onto the boat between Gary and us. Gary waved a hand in front of his nose and said, "Why do you smell so foul?"

"Because Gary, sometimes crappy things happen to people who don't deserve it. Talking of things people need to do, why aren't you waiting for us at the dock?" I asked, turning back to him.

"I was there for a long time, honestly. I would've stayed longer, but eventually, I heard alarms from up the road. I got concerned, so I started the engine and took off further into the middle of the river."

"Fair enough. I suppose there would be no sense in sticking around just to get caught."

"If I had waited any longer, I would have been. Just as I got to the middle of the river, a few German soldiers came running down the stairs to the dock."

"How come they didn't see you?" I asked.

"I extinguished the lamp, I may be out of the know when it comes to things, but that doesn't make me an idiot." He smirked. "By the way, how did you make it out?"

I nodded at Del. "She helped us get out of there in one piece. Del, this is Gary. Gary, this is Del."

"Charmed, nice to meet you, ma'am," Gary said.

"I am Deckard, but you can call me Deck for short," I pointed to Klaus. "That quiet, stoic man is Klaus."

"Nice to finally make a proper acquaintance. My name is Marie Madeleine Fourcade, but you can call me Del, as Deck has already said." She looked at Klaus and continued, "You aren't one of mine. Who are you with?"

Klaus furrowed his brows. "What do you mean?"

"I have a few German defectors on the inside. That's how I got my hands on some blueprints. So, who are you working with?" Del asked.

I cleared my throat and interrupted. "Me, or rather us. The Crown has him working for us."

Del looked at us for a long, impregnable second. As if she was using it to decipher our minds and decide if it was the truth.

Technically, it was, even if it was only half of the information.

"Mhm, well, I suppose that makes sense. Maybe you can help me with something if that's the case."

"And what would that be?" I asked.

"Before I got captured and brought here, I was tasked with meeting our German soldier on the inside. He went missing at some point when he left Parliament and before he could meet at the designated area."

"So, he never showed?" I asked.

"No, we were eventually ambushed while we waited for him to show up. I tried to contact the rest of my resistance group. I wanted help and reinforcements to storm the stronghold before they brought more soldiers in. I sent a message over the radio hoping they would get it in time before I was imprisoned."

"So, what is it you're asking exactly?"

"I am trying to ask, have you been in contact with any other French resistance fighters throughout the area? I was attacked on the way here and lost the small group I was traveling with. I was able to get it out on the airwaves before I was taken prisoner."

I reached down to my pack that lay at my feet. Hoisting it onto my lap, I slipped my hand inside and pulled out the small vial of quicksand. I held it up to the light and saw I had used the last of it earlier when we were in the water the first time. In frustration, I stuffed it back in my haversack and went to put it back near my feet. Before I could, the burning in my pocket returned in force, causing me to jump. I snatched it from the pocket in my pants and put it back in my haversack with haste, wanting to be done with it.

What actually happened when I was near Jakobus? Why did it grow hot and burn my skin? I just don't understand why it did that.

Deciding to forget about it, I turned my attention back to Del. "No, we haven't, but we have been receiving a strange message on a loop. What was it about, the contents of it?"

"It was just a simple one, something that could mean anything to anyone if they didn't know the person that sent it."

"Was it just the word *help* by any chance?" I asked.

"Yes! It was!"

"We actually were trying to locate the source of the message but were attacked before we could even make it to the origin."

"I suppose that means you never came into contact with anyone else then?"

"No, sorry."

She frowned and said, "No matter. I had another question, though."

"What is that?"

"You kept calling Himmler by a different name: Jakobus. Why?"

I exchanged looks with Gary and Klaus before turning back to her, "I can tell you about all that later when we get somewhere safe and build a fire. I am exhausted, hungry and want to dry my clothes off."

"I second that. Gary, can you get us out of here?"

"Yeah, give me a second to get the motor started. She was acting up when I tried to move it earlier."

After a few tries of pressing the starter button, the motor puttered to life, happily chugging to a melody inside its own metallic head. I tried to listen hard enough and could have sworn it was Mozart. But before I could put much thought into it, Gary eased into the throttle and took us out into the middle of the river.

Chapter 22
Seasons Heatings

2:07 a.m.

A strange silence crept in like early morning fog, sneaking in between each explosive heartbeat of the motor. When we reached an area of the Thames far enough away with a bridge crossing it, we decided to stop to rest.

"If memory serves me correctly, there is a church up here to the right. I believe it is All Saints in Fulham. It serves as another safehouse for situations like this," I said.

"Is it like the headquarters?" Klaus asked.

"What do you mean?" I asked.

"As in everything being underground?"

"No, it is just fortified and boarded up. There shouldn't be anyone inside."

"Okay, but we will be safe there?" Klaus asked.

"Relatively," I said as I shrugged. "Gary, just head off to the right."

Gary nodded and aimed the boat's bow in the direction of the church, keeping the speed steady. I enjoyed the repetitious movement of the boat's hull bobbing up and down, letting it soothe my mind somewhat. As we approached the rock wall, a set of stone stairs and a platform seemed to appear out of thin air.

Gary lined the watercraft up with the dock and killed the motor, allowing us to drift to it. I put my foot out to cushion us from ramming into it just in time, slowing us down enough to not crack the hull. Klaus grabbed the rope coiled up on the lamp pole, fashioned a lasso out of one end and tossed it at an anchor point on the platform. He pulled it taut and tied the other end off the boat, securing us in place.

"You sure this will be safe?" Del asked as she stood up.

"As safe as one can be in war-torn London," I said, still perplexed by the repeated question.

Before I stood up, I bent down and grabbed my gear, which included Excalibur, my haversack, and the shotgun. I reached over the boat's edge and placed it all on the stone as softly as possible. "I am going to jump into the water again. I want to try and scrub as much muck from me as possible."

Without waiting for a response, I hopped into the river once more. The frigid temperatures stole my breath away from me as they locked up all of my muscles for a few moments. While submerged in the water, I realized there was something about freezing your butt off. It worked just as well, if not better, than a pear drop to help clear your mind. When I returned to the surface, Gary, Klaus and Del were already off the boat and waiting for me.

"Sorry, I felt like I needed to rinse off again," I said.

"No need to apologize. After swimming through that much waste, I certainly felt the same way," Del said.

Klaus helped me onto the platform, keeping a hand on me as I steadied myself. When I was stable, he handed me Excalibur and picked up the rest of my things. He slung his pack on his back, my shotgun on one shoulder and my haversack on the other. I reached for more to carry, but he held his hand up and said, "I got it. You just lead the way."

I shrugged, slipped Excalibur over my shoulder, and ensured it was snug. My fingers traced over the smooth, worn leather strap Marie, my grandmother, made for my grandad over fifty years ago. It felt right to have it on me again. It just felt right. Not like the feeling I got while carrying the box around, which made me feel angry and desperate. But the more I thought about it, the surer I was that I kind of liked it.

I need to get rid of that thing as soon as I can. It's nothing but bad news, and I can't have anything else convolute my mind like it does. And why did Jakobus mean I had a piece of him? What's in that box?

"Deck? Hello?" Del said.

"Huh? What?" I mumbled.

"You just zoned out for a minute. Are you okay?"

I rubbed at my neck. "Uh yeah. Sorry, that happens once in a while."

She regarded me with thy incredulous look again, causing me to avoid eye contact. I reached into my haversack's pocket to pull out a pear drop while Klaus stood for a moment. My hands shook as I unfurled it and tossed it into my mouth. I focused on that for a second, allowing it to work its magic and help me focus before we continued.

They let me by, and I took the stairs, taking each step with care. It came out into a small, wooded area located southeast of the church. To the left was a large field of snow-covered grass with benches dotting the circumference. To the right was a block-aded bridge.

I motioned to everyone to follow me, and we jogged through the shrubs and bushes that lined the stone wall of the bridge. Even though my mind was elsewhere, I still tried to pay attention to any low-hanging branches that could hit me, or anyone else, in the head.

We stopped momentarily as we saw some light ahead, carefully checking if any German foot soldiers were nearby. From what we could tell, there were none, and about thirty or forty feet away from the church was a Tesla Coil Substation. It was still active, buzzing and humming with raw Wavergy in the early morning hours. We skirted by the brick-and-mortar wall that separated us and the coil, keeping a safe distance to avoid getting zapped out of our wits. The electrical charge surrounding the massive steel and copper behemoth activated our gear, bypassing the grounding process. My shotgun's wires and firing pin started to glow red hot while our spotters lit up, casting cones of light on the trees and bushes around us. I saw the look of terror flash across their faces in response to the discharge of light. Klaus and Gary put their hands over the spotter bulbs to try and keep the semblance of stealth.

It's a good thing we are nowhere near any soldiers.

"Just up here, through the side of the building," I said.

Everyone followed me to the side and watched as I felt around. When Thomas was tasked to design the hidden entrances to safehouses, he needed to get creative. We wanted it to appear that the place was abandoned and not be looked into further. In this safehouse, there was a pull latch behind a specific brick. I found the correct one without much trouble and looked at Klaus. "I know you have a knife. Hand it over, please."

He grumbled a little and handed one to me, handle side in my palm.

The one good thing about him is that he certainly has the tools when you need them. I don't even know where he keeps all these knives.

I shook my head, dug the blade into the gritty mortar, and pried at the brick, causing it to wiggle. Next, I did the same thing with all four sides, "At least we know that no one has been here yet. The access handle hasn't been found. It's still sealed away for us lucky few."

After a little more back and forth, the brick slid out of the slot with surprising ease. The brick was smaller than normal, with a good inch or two cut off the back. Without looking, I reached behind and handed it to Gary, hoping he would take it before I dropped it on the ground.

I looked inside the void, trying to see the latch without much luck. Standing back, I flipped the knife in my hand, and the blade landed in my palm. The blade gleamed as I turned slightly and held it out to Klaus. "Here you go. Thanks."

"Not a problem," he replied.

"Can I see your spotter? I need to see if I actually had the right brick. Chances that another random brick would pry out that easy are slim, but I want to check anyway."

Instead of an audible response, Klaus took his spotter from his haversack strap and pointed it at the wall. The light lit up the small brick-sized hole, revealing a handle set deep into it.

"Do you see it?" Klaus asked.

"Yeah, I don't need your spotter anymore," I said.

"Okay," he replied as he hooked it back into place.

I slid my hand into the hole and gripped the handle. To prepare myself for anything, I took a few deep breaths.

To hell with it.

I turned it and, in the same motion, gripped my forearm with my free hand and yelled, "Ah!"

Klaus, Gary, and Del both jumped back in shock, eyes wide and mouths agape. I heard a gasp escape Del's mouth while Klaus stayed silent.

"Are you okay, Deck?" Del asked, eyes starting to well with tears.

I started to laugh, unable to hold it in. Their eyes went even wider when the realization struck them. Klaus visibly relaxed and smirked, chuckling softly while Del's face switched to anger. Her eyes narrowed, and her lips turned down in a frown.

"You are a Neanderthal," she hissed.

I just laughed some more, enjoying it more than I should have. With little luck, I tried to suppress it as best I could, knowing I wouldn't want to make her even angrier.

I turned my attention to the latch as it clicked in my palm, resetting to the resting position. The door popped open as I removed my hand from the hole in the wall, tilting inward a minuscule amount.

I looked back at Del. "Sorry, I couldn't help meself."

She gave me a frustrated glance. "Shall we?"

I turned back to the door and pushed it open some more. As I peered inside, I could make out little as the door swung inward the rest of the way. It was dark inside, so I decided I would grab my spotter. Since I would now need it more often, I reached into my haversack, pulled the device out, and fashioned it to the strap. I wiggled it to check if it was secure and wouldn't go anywhere. Satisfied, I flicked the switch and banished the shadows and demons from this earth, if only for a little bit.

The door opened into a small broom closet with brooms, mops, and other cleaning supplies. *Perplexing, I know.* All four of us filled the cramped space as we knocked things over and struggled to fit far enough to close the door.

"I certainly hope this isn't it. A bit small for the four of us if I do say so myself," Gary said.

"Of course not." I turned my head. "Klaus, can you shut the door?"

We all had to shuffle some more to give Klaus enough room to close it. I was pushed against the far wall, Del face to face with me. My cheeks ran hot as I felt her curvaceous form fit nicely to my body. Her chest moved against mine, slow and steady with each breath she took. I was feeling myself get lost in her scent as she spoke. "When I said I can get to know everyone later, this certainly wasn't what I meant."

My cheeks flared to the temperature of molten lava as I stuttered. "I– I – that's not what we meant either."

As Klaus shut the door, the pressure of my body against the wall made a new one give way, causing me to fall backward onto my back. Del followed suit, falling onto me and making the air rush from my lungs. I struggled to breathe as she giggled. "Sorry. I wasn't expecting that either."

I strained to talk as she continued to push down on my sternum, "Can't— breathe—"

"Oh," she said as she scrambled to get off me. "Sorry, do you need help getting up?"

Finally, taking a few deep breaths, I said, "No— that's okay."

I rolled onto my side and got to my knees, still heaving for air. It was stale and musty but did the trick. I rubbed my chest, especially the spots she had pushed on to get up, trying to eliminate the lingering pain that stung with every heartbeat. The throbbing sting subsided, and with the change came an aching tenderness. I rubbed at the tears that welled in my eyes from the strain, not wanting the rest of them to see the lapse in stoicism I hold near and dear.

"Whoa, look at this place! It's straight out of a motion picture," Gary said.

I took my hands from my face and took in the church around me, vast and awe-inspiring. Light from the Tesla Coil Substation shone brightly through the tall, stained-glass windows above our heads into the room. It pulsed in irregular waves, jumping over some parts and lighting up others. Row after row of pews stood at attention, neatly aligned from one end of the church to the other.

From what I could tell, even with all the constant bombings and other horrific damage done to the surrounding city, the church was in the same shape it would have been six years prior. Well, minus all of the dust, cobwebs, and grime covering everything in a layer of age, change, and hopelessness.

I stood up and turned to them. "Welcome to All Saints Fulham, everyone."

"Question," Gary said as he raised his hand.

I rolled my eyes. "Yes, what is it, Gary?"

"Why is it warm in here already?"

I tilted my head. "Huh, that is weird, isn't it."

"Yeah, wouldn't it be freezing here since it's winter?"

"Honestly, I am not going to look a gift horse in the mouth. I will just enjoy the warmth while I can."

Gary shrugged and walked past me toward the closet row of pews. "I call this one!"

"Good idea. We should probably get some sleep while we can," Klaus said.

Del walked past me and took a pew three rows down from Gary. She didn't have much on her person besides the hooded cloak, which she slipped off and laid across the top of another pew to dry while she slept. I turned to see Klaus walk over to me and offer a hand to help me up. I took it with appreciation and gratitude, "Thanks, Klaus."

When I was on my feet, he held me back momentarily and said, "I have to talk to you about something first, if that's okay."

I nodded and followed him so as to have some distance between the other two and us. We stopped near the door I presumed was the main entrance and looked at him before asking, "What is it?"

"Do you think we can trust her?" he asked.

"Del?" I thought about it and replied, "I think we can. She got us both out of there alive, didn't she?"

A rare sign of emotion flashed across Klaus' face. Something was troubling him. His lips were turned down in a frown, and his eyebrows narrowed in concern. "She did, but it almost seems too lucky. We happen to solidify our suspicions of Jakobus and happen to make it out with the help of a random Frenchwoman?"

"Klaus, you may forget that you wanted to kill us just two days ago. Me. Circumstances change things dramatically. You know that the most out of anyone at this point."

He mulled it over, eyes darting back and forth at invisible points of interest. He then said, "That may be true. If you trust her, I will too, since I trust you."

I clapped him on the shoulder. "Good. Anything else, then?"

"Yes, she mentioned German defectors. Do you think hers was the body we found in the tunnel of dream gas?"

"Maybe. We can ask her for the name. Do you still have that journal and set of dog tags?" I asked.

He crouched to one knee and swung his bag to the ground smoothly. I aimed my spotter at it to help him search through the contents to find the right items. It took him some time to sift through it all, but he was rewarded for time well spent, pulling the brown leather-wrapped journal. He handed it to me, and I took it while he closed his bag. He then looked in one of the front pockets for the dog tags, this time finding it almost immediately.

"What's the name on the tags?" I asked.

He held it closer to the light and read aloud, "Heinz Richter."

"Hmm, seems like we'll just have to ask Del. If she doesn't lie to us in any shape or form, then I think we can trust her," I said.

Klaus nodded in agreement and stood up, slinging the pack onto his back in the same fluid motion as before. We both did an about-face and started off toward the other two. Gary had already stripped himself of his gear and piled it at the end of the pew. His boots were sitting next to it, letting us see his feet barely covered by socks holier than the church we currently resided in. He was sprawled out on the seat, arms behind his head, and relaxing as best he could.

Actually looks much more comfortable than it probably is.

Del was on her knees in the pew with her head bowed and whispering a prayer. "Please let us make it through these hardships alive and safe so we can return to our families. Please help us prevail over this evil that has spread across the land, casting a shadow of wrathful senseless violence. Amen."

She returned to her seat and fixed her hair, running her fingers over the loose strands to tuck them around her ears. Now that we weren't in danger, I could better take in her beauty.

The warm and vibrant glow of palpitating golden light illuminated her delicate features. Her hair was an auburn brown with some darker highlighted strands mixed into it, mostly pulled back in a ponytail. The skin that wasn't covered by a long-sleeved shirt looked smooth and silky: the color of fresh cream. Her eyes were the same beautiful auburn brown as her hair, sparkling with personality and confidence. I was lost in her luscious rose-colored lips, wondering if they were as soft as they looked.

"Deck?" Del asked.

"Huh—what?" I asked.

"What were you staring at? Is there something on my face?"

I cleared my throat while Gary and Klaus snickered. "No, I was, um, looking at the cross behind you."

She smirked and said, "Okay. Sure."

I chuckled nervously and walked over to a pew across from hers. Klaus took the one down from mine, right between Gary and me. He did the same as everyone else, putting all his gear on the ground in front of the pew, then he sat down with a thud and cleared his throat.

"Right." I paused. "Del?"

"Hmm?" She replied.

"Earlier, you mentioned you were captured after trying to meet with a defector, right?"

She nodded, "Yes, why?"

"What was his name?"

"It was Heinz, Heinz Richter. Why? Did you find him?"

That's a good sign. She is telling the truth so far. I wonder what's in that notebook we found on him. Could it be Jakobus' plans of mass destruction? Could it be the layout of his underground bunkers?

"The last few days haven't been without tribulation for us either. That's more than I want to get into, but we are on our way to meet with our unit."

"Why? What happened?"

"Our headquarters was ambushed by Germans which caused us to be separated from the others. We are on our way to meet at a rendezvous at the moment, actually."

"Does that bring you to the reason why you asked about the defector?"

"Yes, mostly. We escaped through a set of tunnels and rooms that eventually led to a way out. Among one of those tunnels, there was a German soldier in our path."

"What are you saying? Did you kill him?" she asked, eyes narrowing in accusation.

I put up my hands. "No, I swear. We have a feeling it was the man you were meeting. He was deceased. I think he succumbed to pseudo-gas, dream-gas."

"*Gaz de rêve.* Awful stuff. How do you know it was him?"

"He had this journal on him and his dog tags."

I leaned over to her with the journal, passing it to her. She took it from me and undid the leather strap that held it shut. "This is what he was trying to bring back to us."

"We haven't looked at it. I mean, we have been running for our lives for the last few days but still haven't looked at it at all."

She flipped through the pages and muttered under her breath. Her fingers scraped over the paper as she traced words and followed sentences. She stopped in the middle of a page and gasped. "Mon Dieu."

Klaus and I exchanged glances as we both asked, "What is it?"

She struggled to get the words out, "My informant thinks Himmler is trying to open the gates of hell."

CHAPTER 23
Mostly No Ideas

17th August, 1937
Kew Gardens, Richmond Borough, London, England
3:45 p.m.

The room was dim as the picture on the wall shuffled and blurred as Frank replaced it with a new one. The first was a blurry image of Heinrich Himmler, changing quickly to a new image of a painting of the knights of the round table. There were thirteen seats around the table, but only twelve of them were filled.

"The first thing we would've needed to do was to locate all of the artifacts so we could bring as many descendants together in one place. Luckily, we have Davey to thank for that: Deck's grandfather," Frank said.

"Where are they now?" Eileen asked.

Frank turned to her. "As you all know, Deck currently has Excalibur while all the others are held at Nikola's mansion."

"Why aren't they here with us?" Thomas asked.

Nikola Tesla entered the room, his cane clicking on the floor as he walked. "Because, my boy, they are very valuable, and we do not need to be losing them before we can start administering the test."

The top of his cane gave off a miniscule amount of luminosity in the dark room. The glowing wires attached to the top weaved down the shaft of it, all right angles and shapes, mechanical in nature. He walked over to Frank and shook his hand, "Thank you for briefing them on almost everything. Sorry I was late. Car trouble. The shortage of batteries has made us import some from the states. Those damned inferior Edison batteries aren't worth the scrap they are made out of."

Frank chuckled and said, "Not a problem. I think we covered almost everything. All that's left is to make sure no one has any questions about why they are here or what the mission is."

Nikola leaned the cane against the wall and clapped three times. The lights flicked on with such a bright white that they seared spots into Deck's retinas because he wasn't ready for it. He blinked away the manmade blindness just in time to see Nikola grab his cane and start pacing back and forth in front of everyone.

"So, does anyone have any questions on why we are all here again? Anything, in particular, you are still confused about?" Nikola asked.

Deck looked around at Eileen, Frank, Thomas, and Steven. They were shaking their heads in a fashion that specified, 'I understand completely and no need to go over anything again.' Deck still had some questions, so he decided now was as good a time as any to ask away. "So basically, we are trying to locate Heinrich Himmler, aka Jakobus?"

"Precisely. Well, except we aren't one hundred percent sure he *is* Jakobus. We are working on a way to check if he is. We are relatively confident he is, considering he has been on the rise, creating waves and unrest in the German government," Frank said.

Eileen perked up. "What do we think their plans are? World domination?"

"Among other things, yes. For the longest time, we know he was hunting down descendants. We only know this because of

Davey." Nikola paused before adding, "It is a shame we lost him."

Silence fell over the room for a moment to honor Deck's grandad. Some fleeting memories raced through Deck's head, bubbling bittersweet feelings to the surface. One such memory was at the farmers market in the Spitalfields borough. It was a sunny early spring day. Smells and people mingled between the carts and stands in the courtyard. He remembered that day so vividly because it was the first time he ever met Hope, his future fiancée and his one and only love. Deck's grandad knew her parents because they ran his favorite produce cart, always making special trips thereafter to get the freshest sweet peppers.

Nikola began to talk again, snapping Deck back to the present, out of his beloved thoughts. "Any other questions?"

"Have they succeeded in stopping any bloodlines?" Eileen asked.

"Yes, but also no. Since the time of King Arthur, there have been so many different lines of heritage from every knight that he realized his efforts to stop them were moot," Nikola said.

"What do you mean?" Deck asked.

"Every generation of descendants we have found has what are called Dimmers and Brighters. Dimmers cannot access the artifacts, thus not being full-bloods. Brighters, on the other hand, have access to them, but they are limited to just one person." Nikola said.

"There can be more than one Brighter per generation of descendants?" Deck asked.

"Precisely. But after the artifacts are activated by one, the others of that same generation cannot access it, even if they die."

"So we would have to wait 'til the next generation, then?" Thomas asked.

"Yes," Frank said.

The room went silent once more. They all thought about the clarification they had just received, understanding the gravity of the situation to the fullest.

Deck turned to Nikola again. "What can kill him?"

Frank was the one to respond. "From the lore passed down in my family, we have accounts of various attempts to thwart and end his reign of terror to no avail. They have tried swords, fire, poison, and lightning."

"Lightning?" Deck asked.

"Yes, lightning. No, we don't know how they did it, but apparently, it was tried." He paused to drink water from the glass next to him. "The only thing we believe that will kill him is Excalibur."

"Why won't anything else work?" Deck asked.

Frank shrugged. "Honestly, the best reason anyone has been able to come up with is because of his use of magic."

Deck thought about it, sifting through all the memories of his lineage. Something hit him. "But me grandad thought he killed him with Excalibur almost fifty years ago; clearly, it didn't work."

"True," Steven said.

Steven stood up, walked to the front of the room, and stopped next to Nikola. Until now, he was quietly sitting in the back, listening to us talk back and forth. "I believe he has split his soul. Or rather, what one would consider a soul anyways. That's why we didn't achieve what we thought we did on that fateful night."

"Do you know how he did it?" Deck asked.

"The lore states he did it almost the same way the knights of the round table did it. The only real difference is that he split his soul and attached it to objects which enabled him to have influence over the bearer of said object," Frank said.

"Is that what happened to Dr. Henry Jekyll?" I asked.

"No, he was just an unlucky man who was tempted by Jakobus. He allowed him to corrupt his soul, molding him to be in his image," Frank said. "I might actually say he could have been influenced slightly."

Steven nodded and continued. "This was the reason I went to America. In search of his artifact that I believed was still there. I followed the trail of a man for five years, always one step behind. I soon lost all hope of finding him and settled down in New York, started a family, and had a son and eventually a grandso—I mean grandchild."

Was he about to say he had a son? If so, why is his son not here now to help us in this endeavor? I would help no matter what. Why is he protecting him?

Steven cleared his throat and continued. "After that is when Davey came to America for a visit, and we tracked down a few of the artifacts. We also went to a few different countries and found others too."

Steven stopped talking after that and noticeably drifted off into a memory. Deck hoped it was a fond one that he would cherish forever.

"Are there any more questions?" Nikola asked. "No? Then class is dismissed."

CHAPTER 24
Birds Eye View

26th December, 1942
Fulham Borough, London, England
7:39 a.m.

My eyelids fluttered from the bright light shining through them. I lifted my hands up to cover the source of my blindness, blinking my eyes thoroughly to rid myself of the heavy grogginess that plagued me. My body ached from the continuous running and lack of adequate sleep, screaming in protest as I began to sit up. Opening my eyes, I swung my legs off the seat, placed them on the ground, and looked around me.

"Good, someone else is up. I was getting bored," Klaus said.

Klaus was sitting on the back of his pew, feet on the seat with a chunk of wood in his hand. He was whittling it with a knife into the shape of a heart. I squinted to see better, noticing how much detail he could carve into it. He was even able to get it all the way down to the tiny veins that covered the organ. *Amazing.*

"When have you had time to carve a heart?" I asked.

"I have been working on it for a while now. Ever since you gave me my artifact, I have been only able to sleep an hour or two when we take the time to," he said.

"That's only been twice."

He paused before he spoke again, "I whittle fast."

I shook my head and looked at Gary. He was lying on his back with Frank's journal covering his face. Snoring escaped from underneath it, his chest rising and falling after each ragged breath. I looked over to Del, checking if she was awake or not. She was curled up, leaning against the back of her pew, face nestled in the hood of her cloak.

"I got Gary," Klaus said. He put his knife in a sheath between his boot and leg while placing the heart on the bench.

"But—" I protested.

I realized it was in vain as Klaus got up and walked to Gary. He circled the pew and stood behind him, putting his hands between Gary and the backrest. Without warning, Klaus flipped Gary off the bench in one swift motion. It caused him to land on his stomach on the floor, letting out a yelp and groan of pain.

I laughed at him and got up to check on Del, padding silently over to her bench. As I peered down at her relatively still form, a pang of guilt and sorrow fluttered through my heart.

I miss her so much. I know it's been three years, but it feels like yesterday. Why did the lord have to take you so soon? Hope, I miss you.

I reached down to shake her shoulder, being more careful than forceful. The warmth of her skin felt heavenly against mine. Even after going through the vile muck, she smelt like honeysuckle and strawberries. Like always, I didn't notice what I needed to do right away. I was too distracted by her scent to realize the ring on my hand lit up with a faint glow.

What? Is she a Dimmer? Or could she be a Brighter?

"Deck? Is it morning?" Del asked.

I pulled my hand away in shock, hiding it so she couldn't see it glow. I stuttered and said, "Yes, it is, sorry. I didn't mean to startle you if I did."

"You didn't." She sat up and rubbed her eyes. "What time is it?"

"Let me check, one second," I said as I walked over to my gear harness and pulled out my pocket watch. "It is seven forty-two."

"Wow, a whole four hours of sleep. I feel so refreshed," she said, sarcasm lacing her tone.

I glanced down at Gary as he struggled to get up. Klaus now sat on the back of the pew that Gary was previously occupying, a smile stretched across his face.

"I don't know about you, but I don't feel the same way. I think I'm more tired now than before I went to bed, and I hurt more, too," Gary said, glaring at Klaus.

I chuckled. "Sorry, gents and lady, but it's time we head out. We have more distance to cover, and we need to cover it as quickly as possible."

"Since I haven't the faintest idea of where the rest of my group is, can I tag along?" Del asked.

I glanced at the other two to see what they thought. Klaus didn't say anything, shocker, and Gary just smiled and nodded. I turned back to Del and said, "Sure, you can. Another set of hands to take down German soldiers will be appreciated."

Over the next several minutes, we all got our gear back on. I started with my harness first, followed by my haversack and Excalibur. Since Del didn't have anything else to put on, besides her cloak, she wandered around the church in search of anything useful.

I left out the can of tooth dullers and told the two they should eat them for breakfast. Before they could snag all of them, I took two and wandered off after Del, nibbling on my own biscuit. It was dry, dusty, and downright too delicious for what it was. I suppose that happens when you don't eat for a whole day. In my search, I found an office area tucked in the back corner of the church, lights on and movement inside.

"Del? You there?" I asked.

"Yeah, in here," she replied.

I saw her rummaging around in drawers and throwing things around. Papers and books littered the desks and haphazardly dotted the floor in random splotches like a crooked chessboard.

Del turned to me and smiled. "Look what I found."

She lifted up an old-fashioned black powder musket. The tarnished metal sparkled with a faint hue in the morning light, the wood pitted and worn in spots where hands rubbed against it frequently.

"A musket?" I asked.

"And I have some shot and black powder! It's better than not having a weapon," she said as she pointed at two pouches on the table.

I looked at it and cocked an eyebrow. "Do you think it will work?"

"We'll see, I suppose. I'll bring it along just in case."

"Okay, I guess," I said as I rubbed my neck. "Here, a biscuit."

She took it with haste and devoured it in two huge bites. "Thank you so much! I was starving."

"I know they're a little dry, but it's better than an empty stomach. Come on, I think the other two are ready to head out."

We left the office, and she followed me back to the rows of pews where Klaus and Gary stood waiting for us. They looked as if they were ready to go into battle, guns in hand and looks of focus and determination.

"Are we all ready to go out into the unknown? Face evils unheard of on this earth?" I asked.

"As ready as we'll ever be, I am assuming," Klaus said.

"Good. That brings us to how we will proceed. Gary, you will be leading the group. I will be behind you, and Del will be between Klaus and me." I looked at Klaus. "Will you be able to watch our back with the shotgun?"

He nodded as he lifted the shotgun into the crook of his shoulder. Instinctively he turned the gun sideways and racked it, looking in the shell ejection port to watch as the bolt loaded a shell. Satisfied, he looked at us again. "They will not see it coming."

Gary pulled the bolt on the rifle and loaded a bullet into the chamber. "What's the plan?"

"Head back to the boat. We will use that to get up the river some more to the Kew Gardens," I said.

"Why do we need to be ready to fight?" Del asked.

"I think we will need to. I'm not sure why but I just get this feeling. Plus, it's early morning, and that's when I would be patrolling if I was still looking for prisoners that escaped," I said.

I walked between Klaus and Gary to the back door of the church. From the layout of this place, I figured it led out to the same side we entered. Hopefully that would make it easier to get to the boat. I motioned Gary to come over to me. "You go first. We will follow behind."

"Okay, just make sure you guys watch my back," Gary said.

I nodded and grabbed the doorknob. "Ready?"

He smiled. "No, but that doesn't matter."

I chuckled and turned the knob, carefully pulling the door open. It emitted a low continuous creak, stretching along as I kept opening the door. The sun peeked over the tops of the trees and buildings on the distant horizon, blinding us momentarily. A blast of frigid air hit our faces with the force of a brick wall. Our exhalations escaped our lungs, igniting in the freezing temperatures and billowing outward in rolling clouds. As I thought, the door led to the same side we entered last night, only it was ten feet from it. Gary led the group out, and I followed, with Del immediately behind me, and Klaus bringing up the rear.

"Let's keep an eye out and signal if there is trouble," I whispered.

They all nodded, and we jogged to the treeline that acted as a buffer between the field and the bridge. Our feet shuffled through the light dusting of snow that lay like a blanket over the grass, threatening to cause one of us to slip or lose our footing. I saw fluctuating flashes of light in my periphery as we snuck to the foliage. The Tesla Coil Substation buzzed in the background, charging our weapons to the maximum level they could hold. We stopped in the patch of bushes to take stock of the rest of our surroundings, surveying the field once more. My eyes stopped scanning as my heartbeat quickened, sending my brain into overdrive.

"Is that a group of Germans?" I whispered, pointing at the center of the field.

Klaus, Gary, and Del followed my finger, taking in the sight before us. Six German soldiers with a seventh man in the middle were about a few hundred feet away. The two in the front were lookouts, guns ready to punch the cards of anyone who got in their way. There were two in the middle, one carrying a rather large duffel with a man shackled at the wrists and ankles marching along, with two more bringing up the rear. The two in the back glanced behind them frequently, obviously afraid of something.

"Should we help the prisoner?" Gary asked.

Why does it take six people to transport a prisoner? Also, why are they in the middle of the field?

Out of the corner of my eye, I saw a black mass sailing toward the soldiers. It swooped in mere inches from their heads, sending a rush of wind at the ground that caused the thin layer of snow to fly in different directions. They reacted too late, hitting the ground as the mass took to the sky once more. A few of them stood immediately and started shooting at it, barrels flashing in the morning sun as they barked out fiery hot lead.

"What the hell was that?" Del asked, voice cracking from fear.

I looked to the sky and saw the mass circling overhead, righting itself to come in for another pass at them. It came crashing down like a cannonball, patches of red shot out of its back as some of the bullets from the German's guns hit its body. Somehow though, it built up more speed, this time connecting with a soldier shooting at it. It hit him with a sickening thud, carmine splashing out over the pristine white snow. The soldier screamed in agony as he was lifted from the ground with the beast back into the sky.

"We need to help him!" Del said.

I can't jeopardize anyone. I can go up and help. I'm the only one equipped for close-range fighting.

"Klaus, on the side of the sling, there should be slugs. Load those in for longer distance shots." I turned to Gary. "Try and take a few down. I'll run up and try and help the prisoner."

"What about me?" Del demanded, anger in her voice.

I stood up and slapped my boots together to deploy the spikes. The half-inch metal nails sunk into the ground where I stood, instantly adding traction.

I smiled and said, "You have a rifle. Just don't hit me."

Thank God for Thomas and his ingenuity skills. I wouldn't know what to do if he wasn't so eccentric with his inventions.

I dropped my haversack at their feet and took off running, feeling my boots sink into the ground with each step. The biting air stung my lungs and throat as I started to breathe heavily. I looked back toward the carnage that unfolded in front of me. The beast was a few feet from another soldier. I looked up to watch what was happening. It hit him with outstretched legs, gripping him with large sharp claws that tore into his shoulders. He cried in pain, aiming his mp40 at the beast's bloody maw and pulling the trigger in retaliation. It let out a screech that pierced my eardrums, causing me to flinch and lose footing as I slid to the ground. The beast brought its head down, mouth open wide, and silenced the soldiers' screams for good.

What is that? What kind of creature is it?

The beast was the size of a grizzly bear but did not resemble one in any way. It was a mixture of creatures I had seen before, making me wonder if we hit a pocket of dream gas at some point.

The hind legs were that of a lion, with patchy brown fur with large scars littering the skin. Its fur changed from the course hairs to long brown and white feathers nearest the middle of the beast with the front legs, wings, and head of an eagle. Its yellow beak and talons were caked in red and viscera from the mess.

Is that a Griffon?

Another screech filled the air as the beast let go of the soldier and let the body slump to the ground. The large bag he was carrying fell with him, clattering as it hit the frozen dirt. The other three soldiers turned to the Griffon and started to shoot as it flapped its wings and took off from the ground.

I grabbed my pistol from my holster and pulled the slide back in one quick motion, racking a bullet into the chamber. The wires and firing pin were already glowing with charged electricity from our proximity to the Tesla Coil Substation. I lifted the pistol to line up a shot, aiming for the closest soldier. Just before I squeezed my trigger, the head of the soldier lurched sideways, followed by an explosion of red mist spraying out the side of his head. His limbs went slack as his body crumpled to the ground, adding to the pile of bodies. My head snapped back to look behind me to see Gary wave apologetically in my direction.

"Sorry!" he yelled.

The snow between him and I jumped into the air from bullets striking the ground. They peppered all around, urging me to turn my attention back to the Germans behind me. There were two left standing. One was shooting at me while the other still shot at the sky. I went to raise my pistol again to return fire, but had it fly from my hands seconds after I began aiming. It bounced off the ground to my left, skittering twenty feet away where it was too far out of reach to try and grab it. I saw the anger in the eyes of the soldier as we locked gazes, his mouth curled up in a snarl. I could feel death knocking at my door, ready to bust through to claim what was owed to him.

This is it. After everything I have made it through, I will be at peace. Maybe now is the right time, no more struggling. No more quest to stop Jakobus from taking over the world, ruling over all by fear and death. They say life flashes before your eyes when you are about to die. At least I'll get to see you again, Hope. I will be fine if that's the last thing I see.

"Oi!" yelled a voice.

My eyes jerked open, ready to see death at the end of a barrel. Instead, I saw the prisoner tackling the soldier about to shoot me. They wrestled on the ground, gun firing bullets randomly in directions known only to fate. The other was too busy shooting at the sky to notice his cohort struggling.

I took advantage of the situation, drawing Excalibur from the scabbard and sprinting at them to help. I closed the gap in seconds, running with Excalibur out front of me as it gleamed in the sun. The prisoner headbutted the German, sending him into a confused daze, and rolled off a second before me being upon them. I raised the sword above my head and brought it down on him, blade singing from the speed. It sunk into his shoulder and cut clean through bone, sinew, muscles, and flesh. I saw his face and witnessed the life drain from his eyes, glazed over in seconds with the sweet promise of pain-free oblivion.

"Good aim, now get me free of these chains," yelled the man.

I pulled the sword from the man's torso, and a slurping sound escaped the wound from the suction. Another screech pierced the air, making me stagger and look around. Without warning, the Griffon hit the last German like a rugby player. Cracks and snaps sounded just as the ground shook from the impact of the beast. I rubbed at my eyes, taking in the hulking beast that stood before me. A putrid smell of rot and decay struck my nostrils with force, making me gag and cover my nose.

"Don't move," said the prisoner.

I stopped in my tracks and tried not to move, wanting to keep all my appendages in the correct anatomical spot. The Griffon turned its head to look at me, tilting it to the side to take me in. Like a bird, it moved its head in a jolting and jarring fashion, quick and precise movements. We locked eyes, and for a moment, I was lost in them, seeing things even though I wasn't sure what they were.

Why are those eyes so familiar? I feel as if I have seen them before. Could they be from a memory of King Arthur?

It ruffled its feathers, stretching its wings above it to take off once more. Before it could do so, another large mass rocketed into it and sent them both rolling off to the left.

CHAPTER 25
Two Birds, Two Swords

8:20 a.m.

I flinched from the impact, turning as I watched them roll away. My whole world felt like one big fantasy novel at this particular moment.

"What in holy hell is going on here?" I yelled.

"Does it matter? Help me with these chains!" the man said.

I jogged to him. "Which man had the keys?"

He looked at me as his face went pale with realization. "One of the ones it ate."

I looked from him to the beast, then back to him, and shook my head. In an attempt to look for anything helpful, I glanced around at my surroundings.

Guns are lying about, but I didn't think a bullet would get through the steel of the chains.

"Use the sword," the man said.

My eyes met his. "Are you mad?"

"Well, they *do* call me Mad Jack. I didn't get the name for making any sense," Jack said.

More screeching filled the air behind me, sending my heartbeat through the roof again. I shook my head and lifted Excalibur above my head once more.

"Ready?" I asked.

He placed his hands and wrists on the ground before him. "Aye."

The only way to get out of this is to have the two of us ready to defend against an attack. Here goes nothing.

I swung down on the chains, putting as much strength into them as possible. At the last second, I closed my eyes to protect them from shrapnel or sparks that could ricochet off the metal of either sword or chain. The magical steel of Excalibur sunk into the ground, shattering his bonds with no issue. I pried my sword out of the dirt to be ready for another swing to cut into the second set of chains.

Jack put his legs out and pulled the chain as tight as he could. "Let's get the last one."

With haste, I brought the sword down upon the last set. This time I used far less force than before, not wanting to struggle and pry it out of the frigid tundra again. It struck the cold steel and cut with ease, only sending a minimal amount of sparks into the air.

"Aha! Good! We're in business now," Jack yelled.

He leaped to his feet with incredible agility, chains rattling against each other. As he did so, he scanned the bloody ground at our feet. "Did you see a duffel bag?"

"I did." I paused. "Before everyone was crushed to death, though."

Another noise came from the beasts off to the left. This time it was the guttural growl of a lion. Scrapes against the ground sent gravel and dirt into the air. My curiosity pulled my gaze to the second beast, taking it in with morbid fascination. This new monster had the body, head, and legs of a lion. The creature's fur and mane were matted with blood, saliva, and dirt as it fought ferociously with the Griffon. It had the tail of a scorpion's curved exoskeleton with a sharp barb on the end. The wings flapped violently, leathery and somewhat translucent like a bat, as it struck at the Griffon with its hind claws.

It's a Manticore. Of course, it's a Manticore. Can't have a Griffon if we don't have a Manticore to go up against it.

Jack grunted, walking around the bodies and kicking them to turn them over. The last one he rolled over made him smile and bellow with triumph. He leaned down and pulled one end of the duffle toward the sky. Jack fumbled with the knot on the pull string, trying to open it before the creature was upon us. He finally succeeded, prying it open and dumping the contents on the ground before him. A three-and-a-half-foot sword fell out, clanging against the ground. It was followed by a longbow, arrows, quiver, and a bagpipe.

Yep, and honest-to-God bagpipe. Oh, the thirteen arrows are loose too, of course.

Jack crouched in front of his gear and grabbed the quiver first, tucking the arrows back into it that had slipped out when he dumped everything out. He slung that over his shoulder and picked up his sword, fastening it to his belt. The last thing he grabbed was the longbow, gripping it in his left hand.

"Is that a—never mind. Grab your gear, and we'll try and leave before the beasts notice," I said.

At this point, I should know to keep my mouth shut. I really need to know when not to say things to jinx us. After I finished speaking those famous fate-deciding words, the Manticore roared with defiance, shaking the ground under our feet. Jack and I turned our attention to the beasts again, only to see the Griffon on its side, lying motionless in a patch of red-soaked slush. Clumps of feather and fur were strewn about, some floating away with the cool breeze that picked up with the rising sun. The Manticore's paw was resting on the Griffon's shoulder, bloodied and digging into its flesh while it eyed us with intent to kill. Its mouth opened as it flashed crimson-stained teeth, corners of its lips pulled back into a snarl.

I glanced at Jack. "Should we run?"

Instead of an audible response, Jack grabbed an arrow from the quiver. He nocked it to the bow's string and drew it back tight to his face.

"What are you doing?" I asked.

He smirked and said, "Gotta nip it in the bud."

"What? That doesn't make any sense!"

Jack aimed the bow and let the string go, the arrow flying through the air at the Manticore. It sailed easily straight through the wind, flying true toward its face.

My eyes followed as I said, "I guess that decides that."

The beast shifted its stance, front legs in our direction and mouth agape with stained teeth protruding with fierceness. It let out another window-shattering roar, sending a visible shockwave of power at the approaching arrow. The roar sent the arrow into a tailspin, shifting the trajectory enough to fall short of the Manticore by about ten feet.

"That certainly is not fair," Jack said.

"What do you even mean? It's a damn Manticore! How is any of this fair?!"

Jack shrugged and nocked another arrow, firing it within seconds of aiming. He continued to fire them at the beast, each being easily dodged. The beast flapped its wings and ascended to the sky, eluding injury like a ballet dancer balancing gracefully.

"I think you're missing it!" I yelled.

"Close is better than not at all!" Jack hooted.

I looked at the man with confusion and a strange amount of admiration. He was absolutely loony, just a complete headcase. I couldn't believe what I was dealing with right now. Over the turbulent flaps of gravid wings, I heard the echoes of my friends' guns taking potshots at the beast, bullets whizzing by too close for comfort.

My friends. I suppose you could call them that. Weird to think of them that way, though. I just met Del, but I feel I have known her for a long time.

Gary, well, Gary is just a thick-headed American that I somehow love. Then there is Klaus. I'm not supposed to trust him, but he is making it hard for me to stay true to the rift between our people. It's crazy to say, but I would die for the lot of them any day.

"Watch out!" Jack yelled.

My brain heard him, but my body was already moving to avoid damage. I felt the sting of the Manticore's scorpion barb in my left shoulder, shifting to ferocious pain before I realized what had happened. The overbearing force of the harsh impact sent me sprawling to the ground, Excalibur skidding out of my hand. My attention shifted from the cold ground under my hands to the cumbersome beast that crashed to the ground in front of both Jack and me.

I got to my knees and reached over to feel my injury, flinching as soon as I touched it. It felt wet and hot, making me feel queasy from the thought of my shoulder being torn to shreds. The Manticore snarled, teeth bared with saliva dripping like a lethal dose of venom from a rattlesnake.

"The damned beast broke my bow. That was my favorite bow," Jack said.

The beast roared, sending spit flying toward us.

"I don't think it really cares if it was your favorite or not," I said.

"Well, it should," Jack replied.

The Manticore crouched, bowing onto its front paws as it shuffled on them. The gleam in its eye told me it wasn't here to play games, only to kill. Its tail waved in the air back and forth, its exoskeleton clicking and clacking against itself.

"Oh, no," I said.

The thing's gonna pounce. I need Excalibur if I have any hope of staying alive.

I dove to the ground and crawled as fast as my limbs could carry me to my sword. The snow stung my fingertips from the freezing temperatures, eventually numbing them to the bone. I dug and flung large handfuls of the snow as I scrambled, worrying I'd be the chew toy of an overgrown house cat…with wings.

"Watch out!" Jack yelled.

I glanced at the beast to check if it was going to pounce just in time to see it kick off its back legs and launch into the sky. My heart lurched, pumping at full force from all of the stress. I was able to relax somewhat when I felt my fingers wrap around the hilt of Excalibur. The leather wrap felt warm to the touch, sending a sense of calmness through me that I didn't know I needed.

The noise of leathery wings flooded my ears, alerting me to roll onto my back and face what was coming. The quick shift in orientation sent blood rushing every which way, making me dizzy as hell. As a precaution, I brought Excalibur above my body as my eyes focused on the Manticore diving toward me. I braced myself for the impact that would most likely pulverize my bones to dust and squash me like a ripened tomato, and that fell too late.

"Get out of the way!" yelled Jack.

A rush of wind blew my hair into my face, making me realize that death had not come to collect just yet. The crunch of bone never came, nor did the slicing and dicing turn me to fleshy bits. I opened one eye to see if I was being toyed with before getting mauled by the Manticore, not that I ever wanted to know what that felt like.

"Am I alive?" I asked.

Roars and snarls filled the air, prompting me to get to my feet post haste. My attention was brought to the tangled mess of fur, feathers, claws, and teeth gnashing at each other in a battle to overcome the other. I could hear my friends off in the distance yelling to me, warning me and trying to get me to move. Jack was to my right, picking up his bagpipe and cradling it in both hands. I hurriedly slid Excalibur into its scabbard and yelled at Jack. "Just leave it! We need to get out of here while those things are busy!"

"I can't do it, man. I don't have the power to," Jack said.

I ran to Jack and grabbed his arm. "We need to move. Now!"

Jack looked me in the eyes as his lips slowly curled into a smile. "If we are going to march, we will need something to march to!"

I pulled on his arm, prompting him to start running. We both took off as quick as a fresh spring stream to the treeline where my friends were. The threat of danger receded behind Jack and me as we put more of the field between us and the creatures.

I was focused on my breathing, huffing and puffing from the unwanted and unplanned excitement. The music rocked me from my focus, making me trip up ever so slightly. I glanced back in shock and saw Jack was keeping up with me, but that wasn't what surprised me. What surprised me was that he was currently playing his bagpipes while running full-force away from two mythical beasts. Struggling to stay alive. Nothing like having the 'Ride of the Valkyries' be the soundtrack to your death sentence.

"How are you even playing that? Aren't you out of breath?" I huffed.

Mad Jack kept running full steam ahead, not bothering to answer the question. He eventually overtook me and was now the lead.

I suppose that answers that question.

I could make out Gary, Klaus, and Del lined up in the bushes taking shots at the monsters as we approached. The thunderous sounds of their gunfire finally broke through the noises of everything else, sending a little pep back into my step. The air was filled with the static of electrical discharge from the guns and Tesla Coil Substation, giving me a tangy and bitter aftertaste with each new dry swallow.

"Don't look behind you!" Gary yelled.

I realized Gary said not to look behind me, and I knew I should listen to his advice. But alas, I usually didn't listen to sound advice, and common sense often eluded me in life-or-death situations.

While running for the bushes, I made the horrible decision to take a quick peek over my shoulder. I should have listened to Gary when he warned me. I should have decided to keep my eye on the prize, the simple prize of not getting ripped to shreds. My ill decision to look behind us yielded a heart-wrenching realization that the Griffon wasn't able to hold the Manticore at bay for very long; he wasn't strong enough to rip it apart. Once again, our saving grace was lying motionless on its side while the Manticore was on our tail, no pun intended. Okay, maybe it was.

You know what? Screw this. If I die, I don't care what that thing is called. It doesn't deserve the name of what it is.

"Oi! You grown moggy! Leave us alone!" I yelled.

It replied with another roar that shook the snow from the treetops and branches. The frozen water fell to the ground and littered my friends, still hiding in the bushes. I heard Klaus rack the shotgun and aim behind me.

"Go! Get going! We need to get to the boat!" I yelled.

The three got to their feet in acknowledgment. Klaus motioned to the other two and led them along in the direction of the river. I saw Del and Gary flash concerned glances my way, unsure if it was the best thing to do. Jack and I stopped about ten feet from the treeline, giving the others more time to get away. Jack had stopped playing his bagpipe and placed it on the ground next to him, gentle and precise.

I turned to him and said, "Jack, go with them. I can handle the beast, it's the only way you can help them make it out of here. Otherwise, it will just keep following us."

"I cannae do that, me boy," he said as he glanced at me. "What is yer name, anyway?"

"Why does that matter right now?" I shook my head. "It's Deckard. But you can call me Deck."

"Deck me boy, I will be holding ground with you. I have had a hankering for some battle for a little bit now, ever since they captured me."

"I can't believe this, in any way, shape, or form. I suppose two swords are better than one."

Jack smiled a large toothy grin as he and I drew our swords in a quick motion, mirroring each other almost to the t. We both took a fighting stance, bracing our right foot behind us, and we held our swords out in front. The metal of the blades reflected the ever-rising sun off onto the snow in front of us. I watched the Manticore halfway across the field as it paced back and forth with its eyes trained on us, almost as if it was stalking its prey.

"What's the plan, me boy?" Jack asked.

I chuckled. "I don't know. I honestly didn't think that far ahead."

We watched as the Manticore eyed us still. It crouched before launching itself into the air. Its wings flapped with a strength that seemed almost fantastical, something a real-life animal wouldn't be able to do. We stood ready with our swords out in front as it circled overhead above the bloody mess the Griffon created. It continued to do that for what felt like forever, even though, realistically, it was only thirty seconds. The wind picked up across the open stretch of land, howling as silence came from everything else.

What is it waiting for? Why hasn't it tried to take us out yet? We are sitting ducks ripe for the picking. I would have thought it might have tried to take one, if not both of us, at this point.

The Manticore rose into the air even further than it was and righted itself, pointing its head toward us. It then tucked in its wings and started to dive bomb in our direction.

"Here is our chance to catch it off guard. It will be too stunned that it missed us to react fast enough," I said.

"Let's hope it's on its last life," Jack said.

I shook my head at his response and groaned.

Is this how everyone else feels when I say these kinds of things?

"When I say 'now,' I need you to dive to the right and roll. Try to bring your sword back up after getting to your feet and slash at it," I said.

"Sounds like a plan if there ever was one," Jack boomed.

I glanced up in time to see the Manticore reach out at us with outstretched arms, claws glinting off the sunlight. The beast's lips were drawn back in a snarl, revealing its bloodied maw. Chunks of fresh meat were stuck between some of its crooked teeth, stained pink and red from the fresh kill. I looked deep into its eyes, which felt more like black holes, devoid of anything resembling higher brain function other than hunting and killing.

"Now!" I yelled.

I rolled to the left, tucking my chin to my chest as I held the sword out. Jack did the same at the very exact moment as me. The Manticore struck the ground where we were standing, sending dirt and snow flying into the air. The force of its mass striking the ground made it challenging to stay on my feet after rolling to them.

The Manticore roared with rage and swiped blindly at Jack and me, snapping its jaw together at shapes in the dust. I swung Excalibur at it with extreme force, aiming for its legs or paws. I felt the slightest bit of resistance as the blade connected with the flesh of the beast before slicing right through whatever part of it the sword had struck. It roared in pain from the damage both Jack and I inflicted upon it.

"Watch out for its claws," I yelled.

Just as I spoke, a paw the size of a watermelon came soaring toward my face. I ducked just in time, only feeling the wind that trailed behind the force of the swipe ruffle through my hair. In retaliation, I swung Excalibur at the beast once more, aiming for its wing to keep it from flying away or after us. It jumped to the side, dodging my swing and sending the blade sinking into the dirt.

The air finally cleared as the wind picked up the last of the debris and took it away to another desolate field. I pulled my sword from the dirt and looked to Jack to see how he was faring with all of this. He was on the other side of the beast, taking swings at it all while dodging paws himself.

I happened to look up as its tail came down at me with breakneck speed. I brought up Excalibur to block the strike, causing the barb to glance off the side of the sword and stab into the ground between Jack and me. We locked eyes and nodded, both knowing what to do next. At the same moment, Jack and I swung our swords directly down upon the Manticore's scorpion tail. The sharp edges of our swords cut cleanly through two different sections of it, sending it into a frenzy of flailing paws and claws. The Manticore snapped its head to the left of us, toward someone that was yelling.

"Oi, dumb cat!" Gary yelled.

I looked in the same direction, surprised to see everyone standing in the open with their guns held readied. Gary's and Klaus' were glowing blue from the electrical charge of the wires while Del's was a little less intimidating but just as deadly.

"I told you to run!" I yelled.

"We couldn't leave you to be cat treats!" Gary said.

Gary, Klaus, and Del opened fire on the Manticore. They peppered it with charged bullets and old-world lead balls, hitting center mass with every shot. I used the opportunity to do what I could to take the beast down.

It turned in their direction and started to jog that way. Noises of pain and anger escaped the Manticore's mouth as the bullets tore into its hide, causing blood to spill and stain streaks of crimson into its hay-colored fur. I sprinted around the back of the beast and saw that with the initial blow of my sword, I cut off the last third of its right wing, making it unable to fly even if it wanted to. What was left of its tail was swinging wildly in random jerking motions, coming all too close to knocking me upside the head more than once.

Hopefully this works. Otherwise, I will be a goner, and so will everyone else. Here goes nothing.

I picked up the pace to get close and leaped onto its back near the base that connected it to the body. The beast flinched as I hit its back and gripped its fur, moving back and forth and trying to swipe at me with either front paw. I held on to Excalibur tightly and started to climb its back, all while feeling like I was a tick on a mutt's thigh, swinging and holding on for dear life.

It started bucking and galloping faster the further I climbed until I reached its shoulder blades. Once there, I dug into its skin with the spikes of my boots to give myself a better grip, causing it to bellow in anger. In a split second, on the downward motion of the Manticore, I was able to hold myself up with my legs to make my final move. I gripped Excalibur in both hands with the gleaming steel pointing down toward its back and plunged it between the spine and right shoulder blade, aiming directly for the heart. Excalibur sank deep into the muscles and flesh, burying itself to the hilt, causing the beast's knees to buckle beneath me.

CHAPTER 26
The More the Merrier

8:52 a.m.

final roar of defiance escaped the Manticore's maw before it collapsed completely to its stomach on the cold snow-covered ground. I could feel its heartbeat slow to a stop underneath me as its last breath seeped from its lungs into the air.

Is it done? Did I take care of it?

The body of the Manticore lay motionless underneath me as I pulled Excalibur out and slid off the side of it. I hit the ground with a thud, boots digging into the dirt and staining the porcelain white snow with small spots of carmine blood. I slapped the side of my right boot against my left to disengage the spikes as I wiped the blade of my sword on the beast's hind leg. It left thick, deep maroon streaks freezing to the fur as the cold wind brushed past it. I then realized my whole body felt as if I was hit by a train, full steam ahead with no warning. I slid Excalibur back into its scabbard and rubbed my neck as I walked around the beast to see if my friends were alright. I heard them whispering amongst each other, followed by Gary saying something.

"Deck?" Gary asked.

I rounded the front of the Manticore and said, "Yeah?"

Del gasped as she brought her hands to her face in surprise. Klaus, Gary, and Jack all looked at me and started to laugh. This, of course, caused me to laugh as well, sending surges of pain coursing through my body.

"You survived!" Gary said.

Klaus backhanded Gary's arm. "Of course, he survived. Why wouldn't he?"

Gary rubbed at the spot of impact as he frowned. "I don't know, just glad is all."

"Boys, now, now. Let's just get going and head to the boat," Del said as she kicked the Manticore. "Before this kitty realizes it has another life to use."

"Agreed," I said. "Everyone, this is Jack."

I lifted a hand to motion to Jack, turning to look at him. As I looked him up and down, I realized that Jack had retrieved his bagpipe from whence he placed it on the ground and was walking up to the group. He already had his bow over his shoulder again next to his quiver and his sword in its scabbard at his hip.

"Nice to meet you, youngins. Me name's Mad Jack, but you can call me Jack if ya like," Jack said.

"Hey Deck, what the hell was that?" Gary asked.

"What? The flying beasts?" I asked.

"Yeah. I would say the elephant in the room, but they aren't flying elephants, are they?"

I glanced back to our savior, the Griffon, and felt a little sorry for it. At first, I thought it was trying to kill us, but I was wrong; it was only there to help. A pang of sorrow flowed into me at that moment, like a low tide finally returning.

It must've been the same thing that attacked the Germans earlier on before the river. Those eyes too. Why were they so familiar? Why am I sad about this?

"Gary, Klaus, I think the one further away was the same monster we saw after escaping the tunnels," I said.

They both peeked around me and glanced at the still form of the beast fifty feet off in the middle of the field. Gary nodded his head in acknowledgment while Klaus shook his head in pity. They turned their attention back to me for the most part.

"So, it probably wasn't dream gas; we were seeing an actual creature kill a bunch of people," Klaus said.

We all stood in silence, looking at the beast near our feet. The steam from the corpse grew less and less as it started to slowly cool from exposure to the elements. The blood from its injuries began to pool out from the body in a gruesome snow angel, staining the snow in various shades of red to pink.

"Yeah, I guess so. But we need to stay vigilant for safety's sake. Grab your gear and move your feet. Let's get going, everyone," I said.

I took Excalibur in my hand and walked around to the beast's backside. I looked at the barb on the end of the scorpion tail and watched it twitch a few times involuntarily. With a quick flick of my wrist, I chopped the end off the tail, letting it fall to the ground with a soft thud.

"Klaus, come here with some of the extra clothes," I said.

Klaus came around the beast's side with a shirt and pants in his hands. "What now?"

"Put the barb in the clothes and wrap it up tight. I want to bring it with us to get examined by someone."

Especially since I was stung by it.

"Okay," he said.

He bent down and carefully wrapped the clothing around the barb of the Manticore's tail. When he picked it up and folded the edges around the mass, it almost seemed the same size as a pumpkin or melon. He tucked it away into his haversack and followed me back to the other side of the beast where everyone else was. A few members of the group mumbled while others just collected their things for the trip. Gary looked at the Manticore a little closer before shaking his head. In an act of defiance, he walked up and kicked the beast in the stomach. It gurgled loudly and startled Gary, causing him to trip on his feet and fall flat on his backside.

"Scaredy cat," Klaus laughed.

In an act of redemption, Klaus leaned over and lent a helping hand to Gary. He took it and pulled himself to his feet, dusting the trace amounts of snow off his trousers.

"Sorry, I had to," Klaus said.

"Yeah, I probably would do the same," Gary replied.

I rolled my eyes and decided to check my own things before we moved on. Del came up to me with my haversack in hand as I was adjusting my scabbard for Excalibur. She reached out and handed it to me. I was happy to have my bag back and the box near me again.

Why am I happy to have that again? Last time I had it on me, I wanted to rip Klaus' eyes out for no reason whatsoever. I need to get rid of it. I need to tell the others about it and what it's doing to me. Maybe I can tell Eileen when we meet again at the rendezvous. I feel like she would know what to do with it. What did Jakobus mean that he was looking for a piece of him? Is that what's in the box? A way to turn good men or women to his image, evil incarnate?

"Deck?" Del asked.

I felt her put her hand on my shoulder, sending shivers splintering through my ragged and tired body. They weren't uncomfortable shivers, though; they were of want and yearning, of needing someone to care for and someone to get care from.

"Yeah?" I said.

"Are you alright?"

"I think so. It's been a very long and ridiculous couple of days, more so than you could imagine, I'm afraid."

"What makes it so different from any other day here in German-infested London?"

I thought about that and chuckled, "I suppose you're right; that about sums it up."

"So, are you going to tell me what this creature is? It's definitely not natural fauna to London."

I laughed and caused my whole body to hurt. "You wouldn't believe me if I told you. Honestly, I don't even know if I believe it."

"Try me."

I rubbed my eyes. "I think it is a Manticore and the other beast was a Griffon."

She laughed. "You're right, I don't believe you. Next you'll say they are from the gates of hell."

I looked at her and didn't smile or give any inclination that I was joking.

Her smile faded as she thought about it. "Okay, I suppose. By the way, what did Himmler mean when he said you had something of his or, rather, a piece of him?"

I struggled to think of a good lie. "I'm not sure. He seemed delusional to me."

She thought about it for a long moment. "Okay."

I tried to ignore the fact that Del seemed to know what I was thinking about. It seemed like that wasn't the first time since I met her that she did that. What is it about her? She seemed so familiar, but I swore I had never met this woman in my life.

"Everyone? I'll take the lead while Del will be behind me. Klaus and Gary, you two go after that, and Jack will follow up behind." I looked to Jack. "Are you able to handle that, Jack?"

He flashed a grin that would scare the mad hatter. "Aye, I'll be watching behind us."

I gave one last cursory glance at everyone. "Okay, follow me."

I took off at a light jog, allowing everyone to fall into step with me. We made it to the walking path at the river's edge within thirty seconds, keeping our ears and eyes open for any more trouble. The sun was now further above us in the sky, warming things and forcing the chill of the morning wind down to a slight nip at the bare skin.

I led the way down the set of stone steps that we navigated the night before, keeping close to the wall again to camouflage us. The boat teetered gently back and forth as it creaked in the water as we all reached the platform below. Now that there were five of us, the boat seemed smaller than it did the night prior. Or that could've just been because we were seeing it in the light for the first time.

"Gary, you steer again. I'll sit in the front and keep an eye on things." I turned to Del and Jack. "You two sit in the middle with Klaus."

Gary squeezed through the group and got down into the boat first, sitting at the back near the motor. I was next, stepping down into the middle and taking up residence in the front near the lamp. In the middle of the boat, there were two more benches evenly spaced between the front and back. Klaus and Jack hopped down into the boat and took their seats on the bench closest to Gary, sending the boat rocking back and forth with their force of impact. Klaus and I reached up and gave a hand to Del to help her into the boat.

She sat down on the bench and said, "Such a gentleman. It's a shame."

"Why is that?" I asked.

"You don't see too many chivalrous men anymore."

That one hit me harder than it should have, and I was unsure why.

For some reason, it made me think of Hope again, think of the first hellos and goodbyes we exchanged. Why am I thinking of her so much lately? Is it because of Del? Is seeing somebody that remotely reminds me of her bring back all the memories? Or am I just losing my grip on the here and now, eventually forgetting sight of the goals we are after.

I chuckled as I trailed off into thought. "Yeah, that's all too true."

I lost focus on her and half-heartedly looked to Gary. "Ready to start it up?"

"We're all ready, Capitan. Full steam ahead," Gary replied.

He flipped the few switches on the motor, lighting up the bright green start button on the front of the metal casing. A smile crept across his face as he pressed the button, coaxing the old engine to life. It turned over a few times before it sputtered and putted slowly as it warmed up. Gary revved the engine for a few seconds, making sure it was ready for the task at hand of lugging five people through the frigid, semi-frozen water of the Thames. The whole boat shifted as I felt the motor propel us out to open waters. I took in the sight, looking all around us at the crystalized water reflecting an early sun's rays of hope and anticipation.

"Del," I said.

"Mhm," she replied.

I turned to her. "You said in the journal of your defector that Himmler was trying to open the gates of Hell, right?"

"Yeah, that's right."

"How true do you think it is? Or rather, how much do you trust your defector and his journal?"

Jack sputtered and said, "Gates of Hell? What kind of group of people am I with?"

I glanced at him. "Sorry, it's all sorts of messed up right now. I know it sounds crazy, but I assure you, it's all true. For the most part."

"I don't care if it's crazy; I am meself. I just want to know what I am getting myself into, might need some extra arrows is all," Jack said as he shrugged.

A silence filled the air, almost louder than the boat motor. I waited for something to come to my mind, anything to break the silence.

"You know, I like this guy. He seems nuts, but I like him," Gary said.

Del looked from them back to me as she hesitated to continue, "Anyways, I do trust him. Even though it seems far-fetched, I think that Heinz thought Himmler believed he could open the gates of hell."

"I believe him, too," I said. "Gary, Klaus, do you think we can trust her with everything?"

Gary shrugged. "I suppose. Why not? She seems like she is caught in the middle of all of this regardless. I mean, she has seen the beast battle unfold right in front of all of us. How do you explain that away?"

"Fair enough. Klaus?"

He mulled it over before talking. "Like I said before. I trust your judgment, so I trust what you decide to do."

What's the worst that can happen? It may help to have more people to take on Jakobus when we return to the compound. And she seems like she knows it like the back of her hand.

"Okay, I guess it can't hurt any," I said. I turned to her once more. "There's a lot to go over, and I'll give you the highlights. Gary, do you have Frank's journal still?"

"Yeah," he said.

While steering the boat, he reached down into his haversack and pulled out Frank's leather journal. He held it out to Del as she took it from him.

"That is the comprehensive history of The Keepers since its inception in the year five hundred and thirty-six."

"What does that have to do with what's going on?" she asked as she began to flip through the journal.

"In the year 536, King Arthur was at war with a man by the name of Jakobus. He was unable to stop Jakobus when he was alive, so he created the group known as The Keepers. The Keepers have been around since then and are the descendants of the knights of the round table." I paused before continuing. "Are you still with me?"

"Uh—" she began to say.

"Good. My grandad was a recipient of the magical sword Excalibur," I said as I pulled the sword from its sheath.

"That's why you're carrying a sword around? I thought it was just some odd thing British soldiers did." She said, sarcasm heavy in her tone.

I chuckled. "No. Well, for the most part. My grandad was given the sword and was told the same things I am telling you, with a little more to it, but for all intents and purposes, it was basically the same."

"So why did your grandfather get the sword?" she asked.

"Because Jakobus was prowling the streets of London as Jack the Ripper. Or at least Jakobus was the reason behind Jack the Ripper."

At this point, I believe I completely lost her, but I continued on.

"My grandad defeated Jakobus in the end, or so he thought. That is why Himmler said he was looking for something that belonged to him."

Gary and Klaus looked at me, confusion flashing across their faces. I gestured with my hand that I would explain later. The last thing I need to do now is tell them about the box of murderous rage that took up residence in my haversack.

"So Himmler is Jakobus? How?" she asked.

"That's the thing we really are trying to figure out. How he can seemingly go from one body to the next, it's still unknown to us. That's what we are doing in London, still trying to fight back and keep Jakobus from taking the city and then the world."

Del looked at me with determination. "What can I do to help?"

"You can start by reading the journal and learning everything you can," I said.

She nodded and started looking through it. Gary went back to leading the boat down the river as Klaus pulled out his piece of wood and knife to whittle some more. Jack pulled out his bagpipe and started playing a tune to help alleviate the tension in the air. The sweet notes of Beethoven's number nine joined the chorus of the motor and helped me forget about a few of my problems for now. My mind drifted away with the passing winds, fleeting and momentary.

Chapter 27
Training Day

30th October, 1937
Kew Gardens, Richmond Borough, London, England
12:23 p.m.

The previous few days had been quite the ordeal. Deck was brought in for formal training as a Keeper before he could go through the normal military recruitment process. Frank would train him on close quarters combat with swords today, making sure he could handle himself when it came to sharp and pointy things.

Up to this point, Deck was learning some forms of hand-to-hand like muay thai, karate, and a few other useful methods of stopping someone else with his bare hands. At first, he didn't know a thing about fighting because in normal day-to-day life, he tried to resolve things with reasoning and common sense. Deck learned really quick that when it came to offenders of the nefarious nature, they liked to play dirty.

The training center that Nikola had built underneath the Kew Gardens was relatively solid and sturdy. The walls were stone with padding consisting of feathers and cotton to protect you when you were up close and personal with hand-to-hand fisticuffs. At one end of the large fifty by sixty-foot room were targets for archery training, while the wall opposite to that was any weapon you could name hanging from it. At even intervals, there were two five-foot thick cement columns supporting the ceiling, holding the weight of the world above from crushing us in our unawareness.

"Deck, you need to keep your sword in front, steady and strong to deflect any blows that come your way," Frank said.

He circled Deck as he tried to keep up, holding the sword, anticipating a strike from Frank at any second. "I am trying to. We've been at this for hours, and I'm losing focus."

"That's a good thing. The enemy won't care. They will keep coming at you until they take you down."

"Couldn't I be on the defensive the whole time? Wait for them to lose all their energy?"

Frank didn't answer the question. He was too busy leaping at Deck with a lunge, sword stabbing through the air toward his neck. Deck narrowly brought his sword up in time to deflect the blow, steel sparking against steel as the blades bit at each other. Deck backstepped to regain his balance and readied himself for his own strike. Frank was on him as he took his second step, arcing the sword in an uppercut aimed at Deck's forearms. Deck parried it away with a flick of his wrists, this time a little more ready than the last.

"I will take that as a no," Deck said through gritted teeth.

Deck took the initiative and advanced on Frank, swinging his sword in a downward arc. Frank parried with effortless ease and knocked Deck's sword sideways. Deck used the momentum of the deflection to bring it back around at Frank's side, grunting with effort as he did this.

Frank had to jump to the side as he dodged the last swing. "Good! You are learning! Now I won't hold back."

"Wait, you were holding back?" Deck yelled.

Frank came at him with the haste and determination of a lion defending its cubs. The swipes and slashes came in a blur of gleaming metal, sparks, and clangs. Deck was able to keep up but purely on the defensive, being backed into a corner metaphorically and physically. His breathing was ragged and forced as he struggled with the sword, blocking more than attacking.

"If you do not act in retaliation instead of reaction, you will die, Deckard. You need to be able to overcome your enemy if need be," Frank said.

"This reminds me of the memories of me grandad when he was training. Why couldn't that be something that got passed on? Why do I need to learn how to fight when I am literally a descendant of King Arthur? How did Father Hubert teach this to Grandad? He surprised him with a punch to the face, that's it. I need to do something he isn't expecting," Deck thought.

Deck parried Frank's last swing, turning the blade just enough to throw it off kilter and ruin Frank's rebound. As Frank took that two seconds extra to readjust his swing, Deck took advantage of it, swiping his sword at Frank's feet. The look on Frank's face was priceless when he had to jump over the blade, throwing off his rhythm completely.

Deck went in for another swipe from the top left down to the bottom right. Frank didn't have enough time to get his sword up in time to deflect, so he made the split-second decision to jump back once more. Deck's sword sang as it cut through the air just before he felt a thud. He looked to the right and saw Excalibur had sunk three feet into one of the support columns. Surprised, Deck's body moved for him and let go of the hilt instead of struggling to pull it free. He hunched over and charged Frank while he was still reeling from unexpected maneuvers. Deck hit him square in the chest with his shoulder and sent both of them sprawling to the ground. Deck knocked Frank's sword from his hand as he put his forearm to Frank's throat. Deck put one knee on Frank's chest and held down Frank's right wrist with his foot as his left arm held Frank's left arm down.

"Would you call that acting instead of reacting?" Deck asked as he caught his breath.

Frank didn't blink, his gaze on Deck like a cobra eyeing its victim. Deck tried to calm his breathing as he held Frank down, waiting for him to make another move. An infectious smile crept onto Frank's taut face, relaxing his muscles as he started to laugh aloud. Deck couldn't help himself, so he joined in, causing him to breathe irregularly again. Deck relieved the pressure of his heel and hands as he removed his forearm from Frank's throat. Deck stood up and offered a hand to Frank.

"I would say that counts as acting. You're actually learning, aren't you?" Frank said between each chuckle. "Good."

"I am definitely trying," Deck said. "Frank, can I ask a favor of you?"

He walked over to his sword and picked it up. "Sure, what is it?"

"Well, I have been training with you for a little while, and I wanted to ask you something."

Frank slid the sword into its scabbard. "Well, what is it?"

"My brother, I know he isn't a Brighter, but he wants to join the Keepers," Deck said as he rubbed my neck.

Frank paused and pursed his lips. "Deck, you know the rules."

"Yeah, but I wanted to ask. I thought you could make an exception since he's my brother. He really wants to help us. He thinks he could be of good use."

Frank shook his head and turned to walk away. Deck ran after him as he fumbled with his sword, trying to sheath it. Deck caught up to him and put his hand on Frank's shoulder. Deck was about to ask him again, reason with him to persuade him to let Drow join them. But the words were too slow, and Frank spun on his heels, grabbing Deck's wrist in a quick and fluid motion. He twisted Deck's arm, which caused him to turn himself. Deck felt his body leave the ground as Frank flipped him in a forward cartwheel. The ground came fast and hard as Deck connected with it, cracking his back in the process. Frank's knee sunk into his chest as he put his forearm on Deck's throat.

"You cannot let your guard down, Deck, even when you think everything is normal," he said.

"Okay, I get it," Deck choked out.

"Good."

Frank lifted his arm and knee with grace, standing up in an instant. He reciprocated the gesture of goodwill by reaching out his own arm to Deck.

Deck took it and asked, "So, can he?"

"It's a risk."

"I know that. I can keep him in check, though."

"Is that going to be enough?"

"Yes, it will be. Besides, we have loads of soldiers that work in the division."

"That may be true, but they do not know the true reason," Frank paused. "He would."

Deck rubbed at his neck, feeling the pain of hitting the ground run up and down his spine. He flinched and took his hand down. "He's a crack-shot, he can be on my team."

"We will have a team selected for you. We already have a sharpshooter in mind. His name is Carlo Varetto, an Italian chap. He competed in the Olympics last year."

Deck sighed, "I don't want a team selected by you, at least not everyone. I need someone I know I can trust, someone I know would give their all and do what I would."

Frank thought about that, rubbing his chin with his thumb and pointer finger. He walked a little further over to the side of the room where their effects were and bent down to grab his bag. Without standing up straight, he ruffled through it and pulled out his pipe and matches. Frank opened up the box of matches and brought the pipe to his lips as he struck the phosphorus strip with the match head. A flame burst to life at the end of the splinter of wood, burning bright with the same passion of a fleeting teenage summer romance. He puffed on the mouthpiece, coaxing the tobacco to take flame and escape this world of physical distractions.

"He is your responsibility. Whatever happens you need to be ready to take care of it, okay?"

Deck nodded. "Yes, of course. But I promise you sir, he will be extremely useful."

Frank puffed on the pipe a few more times and blew the smoke out through flared nostrils. "We'll see."

CHAPTER 28
Rendezvous

26th December, 1942
River Thames, Fulham Borough, London, England
9:30 a.m.

The sun was at our backs, hot and soothing on my aching muscles and bones. I was distracted, but my daydream wasn't enough to help me feel better about everything happening. Ever since I joined the Keepers, or I suppose drafted into being one, I've been following Frank's lead and making sure I do everything to the T. The situation in which I asked him if my brother, Woodrow, could join my team was still prominent in my mind. I was initially worried when we brought him in because he was known to be a hothead, arguing with most people who told him what to do. After a while, he mellowed out and got along with mostly everyone. I think he was taking Grandad's death quite personally and that's why he acted out.

Never mind that, I should really pay attention to what's going on right now. We should be coming up on the rendezvous soon.

"How close are we?" Gary asked.

I looked around to check the part of London we were in. Because of my daydreaming up to this point, I wasn't quite sure. The scenery changed when I wasn't paying attention, from the cold and unforgiving jungle of cement and glass to the softer embrace of color-fading grass and drowsy trees.

"We are getting closer, just up the river some more," I said.

Everything seemed quiet as we continued on westward. We followed the winding, rushing water that carved its way through the heart of London, keeping an eye out for any more magical beasts hell-bent on our destruction. Gary kept us moving at a great pace while Del was still nose-deep in the journal. When I glanced her way, I noticed she was already about halfway through the worn, thick pages of knowledge. Klaus was busy cutting away slivers of wood from a new chunk of pine, leaving notes of sap and needles wafting in the chilled air.

I pointed to the line of trees and shrubs immediately to our left. "Just up there."

"How do you know?" Gary asked.

"It's just before the bridge."

"And that means something?"

I sighed. "Trust me, I spent months crossing that bridge to the Temperate House when I was training."

Klaus gathered a pile of wood shavings in his hand and tossed it back in Gary's direction like natural confetti. "Stop asking stupid questions."

Gary snorted. "How is it a stupid question?"

Klaus glanced over his shoulder. "Because he answered, and you still doubt him. What does he gain by lying to us?"

He stammered, "I-I suppose you're right. It's not like you could be an undercover German spy trying to infiltrate us while simultaneously twisting our views on the world at large."

After Gary finished his long-winded statement, we all looked at Klaus. An awkward silence filled the air, followed by a couple coughs for good measure.

"Sorry, you're different." Gary smiled and stammered again, "B-but in a good way."

Klaus rolled his eyes and went back to whittling his pocket-sized wooden trinkets. Del returned her gaze to the journal, stifling a chuckle before it got out of control. I turned toward the front of the boat again to make sure we were headed in the right direction. Gary slowed our approach to the left bank by easing up on the throttle, letting us coast instead of being propelled.

"There," I said as I pointed. "Dock us there."

Jutting out from the overgrowth was a larger dock made of massive wooden timbers as round as car tires. A lamp at the end of the platform flickered and danced in its glass and metal cage, trying to burst free.

As we drew closer, I grabbed the rope from the hook attached to our boat's lamppost and started unraveling it in my hands. I stood up and waited until the edge of the wood was about a foot away before putting my foot out to cushion our bow from crunching to splinters.

Del peeked over the top of the journal and asked, "So, let me get this straight, you are a secret brotherhood of grown men that run around pretending to be knights in shining armor, all while hunting an evil warlock?"

I sighed and rolled my eyes, nodding to the statement.

"Yeah, Warlock Hunters. Doesn't it sound cool?" Gary said with a huge grin on his face.

I turned to Jack. "Do you have anything you'd like to add? Your thoughts on Warlock Hunters?"

He shook his head. "After what I saw back there? No sir, I'll just listen and play music."

Jack continued with a serenade of beautiful music while I thought about what they were saying. If it wasn't for the rope in my hands, I would have slapped my forehead. I leaned down to wrap the rope around the cleat that was fashioned to the top of the dock. After I did so I passed the rope back to Klaus, and he tied it off on the boat to hold us in place.

I leaned over to help Del up. "When you put it like that, it sounds kind of strange."

She took my hand. "I don't know. I think it makes it sound fun."

I shook my head and pulled on her arm to help her stand up. The shift in weight distribution from two out of four of us standing caused the boat to rock back and forth. Klaus steadied it by grabbing the dock's rope and trying to hold us still. I let Del get out first, followed by Klaus, Jack, and I. The lively chatter of combustion faded with a few random sporadic spikes as Gary killed the boat's engine.

"We have a mile or less from here to get to the Temperate House. I would like to say we won't have to worry about resistance between here and there, but the last few days have been more than unpredictable." I paused for a moment before continuing. "So, it's best to expect anything."

Gary climbed out of the boat and stood up next to the rest of them. "Is that limited to normal circumstances? Or should we watch out for little devils with pitchforks?"

I cleared my throat. "Like I said, keep an eye out for anything."

"Same formation as before?" Klaus asked.

I nodded. "Yes. Except I will lead, you will be behind me, then Del. Taking up the rear will be Klaus and Jack. Are you okay with that?"

"Yes, sir."

"Okay, follow me."

The group checked their weapons and loaded new bullets for the worst-case scenario. I brought out my pistol and did the same, pulling the slide back to load a new round into the chamber. Satisfied, I led the way up the set of crumbling steps to the area above. It was a husk of what the gardens once were, a painful reminder that the world has crumbled around us.

The skeletons of the slumbering trees were thick, even without their leaves, stretching their limbs to the sky. The bare bushes were so tightly knit that they worked well for concealing things, helping me put my worried nerves at ease.

"Are we sticking to the wooded areas?" Klaus asked.

I glanced around at our prospects of a stealthy approach versus blatant, in-your-face marching in plain sight. The trees would provide quite a bit of cover, but it would be hard to tell if we were going in the correct direction. I think it's safe to assume there wouldn't be much resistance on this side of the Thames because it's mostly wooded.

"We'll try to do both. Stick to the fauna as much as possible while heading in the right direction when we can," I said.

There wasn't much of a reason to run at the moment, so we decided on a brisk walk, fast enough for it to go quickly but slow enough to pay attention to everything around us. As I decided, I was on point in the front while the other members of my makeshift team followed as we made our way.

To the right of us was an open field for rugby, sitting dormant for the winter until the spring came again to melt away the ice and snow for another eight months. Some outlying buildings loomed over us with windows as black as night, hiding whatever may lay inside. The road we were on led to another, taking us in a direction only slightly to the right. We kept the talking to a minimum to keep the attention on us down, only whispering to each other if need be.

"Will we be free of the buildings soon? I feel like a sitting duck, waddling through to the next puddle," Gary said.

I heard Klaus ask, "Why would a duck go to a puddle? Wouldn't it want to be in a pond or something like that?"

"Yeah, yeah. Tomayto, tomahto. Small details."

"What's a tamato?" Klaus asked.

"It's a figure of speech–"Gary began.

"Basically, it means that the person likes to be difficult and says they are right regardless," Del interrupted.

I glanced back and said, "Would you guys keep it down?"

I knew Gary wanted to say something else to Klaus, but he bit his tongue. Thankfully Klaus kept his mouth shut, too; there certainly was no time to waste on bickering about a dammed tomato. We reached a path that cut into the heart of the Kew Gardens, leading to the Palm House, a short walk away from the Temperate House. When we approached the Palm House, a few gasps of amazement left their lips as they took in the sight.

"That's nothing compared to the Temperate House. They both hold beautiful things, though. Amazing it is," I said.

I cut the amusement short and led the group to the south-west on a path that connected the two greenhouses. We kept up a decent pace once again as we navigated the snow and ice-covered ground that lay before us. Before we approached the path that led us from the road to the Palm House, I activated Thomas's very useful spikes for extra traction so that I wouldn't fall flat on my face the first chance I had.

Sorry guys, on your own, I suppose.

"I wish I had some of those. I bet they come in handy quite a bit," Gary said, eying my boots.

"Depending on who made it out of the church in time, you may get your own pair," I said.

After the words left my mouth, I felt a pang of guilt. It was sharp and deep, knowing that I left my team and friends to fend for themselves when we were attacked. I hope to God that they all made it out: Frank, Eileen, and Thomas. I hope my brother made it out. I always said I would keep him from trouble.

I'm sure they made it. Don't fret now, Deck. We haven't even made it to the Kew. For all you know, they'll be waiting for you, just to give you crap for taking so long to get there.

I looked up at the Palm House, rust-tainted white-clad steel in a winter not-so-wonderland. The glass panes would usually be frosted over from condensation of the warmer climate held inside but for some reason, they weren't. Usually, the thick, lush greenery made it hard to see more than five feet in front of you at whatever point you looked in from the outside perimeter. Instead, the vast space was desolate and empty, showing signs of long-forgotten life now wilted to piles of black decay and rot.

"Aren't there supposed to be plants?" Del asked.

"Yeah, there are," I murmured. "The things we destroy in pursuit of our goals."

"This isn't it, is it?"

I backpedaled and turned to head down the path as I shook my head. "No, but it's got me concerned now."

Why would Nikola let this happen to a greenhouse so close to him? Was the rendezvous compromised?

"Just to be safe, we should watch the treeline and check any spots that someone could be hiding behind," I said.

My concern found its way to my feet and pushed them to move faster. It mingled with the slight hope and excitement of seeing my friends again, hopefully safe and sound. It meant we would be one step closer to stopping Jakobus with the help of not only one extra descendant but two, not counting Del and Jack. Their willingness to help was invaluable in times like these.

The area in front of us opened into a larger field with the Temperate House to the left of us, standing tall with pride and dignity. Memories flashed in my head of this place, not only mine but from me grandad as well. I saw the sky shift from a gloomy gray to a deep purple as stars were splattered across it, painting a picture of another lifetime. Through my grandad's eyes, I saw the monumental steel structure lit up in a magnificent glow of gold that radiated from the thousands of glass windowpanes. The next second it switched back to now, tearing me from the bliss I didn't know I needed.

"This is the Temperate House," I said.

I ascended the stairs in front of the greenhouse as the rest of my team followed behind me. The steel stood out in the cold London day, hints of rust peaking through the paint. Some spots were only slightly affected by the oxidation, while others were mocking us as they streaked down in large lines of time.

"What happened to this place?" Klaus asked.

I sighed. "Time. Time and neglect as the world around you crumbles."

"A shame, really. I would have loved to see it in its prime," Del said.

"It was something," I said.

The top of the stairs revealed news I feared. News that could mean life or death for so many people. Like the Palm House, all the plants seemed to have died off. The once great greenhouse filled with plants from around the world was just a graveyard for the shells of what used to be a vibrant place.

"Everyone, stay on the lookout. I'm not sure what's going on here. I would have thought Nikola would keep the plants alive," I said.

"Could it be to keep attention away from him? Or here, rather?" Del asked.

I mulled it over, "I mean, sure, he could have decided that. But that's history he let die. How can one do that?"

"People often let things die when they don't think they mean much or hold any real specific value to society," Klaus said.

Gary gave him a concerned look. "Damn, man, that's pretty deep. You okay?"

Klaus waved his hand in a dismissive motion and continued to walk. Del passed them all and stopped next to me. "Did you have a favorite plant here when it was still as amazing as you make it sound?"

"There were so many plants from around the world. Flowers too. I didn't really have one, but me grandad's favorite was one called birds of paradise."

"Shame," she said.

I didn't give much of a response other than a sigh, not really knowing what to say. It's concerning that everything is dead, but that may be the point. For all I know, Nikola let this happen to draw attention away from what really lay beneath. I shrugged and brought my pistol up, ready to fire at a moment's notice.

You know, just in case a German or cat jumps out, and I need something to shoot at.

I approached the entrance where there used to be a set of large wooden doors. Now, all that stood there was the metal frame that split the entrance and exit sides. With caution, I peeked my head inside, starting with the left and turning my head right to get a look at everything the vast greenhouse had to offer. Besides the lack of green, this house seemed clear of anything that would cause harm to us, so I entered with an air of caution weighing heavily in my mind. The heart-wrenching lack of plants made me miss the days before the war even more, sparking memories of mostly good times. Mostly.

"Now what?" Gary asked.

Without turning, I shushed him, "Could you try and be a little quieter?"

"Oh, sorry," he whispered. "Now what?"

If I hadn't gotten used to him, he would seriously annoy me.

"We will be heading to the right into the smaller greenhouse that's attached to this one," I said.

Out of habit, I followed the path to the middle of the room and took a sharp right. We followed the same path to the junction point of the two houses, gear and guns rattling and shaking in the silence. I tried holding my buckles and sword tight to my body but was only rewarded with an annoying reminder we were walking keyrings.

We reached the spiral staircase that went up to the second level, which consisted of catwalks and balconies. I stopped next to it and motioned to the rest of my group to follow my lead. I looked around once more to make sure we were the only ones there, scanning for movement or life. From what I could tell we were relatively safe to continue, hopefully.

"Okay, what now?" Gary whispered.

I was going to get angry with him, but I realized he actually whispered this time. I turned to them and said, "Magic."

I received mixed expressions in the way of everyone raising their eyebrows in question. As I turned back to the staircase, I chuckled and shook my head. My foot hit the bottom step instead of sliding underneath, reminding me I still had the spikes sticking out of the soles of my boots. Doing that made me feel like an amateur, so instead of looking at them to see if they noticed, I just played it off like I did it on purpose. I slapped my right boot against the left to retract them, making the metal spikes slide back into place. After that, I then put my foot underneath the first step to feel for the pressure plate to activate the trap door.

"What are you doing? Tap dancing?" Del asked.

I dismissed the question. "Just watch."

A few more random taps with my boot were eventually rewarded with a click, followed by a gentle shake of the floor beneath our feet. The bricks underneath the staircase moved and shuffled as a space opened up beneath, revealing the steps to continue below the main level.

"So let me get this straight," Gary said. "We are walking into the darkness down a set of rickety metal steps?"

I sucked on my teeth. "Uh yeah. Why not?"

He shrugged. "No matter. Let's just get this over with."

"Jack, you've been pretty quiet back there. What do you think?" I asked.

"Random staircases that lead into nothing?" he asked. "My kind of crazy."

"Okay, seems like we are all ready," I said.

With that, I reached up, clicked on my spotter, and took the first step down to the lower levels.

Just as before, I feel like this will be it. Honestly, I don't know if I can handle the stress of feeling like I won't survive the next five minutes.

What was I just thinking about? Hope? Oh yeah, the last time she and I went on a date. It was an early fall afternoon with the sun set high in the deep blue sky. The leaves raced around our legs and circled in the wind in random patterns, enjoying the new-found freedom before the long slumber of a dark winter. We stopped in the market to get something warm to drink, enjoying the changing colors that riddled the treetops. It was a simple afternoon of bliss, enjoying the slowness that accompanies normalcy in a regular life. What I would give to have that once again.

Chapter 29
Reunion

10:30 a.m.

The spotter lit up the wall in front of me without adding any clarity to the rest of the staircase. The only issue I ever had with the things was their lack of coverage. Don't get me wrong, they came in mighty handy when you needed to see what was ahead of you, but they weren't as all-encompassing as the old Embyrs the Sparkers carried.

In retrospect, the first dozen years after Nikola created TEA were the golden years of technological advancements. They sent Great Britain rocketing past the rest of the world in terms of inventions that improved the way of life, among other things.

It felt like it took months to descend the staircase to the meeting room. My mind was racing with thoughts of joy, happiness, pain, and of course, a little thing called dread. Up to this point, I was so focused on getting Gary, Klaus, and I here that I really didn't think about what to expect. I entertained the nightmares of bad news a few times, as well as a few bleak daydreams of everyone making it here alive. That was the point, though. The less I thought about it, the less time I had to worry.

My foot hit the stone, changing the repetitious hollow noise of sole on metal to a more solid sound. It snapped me out of my spiraling thoughts of despair and brought my attention to the spacious meeting room that opened up before us. It looked like it did years ago, sans the lively chatter of new acquaintances and wishful thinking. The closest half was lit by the first chandelier while the last two hung dormant on their chains. It shed bright light in the immediate vicinity of us, the staircase, and the bookshelf.

Del whistled. "So many books. I could spend months reading every single word they held."

I glanced at the bookcase. "I spent quite a bit of time here years back. I barely even made a dent in them."

"I was wondering when I would see you here," said a voice.

I whirled and lifted my pistol to the firing position in the direction of the voice. The hammer clicked as I pulled it back with my thumb, followed by the ruckus of the other guns doing the same. I scanned the room, looking for the source of the voice as my heart was forced from my chest.

"Woah there, son," the voice said again.

A speck of orange floated through the dark shadows in the corner of the room. It rose by about an inch and turned a bright cherry red, crackling as it changed colors. I exchanged looks with my team, checking to see what they thought. Gary and Del had their rifles up to their faces, leveled and motionless at the target. Klaus had the shotgun braced against his shoulder, aimed in the general direction. I wasn't sure how, but Jack had acquired a few arrows on the way here, three nocked in the string of his bow, each ready and eager to find their target.

"We all have you in our crosshairs. Walk slowly into the light," I said. "Now!"

The orange dot crackled as it turned bright red once more. "Okay, just don't shoot me."

A plume of gray smoke migrated from the shadows, spreading out in a cloud as it turned to touch the ceiling. A man's leg followed my directions, planting firmly on the floor in front of it.

"Now the rest of you!" I yelled.

"Okay, okay. Still have to work on your patience, I see," said the man.

After another moment, the man finally emerged from the shadows, smoke billowing around him as he took the pipe from his mouth. In my anger, frustration, and worry-frenzied state, I realized who was standing in front of me.

Why didn't I recognize his voice? How could I have overlooked it?

"Lower your guns, everyone. He's one of us." I turned to Jack and shook my head. "And bow."

It took a second, but everyone listened to me and lowered their weapons. They all flicked the safeties on their guns as Jack let the string of his bow slack and then released the energy that he had built up by holding it back.

"Everyone, this is Frank. He's the head of The Keepers," I said.

Everyone's posture relaxed slightly, tension easing with some good news for once. I shook my head and holstered my pistol before walking toward him with my hand outstretched for a shake. Instead of taking it, Frank brought me in for a big bear hug. He squeezed me momentarily before letting me go to catch my breath.

He held my upper arms and said, "I'm glad you made it out, especially with everyone."

"It was hard, but we made it here," I said. "I'm happy to see you made it too."

Frank looked at the two extra people standing behind me. "I see you picked up a few more people along the way here?"

I glanced back. "Honestly, they kind of helped us get here."

"That's great. The more to lend a helping hand, the better. I do like that man's enthusiasm, though," Frank said as he looked at Jack. "With the bow and sword, and what is that? Is that a bag-pipe?"

"Yessir, it is," Jack said.

"Marvelous, and who might this young lady be?"

"My name is Madeleine. But you can call me Del for short," Del said.

"Nice to meet the both of you. We can continue the introductions and backstories soon enough," Frank said, pausing to take another pull of his pipe. "When we get to the relative safety of the rest of the safehouse."

"Fair enough. I'll let you lead the way then, Frank," I said.

He nodded and turned toward the dark shadows from whence he was standing. Gary, Del, and Klaus slid their guns onto their backs via sling while Jack hooked the string of his bow on his quiver. My spotter lit up the dark side of the room as Frank led us across it to the far-left side next to the bookcase.

"What's next? You're going to pull a book, and a secret door will open?" Del asked.

Frank turned to her, a smile spread wide across his face. He held the pipe with his teeth as he chuckled, smoke escaping his lungs in choppy bursts from his mouth like a dragon.

By God, is it good to see him again.

Frank took his pipe in his hands from his mouth, "We aren't that predictable, are we?"

"I would say a little bit, but I haven't seen what you're about to do."

Frank smiled once more and turned to the bookcase. "Often, the best way to keep people guessing is to do the obvious. The thing they would expect to be too simple to actually have been done."

Frank motioned for some light, so I took my spotter off my haversack strap and held it up to illuminate the bookcase in front of him. It was large, made of dark stained oak, with five shelves filled to the brim with scores of books. Some were larger than others, while some were vibrant in color and thick in width. His fingers fluttered over a few different spines of the middle shelf before he made a 'tsk' with his mouth. He did the same with the shelf second to the top before stopping on a red-bound book. The gold lettering on the side reflected the light in my direction, making me chuckle in recognition.

"You can't be serious," I said.

Frank grabbed the top with his index finger. "What?"

"Is that the same copy?"

He pulled it out, making the top of the book tip in our direction. A click followed this action, and he replaced it into its original position, "Treasure Island. It is. Thomas's grandfather donated it to our library some forty years ago. He said it was your grandad's favorite?"

"It is. He told me he read that same copy about a thousand times." I paused and thought. "I remember quite a few of those times as if they were my own."

"Ah, yes. One of the strange things that happen when you get your artifacts. It certainly takes someone with the will of iron to keep everything straight," Frank whispered to me.

"So, we see you are predictable. Now what?" Del asked. "Is the bookcase going to slide to the right to reveal another set of stairs?"

Frank glanced at me and chuckled. "I think we should probably work on our security measures. They might be too easy to figure out."

I grabbed the bookcase on the left and began pushing it to the right. It resisted at first, but eventually surrendered and slid, bottom scraping on the floor with a dry and scratchy noise. As we pushed it out of the way, my spotter lit up another set of stairs that led down even further.

I glanced at Del. "Probably should."

Frank laughed and lifted his arm to gesture towards the stairs. "Go ahead, Deck, show them down. I will make sure the entrance is shut behind us."

I shrugged and began to descend the steps. Just inside the opening was a button that popped with a satisfying auditory response as I pressed it. Lights flickered above our heads, giving us enough light, so we no longer required my spotter.

This set of stairs was a straight shot down instead of the spiraling set we entered with. It was quick work to reach the bottom, with little to see on the way down. The walls were plain and mundane, made of traditional red brick and tan mortar. The Tesla Bulbs hung from single wire fixtures, spaced evenly along the way at three-foot intervals. The rhythmic echo of everyone's boots clanging against the metal steps brought up even more memories of dancing, of the times I went with Hope.

Hope. I wish things were different right now. I wish they were like the times we shared before the war. Before me grandad passed away. The wonderful and beautiful nights we spent together, discovering what life was all about.

The cacophony of voices began to drown out my thoughts and memories of past times. I could pick out random words and phrases from the ruckus ahead of us. The things that stuck out were a word or two here about Germans having issues holding checkpoints against resistance soldiers or small bits of conversation about how many people made it out alive.

Out alive? Do they mean how many people made it out alive from the attack?

"Deck, hold on for a second. I should probably be the one in front now," Frank said.

All of us collected at the bottom of the stairs and allowed Frank to get in front. The pungent stench of his pipe smoke filled our confined space. I pinched my nostrils as we waited for him to open the door in front of us. Frank took the pipe from his lips and tapped the bowl against the brick wall next to him, causing sparks to fly from the impact. Embers cascaded from it, falling in streams of burning tobacco to the ground next to my feet. I lifted my boot and put the sole on the floor, grinding the burning strands to put them out.

"Thanks," Frank said.

He reached for the handle and turned it, opening the door and walking through. I followed right on his heels and braced myself for anything. The first thing I heard was the voices before we entered, and they were definitely ones I recognized, but I wasn't sure who else could have made it.

I would love to say I had the confidence I usually portray, but I was scared out of my wits.

The rendezvous was laid out the same way our previous headquarters was, for the most part. A few minor things were different, nothing too extravagant. Among them was that we had a training center that could accommodate a few different fighting styles. As I mentioned earlier, there was a room used chiefly for sword fighting and learning how to defend oneself in the ancient ways of blade and shield. Another room was devoted to practicing marksmanship, both long distance with a rifle to close range with a pistol or shotgun. The last change was that it was double in size, able to house at least three hundred plus soldiers if needed.

"This is The Keepers, Kew Gardens Training Division," Frank said.

I glanced back at my makeshift crew to see what they thought. Del seemed surprised, mouth agape, and turned up on one end. Gary smiled like a schoolgirl on boxing day, all wide-eyed and excited. Klaus was stoic like always but softer around the edges than the other day. Jack didn't have much reaction either, but he didn't seem bored by any means either.

He's still somewhat of a wildcard. I don't recognize him, and Frank doesn't seem to, either. I'll have to chat with Records to see if he checks out.

My attention was pulled away from them when two hands grabbed my biceps. I panicked momentarily, my nerves still relatively high from the last few days.

"Deckard! You made it out of there!" said the man.

I looked at his face and smiled, worry changing to recognition. "Thomas! You crazy bastard!"

"The one and only! How's the gear holding up?"

"Great, everything is in working order. I have to thank you for the boots, though. They have definitely proven useful."

"Good! I'm glad they have."

"By the way, do you have any more of those nets? I used them before we left the headquarters. They were pretty cool."

We were interrupted by a comforting feminine voice. "He can get you more toys later. First, we need to see if you or anyone else has any life-threatening injuries."

Thomas let go of me, allowing me to look in the direction of the voice. Eileen appeared in my view, beautiful and breathtaking as always. Her flowing brown hair was certainly a sight for sore eyes, even if it usually meant some painful medical treatment.

"Eileen! You made it too!" I said.

She smiled and came in close for a hug. We held it for a moment, short enough to be professional and long enough to show appreciation and love for someone we cared for. I winced from the pain of my shoulder, remembering that I was torn into not a few hours ago. We broke contact, and she took a few steps back, taking in my disheveled appearance.

She walked around me and poked and prodded at my shoulder. "What happened to you?"

I chuckled. "That is something that may be hard to believe."

"No matter. They have a mender here that we can use to make you good as new."

"Can it wait?" I asked. "We need to have a debrief of everything that's happened the last two days. I have seen a lot and found a few important things for everyone to hear."

She shook her head and frowned. "We can do both. You just have to stop being such a baby about it."

"Sure, we can," I said. "Speaking of everyone, where's Woodrow?"

I looked around at everyone in the large expanse of the room. Then I realized I didn't hear his voice arguing with anyone else's. It struck me that he wasn't the first to come to greet us or wasn't on Thomas's heels complaining about being referred to by his full name.

I looked at Eileen and Thomas, "Where's Woodrow? How come he isn't over here yet?"

They both stayed silent and looked somewhere other than my face. I started to get worried, fear bubbling to the surface. My eyes darted around frantically again, hoping he was playing a trick on me and hiding. To jump out when I least expect it and scare the boots off me.

I looked at Frank as my heart pounded in my chest, feral and hectic. He looked me in the eyes, a frown overshadowing his face's usual smile. Frank shook his head and looked as if he was going to say something but stopped just beforehand and turned to the other two.

"Frank. Where's Woodrow?"

My heart just about had it. Did everything I worry about actually come true?

I walked up to Frank and grabbed his shoulders. "Frank. Where. Is. Woodrow?"

He stayed silent. Thomas stayed silent. Eileen shrunk away. My fear, fluid and cold, ignited to fury. I shook his shoulders as I yelled again. I couldn't help myself. I couldn't keep myself from lashing out. In my blind rage, I pushed Frank across the room, causing him to trip over a chair and fall to the ground. All I wanted was for Woodrow to be there. That's the only thing I could think about. I lost control of myself as I drew Excalibur, not caring who I hurt as long as I was told what happened. I could hear everyone yell at me in my daze, voices barely breaching the fog of fury I was now swimming in.

"Deck, what are you doing?" Thomas asked.

"No, stop!" Eileen yelled.

More pleas for me to stop inched their way into my mind. I felt myself push back against them to clear them from my head.

I didn't care what they said. I couldn't. All I needed to do was keep Woodrow safe and keep him well. It was a promise I wanted to keep, something our mum needed me to do.

As I was about to start my mindless rampage, I felt a pain shoot up my arm from the wrist of my hand that held Excalibur. It was electric, shocking my tendons and muscles, jolting me, and causing tremendous agony. I felt my fingers uncurl from around its hilt, making the pain lessen as it left my hand.

An intense, deafening clang pierced my hazy mind as the sword rattled to a stop on the floor. The congestion of awful thoughts immediately cleared with the sound of metal on stone. Everyone's pleas made it through to me, making me realize what I was doing.

What am I doing? This isn't who I am, and this surely isn't what Woodrow would want.

I collapsed to the floor, hitting my knees violently. The world felt heavy as I kneeled there, thinking about what was happening around me.

Is this how Atlas felt as he held the world on his shoulders, alone?

Tears started to form and stream down my cheeks like rivers and onto my hands. I looked up and saw Frank kneeling beside me, hand on my shoulder. I felt ashamed for lashing out like that, for trying to hurt someone.

"It's—"Frank began to say, "it'll be okay."

I struggled to look at him as I held back tears. "Frank, what happened to Drow?"

Chapter 30
Group Effort

25th December, 1942
Hackney Borough, London, England
1:15 p.m.

The ground shook and Frank tried to steady himself as Deckard, Gary, and, Klaus left him to collect their things to escape. Frank then looked around the room, watching everyone rush to grab their gear and weapons. Eileen, Thomas, and Woodrow were the three people he needed to make sure he got to safety. The Keepers had contingency plans set in place for this very kind of situation. One individual, usually a higher-ranking officer, would ensure they knew where their three specified people were at a given time. They were in charge of their safety in the event of an ambush, attack, or separation.

Frank squinted to see if he could make any of them out in the crowd, struggling to look at faces as they moved with haste. He wanted to help everyone but realized he couldn't, that they all already had someone to keep an eye on them. It still didn't make ignoring them any easier to do by any means. In fact, it made it weigh heavier in his mind.

He spotted Woodrow across the room to the left, ushering people past him as he looked around frantically. Drow was helping who he could by telling them where to go to leave through the escape tunnels. Frank looked around for any sign of Thomas or Eileen, hoping they would be just as easy to find.

"Frank!" Eileen yelled.

As Frank turned in the direction of Eileen's voice, he saw her jog up to him. When she reached him, he could see she was breathing heavy and ragged, concern and panic plastered across her face in the form of a frown and knitted brows.

"Frank, we need to leave," Eileen said.

Alarm sequences blared through the speaker system around the bunker as they tried talking. The noise did its best to interrupt them whenever possible, causing issues for fun.

"We need to get Thomas and Woodrow before we leave," Frank said. He pointed to Drow in front of them in the middle of the rushing soldiers. "You go get Drow while I get Thomas. After you get him, meet me at tunnel entrance B12."

"Okay, I will," Eileen said. "Be careful."

She looked at Frank for a second, almost as if she wanted to do something. She decided against whatever she was thinking and turned to leave.

"Wait," Frank said.

Eileen turned back to Frank as he walked toward her. He took her hand, drew her close, and wrapped his arms around her. Frank bent his neck down, and their lips connected. They kissed like it could not only be their first time but also like it would be their last. The smoke and alarms felt like they were a million miles away at that moment, time slowing to a crawl as they embraced each other. They pulled away from one another, remembering they were on a literal battlefield.

He looked at her, staring deep into her eyes. They held that as he said, "I will. You do the same."

She took off toward Drow, weaving between other soldiers and personnel as they rushed by. Frank watched her as she went, wishing he could have done that sooner than he did.

Frank shook his head and looked around for Thomas as everything fell apart around him. He looked to the left and saw Deck, Gary, and the prisoner approach the headquarters' main entrance. The ground shook as the doors in front of Deck, and the other two blew inward, sending them sprawling to the ground. The blast was lessened at this distance, but Frank had to steady himself. He saw Deck dodge and roll as the German soldiers entered through the smoke of what used to be the main entrance.

Deck finally got to his feet and sprinted to the armory where Thomas most likely was. Frank looked around for something to use as a weapon, anything to help suppress the Germans, as he made his way to Thomas and the others. In the red light, a sparkle out of the corner of his eye caught his attention, making him turn to one of the desks in front of him near the railing.

Frank jogged to it and picked it up. "Thank God for soldiers that forget to put their rifles away."

Machine gun fire caught his attention, putting him on edge again as it tore him from his small piece of excitement. He crouched as his eyes snapped toward the armory where the gunfire was coming from. Streaks of azure raced in bursts at the Germans, most meeting their targets with ease.

The firing stopped momentarily, giving the opposing soldiers a chance to return fire. A pulsing red glow lit up the space behind the counter to the armory for a moment or two just before Deck stood up with the glowing mass in his hand. He threw it at the soldiers that drew closer to them, tendrils splitting from the mass. They turned from bright red to a blinding blue-white and spun around as it flew in their direction. It hit with force and wrapped around them, sending electricity coursing through their bodies at thousands of volts at a time.

Frank chuckled. "Thomas certainly comes up with the most ridiculous things."

Frank stood up and ran in their direction, deciding it was safe enough to do so. As he drew close, he saw Deck, Gary, and the prisoner enter through an escape tunnel in the back of the armory. He tried to reach them in time to wish them luck but needed to be faster. As Frank reached Thomas at the counter, the door slid shut with a clunk.

"Damn," Frank said.

"Glad you're alive," Thomas said.

Frank turned to him. "Thanks, same to you. We should probably leave now."

"Yeah, you're right. It would be nice to keep it that way."

They both picked up what they could for gear while they had a moment of cease-fire. Thomas grabbed his light machine gun and a haversack tucked underneath the counter while Frank snatched two more bags hanging on the wall to the right of them. Just as they finished collecting what they could, bullets resumed flying in their direction. They flew dangerously close to them, missing by mere centimeters as they dug into the cement walls. They both ducked behind the counter again, taking cover to not get shot.

"Have any more of the doohickies that Deck threw?" Frank asked.

Thomas smiled with an ear-to-ear grin. "Of course I do."

He lifted his shirt and unhooked a small metal sphere on the end of a short three-inch chain. Thomas tossed it to Frank, slow enough for him to catch it with ease.

"This is it?" he asked.

"Yup, just press the red button and throw it," Thomas replied.

Frank pressed the button that initiated the priming sequence for the device, triggering the same red strobing light he saw earlier. It started slow and grew in speed as each second ticked by, warning him of an explosion waiting to happen. Frank stood up and scanned the area before him to ensure he had a target close enough to hit. He saw five German soldiers rise from their positions to sprint in their direction, causing panic to wash over him.

When they were about thirty feet away, he tossed the device with as much precision he could muster with the strength he put into the throw, arcing it high into the air. A few feet from his hand, the electrified net expanded and wrapped itself around the closest soldier and causing him to topple back into the other four.

"This thing is great!" Frank yelled.

"Yeah, they are," Thomas said as he grabbed Frank by the shoulder. "You'll have more things to try out when we get out of here."

The two turned and ran to their designated exit, grabbing their supplies as they left. Most of the headquarters was vacated at this point, giving them more room to escape, making it easier to find Eileen. Woodrow and Eileen were helping the last few people to their exits as Frank and Thomas jogged up to her.

"You both made it. Good," she said.

Eileen's eyes met Frank's, holding the stare longer than needed. Woodrow cleared his throat and said, "Some other time, you two can work through your feelings. Now is not the time."

Frank nodded and tossed a haversack to Drow as Eileen blushed, her rosy-red cheeks shining through the scarlet light that still bathed them. Drow leaned his rifle against the wall as he slid the haversack over his shoulders. Bullets ricocheted off the support column next to them as Drow reached for his rifle, prompting a quick retreat without much more argument or fuss. Eileen, Drow, and Thomas jogged through the doorway with Frank behind them. As they crossed the threshold, he slapped the button on the way to shut the door behind them.

Dim light from Tesla Bulbs pulsed with the excess energy flowing through the air as they moved with haste down the corridor. The shouts from the German soldiers were muffled from a distance, and the solid metal reinforced door separated them, giving a false sense of security that would soon be nonexistent.

The group followed the cold and damp corridors infested with rats, mice, and other animals that could or could not have been a mystery to humankind. After they reached a certain point, it was quiet for the next twenty or thirty minutes. Eventually, Frank was the first to break the silence.

"Everyone make it out of there, okay?" Frank asked, breathing heavily as he ushered the group along.

"As far as we know," Eileen said. "It was a mess in there."

"And the self-destruct sequences on the equipment? Are you sure it will all work?" Frank asked.

"Of course it did. I designed it myself," Thomas said.

"Uh, Frank, which way do we go?" Drow asked.

Ahead of the group was a four-way intersection with the left-most door closed, barred, and locked. The middle door was blocked by wood, stone, and other debris, while the right was open and led to a set of stairs.

"To the right," Frank said.

"Are you sure?" Drow asked.

"Yes, but the door in the middle shouldn't be covered with debris. Be careful, Woodrow. Anybody could be around that corner."

Drow took the door to the right, caution front a foremost in his mind. He pulled up his rifle and readied the electrical charge for a shot. Eileen, Thomas, and Frank followed behind as Drow ascended the staircase. The light faded as they reached halfway, now only having the glow of the charged rifle to show their way.

They reached the top without incident as Drow began to open the door, peaking through the crack and scanning the room at the top. It was large and well-furnished with comfortable-looking couches, chairs, and decorative Persian rugs.

"What is this place?" Drow asked.

They all filed into the room, allowing Frank to enter and take a look for himself. He quickly glanced around for anything that seemed out of place. Anything that could tell him if the place was disturbed by someone that wasn't supposed to be there.

"It's a safehouse. One of many spread throughout the city," Frank said.

Frank turned and closed the door behind them, locking it with the deadbolt. He then grabbed a wooden kitchen chair and propped it underneath the doorknob to keep anyone from entering through the tunnels they had just left.

Drow took a few more steps into the middle of the room. "Will it be safe enough for us to wait out the siege the Germans are laying waste to our old headquarters?"

"It may be, but we would have to have a lookout while the others try and rest a little bit. It will be a long and treacherous journey to the Kew," Frank said.

Drow walked over to a window and pressed himself against the wall. He peeled the curtain back and peeked outside, seeing if any of the Germans had patrols scouring the area for anyone who made it out of the attack.

"I can be the one to keep watch. You guys should try and get some rest," Drow said.

"Okay, just make sure to wake Thomas or me to take your place after a few hours," Frank said.

"Will do. At some point, I want to take a look around outside. Just to see if there is anything useful for us to take with us or if there is any way I can deter any Germans from finding us while most of us sleep," Drow said.

Frank nodded. "Just be careful."

CHAPTER 31
The Test, Once More

26th December, 1942
Kew Gardens, Richmond Borough, London, England
11:00 a.m.

Silence filled the air after Frank stopped talking. I still couldn't understand why this happened and how they couldn't stop it. Even though I knew what happened to the others when they were split up, it still didn't make things any better than they were.

I stood up, struggling to keep my balance as my body was on autopilot and my mind was elsewhere. Frank walked over to me with Excalibur in his hands. He lifted the sword up for me to take, face still dark with shame and guilt.

"What happened then?" I asked. "That doesn't answer my question."

Frank cleared his throat. "We all awoke after about five hours. I knew something was amiss because Drow had never woken either of us to take his place."

I walked away from them and began to pace.

My greatest fear was coming true. I should have just brought him with us.

"It was his rifle I saw, then," I said, voice distant and distraught.

"What?" Frank asked.

"It was his rifle. I saw Drow's rifle at the German compound," I said.

Frank and Thomas exchanged glances. "What do you mean, German compound?"

I shook my head and rubbed at my neck.

"We infiltrated the German compound in Parliament. That's where we found Del," Klaus said.

"Where I saved you," she interrupted. "If you want to be exact, that is."

"Yes, she saved us," Klaus said.

I ignored what Klaus said, focusing on one thing. At this point, it felt like nothing else mattered in this world or any other. I needed to find Drow. I needed to find my brother.

I looked back at Frank with the need to know more. Anything that could help us find him. "After?"

"We looked for him. We looked for as long as possible without getting caught by the enemy." Frank said.

I need to calm down. Getting angry with them will not help nor bring Drow back to us. They must have him alive. I mean, why wouldn't they? He would be spouting off about how his brother was a round table knight and that I would rain hellfire down upon them.

"He must be at Parliament. He must be," I said.

"Well, then, we need a plan. If Drow is there, and so is Jakobus, then we may be able to take him out while rescuing Drow in one fell swoop." Frank said.

I stopped pacing and looked at Frank, "What do you have in mind?"

"Well, after we looked for Drow and came up empty-handed, we had a run-in with a group of people," he said.

"Who?" I asked.

"It seems you weren't the only ones saved by the French."

"What do you mean?"

"We were ambushed by the group sending out the distress signal. The one you were looking for a few days back."

"The rest of my resistance fighters?" Del asked.

Frank snapped his thumb and middle finger together and said, "Bingo. They also came with us back here to the Kew. In all, there were about fifteen of them, I believe?"

"That settles it then, Deck. We will help you get your brother back," Del said.

"Thank you. But before we can do that, there are a few things we need to take care of," I said.

"What's that?" Frank asked.

I turned to him and said, "First, we need to get Gary his artifact."

"What's next after that?"

"Then we need a plan to get through their defenses and into Parliament. They are heavily fortified and most likely have things we have never seen," I said.

"Like that man you called Spike, right?" Eileen asked.

"That, among other things," I said.

"What do you mean by other things?" Thomas asked.

Jack laughed at that question. "Do you believe in monsters?"

Thomas shifted uncomfortably on his feet. "Like how all men have monsters in them?"

That response made Jack laugh more. "No, by monsters, I mean ones with wings, fur, and gnashing fangs."

The room stayed quiet for a moment before I spoke, "We've seen some crazy things on the way here. Eileen, by the way, were you able to find anything out about that blood sample I gave you?"

"I did," she said. "It's not blood."

"What do you mean?" I asked.

"Or at least it isn't anymore. Whatever it is, there are remnants of what used to be alive, but it seems it's from more than one deceased being."

"But he was moving, running, and spitting balls of fire at me. How was he not alive?" I asked.

She shrugged. "Your guess is better than mine."

I shook my head. "I mean, we have seen a Manticore and a Griffon."

"A what and a what?" Eileen asked, eyes wide.

"You can tell us more about these monsters you have seen after we get Gary tested," Frank said. "Jack, you can go with Thomas and help him with supplies and weapons."

"Alright, sir, I can do that," Jack said.

"Good, Del, you can go with Eileen, and she will bring you to your agents. You can go over things with them. We would be entirely grateful if you help us."

"I can do that. We wouldn't want to miss an opportunity to take down a key member of the Reich," Del said.

Frank nodded. "Deck, bring Klaus and Gary with us. We need to test Gary and find his artifact. Better if we have another knight on board to help."

Gary turned to me, face stricken with fear and surprise. "Why would we need another knight to help?"

I laughed and said, "Oh, no reason. It's just sometimes the process doesn't work correctly."

Klaus chimed in, "I fainted when I touched mine."

"Is that what you meant, Deck?" Gary asked.

"No." I laughed again. "Another descendant that tried their artifact ended up going crazy."

Gary gulped hard and started to sweat profusely. It dripped down the side of his forehead as he shook his head. "Oh, is that all? I can handle going crazy and hitting my head as I faint."

I slapped him on the shoulder. "Attaboy. We knew you could handle it."

We all followed Frank to the small conference room in the back. As I said before, the layout of the underground headquarters of the Kew was quite similar to the one we had underneath St. Bartholomew's but on a much larger scale. There was so much more space to expand because there were no restrictions of other buildings and their structural integrity of having a solid foundation. The double doors to the conference room were propped open, revealing Frank already taking items out of the trunk and placing them on the massive round table.

I walked into the room and peered at the table. "Frank, is this the same table from St. Bart's?"

He finished placing the last item on the table and turned to me. "It must be. There wasn't a table here before."

It will never cease to amaze me the things that happen. From all-powerful swords and flying mythical creatures to magic artifacts and mysterious appearing tables.

The items were all laid out on the table, nine in total, with no chair in front. The plan must be to just go down the line as quickly as possible.

"Gary, go ahead. No sense in drawing it out," I said.

Gary gulped hard again as he wiped at his brow. He rubbed his hands together, trying to delay the inevitable. He inched up to the table, carefulness the main thing on his mind.

"Go on, the artifacts won't bite," Frank said.

Gary scoffed, "Yeah, but they could send me into a coma."

"You'll never know unless you try," Klaus said.

Gary sighed and looked at the far most left item on the table. It was the dagger that Klaus first tried a few days ago. It felt like thirteen minutes before he finally placed his hand on it with haste.

We all waited. We waited in silence and curiosity, wondering if the first object would be the right one.

"I don't believe it is that one," Frank said.

Frank's voice scared Gary and caused him to jump. He must have launched himself three feet into the air. As he fell back to the ground, he put his hands out to catch himself with the edge of the table. The right hand landed between two artifacts, while the left landed on the rosary next to the dagger.

"Convenient," I said.

"Not funny," Gary whispered.

We all waited patiently, curious to see if the rosary was correct. Time ticked by once more as we waited for something to happen. Nothing did. It was becoming apparent that it may take quite a few tries to find the right one. Gary tried three more, waiting a few seconds before going on to the next item to try and see if it was the right one.

All while this was happening, I started thinking about Drow again. I hadn't forgotten what had happened or what I was devastated about. Still, the distraction of Gary was a welcome one. It kept me occupied from overthinking the current situation and lashing out again.

I turned to Frank and asked, "When I lashed out earlier, Excalibur shocked my hand. That's what caused me to drop it. Why did it do that?"

I could hear his teeth clack against each other as he thought. "Excalibur is a holy weapon. It is meant to be used for all things good and righteous. I think that is why it shocked you and flew from your grasp. It must have sensed some ill will and wanted to prevent anything from happening,"

It knew something was happening to me. It knew this wasn't who I was or how I usually acted.

What did Jakobus say when I was near him? I had something of his he was waiting to regain for a very long time? That must be what is causing the evil thoughts and bad intentions. I only feel that way when it is on my person.

"I think I know why I have been lashing out and getting angry," I said.

"Why is that?" he asked.

"When we escaped through the tunnels, we encountered an underground study. It contained a multitude of books, trinkets, and things in jars."

"Did you find something while you were down there?" he asked.

"Yeah, I did. I saw a podium in the middle of the furthest wall, and I looked closer. On top were a letter, an inkwell, and a quill. I suspect the contents of the inkwell were old, dried blood. I think Jakobus used the room over forty years ago."

He turned to me. "So, what did you find there? What do you think could be altering how you act?"

"There was a box. A small one, about the size of a jewelry box you would have a ring in. It called to me when I first laid my eyes on it. It beckoned me to take it with us."

"Let me guess. You took it?"

I looked to the ground and felt ashamed. "Yes."

"Where is it now?" he asked.

"It's in my haversack that I left near the front. That's how I know it was Jakobus we saw at Parliament. He said I had something he was trying to retrieve for years."

Frank rubbed his chin. "We should have Thomas and Eileen take a look at it. Maybe there's something they can tell us about it."

He reached over and patted me on the shoulder. "Don't worry, Deck. Sometimes things happen for a reason. Finding this may have been a stroke of luck."

I nodded, still ashamed of what I did. Frank let go of my shoulder, which prompted me to look up. Gary was on the last artifact with his hand waiting inches above it.

"None of the others worked?" I asked.

I was so distracted by what Frank and I were talking about that I forgot what was happening in front of us.

Frank sighed. "No. I thought it would be the helmet, but that hope was quickly dashed."

"Well, we knew this could happen, especially when you're talking about chance. We still have the last one to try," I said.

I peeked around Gary and looked at the artifact to see what it was. "Is that a hairclip?" I laughed aloud when I saw it.

Gary glanced over his shoulder, "No. I think it's a brooch. It holds a cloak around your neck."

I stifled my chuckle. "Okay, your mightiness, here's to hoping your artifact used to hold a cape."

He rolled his eyes and picked it up, turning it around in his hands. I walked next to him to see for myself. It was made of bronze, immaculate, and free of any form of wear you would expect for something that's been around for a millennium. To everyone's surprise, nothing happened—no sudden frothing at the mouth or immediate collapsing of his body.

Gary gently placed it on the table and turned to me. "Why didn't any of them work?"

A voice from behind interrupted me before I could say anything to Gary. "Because."

We all turned to see Steven and Nikola walk into the room.

"He's my grandson," Steven said.

Nikola's cane clicked on the floor as they approached, only stopping when they were a couple feet away from us. I looked at Steven, taking in his appearance and thinking of time gone by. I thought about my grandad's memories and how he and Steven spent all those years together. It was a strange feeling, knowing someone but also understanding it wasn't your memories you recollected so clearly.

The years had been kind to him for an eighty-year-old. Steven had grown old and gray, age and gravity pulling him closer to the earth. Nearer to the eternal slumber that awaited everyone. The wrinkles that accentuated his expressions told almost as much about his life as the memories I had of him. He wore the same outfit he wore the day my grandad met him, albeit bigger around the gut and shorter in length.

"What did you say?" I asked.

"He's my grandson," Steven said.

"But you said you didn't have any. You told us when we first met that you only had granddaughters."

The rage swelled in my gut again, churning and crashing against my common sense and understanding. I knew I needed to calm down, so I closed my eyes and took deep breaths. With the aid of my makeshift mantra, I counted to ten and then looked at Steven again.

"Why lie?" I asked.

He walked closer to me, putting both hands on my shoulders. I looked at his face and took in the sight before me. His smile lines showed happiness on the outside, but behind them were years of regret and torment.

"I thought if I lied, he wouldn't be pulled into this. If I sheltered him from all of this, he wouldn't have to live a life of regret or failure for not being able to do what he needed to do," Steven said.

"But I'm here anyways, Grandpa. I'm involved, and we are further behind than we could've been if I knew all along," Gary said.

I glanced in Gary's direction and saw a change in him. It was subtle but noticeable, switching his demeanor to determination and anger.

"I know that now. That I shouldn't have prevented you from knowing your true destiny," Steven said. He looked at me again. "Please, forgive me, Deckard."

I felt hurt and upset by what he did. We all have lost people we love in this war; we couldn't make an exception for anyone at this point. I looked at Steven, not knowing what to say. Not knowing if I actually had anything to say to him. The war has ravaged all our lives and taken things from everyone. What made Steven think he could protect anyone from Jakobus?

"Where's his artifact then, Steven? Where is the Spaulder?" I asked.

Mentioning his artifact made memories of a past life rocket to the surface of my mind, causing me to drift off in times gone and past. It was vivid, like a movie or picture, rather than a memory from my grandad. Not only did I see it, I felt it, smelt it, and tasted it. From the frigid, icy air against my face to the ash and dirt smelling like death and tasting of people and things long forgotten.

A metallic thunk brought my attention from my memories to the situation in front of me. I glanced at the table in front of Gary, seeing the answer instead of hearing it.

"I'm sorry, Deckard," Steven said. "And I owe an apology to you, Frank."

I shook my head and sighed. "What has past is never done."

Steven nodded. "Thank you."

Steven, Frank, and I turned to Gary and watched with held breath as he reached for the Spaldur. His fingers hovered over it, shaking for a moment before becoming very still.

"It's time I play my part and help," Gary said.

He took a few deep breaths and touched his artifact.

Chapter 32
Strained

12th May, 1938
Kew Gardens, Richmond Borough, London, England
1:45 p.m.

The metallic melody of swords clanging against swords filled the training room, echoing off the pitifully padded walls and bouncing around Deck and Drow's heads.

"I see you brought in more wicks. You know, more recruits?" Drow said as he strained from the last impact of the swords.

"Yeah, we did. Why?" Deck asked.

Drow swung his sword with more determination this time, force and anger fueling the action. Deck brought his sword up in time for them to connect, just to have it ricochet back from the force. Before Deck knew it, Drow swung the sword at him again, barely giving Deck enough time to defend himself. Anger hit Deck like a freight train, providing speed to his reactions of defense that then turned to actions of attack. It turned from Deck defending himself from the unwarranted onslaught from Drow to him pressing him back further and further. Deck came in with one last strike, causing them both to lose their grip on their swords. They flew to the ground and skittered in different directions, sparking against the rough stone floor. Deck turned back to Drow and pushed him with both hands, sending him back a few feet.

"Drow, what gives? Why are you angry?" Deck asked.

In a fit of rage, Drow pushed back at Deck. A look of feral anger sparked behind Drow's eyes, his nostrils flaring with such violence it seemed smoke was about to pour from them. The tension in the room grew to extreme heights, weighing heavily on their shoulders. Drow let out an angry growl before speaking. "You just don't get it, do you?"

"Of course I don't! That's why I'm asking you!" Deck yelled.

Drow shook his head and shrugged off the anger. Or at least he tried to. "You just don't understand. You never will."

Deck watched as Drow started to pace back and forth, stomping his feet to the ground with enough force to wake the dead. He stopped to look at Deck once more. "You and your stupid little sword."

Deck scoffed, "What's that supposed to mean? Help me understand why you're so angry."

Drow started to pace again, making three more turns before answering, "I thought I could do this. I thought I could be okay with it all. I mean, what could ever come between us?"

"I'm not following."

"I thought that even though you were chosen, I could still handle not being anything special. As long as you were my brother, I would be okay with being normal. Nonessential to the Keepers."

Deck sighed. "Of course, you're important. You're my brother."

Anger filled his voice. "But that doesn't make me of any use to the team or the mission."

"Of course, you matter. You add a multitude of skills to the group."

He shook his head as he put his hands to his head. He ran them through his hair with force. "That's not all of it. I may be your brother, but I am no longer the only one with a special bond with you. In a way, the people you have known in other lifetimes are more important to you than I will ever be."

He threw his arms to his sides, grunting in anger and frustration. Drow walked over to the far wall and turned to lean against it. He let his back inch down the wall, feet sliding out as he reached the floor. Drow pulled his legs to his chest and rested his face into his hands, body shaking from silent tears.

Deck walked over and knelt beside his brother. He put a hand on his shoulder and patted it before turning and sitting next to him on the ground. They both sat there while Drow let it out, all the frustration and anger that had built up over the last few months.

"Drow." Deck paused. "The bond we share as brothers is stronger than anything I could ever have with anyone else. Those new Wicks will never have what we have."

Drow's body stopped shaking from the tears and adrenaline. "Are you sure?"

Deck smirked and looked at his brother. "Of course."

Chapter 33
Things That Go Boom

26th December, 1942
Kew Gardens, Richmond Borough, London, England
12:03 p.m.

I dle, mumbled chatter from random radio signals filled the common area of the Kew headquarters. After Gary touched his artifact, Steven took him aside to talk with him. From what I gathered, it was most likely to apologize and help him sort through things. The initial first few minutes are crucial for a stable mind and ease of memory transfer.

The rest of the group was looked at by the attending field nurses and Eileen to make sure they were of sound mind and able body to continue with the hard decisions they would be making later that day.

"So, Eileen," I began. "Any theories about the blood yet? Anything I could go off to make sense of the man, or thing, I took the sample from?"

I sat there on the stool in the infirmary and waited with patience for her response. My shoulder ached from all the abuse she was putting me through. Okay, maybe it wasn't as bad as I am making it seem, but it certainly didn't feel very good.

"When you were busy talking with the boys in the conference room, I took another look at the sample," she said.

I felt a sharp pain shoot down my arm as she spoke, making me yelp from surprise more than anything. My eyes snapped to her to see what kind of inhumane torture she was doling out. To my astonishment, she had only removed the tattered and torn, sorry excuse for clothing from my shoulder.

"That's all you've done?" I whimpered.

She rolled her eyes at me. "You're such a baby."

"I resent that; I am far from it."

I was interrupted from saying anything else by the immediate pain the mender caused when applied to an injury. My shoulder wound began to heat from the electrical impulses the device sent into it, stimulating the healing process. It turned weeks and months of healing and recovery into mere minutes.

"You should work on your bedside manner," I mumbled.

She rolled her eyes again.

"And you should stop rolling your eyes. I wouldn't want them to get stuck in some random spot," I said.

"You need to work on your understanding of anatomy." She chuckled. "Then I will start taking advice about bodies from you."

She held the mender to my shoulder for a few more seconds and then removed it. I looked down at the new trophy from surviving another run-in with good luck, bad luck, and dumb luck all rolled into one.

"You're going to have more scars than not eventually. Maybe you should think about another career path."

I laughed. "I'll keep it in mind. Maybe after this is all over. I might get into writing or something. Seems safer to me."

In surprise, she laughed instead of her regular rolling of eyes. "As for your first question: It's an odd thing you have here."

"How so?" I asked, rubbing at my new scar.

"The blood, or whatever it may be, is alive in a sense."

I cocked my head. "What does that mean?"

"Well, when you look at a blood sample underneath a microscope, you see red and white blood cells, among other things."

"That's what you meant by alive? The blood cells?" I asked.

"Well, that's where the 'sort of' comes in. See, the blood of whom you called Spike has both of those. A huge number of them."

"So then, what are you getting at?"

"The strange part is there is something else I haven't seen before, something attached to the cells in his blood."

I stayed quiet, waiting for her to continue.

"The cells themselves aren't alive, at least not anymore. Whatever has attached itself to them is what's alive, and I feel that's what is keeping the man alive."

I thought for a moment. "So, what you're telling me is he is being kept alive by the cells attached to his blood cells?"

I glanced at her as she spoke.

"Precisely. And to top it off, mixed into the substance we are loosely calling blood cells, there are other types of cells from different sources."

I shook my head and blinked. "You mean as in different people?"

"That," she started, pausing as she put the mender on a bench, "and animal blood cells too."

"What?"

She nodded. "It seems we have a physical melting pot of different elements in this blood sample. In any respect, the man, or creature rather, shouldn't even be alive. Let alone shooting balls of fire at you."

This certainly brings a lot more questions to mind. Questions that seem unexplainable in our current situation. We have never encountered biologically enhanced individuals or creatures during our recons. The reign of Jakobus has brought several destructive inventions and weapons to play in this astronomically long game of figurative chess, causing us to keep up and out-think him. For the most part, I'm not sure we have been doing an excellent job with any of that up to this point.

I thought it over. "Whatever he was, I hope we don't have to deal with him again, I suppose I should also ask you about the box from earlier."

"Yes, the box," she said. "I took a preliminary look at it while you were busy administering the test to Gary."

I waited a moment before asking, wanting to make it seem I wasn't that curious. That I couldn't care less about what it was, that I wasn't obsessing over getting it back into my hands where I knew it was safe.

Stop thinking about it like that. You know better than anyone what it did to you. What kind of chokehold it had you in.

"What could you tell from it? Since I found it in the catacombs underneath London, I never once opened it to look inside," I said.

She sighed and pulled a stool closer to me. She sat down and rubbed her temples with some force, either to push the migraine away or to take her mind off it. "Really? I suppose, when I took a closer look at it, all I could tell is that it's a lock of hair suspended in a cut gemstone made of amber."

The mention of hair struck me, specifically a lock of hair. Somewhere in my mind, I felt a tingle, a tiny iota of thought. It grew the harder I tried to think about it, to recollect what it was from. I focused as hard as I could on it, to remember what it came from and what it could tell me about the mysterious box. Images and scenes of other people's memories drifted languidly through my mind while others rocketed past with haste greater than ancient Chinese black powder fireworks. Before I could tell what was in front of me or what I had failed to notice, a certain specific memory stopped front and center for me to see.

It was a bustling, busy street with cars and people zipping by. Most everyone moved with determination as they went about their own business. I tried my best to focus on the faces of the passerby but was rewarded with a fuzzy and muted tone where the face should have been. It was strange. On the other hand, I could make out smells from the surrounding restaurants.

The most prominent one was roasted beef, freshly baked bread, warm cheese, and cooked peppers and onions. I heard someone yell to my left, prompting me to look for the source. I scanned the sea of blurred-out faces to find two men separated by a street of cars and people. The one closest to me was my grandad when he was young, back when he first got the sword. I remembered what I was witnessing now. It was when he and Steven had to escort Nikola to America. It was when they saw the man with the cane. That's why it was so familiar. It's the stone from atop his cane. It must be a lock of Jakobus' hair. It's the only explanation for why he could control more than one person at a time.

"I know whose hair is in the amber," I said.

"Who might that be?" asked Eileen.

"It's Jakobus' hair. It's the only logical thing I can think of. The only way those kinds of thoughts could creep into my head. The only way my behavior could change from how I normally am."

She pursed her lips. "I would say that you're crazy, but there seems to be a lot that happens that doesn't quite add up to be normal. Especially when it involves Jakobus."

I sat there for a moment to gather my thoughts. There are a few things I need to take care of still before we can tackle Parliament. First off, I need to check with Thomas to get Del a weapon, something a little more reliable than the black powder musket she was using earlier. Maybe he has a few more gas masks we can bring with us, just in case. Del says she knows the underground tunnels well, but we need to be ready for anything, including more dream gas.

"I need to talk to a few more people," I said.

I sat up from the stool I was sitting on and turned to Eileen. "Thank you for the help, Eileen. It certainly helps."

She nodded and said, "my pleasure. Now go on and take care of things. We have a war to finish."

I smiled half-heartedly and turned to leave the infirmary. Already my shoulder felt a hundred times better than it did not five minutes ago. I rotated it in a circular motion testing my mobility. To my surprise, it felt as good as new. All traces of pain and discomfort were gone as if it were magic.

If only magic were something we could utilize to our advantage. It would make things go a lot quicker and maybe even more smoothly.

As I walked from the infirmary to the armory, I looked over the common area and felt an aching pain. It felt desolate compared to the headquarters we had underneath the church. When the Luftwaffe ambushed what we called home, we tried to get as many people out during the mayhem. Sadly, we did lose a few good soldiers in the process.

Thomas was in his element, tinkering with something at the counter in the armory, when I neared him. I peeked around his arm to see what it was. Usually, whatever he came up with was quite interesting.

"Thomas! How are you?" I asked, patting him on the back.

"Good, thank you for asking," he said.

I took a step back to give him some space, allowing him to turn toward me. He wore thick brown leather welding clothing, including a long sleeve jacket and pants. With a loud clunk, he placed whatever he was tinkering with on top of the counter behind him.

"What are you working on there?" I asked.

I tried peeking around his side to get a look at it, only to have him move in the way. I smiled and stood straight. "What are you trying to hide?"

He chuckled and said, "It's for another time. What can I do for you?"

My smile faded somewhat. It wasn't from him not wanting to show me but because I thought about Drow. Usually, he would have a quick quip to reply with, something to get under Thomas' skin. It was a horrible feeling to know that you failed at something you promised to do.

Thomas cleared his throat and said something, snapping me out of my trance, "I'm missing it too."

I nodded and said, "I wish I would have something readily available as a response, but I don't."

"We will just have a lot of catching up to do when we get him back," he chuckled. "What can I do for you?"

"I need a weapon."

"Well, you've come to the right place. What do you need? Something that explodes? Something that implodes? Oh, what about something that disintegrates?"

I was about to say something, but I paused, thinking about the last thing he had said. "Something that disintegrates? You know what? I'm okay. I don't need that. What I need is a gun for Madeleine."

"Does it need to have a bio-electric connection? Or just a generic, run-of-the-mill rifle anyone can use?"

"It doesn't need to be connected to her, but I expect more from you than something generic."

He smiled. "You know me too well."

He turned around and walked behind the counter. His head moved from right to left, looking for something in particular. Not seeing what he wanted to, he walked down the first aisle of many, running his finger up and down as he passed each section of shelves. Lining every square inch of the aisles were guns, weapons of some sort, and doodads that were completely new to me. He made it halfway down and stopped. "Aha!"

"Find what you were looking for?" I yelled.

He plucked something from the top shelf and held it for a moment in the light. As he turned, I could see an ear-to-ear grin resembling a child on Christmas getting gifts at six in the morning.

"I think this will do," he said.

Thomas walked back to me with the weapon in hand. When he got close enough, I could see it was a semi-automatic bio-electric repeater. It was a beautifully crafted rifle with a mother-of-pearl inlay and an old western scene engraved into the stock. I put out my hands, and he gave it to me to look at.

"It's gorgeous. But I have to ask, why an American gun? I have nothing against a nice Torrance repeater, but does it stack up against anything we have?" I said.

"Surprisingly, it does. At first, the early models of this gun had a habit of going off without the user shooting it. They had to revise and improve it after some of the owners' families got shot and killed by them."

I held it at arm's length. "But this model works just fine?"

He laughed and took it from me. "Of course. I tore it down and added some British parts to it. And you know, converted it to an enhanced bio-electric version."

"I suppose I'll take your word for it. This is definitely more than something generic."

Thomas placed the rifle on the countertop and reached underneath to grab something. He was making faces as he struggled with his tongue pinched between his teeth. I heard his hand scuffling about, looking for something in particular, slapping against cardboard and bare wood. He stood up and pulled a box of ammunition about the size of five stacked decks of playing cards out from underneath the counter.

"This repeater uses clips of bullets," he said.

He opened the end of the ammunition box and pulled out one of the said clips. It had a curved design and held eight bullets connected at the back end via a metal clip.

Thomas used his index finger and pointed to a specific spot, and said, "The clip has notches on either side of the ends of the bullets to help move the clip along when you engage the lever action."

"Does it ever jam?"

He snorted. "I built it."

I smiled. "So, every other bullet?"

He cleared his throat. "I resent that remark, but alas, someone needs to keep my ego in check."

"I'm glad we're all on the same page," I chuckled. "Would you mind if I took it to bring to Madeleine?"

He eyed me quizzically and raised an eyebrow. "I suppose. Just don't let there be an accident."

It took me a second to realize he wasn't referring to the gun going off. I could feel my cheeks burn hot with embarrassment; up to this point, I didn't know you could feel yourself turn different colors. I stuttered momentarily before getting the words out. "I have no idea what you're talking about.

To take the spotlight off me and my molten lava cheeks, I held my hands for Thomas to give me the gun. He smiled and shook his head as he handed the Torrance repeater. I snatched it from his hands and turned. "Thanks, Thomas. I'll check back later for any goodies."

He shouted back as I walked away from him, "Okay, boss!"

Chapter 34
The Plan

26th December, 1942
Kew Gardens, Richmond Borough, London, England
12:45 p.m.

I tucked the repeater underneath my arm and headed to the chapel. The only difference between this headquarters and the one underneath the church was that we had a chapel. The decision made before building all the safe houses was that we would like to have a place for the soldiers to pray when the goings got tough. Madeleine told me she would be in the chapel earlier on, just before I went into surgery.

For ease of movement and security purposes, most departments or sections did not have doors leading to them; instead, the whole safe house was a relatively open space design. I walked to the chapel area and looked at the three rows of pews tucked tightly together, only a mere couple of feet from the altar and podium. While looking at the ornate and intricate designs carved into the wood, I saw Del sitting in the front pew closest to the lit candles behind the podium. The flickering of the fire made me realize that life was but a flame. When it boiled down to it, all we could do for ourselves was burn as hot and bright as possible when the moment was right and make the best of the dark days that followed.

She looks so beautiful sitting there. If I weren't aware of the current situation, I would almost say she seems at peace.

I watched as she stood up, fatigues settling elegantly on her form. Somehow it accentuated her curves nicely, causing my eyes to wander farther than they should. Feelings tugged at my heart, pulling me away from the welcome distracting thoughts.

Hope, I miss you.

"Deck? Are you okay?" Del asked.

The question took me by surprise. I'm not sure why it did; I was just standing there staring at her like a crazy person. I shook myself from the thoughts and focused on her. "Sorry about that; it's been a little difficult lately. I didn't mean to startle you."

She reached up and tucked a few stray hairs behind her ear. "You didn't. But if you're going to stare at someone, you should be a little more discreet about it."

I blushed at the accusation. It may have been accurate, but that didn't make it any less embarrassing. I rubbed at the back of my neck. "Sorry, I didn't mean to. You just remind me of someone. It's a bit jarring and brings up a lot of feelings."

She shifted on her feet. "What was her name?"

With the question, I let my attention and focus relax and wander off.

"Sorry, I don't mean to bring up things that hurt," Del said.

"No, that's okay," I said. "Her name was Hope."

"Is she waiting for you somewhere?" Del asked.

I felt tears well up in my eyes. "Somewhere, yeah. But it may be a while before I see her again."

"Oh, I see. I'm sorry, Deck."

Out of my periphery, I saw Del walk closer to me. I felt her take my hand in hers as she squeezed softly.

"It happened the day they attacked. There was so much panic everywhere we looked. We didn't have much of a warning," I said.

I squeezed her hand back and then let go of it. Without much thought, I walked over to the closet pew to take a seat. I leaned Del's new rifle against the back of it before I eased myself down. Del followed and took a seat next to me.

"We got as many citizens out as we could; most escaped the city and fled north past the wall. I tried to find her in the fray of ash and fog." I turned to Del, tears flowing freely down my cheeks. "We were supposed to go on holiday that day. Her grandparents had a home in West Mersea, Essex that we were going to go spend a few weeks at."

Del placed her hand on mine as it rested on my thigh, giving it a slight squeeze again.

"She didn't make it out of the city that day. When they attacked, they hit some of the Tesla substations to cripple our power supply and our ability to defend. One of the substations they targeted was one at the hospital she worked at as a nurse. The building was decimated in seconds."

I felt like sobbing. I felt like lying down and never getting up again. I wanted to drift off into a sleep so deep and distant it would feel like nothing had happened. It would be as if I never lost Hope or anyone I cared about. But I couldn't feel this way. I was chosen to help end this war once and for all. I needed to stop Jakobus.

"I'm sorry I asked you, Deck. It must be a painful subject," Del said.

I looked at her. "It is. But time has dulled it a little, and I will always remember her."

Del nodded. "We have all lost someone in this war. I am glad to have met you and the rest of your merry men. They all are a bit strange, but I have faith in you and your plans."

I chuckled half-heartedly. "Well, that's good. Sometimes, I don't even know how we will make it the next day, let alone find and defeat Jakobus."

Del lifted her hand to my face and helped wipe away some of my tears. "I agree." She paused before continuing. "By the way, here is your journal back. I think you said it was Frank's?"

Del reached into the bag that sat next to her on the pew. She pulled out Frank's journal and handed it to me.

"Thanks. Was it an interesting read?"

A smile curled on her lips. "It was, to say the least. I have a hard time thinking all of it to be true, but I have seen things today that would make me sound like a madwoman if I mentioned them to anyone."

"Good thing we're all mad here."

I put up my finger. "Hold on, I have something for you."

I got to my feet and picked up the repeater that I leaned against the pew. My fingers found the lever and trigger assembly without effort, years of muscle memory doing what they were supposed to do. I flipped the lever toward the front of the gun and opened the breech, where the casing fell from. In the same motion, I pulled the clip from the gun to make sure it was unloaded before I handed it over to Del.

"This is a Torrance Repeater, American-made but perfected by Thomas."

Del came over to me and took it from my hands. She looked at it in the light from the central commons area of the safe house. She traced her fingers over the pearl inlay. "It's beautiful."

"It isn't connected to your bio-electric signature, so you will not have an issue with it. Sometimes the specific connections cause problems, even for those supposed to be connected to them."

It must have been Drow's rifle; there wouldn't be another explanation. Why would the Germans have a bio-electric rifle that had signature-specific parameters to them?

Someone cleared their throat behind us.

"Am I interrupting anything?"

We both turned to see Gary a few feet behind us. He had a sheepish grin as he waved awkwardly to us.

I looked at him and thought he seemed more confident, or rather, a little less uncoordinated and bumbling. He was in his American battle dress still, with a familiar addition. On his left shoulder and upper arm was the piece of armor that was his artifact. The light of the candles and other sources around us bounced off the surface of the dark gray metal as it accentuated the gold designs inlay on it. A few memories flashed through my mind of the years my grandad spent with his and the wild and dangerous adventures they got themselves into.

"Gary, you made it through the merging," I said with a smile.

He reciprocated the sentiment, "You made it through your surgery."

"'Tis but a wound of the flesh, much easier to deal with than the melding of thousands of minds."

"Fair enough."

I walked over to him and asked, "How does it feel?"

"It's a little clunky if I'm going to be honest. I kind of wish it was a cool weapon or like a necklace, something like that."

I sighed and shook my head. "I meant the memories, not the armor."

"Oh, that was uncomfortable too. But I think I will be able to deal with it."

I fumbled with my pockets to find what I was looking for. On the second to last, I found the candy, still neatly wrapped in its wax paper. I pulled it out and handed it to Gary.

"What's this?"

"It's a pear drop. It will help if you ever get confused."

"What's a pear drop?" he asked. "And how will it help?"

"You don't have pear drops in America?"

"No, we don't."

"Hmph," I said. "Well, it will help you keep yourself grounded in the present. If you find yourself getting lost in all the memories, pop one of these in your mouth, and it will pull your mind back."

He nodded as he took it. Without hesitation, he popped it into his mouth and moved it around with his tongue. I heard it clack around against his teeth before he spoke. "I don't care for bananas."

I rolled my eyes at him. "It'll do a better job if you don't like the flavor."

He made a sour face before shaking it away. "Frank sent me over here to get you two. It's time to start talking about the plan we have in place."

I glanced at Del before looking at him again. "I think we all are ready to take him down."

We followed Gary over to the Conference room located in the back. It was the only room separated by large, stained oak doors. They were already open, allowing us to see everyone waiting for us. Spread around the massive round table were enough chairs for us all to sit on. Seated at the front of the table was Nikola himself, dressed to the nines in an immaculate black and gray suit.

To the left of him sat Frank with a pipe to his lips as he looked at me behind his horn-rimmed glasses. He bowed his head as he took a pull from his pipe before exhaling it through his nostrils. I saw Eileen sitting near him, beautiful as always, in her nurse uniform. She glanced at me and winked before looking back toward Nikola. Next to her sat Steven, looking calm and collected as everyone else went about their business. To the right sat Thomas with his face and neck smeared in grease. Denim overalls were hooked over a light blue button-up shirt with the sleeves rolled up to his elbows.

At least he's wearing work gloves. Maybe his hands are clean underneath them.

Next to Thomas sat Mad Jack with his bagpipes resting on his lap. Part of me assumed he doesn't go anywhere without it, so he had it there. Last but not least was Klaus, sitting at the end on the right. He was carving a new piece of wood in his hands when I looked at him. For a moment, he stopped and looked at me, nodded, and returned to his newest creation.

Nikola stood and clapped his hands together before grabbing his cane. "Good, we are all here."

He motioned for us to take a seat. "Now we can get the ball rolling and figure out our next move."

I first met Nikola in 1937. He was at the spry young age of eighty-one. For the first year or so, he moved around with relative ease compared to most people I knew at that age. It wasn't until the year that the streets went dark that he picked up a cane to help him walk. He, like many others, managed to escape the city without losing his life. But making it out alive didn't account for the damage he received trying to do so.

When the day was done, and all of the bombs had whistled down upon the streets I walked as a child, I too made it to a designated rally spot deep in the hills of Wales. For the following year or so, we, as in what was left of the British armed forces, fortified the defensive line that we cobbled together in the early days of the attack. Named The Churchill Wall, it spanned from Boston as the starting point and stretched across the country to Nottingham, Birmingham, and Worcester before ending in the bay near Gloucester. Over the next few years, we made tremendous advances back into London, taking back the heart of the country one German checkpoint at a time.

Nikola rubbed his hands together again before speaking, "Frank, how are we looking in the way of personnel?"

Frank pushed another stream of tobacco smoke through his nostrils before he spoke. His expression stayed stoic except for a flash of sorrow and regret. "We have the three of us that made it here about a day ago. Deckard and company made it here this morning, bringing not only Klaus and Gary, but he also managed to pick up two strays."

Mad Jack looked at everyone and played a quick little jig on his bagpipe. After he finished, he spoke up. "Nice to be in the presence of knights of the round table."

Del lifted her hand as a friendly gesture. "Nice to meet you all formally."

Nikola smiled and nodded at everyone before walking around the room. "It seems we have a good group of people to start with. Frank, how many soldiers made it out from the church?"

Frank had the pipe to his lips, embers pulsing as he puffed at the dried shredded plant matter. "Well, thirty or so made it out, but only seventeen met up with us here. While thirteen went south then west across the Thames to the other safe house in Gravesend."

Nikola's cane clicked and clacked against the worn stone floor as he walked around the room. He made two whole revolutions before he spoke, "Seventeen soldiers, three Keepers, a German POW, and a music-playing madman to get the job done."

"That sums it up," Frank said.

Del cleared her throat to get his attention. "Not quite. You have me, sir."

He stopped walking and turned to her. "Are you sure you want to be involved in this, young lady?"

Del stood up and looked him in the eyes. "Yes. I am, and I think I have something that could help us. Or rather two some-things."

He regarded her with tired, old eyes. Eyes that have seen years of prosperity as well as years of pain and suffering. He tapped his cane on the floor three times and said, "What do you have in mind?"

CHAPTER 35
Take Two

26th December, 1942
Kew Gardens, Richmond Borough, London, England
1:00 p.m.

Del rummaged through the bag she brought to the conference room. She was searching for the journal that Deck, Gary, and Klaus found on the French spy in the tunnels beneath the streets of London. After a moment of silence, as everyone stared at her, she found what she was looking for. "Early in the year, we had come in contact with a German soldier. We, as in my team and I, convinced him to relay information to us that he gathered on the tunnels and rooms Himmler was having constructed underneath Parliament."

Del walked around to where Nikola was standing and handed him the journal. "Inside these pages are somewhat comprehensive notes about what he has been doing underneath."

Nikola took it from her and used both hands to skim the pages. He balanced on his feet as he held his cane in the crook of his arm, staring intently at the words written before him. He flipped through the whole thing before looking at Del once more. "Do you believe this?"

Del pursed her lips. "I wouldn't have a week ago. But meeting you and seeing those beasts in person has made me feel otherwise."

"If you believe it, then we need to be very, very, very concerned," Nikola said.

Del nodded. "I also think we need to work fast."

Thomas spoke up, "Just so we all are on the same page, what are you two talking about? What's in that book?"

Del looked at him and said, "Himmler plans on opening a rift or door in the fabric of space and time."

Everyone in the room started to murmur and mutter.

"Do we know what he is trying to do? Let alone how he is doing it?" Thomas asked.

Frank spoke up this time. "I spoke with Del earlier while everyone was busy. I took a cursory glance at the notes and referenced it with what we have accumulated on Himmler, which we are now assuming is Jakobus. Since Jakobus was a force that the great and wise Merlin couldn't overcome, we have reason to believe he has access to magic, or at least something equivalent to that."

"That can't be the only thing he's using to open a rift," Eileen said.

"You're right. We believe he has been using the third Reich to build their own technology to harness his magic. We will call it that to make it easier to explain," Frank said.

Nikola pulled his chair out and took a seat. He hooked the cane on the edge of the table and flattened the journal out in front of him to look at it some more.

I thought about what they were saying, and something hit me. "I was thinking about the Manticore and Griffon we saw earlier this morning. They must be the products of his attempts to open a rift, to see how much he could or couldn't do with it before it shut on him."

"Where could the rift lead that would let a Griffon and a Manticore out?" Eileen asked.

I rubbed at the back of my neck while I thought about it. Memories swirled around my head as I struggled to find anything relating to magical beasts and where we could find them. After a second, it came to me. "They are from the sixth century when King Arthur was alive."

The revelation caused the room to stir more. Murmurs and muttering became an audible discussion of the ramifications this could have. Not only on the war we have at hand but the fate of the rest of the world in general.

Nikola steepled his hands in front of his face. "We will need to move with haste if this is the case. Del, you said there were two ways to help. What is the last way?"

"The source of the radio signal that has been broadcasting is coming from within the city. I say this because it means I have some soldiers of my own that can help infiltrate Parliament to rescue Deck's brother and stop Jakobus."

"Good. How can we get in touch with them to coordinate the plan's next steps?" Nikola asked.

"I can get through to them by an encrypted message on the same radio channel," Del said.

The room grew silent as we all thought about the plan. We realized the risks that were involved in this kind of decision, and we all knew it was the right thing to do. Once and for all, we can stop Jakobus before he reaches his goal, or die trying.

"We will have you contact them soon. We will take a few hours to rest up, regroup and reorganize," Frank said.

"Good, good, good. I think we have a plan that will be successful," Nikola said. "Do we have a name for this operation?"

We all muttered thoughts to each other before Mad Jack spoke up above everyone. "Since we will be in the tunnels, I think it would be fitting to call it Searchlight."

Nikola rubbed at his chin. "Operation Searchlight it is."

We all nodded in agreement, not having an issue with it. Everything seemed like it was all wrapped up before Eileen shifted in her chair.

"I also have something we need to address," Eileen said. "When Deck arrived, he had a moment of distress."

I looked up and noticed everyone look away from me, pretending to be observing other things.

"We can all understand why he reacted the way he did, but I have concluded that lashing out like that was also the result of an outside force compelling him to act on emotion, especially anger," Eileen said.

Nikola looked at Steven. "You've been quite silent this whole time. What is your opinion?"

"I am inclined to think that Eileen is right. Young Deckard was influenced by a source of evil, an object containing the will and essence of Jakobus himself," Steven said. "I spent many, many years searching for this exact object in America."

"We were always curious about how Jakobus survived his encounter with Deck's Grandfather years ago. It was brought back here to London sometime between 1920 and 1937," Frank said.

Eileen nodded and reached into one of the pockets on the front of her nurse's uniform. She pulled out a black cloth wrapped around a small object. It immediately pulled and tugged at the edges of my mind. I hadn't known she had brought it with her, but now that I did, it was beckoning me to take it from her. My blood felt as if it heated to the temperature of molten steel as my heart rate hammered against my rib cage. I tried to block it out and think of something else, anything other than the stone. Eileen's words were slowly fading away from my senses, shifting to a muffled buzz that droned softly in the distant part of my mind. My vision went from being clear and competent to blurry everywhere except the ebony cloth and amber stone.

"Deck?" asked a voice.

At first, my mind didn't register that someone was trying to get my attention. It was hard to lift my head and look away from the stone, to focus on anything but that. The world was closing in on me as my eyes stayed stationary, vision sinking like lead weights.

Feet shuffled somewhere behind or around me; at this point, I couldn't tell. The rage and anger simmered and boiled over, inciting my thoughts to think the worst, to want the worst. I felt a hand being placed on my shoulder as it gently shook me. A sense of comfort and reassurance started where they touched me. It spread, picking up as it cascaded over the rest of me. I sensed the feeling as it reached Excalibur, resonating as it struck the magical steel. It reverberated tenfold as it reflected the pure power of decency and good back. It washed over my chest and extended outward over my arms, legs, hands, and feet. It made its way to my head, my mind, pushing out all negative feelings and replacing them with ease.

"Deck?" asked the voice.

I turned my head to see Eileen standing next to me. "I'm sorry. I-I—that thing, that stone. I need to get it away from me."

She frowned. "I can't believe it has that kind of control over you."

I stayed turned away from it and focused on her.

"It would benefit your health and our safety to destroy it. I also believe it will weaken Jakobus in the process," she said.

"How do we do that?" I asked.

"Excalibur would do the trick," Frank said.

That would make sense. He's afraid of its power; why else would Jakobus try to destroy my Grandad and me? Fifty odd years ago, Davey thought he killed him with Excalibur; it seemed to destroy part of him, at least.

"It has refused you once for being tainted with the stone's macabre, dark power," Gary said.

"Yes, but he doesn't have possession of the stone now, and he has the sword on his back, so who's to say it won't do the trick?" Frank said.

I closed my eyes and took a few deep breaths to push out any residual ill intentions. I counted to ten and opened them again. "I can do it. Let's destroy it."

I glanced at all the people in front of me. The last five years have been taxing, and almost impossible for us to keep ahead of the curve. They are no longer just people to me; they are family.

"We will tend to the stone now. After that, we will collect all of our supplies and weapons." Nikola said. "Thomas, take Deckard with you and try to take care of the stone by any means."

Thomas and I nodded.

"Gary, you can go with Eileen to ensure the merging took. We don't want any adverse effects to appear while we are in the middle of an important battle."

"I would like to go with my grandson and Eileen," Steven added. "If that is alright."

"That is fine," Nikola said before relaying more orders. "Del, you will go with Frank to send a message to your group. Hopefully we hear back from them within the hour. By the end of the evening, we will be storming the tunnels and laying siege to Jakobus' plans."

Del and Frank both said, "Okay," at the same time.

Nikola nodded. "Klaus, you can tag along with Frank and Del, just in case there is anything in the journal they can't make out."

Klaus looked up from his latest whittle project. "*Ja.*"

"Okay, before we all separate, I want to make sure we all know what is expected. I'll go over the plan one last time," said Frank. "Those who are able-bodied will meet with Del's soldiers near Parliament. After we are all together, we will follow Del into the tunnel system that connects with the setup Jakobus has been building. When we reach the main area, we will plant explosive charges and hightail it out of there in time to blow it all back to hell."

"What is our plan for killing him?" Steven asked.

"I'll have to get close and use the sword on him. It worked before, at least on an incarnation of him," I said.

"What if it doesn't?" Del asked.

I glanced at her. "It will have to, or I will die trying. Besides, if I successfully destroy the lock of hair, it should weaken him enough for the sword to work."

"What about me, sir?" asked Jack.

Before I could respond, Nikola did, "You can come with me. It's been a dream of mine to have my own theme music."

"Can do," Jack said.

The room fell silent for but a moment. Shuffling of chairs and feet followed as we all got up to go about our tasks. Del and Frank exited the room, presumably to send a message to her soldiers, tobacco smoke trailing behind them. Eileen and Gary followed on their heels, heading to the infirmary to run diagnostics on him to check his vitals and things of that nature. All while this was happening, I tried to think of anything except the stone sitting in the middle of the table. Calling me, taunting me to come to pick it up.

Thomas came over to me. "Are you ready to destroy it?"

I nodded. "I am. But I will have you bring it with us. I do not want to get sucked back in if I touch it."

"I can do that."

Thomas leaned over and picked up the stone. I turned quickly to avoid staring at it and walked out the doors. We made our way back to the armory, where there was a shooting range tucked back in the corner. It had enough room for two people to stand side by side to shoot simultaneously.

Usually, the walls and ceiling of a normal range would be relatively unscathed, besides a few gouges here and there from stray bullets. This one was not the case. With someone as eccentric as Thomas regarding new inventions, most of them explode in some form or fashion. That caused the walls and ceiling to be charred black from fire and shrapnel.

"Let's go down range about halfway to do this," Thomas said.

"Might be a good idea," I agreed.

I started down to the middle while Thomas grabbed two wooden crates. He was a few steps behind me when I reached the spot, giving me time to turn toward him. He placed the wooden crates on the floor in front of me, stacked on top of each other to create a flat surface. After that, he placed the stone on the top and gingerly grabbed the edge of the cloth to pull it from covering the stone. As the last corner slipped slowly from the amber, it revealed the stark black lock of hair.

I felt the gravity of it pull me down and inward toward the stone. The world around me started to spin and shake, making me slightly nauseous. I reached up and put a hand on Excalibur's hilt, hoping it would help me combat the effects. Immediately upon grasping the worn but crisp leather wrap, the spinning stopped. The pressure of my surroundings returned to normal as my mind grew clearer.

"Deck, are you ready?" Thomas asked.

I nodded and pulled Excalibur from its sheath in a smooth and rehearsed move. The blade sang like a thousand angels praising the lord's word. I closed my eyes and took a few focused breaths, thinking about ending something evil, vile, and wicked. Stopping part of him from tainting anyone else. Images flashed through my head like pictures and movies plastered across the inside of my eyelids.

The memory of King Arthur gaining Excalibur from the stone at the bottom of the well was the first thing I saw. With a flash of light, I saw a view of the night sky lit up by millions of lights. People walked about with foods of many kinds, laughing and smiling as the morning drew closer. I recognized some things my grandad would have seen. Canals and lagoons stretched far and wide over a vast layout with neoclassical buildings erected for what seemed overnight. It shifted to other scenes I had never seen, changing faster and faster like slides on a wall.

I pried my eyes open and looked at the amber stone, focused on destroying it. My grip on Excalibur's hilt tightened as I brought it above my head. Without hesitation, I swung it down onto the stone with the strength of a thousand men. Time slowed as it struck, sending a flash of light searing through my brain.

An invisible force sent a shockwave outward from the point of impact. I felt it hit me square in the stomach, knocking me backward and causing my body to strike the wall. It knocked the air from my lungs as I slid to the floor. The same wave of energy sent Thomas flying as well, hitting the opposite wall at almost the same time. I wheezed hard, trying to gulp in lungfuls of air to replenish what I had lost. My vision was blurry from the tears welling up in them. The only thing I could think to do was rub them away with my sleeve, hoping to wipe the dust from them as well.

"Thomas? You okay?" I choked out.

Dust filled the confined space, limiting our visibility.

"Yeah, I'm okay," he wheezed.

I laughed. A hearty, much-needed one.

Not to sound I, but it felt as if a weight was lifted from my shoulders. The sense of the overbearing dread that's been floating over my head for the past few days disappeared with the stone.

Thomas began to chuckle after hearing me laugh. Soon we both sat there for a moment laughing, letting the worry melt away for the slightest reprieve.

The air in the room began to clear up, allowing me to see the grin on Thomas's. It was ear to ear and pearly white, while his skin was covered in sand, dirt, and dust.

"I wonder if I can get that kind of boom out of something again. What a blast," Thomas said.

Of course, that's the only thing on his mind. I just shook my head. In doing so, I saw Excalibur lying three feet from my hand. I leaned over on my side to grab it, adding more grime to the layer already on me. When I grabbed it and pulled myself up, I saw something I didn't think would ever happen.

Halfway up the shining, gleaming steel, there was a crack spidering about an inch into the blade. Electricity, or at least that's what it looked like, snapped and arced from the crack, curling back to itself and connecting to the chips at the edge.

"Bollocks," I said.

CHAPTER 36
In Motion

26th December, 1942
Kew Gardens, Richmond Borough, London, England
2:00 p.m.

I carefully stood up to not disturb the crack any more than I needed to. The sparking subsided after a few moments had passed, giving me a slight amount of relief. It wasn't a lot, nor was it good in all actuality.

"Who would know the most about this?" Thomas asked.

"Frank has the most knowledge regarding the artifacts and the powers they contain. His grandfather, Hubert, was a great man and an even greater guardian. In the years he spent waiting for me grandad and Steven to eventually show up, he learned as much as he could regarding everything Keeper-related," I said.

We walked past all the radio banks to the last one at the end where Del, Frank, and Klaus were. Del was sitting in the chair in front of the control panel, Klaus on the left of her leaning over the journal, and Frank standing to her right.

"Frank, we have a problem," I said.

He turned to me. "What is it?"

I feel ashamed to show him, but I need to.

I pulled Excalibur from its sheath and rested the blade in my left hand, hilt in the right. To make sure he could see the cracks as I lifted it to chest level in the light.

I wasn't quite sure why I was ashamed. All I did was do what I thought was right. What I thought needed to be done. I destroyed a piece of Jakobus to help rid the world of his vile and evil soul. How was I supposed to know Excalibur would become damaged in the process?

Frank leaned closer to inspect the damage on the blade. He pinched the frame of his glasses and wiggled them to get a better look, focusing on Excalibur through the bifocals at the bottom half of his lenses. The crack sparked, and small arcs of pocket-sized lightning skittered across the sword's metal.

Frank let out a few obligatory hmphs and hmms before saying, "Well, this may not be very good."

What? He's supposed to be the expert.

"Is that really all you have to say?" I asked.

He straightened. "Yes."

I sighed and slid the sword back into its sheath. It nestled into it without so much as a bit of friction or resistance. My hand found my neck and rubbed at it. "Do you have anything a little more helpful than that?"

Frank rubbed at his chin. "For one, this kind of thing has never happened. I didn't think anything could damage Excalibur, let alone to this extent."

"So, what does that mean for the plan?" Del asked.

"Nothing. This changes nothing. I will have to face him regardless," I said. "Maybe it won't make a difference anyway since I was able to destroy the stone."

"You may be right. He could be weak enough because of that," Thomas said.

The rush of release and freedom that came from destroying the amber was quickly fading. I now started to worry that our plan would fail, and that once we reached the inside of his lair, we would fall to his power. Worst of all, I wouldn't be able to keep my promise of saving my brother.

I immediately felt terrible for thinking that was the worst thing. The whole world is relying on us, The Keepers, to stop Jakobus from opening a rift to God knows-where. Suppose he was able to have a sustained door to another time, who knows what could come from beyond? I saw firsthand what the Manticore and Griffon could do to a man. In my mind's eye, I could still see the beasts, the horrid smell accompanied by the matted fur and ruffled feathers. The hairs on the back of my neck stood on end as I remembered one of the German soldiers getting airlifted off the ground, nothing left but red mist floating like a deathly fog in the morning sun.

Regardless of what happens, I need to try.

"Were you able to send word to the rest of Del's people?" I asked.

Del and Frank nodded.

"I was able to send an encrypted message like the one we had on loop before," she said.

"A Polybius cipher?" I asked.

Hang in there, Drow, we'll get to you soon.

"Yes," she said.

"What did you say to them?"

"To meet with us somewhere in particular."

"Where is that?" I asked.

"I spoke with Nikola about any other safehouses in the area near Parliament. He said the best one would be St. Peter's Vauxhall would do the trick. Apparently, the crown hired a few architects to connect some of the surrounding churches to Parliament for this specific reason, in case people need to travel around the vicinity without anyone else knowing," Frank said.

I glanced at him. "Isn't that across the Thames?"

"Yes, but we needn't worry. Even though it is across the way, there still is a tunnel underneath the water," he said.

"It may work. A little bit of a walk, I assume but hopefully that way, we won't see anyone we don't want to see," I said.

Frank nodded. "And Del said that specific tunnel leads to a few others, eventually meeting with the ones Jakobus built. So, we are assuming that they most likely haven't been through them.

I gave a cursory thought, thinking of the dangers involved in running through a tunnel underneath a raging river moving tons of water daily. Safe. I heard the radio's speaker give off some static, followed by Del's broadcast.

"Trois-cinq attendez, un-cinq attendez, quatre-quatre attendez, un-cinq attendez, cinq-un attendez, un-un attendez, quatre-cinq attendez, cinq-trois attendez, deux-trois attendez, un-un attendez, trois-un attendez, trois-un, terminer," said Del's voice over the radio.

"What does it say?" I asked.

"It says Pete Vauxhall," Del said.

"Do you think they will understand?"

She nodded. "Yes."

The broadcast repeated twice more before returning to static. It would stay like that for another five minutes before replaying, hoping the intended receiver would get it. Before I realized it, I drifted off into a daydream, thinking of her voice.

I shook my head and looked at Frank. "Do you need us for anything else?"

He shook his head. "Just go get all the gear you can, and we will have everyone come by to load up on weapons and any protective gear we have."

"May I come along?" Klaus asked.

"I don't mind, Thomas, do you?" I asked.

"No," he said.

I motioned for him to follow us. As I did, Thomas bumped my arm.

"Do you have those metal cylinders still? They were in one of the packs you took when we left the church. I looked for them as much as I could before I left," Thomas said.

"Yeah, I do. I can go get them."

"No, that's okay. As long as you have them, we will grab your pack when we leave for the tunnels."

"By the way, what are they?"

He smirked. "Oh, just a little something I have been working on."

"Come on now, don't leave me in the dark."

"Okay, I'll tell you." He stopped and turned to me. "The two metal rods use the electricity in the air to create their own electro-magnetic field."

"In English please."

Klaus interrupted, "What he is saying is they will create a force field. Effectively blocking out any force that comes in contact with it."

Thomas smiled. "I like this guy. Yes, to put it plainly. If we get caught up underneath and can't get away to blow the charges, we will have a way to try and protect ourselves from the blast, debris, and other things that go with big explosions."

"Klaus, you go with Thomas and make sure everything is ready for us to grab and go. I will check with Steven and Gary before I meet with Nikola for the last time," I said.

In Klaus' fashion that I was getting used to, he gave me a silent nod as he followed Thomas. I turned to check with Gary, walking briskly to them to not waste any time. I passed Del and Frank again, still focused intently on the radio. They were probably double-checking with her men, sending another message to confirm they understood. I neared the infirmary and saw Steven standing next to the first cot.

"Steven, everything all right?" I asked.

He looked up from the spot on the ground he was staring at. A half-hearted smile flashed across his face.

"You remind me so much of your grandfather," he said.

Some of my grandad's memories drifted closer to the sur-face, reminding me that he was never truly gone. He would be with me forever and always, in a way.

"Sorry about that; it might be painful."

He chuckled. "No, not at all. It is nice, actually, to see so much of him in you."

I walked closer to him. "How's Gary?"

"He's doing well. Eileen says all his vitals are strong, and his mind is relatively in one piece. I think that last statement was par for the course, but he's always been a little interesting," he said.

I smiled. "He's definitely grown on me. I'm glad the process took well."

I thought about me grandad's memories. "Do you miss him?"

Steven smiled. "Everyday. We had very many good years to-gether. I especially enjoyed the ones he came to visit me in Amer-ica."

"He did? He never told me of those," I said.

He cocked an eyebrow. "Really? No memories from those times?"

I shook my head. "No. I have a lot from him, but only the most crucial ones I remember well. You know how it is; a lot of other people's memories are floating around in here too."

I tapped my temple to get the point across.

"Fair enough, maybe some time I'll tell you about them. But for now, you should grab Gary and get the ball rolling on the plan. Nikola and I will sit this one out. The years are finally catch-ing up to us, and I fear we will just hold you back," he said.

"I understand. I don't think any of us would want you two to get hurt. I would have to agree that it's best," I said.

I heard some rustling from inside the infirmary. Turning to see what was causing the noise, I saw Gary walking toward me. The light reflected off his spaulder as he moved; definitely a sight to see an American soldier wearing a piece of medieval armor. I mean, I ran around with a sword strapped to my back, and that probably still wasn't the weirdest thing. Mad Jack not only had a bagpipe glued to his hip, but he also had a longbow, arrows, and another sword. In a word or phrase, we were definitely a band of merry men. Thanks, Robin Hood.

"How do you feel?" I asked.

Gary rolled his left shoulder as he tightened and adjusted the leather straps of his armor. He smiled as he looked up and saw me. Finally, he put his arms to his sides as he finished fidgeting with it and said, "Pretty good, actually. The shoulder is just a bit sore from having the armor attached to it all the time."

"You'll get used to it," Steven said.

"Well, seeing as you are doing okay, we should talk to Nikola and tell him everything is in order. In a few hours, we will be on our way to fight the good fight," I said.

2:30 p.m.

Another difference of the Kew Gardens version of the headquarters was a specific office built just for Nikola. During the year I spent training underground with Frank and the Keepers, he often stayed with us. I figured with his old age, he didn't like people or the outside world as much as he used to, but I think I understand now that it was something else entirely. He wanted to be here because he strived to improve the world. Not only have his inventions made modern-day life so much more efficient and enjoyable, but they have also made existence as humans as equal as possible. Even though he was never a Brighter, he wanted to ensure he did everything in his power to keep King Arthur's oath alive.

Gary and I turned the corner just before Nikola's office, only to stop halfway. In front of his door were Frank and Klaus, busy talking to each other. I only thought it was strange because the conversation seemed heated.

"Frank, Klaus, you two okay?" I asked.

Frank gave me a glance. "Klaus says we should wait to talk to Nikola."

I looked at both of them. "Why?"

Klaus turned his gaze to me. "Jack is busy playing his music in there. We should let him finish before we bother them."

I paused for a moment, unsure of what to say. "Why should we wait?"

Klaus sighed. "Do you not have any appreciation for the fine arts?"

Frank scoffed, "For a squealing bag of air?"

I looked at the two again and laughed. "I'm sure Jack is almost done. Let's wait the few seconds, okay?"

The sweet serenade of the bagpipe stopped moments after I said we should wait. I could hear Nikola and Jack let out hearty laughs beyond the door. Hearing Nikola sound happy was a good change of pace.

"Alright, now let's go talk to him," Frank said.

Frank gave the door three knocks before entering. When he opened up the door, we saw Nikola was at his desk, a drink near his left hand and a cigar in his right. Jack was standing near him at the edge of the desk with one foot on a chair.

"Nikola, I didn't think you smoked," I said.

He smiled. "I don't. But when it may be one of the last times you can enjoy yourself, you need to try new things."

I chuckled. "Aren't you staying here with Steven?"

"Yes," he said. "But one thing I have learned from a long life such as I have lived is that sometimes you need to plan for anything."

The statement struck me as odd, but I didn't read much into it. We all walked into the room and took our spots around his desk.

"We contacted Del's people and received word back. They will meet us at the church of our choosing within the next few hours," Frank said.

Nikola took a sip of his drink. "And of you? Did you take care of the stone?"

I nodded. "I did. But the sword took damage in the process."

"Hmm, is it dire? Enough to stop the attack and try another time?"

"No, I believe it will still work."

I hope to God it does. Otherwise, we all die for nothing. Or at least I will.

"So, it seems everyone is all set," he said. Nikola turned to Jack. "Thank you, my friend, for the wonderful music."

"Aye, my pleasure, sir," Jack said. "When this is all done with, I'll be back to play you some more."

"Good, I'll be waiting for it."

Nikola took another sip of his drink and looked at all of us.

This may be the last time I see him, and it may be the last time I see everyone together. I pray we find Drow, destroy Jakobus' lair and kill him in the process. We cannot fail. If we do, we fall.

"Good luck to you all. May the light guide you to the end, as swift and just as a swords blade," Nikola said.

CHAPTER 37
Wet

26th December, 1942
Vauxhall Borough, London, England
6:00 p.m.

We stayed in the shadows most of the way to the new rendezvous. After talking to Nikola, we met with Thomas in the armory. He had a plethora of guns, explosives, and doodads I had never seen before.

One of the benefits of knowing a mad scientist is that he always has something new for you to play with.

The decision of who would be involved in Operation Searchlight came down to Frank. Nikola and Steven would stay behind, of course, while every other able-bodied person would come with. That included me, Del, Gary, Klaus, and Jack. We all agreed with Frank's decision that he would also stay behind. We would be back to keep the order alive if all went well. But if we weren't back, he would be there to continue without us.

About seventeen other men and women could have come with us, but we decided to take five instead. It was agreed that a smaller group would have a better chance of keeping a low profile. Having the other twelve at the gardens would be ample security to protect the people left behind.

Besides Excalibur and my Kestler Mk IV, I brought along my haversack containing food rations and the two metal cylinders from Thomas. Gary had his pack, armor, and shotgun. Klaus was given the rifle that we took before leaving the church. Del had her repeater, locked and loaded, slung on her back. The other five men and women were given an array of guns, all slightly different versions of the ones we carried.

We had one edge over the German soldiers we were about to face: all our guns were bio-electric. This meant they had a little bit of an extra zing to them when they shot. From our intel, they still used the plain Jane lead slingers from the start of the war. It seemed odd that they never started using something with a bit more punch. From experience and all the other information we'd received, they liked to be at the forefront of technology.

"Jack, couldn't you have taken a gun?" I asked.

He eyed me and whispered, "What be the fun in that? Not much of a challenge either."

I sighed and rubbed my neck. "You could have at least brought a pistol or something. A sword and a bow will only get you so far."

"I also have my bagpipe."

I shook my head in disbelief. "How did you bring that without me seeing?"

He smirked. "See, all I need is a bow and a sword."

I paused. "That doesn't even make sense."

He shrugged his shoulders and smiled again.

"Okay, whatever," I said.

I turned my attention to the rest of the group, counting heads to ensure everyone was there. We met with Del's men about ten minutes prior, just as planned. When we arrived at the next rendezvous, they were already there, waiting for us in the shadows of the old brick church. It towered above, casting the thick black curtain far enough for us all to crouch and lean against the wall. As promised by Del, there were fifteen other men and women ready and willing to help in any way they could.

I walked close to Del and tapped her shoulder. "Are you and your people ready?"

She glanced at me. "Yeah. They aren't quite used to your weapons, but I gave them a quick rundown."

"You think they'll be able to handle them without shooting one of us?"

"I believe so," she said.

"I mean, that's more reassuring than a no. I'll take what I can get."

"One of my men did bring up an important detail," she said.

I cocked an eyebrow. "What's that?"

"If the guns run off electricity in the air, how will they work underground?"

At some point, Thomas must've walked up behind us because I heard his voice answer the question for me.

"This," he said.

We both turned to look at him. He had slung a bag down from his shoulders to one arm. It was a normal-looking haversack except for one detail. Coming out of the top of the pack were two antennas about a foot in length.

"Uh, what is that?" I asked.

He smiled. "It's a mobile Tesla coil. Electricity bridges the gap between the two antennas giving off a charge in the air. Your receiving pads on the guns will use your body as an amplifier and charge that way."

"Sounds dangerous. Electricity, gunpowder, and explosives in confined spaces?"

Thomas' smile widened. "I suppose you could think about it like that. Honestly, I like to live on the cusp. Why play it safe when you can have fun?"

Del and I were quiet for a moment, waiting for Thomas to say he was joking or something along those lines. After some time, we realized he wasn't.

"I suppose that's a way to look at it," I said. "If you two are ready, I'll check with Klaus and Gary quickly. I know Jack is."

We all turned and glanced at Jack. He was near the French soldiers sharpening the heads of a few arrows…with a rock.

I left Thomas and Del and walked over to Gary and Klaus. They were between Jack and me, pulling on their straps and ensuring their gear was situated well.

"Gary, Klaus, are you two ready?" I asked.

They both looked up from what they were doing.

"I am," Gary said.

"*Ja*," Klaus added.

"Good. We will be heading out now. I will be on point. I want you two behind me," I said. "Behind that will be Del and Thomas, followed by her ten soldiers and our seven."

"What about Jack?" Klaus asked.

"He volunteered to hold up the rear," I said.

They both nodded.

"That's a lot of boots. You think we will be able to catch them by surprise with that many people?" Gary asked.

I shrugged. "I'm not sure, but I want to have this many soldiers just in case everything goes sideways."

"That's fair. Then I guess we are ready," Gary said.

I walked to the front of the group and did an about-face, turning to see everyone. They looked at me with all their attention, a look of fear in their eyes. Apprehension and eagerness to get this over with boiled inside them. Others seemed distracted with thoughts of death and pain from not making it out of this alive. But some of them seemed ready to follow me. They knew what needed to be done and why it did. While they weren't Brighters, Dimmers, or Keepers, they were briefed on the situation and wanted to end this long and destructive war.

"Alright, everyone," I said. "This is it. We have one chance to do this, so let's do it right. You all know the order we will be in, so watch each other's backs. If you see something, say something, and shoot anyone you don't know. Once we get through the tunnels to where the machinery is located, we will set the explosives and head for the hills."

They all looked at me anxiously as I continued to talk, "While the charges are being set, I will try to locate my brother and take out the man known as Himmler. Do not, I repeat, do not wait for me. Follow Del's lead if you cannot find me. I want as many of you to make it out of there alive."

Everyone nodded in agreement. I glanced at my friends and saw that they looked worried and scared. They knew what might need to happen, and that included leaving me there.

"Let's head out. Follow me and keep your firearms charged," I said.

I sighed, turned, and walked toward the wooden gate leading to the church's back. The sun was almost buried beneath the skyline, only letting a small amount of its light crest above the shortest buildings in the distance. A light dusting of snow began to fall minutes after we reached the church, accumulating on any stationary surface. It seemed peaceful for the few moments I paid attention to the world around me, devoid of gunfire or shouting anywhere near us.

Maybe we will make it out of this in one piece, Drow. Maybe.

I reached for the latch of the rickety, ancient wooden gate and unhooked it. It creaked as I pushed it inward, causing me to wince. Someone coughed behind me and cleared their throat. I took a few deep breaths, cleared my mind, and pushed on.

Maybe I need to be a little quieter too.

Though there were almost twenty-five people behind me, they were all pretty quiet. We quickly crossed the small yard behind the church and got to the side entrance. It opened into a church like most I've seen and some I haven't. It had all steepled ceilings with arches and archways, with each and every nook and cranny having either a statue of an angel, a son of the lord, or a ridiculous number of candles. Stained glass windows let in a flood of ever-dimming light, bathing the floor in front of us with crimson, indigo, and goldenrod. I glanced back at my men as we walked beneath them, streaks of red and blue stretching across their faces like fresh blood and pained tears.

We passed the pews and turned to go near the offices in the back, being mindful of our surroundings of anything that could pop out of the shadows. The church as a whole was relatively well lit from the light coming in from outside except for closer near the back.

"Spotters up," I said.

I reached up for my own, clipped to the strap of my haversack. Just as I clicked it on, a plethora of other streams of incandescent light flooded the area in front of us. I glanced around and saw the offices were on the right while a small broom closet was on the left. I walked to the closet, opened it up, and went inside. It was small and cramped, only six feet tall, and had little elbow room. I moved the brooms, dust pans, and cleaning utensils to the side and looked at the left wall. Halfway down was the same symbol on Frank's tie, a silhouette of a sword with wings on either side.

I reached out and pushed on the burned-in design, depressing it inward. A loud click and thunk sounded, followed by the whole wall popping toward me. I grabbed the side and slid it out of place, revealing a staircase that led down at a slow angle.

My spotter's light danced around as I shifted and moved down the stairs. Boots slapped against the stone steps as they followed behind me, adding a thundering rhythm to the strange and stressful situation.

It was cool and damp, with an odor of wet dirt and worms. The walls were made of old field stone, jagged more in some spots than others. I felt a sense of dread as we moved further toward the center of the earth.

If it kept going, what would we find? Jules Verne thought we would find ancient dinosaurs. Was there ever any real merit to that?

We reached the bottom of the stairs as our spotters illuminated a large room in front of us. It was vacant with no furnishings of any kind. The floor was barren dirt in some spots and cobblestone in others. To the front and left of us was a wooden door set into each wall, ordinary and plain. My attention was brought elsewhere as everyone else filed into the room. All the gear and guns shifted, causing the buckles and buttons to clack against the metal of the weapons.

I turned to the sound of footsteps coming up from behind me. It was Del with her nose glued to the journal, a spotter in one hand shining light at it to read the contents. She looked up, light following her gaze from one of the doors to the other.

"Which way?" I asked.

She hooked her spotter on a harness strap and reached up to tuck a strand of her auburn hair behind one ear. I couldn't help but watch as she did, taking in her beauty. She had such a strong will; confidence and intellect were no strangers to her.

"Deck, you're staring again," Del said.

I felt my cheeks burn hot like coals. "No. You are."

She rolled her eyes. "The notes say straight. Which makes sense if you think about the direction we are facing now."

I thought about it. "Right. Because we are now facing the Thames."

She nodded. "Do you want me to take the lead?"

"No, I will stay in front. You can be behind me, though. Tell me whatever I need to know when I need it."

She fell back behind me. "Ready then. Straight through the door, the tunnel supposedly goes for about one thousand feet."

I knew it wouldn't be a walk in the park. Still, a thousand feet underneath a massive river pushing tons of water at high speeds wasn't something I looked forward to.

"Okay, keep up and follow me," I said.

We walked to the door, and I took out my pistol from its holster, unclipping the button that held it securely in place. I brought it close to my face and pulled the slide, loading a round into the chamber. The contact with my skin triggered the charging sequence, lighting up the exposed wires and turning them into a beautiful hue of sky blue.

I'll just watch out for anything that may be out of the ordinary. I mean, a Manticore and a Griffon are definitely normal...

This door opened normally. No special key, no intricate locking mechanism, or pressure plate. Just a good old-fashioned door and knob. Splendid. No need to worry about secret tunnel security when it's supposed to be exactly that: a secret.

As expected, my spotter showed me down a long, ever-stretching tunnel that felt as if it would never end. There were a few odd things about this, though. For one, when the door did open, a small, and I do mean a slight amount, of water spilled out onto my boots.

"Great. A tunnel that's supposed to be waterproof has some water in it," I muttered.

Without wasting more time, I went in, all twenty-five sets of feet on my tail. We made it almost three-quarters of the way down before I noticed the walls around us. They were the same field stone with mortar as the room before this but with the added extra layer of clay protection. The cracks and seams were reinforced to help waterproof the tunnel. This was a reassuring thought until I noticed the many small streams of water trickling from various spots around us.

Bollocks, that's where the water came from. I wouldn't be too worried, but to have built up that much water in a thousand-foot tunnel probably isn't a good thing.

I looked at them again, this time with my spotter to check for how much was actually pouring out from the intrusions. It certainly did worry me; definitely not something we want to happen now.

I glanced over my shoulder to tell behind me to everyone. "Be careful, everyone, the tunnel walls have water coming from—"

CHAPTER 38
Lost Souls

A stream of water broke through the wall in front of me, striking me in the head and chest. The pressure pushed me against the side of the tunnel, bouncing me off it and back into the stream. I tried to yell back at the men behind me. "Thomas! Turn off the coil!"

Shouting from behind crashed through the noise of rushing water. I could feel multiple hands haul me up from the ground, pulling me to my feet. They pushed me forward past the stream that hit me. I quickly looked back to see if Thomas had put out the coil but was blinded by all the spotters worn by the other soldiers.

"Thomas, did you turn it off?" I yelled once again.

Panic filled the air as I tried to focus on the voices beyond the stream.

"It's off! We need to move now!" he yelled.

"Follow me, everyone!"

I turned and started to sprint down the tunnel. My boots sloshed in the already rising water level, making it harder to run through the muck. I slammed my pistol in its holster and clipped it shut, allowing me to focus solely on escaping and not losing my gun. More shouts came from behind me, followed by a loud and large crash of rushing water.

I knew I shouldn't have looked, but I did anyway, needing to see how my men were faring and if they all made it past whatever was happening right now. To my horror, I saw the water flowing from the wall with the force of a tsunami. It swept soldiers away like they were nothing, sending streaks of incandescent light strobing around the ceiling and walls. Cries for help escaped their mouths only to be abruptly silenced within seconds of being swallowed by the Thames.

I couldn't help any of them. The only way I could do anything was to keep running. If I got to the end, I would seal off the tunnel and stop the water from filling up anything else.

The frigid water rushed by even quicker now. It was up to my waist, chilling me to the bone as it surged by in waves. As I got further away and closer to the other end of the tunnel, the water level lowered to my knees. I focused on breathing and kept my feet moving, left then right, and repeated. I could make out my friends' raspy, ragged breaths behind me, still somehow on my heels.

"We need to get out of here!" Gary yelled.

"We are only a few hundred feet away; come on!" I replied.

I turned back to the tunnel in front of me. We were almost there. I could see the end in sight. An eagerness filled me, causing every fiber in my body to shake and shudder with adrenaline. I made it to the exit and burst through, dashing to the side to let everyone else by. Gary, Del, Klaus, and Jack whizzed by me with ease, all turning to help me with the door when our men made it through.

I looked down the tunnel, yelling to them that they only had a little further. To my horror, my spotter lit up the water, which filled the tunnel behind the rest of the soldiers. It quickly gained on them, engulfing another person right before my eyes.

"Come on! Keep going!" I yelled.

One by one, they flew from the doorway, spraying water everywhere from their sloshing footsteps. My eyes followed one of the last to make it through and saw at the end of the room, there was a large clump on the ground. Without wasting any more time, I started to push the door shut as the water bit back with the force of a circus-strong man.

"Help me!" I shouted to anyone

More hands started to push on the door next to mine. We moved it inch by inch while the water seeped through the cracks around it. It felt impossible to keep pushing. It was getting heavier and heavier to hold off the water. We could get it to shut, but I knew that wouldn't be enough. There were hooks on the sides of the door jam, prompting me to look for a board or something to put in place.

"Is there any wood around? We need something to hold the door shut!" I shouted over the roar of the water.

I frantically looked for something, glancing to my left and right. In the corner of the room was a large four-by-four piece of wood about five feet long.

"Del, go grab that piece of wood," I said.

She sprinted over to it and grabbed it quickly, returning it with the same haste. I kept pushing against the door and arched my body back to allow her to slide the end into the first hook. We had to redouble our efforts to push the door back because when she first tried to put it in place, it caught against the door. I counted to three, and we heaved again, keeping the door and water at bay for her to get the wood in securely.

"Should we let go?" Gary asked.

I leaned against the door with my shoulder, feeling it pulse from the force of water against it. More spurts and streams flowed from the cracks. I weighed the options and decided we would have to let go of it at some point, regardless of how we felt about the situation.

My eyes scanned the room to see what we had to work with and if there was a way to put another barrier between us and the frigid fingers of the Thames. I then noticed how many soldiers we had in the room, only counting nineteen people. Four of Del's soldiers and one of my own were lost. They all stood soaking wet; ready, but visibly distant and exhausted.

"Dammit! Why didn't I know this would happen!" I yelled.

I can't believe I didn't think of this happening. Why didn't I just go myself? To make sure it was safe for everyone?

I felt a hand rest on my shoulder, so I looked up to see Del, a frown pasted across her face.

"There's no way we could have known that would happen. Don't beat yourself up over it." Del said.

I shook my head. "I should have."

My eyes scanned everyone's face again, feeling the dread and sorrow of losing some soldiers. I squeezed them shut for a moment and opened them before talking.

"Del, where do we go from here?" I asked, still heaving from the strain of holding the water at bay.

"I don't know. The water washed away my journal," she said. "Let me think."

She closed her eyes and made quick motions in the air. I assumed she was mapping out everything in her head, thinking of the right way. Her eyes shot open as she looked at me.

"Through the next door, there will be a four-way intersection of tunnels. We need to go left," she said.

"Okay, everyone on me. I'll follow Del, and don't fall behind!" I said.

Before I could give anyone time to confirm or argue, Del ran for the door opposite me and threw it open. I sprinted to her and went through myself, allowing everyone else to fall in behind.

This next tunnel was just as dark as the first, all our spotters bouncing off the walls in jagged arcs as we ran. I didn't hear an immediate crash of splintering wood or rushing water, so that was good. After everyone made it, the last person shut the door and immersed us in a blanket of darkness save for our spotters.

"Keep moving. I'll make sure it's wedged shut," Jack yelled.

"You better catch up with us!" I shouted as we ran.

I hope that crazy bastard doesn't try anything stupid. I better see him again.

We reached the intersection, and Del turned to the left, keeping up a good pace. After about a few hundred feet, we came to another four-way intersection. Del stopped momentarily, head shifting from left to right, then straight. Without saying anything, she turned, heading down the right tunnel.

All the passageways started to look the same. The fieldstone had now turned to neatly stacked bricks of the same color. We jogged for about two hundred feet, breathing and focusing on staying ahead of the promise of a watery grave if we tripped up. Finally, the tunnel opened up to a large, well-lit room.

I wasn't sure if it was surprise or shock, but we all skidded to a halt a third of the way into it. In our situation, I'm sure none of us thought we would stumble into something like this.

The room itself was most likely thirty feet wide by eighty feet long. Men lying dormant in metal and glass tube-like equipment set at fifteen-degree angles covered every square inch of the walls. Wires and pipes came from the tops, curving to the walls and climbing to the ceiling. They all flowed together in the center of the room, disappearing into a grated hole. A green, phosphorus light radiated from each tube, competing with the bright white strips of Goebel tubes built into the rock.

"*Oh mon Dieu,*" Del said.

I looked around us, horror slowly building in my guts. My eyes scanned each tube to see any sign of movement, senses on edge, and fraying faster than spun yarn. Each of the strange equipment pieces had the same thing in them: more Spikes. Exact, down to the baseball stitching scars on his, or their, heads.

"More Spikes," I muttered.

I saw in my periphery that Gary had walked up next to me. He had a look of fear and bewilderment on his face. He whispered something I couldn't make out.

"What? What did you say?" Gary asked, his voice louder now.

"They're Spikes. I fought someone, or something, like this before," I said.

"Something?"

"Yeah, he was as fast as a raging bull and about as bright as one too."

"You sound like there's more to it."

"He is really strong, like throw-a-small-car strong."

"Oh, well, that's not too bad. We just have to make sure we take them at a distance from us."

I turned to him. "He spits fire too."

I saw the color drain from his face. "That's bad."

I pursed my lips and thought about what to do next. From the looks of it, they all seemed unaware of us being here. By my count there were fifteen on either side, making thirty in total.

One of them was hard enough to take out. I knew I had more people with me this time, but I still don't know how effective bullets would be.

"Spotters off, everyone, just in case," I said.

All the extra added lights clicked off in succession. After everyone turned theirs off, I reached up to mine and flipped the switch.

"Nobody touches anything. We don't want to wake them up or alert anyone," I said. "Del, which way after this room?"

She stammered, "I-I don't know. This wasn't in the journal. It was supposed to be another intersection of tunnels."

I shook my head. "Well, we need to do our best then."

I looked at the rest of the soldiers, pained by our loss already. If I had vetted the tunnel first, we wouldn't have lost anybody because it would have only collapsed with me in it. Now we were short another man too because Jack hadn't shown up behind us. I hoped he had the common sense not to touch anything.

"Thomas, turn the coil on again. We will need our guns charged and ready for anything," I said.

He nodded and reached back to the haversack with the coil in it. Flipping a switch, the two antennas sparked to life as they emitted electricity, bridging the gap from one another. All our weapons started to cast a brighter, more vibrant blue hue as they collected energy once more.

Now or never, let's get moving.

I led, keeping quiet as we walked the length of the test tube room. A buzzing from the overhead Goebel tubes cut through the ringing in my ears.

What was the source of the ringing? Perhaps it was the change in pressure or the fact that I got hit in the ear by a blast of river water. It could even be from the frayed nerves. Pick your poison; it's probably one of those.

My eyes darted nervously back and forth from either side of the room, watching each Spike closely and waiting for them to open their eyes and jump out at us. But, to my relief, nothing happened when we reached the opposite door. I signaled for everyone to crouch as I put my ear to the cool, rough metal to listen for anything on the other side.

A plethora of incoherent noises came from the other side. I focused and was able to make out men shouting in German and machinery whirring and clacking. I was about to pull my ear away when I heard him. His cruel, vile voice slithered through the rest of the chatter, sticking out like a sore thumb. I closed my eyes and thought about what he was saying, allowing my mind to drift and actually listen to what he was saying instead of just hearing it.

I pulled my ear from the door and looked at everyone. "I have good news and bad news."

Murmurs ensued, eyes shifting on each other and then back to me.

"What's the good news?" Gary asked.

I reached up and rubbed at my neck, wishing I had brought more pear drops with me. "We don't have far to go. I think what we were looking for is behind this door."

"Well, what's the bad news?" Del asked.

"I have no clue what to expect. We have no idea what we are getting into."

Del rubbed her temples. "From what I remember from the journal, if it's the right room, it's a large open area. Almost like a hangar or warehouse."

"Okay, then let us plan on setting the charges. We will look for cover to stay low. Try not to be seen while you move about," I said.

A lone soldier from the back of the group raised his hand. "Sir, we only have half of the charges left."

"Bollocks, we lost the others?"

"Yes sir, sorry."

"No, I am. Well, I suppose we will have to make do." I cracked my neck. "Place them on any integral pieces of machinery. We need to stop their equipment."

"Give me the remote. I'll trigger them after I take out my target. When you are done with the charges I need you all to find a way out. Del, do you think you could lead everyone out?"

"I can. I will be able to reorientate myself."

"I'll get as close to Jakobus as possible," I said. "Del, you stay in the back and watch my back. Gary, you'll be with me. I may need another gun. Klaus, you'll do what you can. Help Del if she needs it or come help me too."

He and everyone else nodded.

I took a few deep, shaky breaths and reached for the door handle. With my hand on it, I eased and slowly pushed it open. At first, I peeked through the crack to see if I could make anything out. Flashes of light flickered next to me, the electric crackling of somewhere close. Del was right: so far the room was enormous and I was just looking at a corner of it.

Stop wasting time. You need to find Drow. He's counting on you. The world is counting on you.

Chapter 39
An Oath

I snuck through the doorway and looked around. Directly in front of me was a set of metal steps that led up to a platform with rows upon rows of electrical panels. Switches and buttons lit up the fronts of them, blinking and pulsing in random intervals. A few men in white coats stood in front of them with clipboards, writing things down and marking them off.

I looked beyond them and saw something that took my breath away. In the center of the hangar, about a hundred feet away, was a larger platform raised about fifteen feet off the ground on metal supports. More electrical panels surrounded the circle's circumference, a dozen or so more men in white coats manning their own portions of the controls.

I watched in awe as something strange happened in the middle of the platform. The air became distorted, almost as if superheated before our eyes. It resembled the warped images of the warmth and steam that an engine causes as it heats up in the middle of a desolate winter. It started to ripple, like waves cutting through still water, when a few flashes of blue appeared in the same spot before a lightning spark ripped through thin air.

What the hell is going on? Are they opening a rift?

Instead of disappearing, the arc of lightning shifted in the air. It started with a metal ball built into the floor and connected to another in the ceiling high above. An unusually familiar buzz filled the air accompanying the electricity, bringing back memories from my grandad's past life. In a split second, the lightning widened into a triangular rift of pure black void. The point of the triangle stayed at the top while the bottom connected to two more metal balls. A heavy and forceful wind swept through the room, whipping my hair around, picking up random debris, and carrying it about.

We needed to hurry.

I glanced right and saw a staging area, large bundles of wires leading to and from a metal platform. To the left were five or six stacks of pallets containing various items, just enough coverage for the lot of us. I duck-walked to the makeshift cover, getting far enough to let everyone get behind me. When I could see all their faces, I made a few gestures, indicating the bomb squad to carefully go set the charges.

Without thinking, I pulled out my pistol and turned the safety off. Luckily there was enough sound and random noises to provide ample cover for Thomas's portable coil. I peeked over the top of one of the pallets to see where Jakobus was, surveying everything. Further down the warehouse were a couple of half-tracks, panzer tanks, and other experimental vehicles. A strange shape caught my eye, stopping my gaze for a second. The device, or whatever it was, stood quite tall and bulbous in shape. It was round at either end with a flair outward like a bell at the bottom of it.

Is that a bell?

Whatever it was, I didn't need to worry about it. I needed to focus on the task at hand, so I kept looking. My eyes glanced back to the equipment to the right of me once more, following our troops as they crouched and placed charges on various pieces of equipment.

I went to look back at the expanse when I felt a cold metal barrel press against the back of my neck. My body froze, and my heart jumped, adrenaline pushing my mind off the deep end.

"Don't move," a voice said.

A voice. A familiar voice. More than that, actually, it was one I knew. One that I spent my whole life near. It was Drow.

"Drow?" My voice cracked as I asked.

"Shut up," he said with a snarl. "Don't say my name."

"What—what's going on? What are you doing?"

Drow's knee struck me hard and I felt a sharp pain in my ribs. I flinched and grabbed at it, feeling like doubling over from the pain. Out of reflex, I rolled onto my side and put a few feet between Drow and me. My eyes met his as I clutched at my side. A pure hatred smoldered behind them, burning and smoking as he traced my movements.

His eyes were sunken with deep purple bags under them. He looked malnourished, almost like he hadn't eaten or drunk anything in days. His usual clean-shaven face was now an unkempt mess of stubble, smudges, and scratches. There was something wild about him: feral fidgeting and awkward jolting movements.

"Drow— you're alive… we need to get you out of here. What are you doing?" I pleaded.

"Shut up!" he said, voice close to a whisper. "I'm not going anywhere."

"Why not? You're worrying me, Drow."

He scoffed, "You care now?"

"What do you mean? Drow, of course, I care. What are you talking about?"

His gaze shifted from me to other unseen things around me. He was swaying, having a hard time keeping his stance solid.

"Did you bring any other knights with you? The people you share a forever bond with?" he said.

What was wrong with him?

"I did, but why does that matter?"

"Of course it doesn't matter to you. You'll see them in another lifetime. I'll just be forgotten about."

I shook my head. *What?* "Drow, what's gotten into you? Of course you're important. Why are you saying these things?"

His frown deepened as he pulled the gun to his cheek. A flash of sorrow flew across his face, switching back to hatred just as fast.

"Just shut up. I've never been anything to you. You were destined to be important the second you were born. He was right. I'll never be anything to you."

"Who? Who are you talking about, Drow?"

"Him. Jakobus," he whispered. "He has a plan, you know. A way to make everyone important. A way to make my name last forever. For me to last forever."

I can't believe he got to him. I destroyed the amber. He shouldn't be able to keep a hold on him like this.

"Drow, don't listen to him. He's dangerous and doesn't care about you."

Out of the corner of my eye, I saw the rift change from bleak black nothingness to a lighter shade of gray. It kept getting brighter by the second, shifting like a mirage.

"No!" Drow yelled. "He is the only one that's told me the truth. You said the team needed me."

He inched closer to me, the gun now pressed against my chest.

"You said that I was important! If I was so important, how did you get here? See! You never needed me!"

I faltered. I knew I needed to say something to get through to Drow, but I couldn't get it out. My voice abandoned me, and I was left with nothing but silence. I knew I should have told him about Dr. Henry and how Jakobus used him to get to Grandad. Or how he used Herman Mudgett to speed his evil in different countries. He needed to know he was only being used, but somehow, I didn't feel like any of this would get through to him.

An alarm sounded just then, loud and ear-piercing. Drow and I snapped our heads to the rift in the center, watching what would happen next. Red lights bathed the entire warehouse in a bloody glow, now offset by the bright white coming from the door to nowhere.

While we looked that way, Drow started to smile. It was a strange, animalistic-looking smile that scared me to my core. "You will see what he has planned. Just wait—"

Rustling and noise turned my attention to Drow instead of the rift. One second, he was standing there, reveling in the awe he felt. The next second he hit the ground, Klaus on top of him as the gun skidded toward me.

"Don't kill him! That's my brother!" I yelled.

Klaus looked up at me in shock. Before he could say anything, he was thrown back off of Drow. Klaus hit the wall fifteen feet back. I watched in horrified surprise as Drow shook violently on the ground, pained whimpering escaping his lips. In the crimson light, I saw his body shift in ways it shouldn't have. Muscles and bone rippled underneath tautly pulled skin, bulging and ripping the fabric of his clothes.

What did he do to you? Why is this happening? I need to think of something to knock him out. Or keep him from getting back up. I can't risk him getting hurt or worse.

I patted the pockets on my uniform for something to use, anything to help. I brushed over my spotter. No that wouldn't help. Finally, I felt two small metal balls in my left breast pocket. I pulled them out and lifted them to the red-stained light to see.

Finally, something to help. Hopefully, no one heard the noise these will make when I used them.

I depressed the red button in the center of either of them, initiating the countdown sequence. They began to blink, starting slowly and building to a faster pace. At the same time, they began to emit a beeping noise. *Thanks for telling me you're going to go off.*

I tossed them both next to Drow lightly, not wanting to have them bounce away before they could go off. Drow began rising to his knees and hands, trying to stand up. Before he could get any further, the devices went off, and nets wrapped themselves around him completely. They surged with electricity, flashing a neon blue as they shocked him multiple times. His body hit the floor with a thud as he squirmed in pain from the nets. It hurt me to see this happen to him, but I couldn't afford anything else to happen to him or us. He curled into the fetal position, electricity still shocking him every few seconds.

"I'm sorry, Drow! Just hang in there, and I will be back for you!" I yelled over the alarm.

I glanced at Klaus in time to see a barrage of bullets whiz past him and hit the wall with a thunderous thunk. The hot lead tore through the pallets of equipment in front of me, inching closer as I watched. I rolled out of the way of the steady stream of molten metal to the left some more. Shouting ensued as Klaus started to shoot in the direction where the gunfire was coming from.

When I got to my feet further away, I saw Gary running in our direction, shotgun firing and shooting charged pellets at the nearest German soldier. They struck, hitting center mass, tearing a chunk of flesh and cloth from the right side of his body. The edges of his clothes caught fire from the electrified shot, cauterizing the wound. Gary jumped over an exploding area of the ground where someone shot, sliding feet first the rest of the way to us.

"I think they heard you!" he yelled.

"Sorry, next time I think I'm going to die, I will just lie down and take it," I yelled back. "Where's Del?"

I scanned the area where we came in, trying to see if she was safe, far enough away from all the gunfire. Near a stack of crates in the far corner, I saw her pop up and make a quick shot at a German across the room. I followed the glowing mass of lead as it soared through the air, right into the skull of a poor soul. Next to her was Thomas, staying in cover, so we all had a source of power still. He, too, peeked up over the crates and took a few potshots at random people.

"She's handling it herself!" Gary said.

I smirked. "Good!"

My eyes shifted to the central platform where the rift was, checking for Jakobus to ensure I still had a chance. The door was no longer just gray. I could now make out a countryside scene through the distorted layer of superheated air. I tilted my head to the side, causing the rift to shimmer as the view changed from the idyllic view. It was now one of red and black, arcs of flames blasting all around wherever the door was open to now. Jakobus stood in front of it, arms outstretched as if beckoning something to come forth.

"We need to get him now while he is preoccupied!" I yelled.

Gary and Klaus looked at me and nodded.

I got to my feet and ran, dodging bullets that flew my way. Without much of a plan, I pulled out Excalibur and readied it for a strike on Jakobus when I got near him. A German soldier to my left pulled up his gun, ready to shoot, only to be stopped before he could act. His shoulder was blown away by another shot from Gary's shotgun. Glistening viscera spewed in a cloud of vaporized blood and cloth as the soldier fell backward from us. I ran to the steps leading to the center platform, swinging my sword at anyone I could reach. It cut through their guts like a knife through butter, cleaving them in half without any effort. The sound of intestines plopping against metal rang through every other noise and seared itself into my brain.

I reached the top step and saw that Jakobus had turned to me. Competing lights of ethereal blue and maddening red danced across his face as an evil grin was stretched across his face from ear to ear. I saw the men in white coats cowering in the corner beyond the rift, praying and covering their faces.

"You are simply too late," he said. "It's already open, and you won't be able to shut it. I will have what I wanted all along."

I took a fighting stance. "We have charges set all around us on your equipment!"

He sneered, "That won't be enough. It's already begun!"

A rage filled me once more. One that wouldn't let him get away this time. It was like the rage I felt when I held his piece of amber, but this time it was for one thing: him. I thought of all the lives lost because of his quest for true and ultimate power. Of all the innocent people that had been manipulated by him so he could get what he wanted.

Excalibur started to glow a faint blue, electricity crackling and spidering out into the air from the splinter in the blade. I could feel the will of a thousand descendants fill me with courage, with the strength needed to do what needed to be done. My rage turned to understanding and confidence, a sense of duty and honor I always carried with me. It was time to end this. It was time to stop the games he was playing and kill him.

I bolted in his direction, alarm noise blaring in my ear as the blood-red light stained everything around me. He stood there and laughed, cackling as he held his hands to the heavens. Excalibur found its mark and sank deep into his gut, sparks of electricity coming from the crack in the blade that nipped at random spots on Jakobus.

He lowered his gaze, expression slowly fading from a maniacal madman's smile to one of anger and despise. Panicking, he put his hands around the blade and tried to move it and me. The sharp, magical blade bit into his flesh, causing thick black sludge to ooze from the wounds it was causing,

"How?" he snarled.

I dug my feet into the ground, engaging the spikes Thomas built into my shoes so I could keep him in one spot. I couldn't let Jakobus go. The rift's heat felt like it was searing the flesh from my bone. I glanced at the picturesque landscape, and it seemed so inviting, causing me to second-guess what I was doing.

"The stone! We destroyed it!" I gloated.

Jakobus let out an earth-shattering bellow, rage filling every aspect of it. He pulled and shook at the sword, but I held it in place. I felt a helping hand and realized Gary and Klaus had grabbed onto me to help me stay still, to help me from letting Jakobus go.

Time slowed for what felt like millennia. I looked around me as the gunfire ensued, people falling from wounds all around us. In the distance, I could see what was left of our soldiers being ushered by Del and Thomas to a set of doors further away toward the edge of the warehouse. I held Excalibur in place with one hand as I reached into my breast pocket for the remote of the explosives.

"You can't defeat me. Not like this!" Jakobus howled.

"I can try," I said.

Tears welled up in my eyes as I thought about my grandad. As I thought about Hope and my Mum. I pictured my brother being captured and turned against me, hating everything about what had happened. The tears grew, and I pinched my eyes shut, pushing them away with every painful memory.

I opened them one last time, checking to see if everyone left made it to the exit. Del and the last remaining soldiers escaped to the door, all filling through to make it out alive and safe. At the last second, I saw her turn to me, eyes locking with mine, and sharing one final moment. Feeling the connection once more before being severed forever.

"Go," I said, knowing she couldn't hear me over the alarm.

Tears fell down her dirt and sweat-caked cheeks, leaving behind clean lines of pain. I glanced at Klaus and Gary for what I felt was the last time, seeing my men, my friends here by my side when the world was going to fall down around us.

Would Atlas crumble under the same circumstances? Maybe.

Jakobus stood snarling over me, Excalibur still sunk halfway through his chest. I depressed the plunger for the remote, and the explosive charges went off. Equipment erupted in flames all around us, causing the rift to flicker and spark with an unknown force of energy. I could hear Gary and Klaus yell at me, but it somehow seemed far away. Miles from me in a distant land.

I felt a tug at my haversack as someone reached inside. In my periphery, I saw Klaus' hand slam a metal cylinder into the ground in front of me, completing the force field to protect us. A dome of yellow, frosted light wrapped around us, starting above my head. It slowly continued toward my sword as more explosions went off around us. As the edge reached the ground, I felt a shock wave of energy rock everything around us, causing the dome to light up to unbearable blinding white.

I closed my eyes for the last time and waited for what came next, knowing exactly what to expect.

Epilogue
The Unknown

South-West England
8:30 a.m.

Before anything else, I felt the searing, early morning heat on my neck and the left side of my face. The right side of my face was chilled, albeit uncomfortable, but at least protected from the sun's rays. I tried to pry open my eyelids to see what was happening around me but couldn't get them to budge. Chatter from people filled the air around me, adding to the clang of metal on metal and the crackling of fires. The one thing I didn't expect, though, was dirt to hit me square in the face. Clucking followed on the heels of the spritz of sand, scaring me and sending my heart into overdrive. I flailed as my reflexes kicked in, slapping at open air as I tried to open my eyes once more. Eventually, I was triumphant, eyelids rocketing open to see the view before me.

The bright light of a rising sun caused my pupils to dilate, making my surroundings a blur of brights and darks. I pulled myself upright and rubbed my eyes to clear the fog and haze away from them. After a moment of vigorous purging, I opened them to look again at what lay around me.

I was sitting in a clearing near the edge of a small village. Further down the dirt path, there was an oxen-drawn cart heading in the opposite direction. Gold and tan hay piled high on the back, covering whoever could drive it. Chickens clucked and marched around me in zigzagging patterns, either busy with important nothings or lazily going about business.

What the hell?

ACKNOWLEDGEMENTS

As always, a thanks to my parents, David and Kim, for if not for them I would not be who I am today.

I can't forget about Ward: he will always be an important part in my life. Thank you.

A thanks to Cole, my editor, for making this crazy dream a reality.

Both Maddy and J. deserve an enormous thank you for being an integral element of the final parts of this long process.

A thanks to Andrea for the beautiful illustrations, and to Stefan for the amazing cover.

And last but not least, Bryan and Eileen for reading the first few drafts.

Thank you all for the support.

Contact Information

Email: adavidbarrett@gmail.com
Instagram: adavidbarrett
Twitter: adavidbarrett
Facebook: theadavidbarrett